THE SPIRIT IS WILLING

She was curled up on the love seat, one foot tucked beneath her, Britt's journal cradled in her lap. She went back to his scribblings, savoring all the words as if they were part of a love letter written just for her.

Intrigued, Britt peered over her shoulder to see what exactly held such interest.

Dreams are as important to life as food and drink, often more. They flavor the plainest bread and give water the quality of a fine wine. It's only when we fail to lay them down at the proper time that they ruin us.

Crouching down to see her face, he discovered a tenderness shining in her eyes.

Reverently, she turned another page. Longing and affection radiated from her like a comforting fire. For over twelve decades he'd been cut off from God and humanity. Suddenly learning that a living, breathing human cared about him was a priceless gift he'd never thought to experience again.

Lord, he wished he knew what to do . . .

HAUNTING HOPE

RAINA LYNN

JOVE BOOKS, NEW YORK

HAUNTING HEARTS is a registered trademark of Penguin Putnam Inc.

HAUNTING HOPE

A Jove Book / published by arrangement with
the author

PRINTING HISTORY
Jove edition / October 1999

The Penguin Putnam Inc. World Wide Web site address is
http://www.penguinputnam.com

ISBN: 0-515-12655-1

A JOVE BOOK®
Jove Books are published by The Berkley Publishing Group,
a division of Penguin Putnam Inc.,
375 Hudson Street, New York, New York 10014.
JOVE and the "J" design
are trademarks belonging to Penguin Putnam Inc.

PRINTED IN THE UNITED STATES OF AMERICA

10 9 8 7 6 5 4 3 2 1

HAUNTING HOPE

Chapter One

Thunder echoed across the canyon, and the tension that coiled around Sheriff Britt McLean's spine tightened another notch. The clouds had darkened again, threatening another downpour. The last thing these mountains needed was more rain. He studied the oozing mud that only last week had been a passable mountain trail. Descending the steep, rock-strewn canyon wall to the rain-swollen stream at the bottom would be dangerous enough for a man alone on horseback. But he'd arrested Tyler Carbow that morning and had the man tied to the saddle horn on a horse behind him. If the animals lost their footing, it could prove fatal. But the other crossing sites farther down would be just as bad. He had no choice but to risk this one.

Dan, his sorrel gelding, shifted his weight in subtle protest at the nudge from Britt's heels. The big horse was cold and covered in mud from similar crossings. He'd submit to more, but his exhausted bearing made it clear he'd rather not. Britt gave him an apologetic pat on the withers.

"McLean, you can lock me up in Manzanita's shiny new

1

jail if you want to,'' Carbow sneered, "but you'll never get me to the courthouse in Breford.''

Britt had arrested the scrawny bastard less then twenty-four hours after he'd robbed the Manzanita Bank and murdered the old man who owned it. "For someone facing the gallows," he drawled, "you're certainly full of yourself.''

Carbow snorted, his small eyes glittering. "A whole lot of people in that town need to learn to mind their own business—including that little wife of yours.''

Rage flared hot, but Britt willed himself to show nothing. Lucinda had been in the bank that morning. Old Parker Simple had given over the money as they'd demanded, but Carbow had shot him anyway. After they'd left, she'd cradled Parker's head in her arms as he'd died. If Britt lived to be a hundred, he'd always remember the hollow-eyed shock in his wife's pretty green eyes. No woman should experience something like that. He'd wanted to stay home and comfort her, but the people of Manzanita and three other neighboring mining towns counted on him to do his job. He couldn't let all of them down.

"Ain't you even a little bit concerned about what I plan to do to her before she dies like the others?''

The mental picture of this filthy, gap-toothed buzzard touching Lucinda fanned the rage to nearly uncontrollable levels, and Britt trembled from the force of it. His bulky oilskin and rain-soaked hat pulled down low probably hid his reaction. He hoped. With deliberate slowness, he gazed over his shoulder. "Aren't you afraid of not making it back alive?" he countered in a low drawl. "It's a long ten miles, and you're trying my patience.''

That earned him disbelieving laughter. "You're too much of a do-gooder to scare anybody, McLean.''

"You're that sure of me, are you?" He put an edge to it that took the gleam from Carbow's eyes and the arrogance from his shoulders. Nudging Dan forward, Britt played out the lead rope on the second horse. Dan picked his footing, and both animals moved reluctantly down the steep canyon.

Britt's arm brushed the gun at his hip. The reminder of its presence comforted him. He'd get Carbow back to Manzanita alive if possible, but he refused to take any unnecessary risks. What made his skin crawl was that Ira Fleming, Carbow's partner, hadn't made a single attempt to free him. From what little Britt knew of the pair, that was out of character. Without making an obvious show, he scrutinized every shadow and hiding place for a raw-boned bearded man with a scarred-up rifle.

As they reached the water, a blast of wind howled through the pine and oak trees. Lightning ripped open the muted gray sky, thunder booming on its heels. Then, as he'd feared, the clouds opened up. Britt hunched deeper into his oilskin against the fresh deluge and kept the horses moving forward. Carbow picked up his taunt again, raising his voice to be heard over the roar of the freezing rain.

"My offer still stands, McLean," he yelled. "Let me go. I'll give you half the money and leave everyone alone. If you take me in, Ira won't like it much. Neither will I." He chuckled loud enough to be heard. "Your Lucinda sure has nice yellow hair."

The callousness in Carbow was like nothing Britt had seen in the ten years he'd been sheriff in these mountains. There was no question in his mind that if Carbow got loose, he'd carry out his revenge.

They reached the other side of the stream, and Dan lunged up the saturated bank. Icy water sluiced off his legs and belly. Britt silently apologized to the tired horse. Then, an impact like a hammer blow knocked him to the ground. His right side erupted in white hot agony.

Gunshot!

Shock and disorientation clouded his mind, and he felt himself fade. But he struggled against it.

He'd been shot before, and survival instincts screamed that if he lost consciousness, whoever had ambushed him would finish the job. Fighting to clear his head, he forced himself to roll onto his back and reach for his holster. Gritting his teeth against the pain, he closed his fingers on the pistol. Bearded Ira Fleming stepped from the heavy brush at water's edge, and Britt found himself staring down a rifle barrel less than a yard from his nose. Frigid rain pelted him in the face. Each breath became harder, more painful to draw in than the one before.

"You should have taken me up on my offer, Sheriff," Carbow yelled over the downpour. His lips thinned into a gap-toothed grin. "You coulda been a rich man and bought your little wife all the pretty dresses she wanted. Now all she'll be wearin' is black. If she lives that long."

Shoving away tendrils of panic, Britt cursed the overconfidence that sent him out alone after these two. Lucinda's involvement had made the robbery too personal and he hadn't taken the time to gather up help. Now, unless he found a miracle, he'd pay for that carelessness with everyone's life. His fury at himself and at Carbow grew with each hard-fought breath.

"If you touch her, you won't find a hole in hell dark enough to hide from me."

Carbow's lecherous smile became fixed. "Brave talk for a dead man."

A wave of dizziness rolled through Britt, and he tasted blood in the back of his throat. Chances of survival weren't good. Somehow he needed to find a way.

"If being dead is what it takes," he said, staring Carbow hard in the eyes. A strange sense of invincibility settled over him. The wind and rain probably drowned out his words. He'd declared war, and he didn't care whether or not those two animals had heard him. No matter what it took, they weren't going to lay their hands on his wife.

Britt didn't know what kind of expression was on his face, but Fleming's lips pursed at a nervous slant. The man's gaze locked on to Britt's eyes and never moved as he maneuvered the rifle into one hand, drew a knife and cut Carbow's ropes. The barrel held rock-steady. Carbow hopped to the ground.

"Finish him," Carbow ordered, watching Britt as he rubbed the circulation back into his wrists.

Fleming didn't hesitate.

Britt heard the shot, saw the puff of smoke, but didn't quite feel the impact as a second bullet slammed into the center of his chest. A strange detachment settled over him as he rolled down the embankment into the water. Limp, he floated a few feet downstream, then came up against a fallen tree.

"I want McLean's horse. Bring him over here." Oddly,

Carbow's voice had an unnatural clarity to it like nothing Britt had ever experienced. It was like hearing sounds with more sensitive ears.

Britt rose free of the water. He had no sensation of hot or cold, comfort or pain. He simply *was*. That worried him, but it paled compared to the shock when he glanced at his hands. They were so translucent he could see the rushing stream through them. A panic too fast to stop tore into him. He stood, turned and looked back toward the fallen tree. His body lay in the water, eyes closed, the current pressing it against the branches and collected debris. In disbelief, he stared at his translucent hands, torso and legs. The bullet holes in his chest and side were fading, leaving his strange spirit-self whole. Even the bloodstains had vanished from his shirt and oilskin. Sinking horror filled him.

Carbow slogged through the water toward the fallen tree and what was inarguably Britt's corpse. Mentally, Britt shuddered, trying to deny what his eyes told him.

"Is he dead?" Fleming yelled over the roaring deluge.

"Yep. Bring me that horse before I decide I don't need no partner. I got business in town."

Fleming laughed thinly.

Waves of raw emotion blasted Britt from all directions. Paralyzed by the their intensity, he had no defense against them. He recognized the fear, confusion and frozen disbelief as his own. But the rest belonged to the other two men!

Ira Fleming mostly felt irritation over being soaked to the skin, cold and inconvenienced. He feared Carbow, though, and hated how that weakness made him feel. From Tyler Carbow came a solid wall of bottomless hatred, evil and a sick satisfaction of having taken another life.

How did he know all that! Britt wanted to believe this was some sort of hideous nightmare, that in another moment, he'd wake up with a start and find Lucinda sleeping peacefully beside him. But instinct rebelled at that willful fiction. This was real—whether it made any sense or not.

Panic burned through him. He tried to block out the strange *knowing*, but couldn't. What was happening to him? From behind, a soothing warmth beckoned. He turned and saw a cloud-lined tunnel of light spiraling in close. From it billowed a silent invitation to let go and come to a place of peace where the tragedies of the world lay beyond his concern.

Death. How could he be dead when only moments ago he'd been heading home? Recoiling from the concept, he moved away.

"*No!*" he screamed. Carbow and Fleming didn't appear to hear or see any of this. "*I have to stay here! They'll kill Lucinda and the others who were in the bank yesterday. I've got to save my family!*"

No angel came forth, giving him an opportunity to plead his case, and if the light was capable of hearing or responding, it gave no indication. He was dead, and the time had come to go.

Turning away from the light, Britt ran up the side of the hill where Fleming had caught up with Dan. Carbow took Dan's reins. The light's pull became more insistent, nearly jerking Britt off his feet. He made a grab for his pistol which was now stuffed in Carbow's waistband, but his fingers went through the steel and wood, closing on nothing.

Carbow jumped. "What the hell was that!" he demanded, whirling around and patting at his side.

"What was *what*?" the other man demanded.

"It felt like someone shoved a hunk of ice up my shirt. Coldest damn thing I ever felt."

"Ain't nothin' there." Ira gave him a sideways frown, and Britt felt him gauging Carbow's sanity.

The truth of the situation took on a deeper level of reality, but Britt closed his mind to it. His family couldn't afford for him to be dead. They needed him to keep them safe! Again, he tried for the gun but still couldn't get hold of it.

Carbow jumped again and swore. Britt tried for his throat, but his hands went straight through. Carbow screamed in terror and pain. The horses shied.

"What's *wrong* with you!" Ira demanded, his fear of Carbow deepening.

Wild-eyed, Carbow shook his head and mounted Dan. "Let's get outta here. I don't like this place."

Overwhelmed, Britt stood for a moment on the trail,

watching them ride off. Rain poured down in sheets through and beside him. He had no physical sensation except the pull of the light. The tunnel drew ever closer, its seductive tug increasing. Involuntarily, his gaze tracked back to his body still lying limp in the rushing water, then swung to the light.

"You don't understand. I can't go," he pleaded. *"They're going after everyone who can identify them."*

Still, no answer came.

Britt couldn't bring himself to admit defeat. Without any idea how to fight this, he turned and ran with everything he possessed. There was a strange nothingness to the effort. No pounding heart. No straining lungs. Then he noticed that his strangely transparent legs had stopped pumping and he moved by force of will alone. That bothered him, but given everything else, he didn't question it. Then he caught sight of his surroundings. He was passing by and *through* trees so fast, they blurred. Yet the light kept pace, its pursuit relentless. Terror clawed at him.

"For God's sake, don't do this!" he cried out. He "ran" harder. The mountains gave way to the Sacramento Valley, then to the ocean hundreds of miles from Manzanita.

Suddenly, the light sputtered, the first indication of change he'd seen. It birthed a fragile hope, and Britt hung on with everything he had. How much time had passed? He had no sense of that, either. Was he already too late to save his family? Turning back in a wide loop, he kept the tunnel behind him. He didn't understand the impossibility of what he was doing, merely accepted it and pushed on.

The light sputtered again. Had it lost some of its brightness, too, or did it appear that way because that was what he wanted to believe? Could he trust any of his senses now? Still keeping out of reach, he resisted with his mind and fled back toward the mountains. Twice, he overshot the town before figuring out how to slow down without the light gaining any ground. The pull weakened. He moved along Main Street, turned left at the jail, then wove through two more blocks. Finally, the whitewashed cottage came into view. His best friend was tying his horse to the hitching post out front.

"Nestor! Thank God!"

Lanky Nestor Hawkings gave no indication that he heard him as he hurried from the rain to the dry, covered porch. The light flickered, crackled and began to pulse. Even at its brightest, its strength had definitely faded, and Britt dared believe he might win this fight.

"Nestor!" he yelled in the other man's face. *"Carbow is loose. He's coming here first. You've got to protect my family!"*

Oblivious, Nestor rapped on the door. A moment later, Evie, the oldest of Britt's five children, opened the latch and peeked out. Her seven-year-old face broke into a wide smile. Britt felt her surprised joy.

"Uncle Nestor!"

"Hey, squirrel," he said, scooping her into his arms. His homely face warmed with a genuine pleasure, and his affection for the little girl filled Britt's senses. "How's the prettiest lady in town?"

Britt grabbed at Nestor's arm to try to turn him around and get his attention. His hand passed through.

Nestor spasmed. "Lord Almighty, the temperature's dropping fast. Let's get you by the fire." He set her down and steered her inside as Lucinda came from the kitchen carrying baby Katherine on her hip. Wisps of long, blond hair had escaped the bun at the base of her neck. Her face was flushed as if she'd been bending over a hot stove.

"What brings you to town in weather like this?" she scolded, shutting the door on Britt. It passed right through him. "Take that wet coat off before you catch your death."

Britt could see the tunnel of light even through the walls of the house. He struggled once more against its pull. With a hissing crack that sounded as if creation itself had ripped apart, it disappeared, leaving an echoing silence behind. The nothingness was so profound, he stopped and listened. A gut-level sense of doom worried at him. Had he accomplished something no man should dream of even trying? He didn't know, but in the face of protecting his family, he couldn't let it matter right now.

"Can't anyone *hear me?"* he yelled, frantic.

From behind him, he felt a familiar evil, only a hundred times more clear than in the moments after his death—

Carbow. Whatever these strange new senses were, they were developing with stunning clarity. Britt walked through the wall into the yard where he could see better. Carbow rode up on Dan, gun drawn. But Nestor and Lucinda were too busy swapping small talk by the front window to notice. The roar of the rain should have masked the sound of the hammer being drawn back, but Britt heard it like a death knell.

He thought about calling to Nestor again, but it was obvious the living couldn't hear him. So far, the only reaction he'd gotten from any of them was a violent shiver. But that still gave him *one* chance. Desperate, he ran to Dan and dove straight through the animal's body.

The big gelding squealed in pain and terror, rearing as Carbow pulled the trigger. The bullet shattered the front window but went wide. Nestor shoved Lucinda, Evie and the baby to the floor. He didn't carry a gun, but Carbow's struggles to regain control of the panicked horse gave Nestor the chance to grab Britt's spare rifle mounted on the wall. Nestor peeked around the window casing as Carbow fired off another couple of rounds. Nestor wasn't fast, but he was accurate, and when he finally took his shot, Carbow dropped from the saddle like a stone.

Britt sank to his knees in relief, then watched in eerie fascination as Carbow's spirit left his body. The tunnel of light returned. A split second before it drew Carbow inside, Britt saw the dark fate that awaited him. Tyler Bartholomew Carbow barely had time to scream before he and the light vanished. Shaken, Britt rose to his feet.

By now, Nestor had run outside and was kneeling by the body. Straining to see through the worsening rain, he stared at the horse across the street. "Oh, God," he murmured. "That's Dan. Britt's in trouble."

Lucinda, trailing behind, sucked in her breath. Fear clung to the air around her, and tears tracked down her face. She knew.

MANZANITA, CALIFORNIA
SPRING 1999

The downpour hit just as Hope McLean and her coworker, Pat, reached the covered porch of the century-old Victorian.

In its day, Hawkings House had been one of the finest homes in Manzanita. Now the mansion Nestor Hawkings had built as a wedding present to his bride, the widow Mc-Lean, was just an oversized relic of a bygone era, a semi-neglected curiosity on the town's Points of Interest map. By modern luxury home standards, it wasn't even that big, certainly no longer thought of as a mansion.

Hope knew that her husband didn't care whether or not it had been brought back into his family. But she did—with all her heart.

Streetlights flickered once, then plunged the mountain town into darkness.

Pat squawked in mock rage. "I finally get the chance to see the inside of this place, and Mother Nature gets rude."

"Well, you know what they say about Murphy's Law." Hope tried to sound lighthearted, but her ulterior motives for extending the invitation were making her feel more than a little guilty. In the month since Pat had come to work at the realty office, they'd become remarkably good friends, and she'd begun to feel that maybe she could risk a big imposition. Still, Hope's conscience complained that she should at least have been up front with her. Then again, courage had never been her strong point—which was why she'd decided to dangle this carrot in front of Pat's nose. Drawing in a short breath, she put her key in the lock and opened the door.

"Is your husband home tonight?" Pat asked.

Hope didn't miss the subtle disdain in the inflection. "His car wasn't in the driveway, so probably not."

"Unless he got so drunk that he forgot where he parked and had to walk home."

Having a friend and coworker know the situation so well was alternately a comfort and a humiliation. Hope sighed. "Maybe you'd better wait out here. I'll see if he's here and try to gauge his mood. If he's too surly, maybe we can do this another time."

Pat shrugged. "I've wanted to see the inside of Hawkings House ever since I moved here five years ago, but the old coot who used to own it wasn't interested in giving a tour to a history junkie." Her gaze caressed the hand-carved front door and the stone columns that supported the porch roof. "If making nice to Richard is what it takes, I'm game."

Her take-life-as-it-came attitude was one more item on the list of traits Hope envied about Pat. Her friend was tall and willowy and blond, beauty's ideal, while Hope saw herself as being about as unremarkable as she could imagine. If she stretched to her full height and cheated a little, she just reached five-five. She'd lost track of how many times she'd dreamed of coloring her hair from its mouse brown to something glamorous—like flaming red. Her worst feature was without doubt her eyes. Who on earth but her had purple eyes? They looked ridiculous. Elizabeth Taylor was known for her violet eyes, but movie stars had help with lighting and makeup and who knew what all else. Taylor probably hadn't had to endure a childhood of being known as the Purple People Eater, either. Why were kids so cruel?

Hope shook off the old pain and refocused on retrieving a flashlight from the drawer of a curio cabinet by the door. "Just remember. I warned you how little time I've had to work on the restorations." *And even less money,* she added silently.

Lightning tore open the night sky as they stepped inside. The multiple flashes cast eerie shadows into the main hallway and the matching parlors that flanked it. The heavy coat of faded pea-green paint had begun to lift from the walls, exposing an equally ugly, dirty-mauve layer of wallpaper beneath. She thumbed the switch to the flashlight. The powerful halogen beam illuminated the hallway with a steady glow. Every time Hope looked at these walls, her mind's eye saw the fine woods that had endured years of desecration from color-blind Philistines and their paintbrushes. Her hand itched for a paint scraper to set the captive free. She adored this old place, and it deserved so much better than what she'd been able to give it during the two years she and Richard had owned it. At least the structure itself was sound.

Ear-splitting thunder rattled the walls. Both women jumped.

"You don't have any resident ghosts, do you?" Pat

quipped. "If not, they're missing a great place to haunt. Thunder. Lightning. Shadows that go back forever." She craned her neck to see down the long, dark central hallway that ended in the door to the old-fashioned music room.

"Only a couple of realtors like us would look at it like that." Hope dropped her voice into an appropriately somber sales tone. "Plenty of gracious living for the well-to-do specter and lovely playrooms upstairs for the little ghost-lettes." Unexpected laughter burst from her lips before she could stop it. Self-conscious, Hope cleared her throat. She didn't crack jokes very often—too afraid that they'd back-fire on her. Pat didn't seem to suffer from that affliction.

Pat shrugged. "Are you sure about the ghosts?"

"Positive. I even checked out the attic once."

"You scoped out the place for spooks?"

"No," she chuckled, "just junk that previous owners forgot about, something that had since become an antique."

Pat's eyes gleamed with interest. "Find anything good?"

"Nothing. Not even a shoe box. I swept out all the dust and haven't been up there since. I closed off the third floor to save on electricity." Keeping the door locked at the base of those stairs also eased the temptation of constantly going up there to dream about what she could do with this place if she only had the time. It also kept in check the fantasizing about all the events this wonderful old house must have seen.

"No ghosts. No treasures. Major bummer."

Hope grinned. "Sorry."

A rapid-fire series of lightning flashes lit up the house, and Hope used the moment to point the flashlight beam to the room on the left. "This used to be the ladies' parlor. We use it as a den." There wasn't much there. Just furni-ture odds and ends to keep it from looking completely bar-ren.

Pat nodded, then turned to the room across the hall. "I take it this was the gentlemen's parlor?"

"Now it's the family room." Hope deliberately didn't shine the light in there. But a new series of flashes hit, clearly showing a room in shambles. Beer cans littered the couch, coffee table and the top of the entertainment center. Papers and the remains of a sandwich and chips were strewn across the floor. An empty beer bottle lay on the china hutch.

Hope cringed. At least Richard was nowhere in sight.

Pat put an arm around her in support, and Hope's face heated in humiliation. Women of spunk and courage like Pat wouldn't have put up with this for even a month, much less the two years since Richard's drinking had gotten completely out of hand. All Hope's life she'd been taught that any problem in a marriage was solvable if she tried a little harder, loved a little more and never gave up.

That philosophy was all well and good if both people involved were basically normal. But some situations just weren't worth salvaging. She knew what she needed to do. She just couldn't do it by herself. Nor could she stand here and let her new friend survey the evidence of Richard's excesses. "Come on. I think there's a couple of diet colas in the fridge."

"I wish you'd had a candle in that drawer instead of a flashlight. The aura of a flickering flame would be so much more appropriate for this place." Pat gave a credible ghostly moan.

Rolling her eyes, Hope shook her head and walked down the hall, through the dining room to the kitchen. "You're really disappointed that Hawkings House doesn't have any wayward spirits, aren't you?"

"Aw, come on. Don't take all the fun out of it for me. Can't you just *pretend* something goes bump in the night occasionally?"

Hope chuckled to herself as she snagged the two sodas from the fridge. She'd remodeled the kitchen right after escrow closed. She and Richard had been married only a year and, at that time, he still had an extremely well-paying job. After rewiring the entire house, she'd indulged a whim and purchased appliances with expensive antique fronts. Even the microwave oven was masked to look old. She had all the modern comforts yet the feel of a bygone era. Little had she known that her dreams for her marriage and of restoring the rest of Hawkings House were about to crash down around her.

"I've had time to think about this invitation," Pat observed, nodding her head in apparent approval over the de-cor. "Why am I here? Really." She took one can of soda and popped the top. "Granted, I've groveled shamelessly for an invitation, but why tonight? Even without the storm and the power failure, I can't see much at night, certainly none of the grounds."

Hope started to answer, then changed her mind. "Let's go into my office." She went to the back of the house and opened the door at the end of the hall. Originally, it had been the music room. Now it was her sanctuary, the one other room besides the master bathroom and kitchen she'd been able to do something with before the bottom had fallen out of her life. Even in the darkness, in her mind's eye she could see the gleaming hardwood floors and the frescoes and mouldings that she'd lovingly restored. In here, among the McLean antiques she'd collected, she felt safe and warm. The electricity flickered twice, then flooded the room with bright light, dramatically unveiling her hand-iwork.

Pat's jaw sagged open as she took it all in. "Hope, this is incredible!" she squealed. "I feel like I stepped back in time!"

Her friend's appreciation meant the world to her. "Ev-erything in here is genuine, no reproductions except the rag rug. Bought that at Wal-Mart. The rest were once owned by descendants of Britt McLean, Richard's great, great, great-grandfather."

Pat's expression became even more enthralled, if that were possible. Reverently, she trailed a finger along a book-case.

Hope wanted to talk about the real reason she'd invited her friend here, but she didn't want to spoil the rare moment of someone else appreciating her obsession of her in-laws' family history. She pointed to each of her treasures in turn. "The desk was owned by Robert McLean, Britt's oldest son."

"He's the one who became the judge, right?"

Hope nodded.

"What about this safe?" She pointed to a battered lead-and-steel cube in the corner that stood nearly six feet tall.

"That's not something one sees in every home in America."

"It's the original vault from the old Manzanita Bank." Inside lay the greatest treasure of all—the single remaining original journal of Sheriff Britt McLean—but she shared that with no one. "Evie McLean Carringer's husband built the love seat for her in 1882, and their youngest son imported the grandfather clock from Germany in 1910." She ran through the history of each piece, including a sideboard, three curio cabinets and portraits and old photographs of the various McLeans throughout the years. What pictures weren't on the walls were in albums in a glass-fronted bookcase. Pat hung on her every word.

"You're a walking history book on the McLeans," Pat observed when Hope finally wound down. "Have you ever thought of recording all this for future generations? Or did someone born into the family already do that?"

"I have a computer hard drive full of stuff, but most of the McLeans take their family history for granted and don't really care. The museum curator suggested I approach a university press, maybe the same one that published Britt McLean's journals twenty years ago. I still haven't decided." Hope tried not to look self-conscious, but had no idea whether or not she succeeded. "Pat, I was adopted. When I was three, my birth mother dropped me off at a church and disappeared. No one ever found her, so I have no stories at all. No roots."

"How horrible," Pat said, her baby-doll blue eyes soft with compassion. "I can see why a family history is probably more important to you than for most people."

That was another thing Hope liked about Pat—her perceptiveness. "To the point of unhealthy obsession," she confessed. "I think much of what appealed to me about Richard was that he knew quite a bit about entire generations of his family. And the stories his great-aunt used to tell . . ." A twinge of sadness tugged at her heart. Hope hadn't had the chance to get to know the old lady well, but she'd loved talking to her. "I used to sit with her at the nursing home for hours, writing out stories in longhand, then transferring them to the computer when I got home."

When she'd married Richard she'd thought she'd found paradise, a family of her own. Mostly, she'd thought she'd found an echo of the historical figure she'd obsessed over since a teacher had assigned him as a research project—Britt McLean. But she'd go to the grave before admitting the extent of that foolishness to anyone.

Pat's gaze became uncomfortably speculative. "Your voice has been off all evening. I noticed it when we finally finished with our respective pokey clients, but didn't think I should say anything. Now, I'm really worried. You're upset. What's bothering you?"

Getting cornered wasn't exactly what she'd planned. In the long term, it didn't make that much difference, but she didn't know how to begin. She perched on the edge of Evie's love seat and laced her fingers together in her lap. Pat leaned back against Robert's desk and crossed her arms, waiting, her expression tense.

Hope took a short breath. "I'm a mouse. I've been one my whole life, and I hate it. I want to be an up-front, in-your-face kind of person. Like you. Can you teach me?"

Pat's eyes widened, her model-perfect face smoothing in shock. "Come again?"

Hope blushed clear to her toes. "I'm sorry." Her gaze dipped to the floor. Determined, she squared her shoulders and looked Pat straight in the face. "I shouldn't have asked. It's not fair to put you on the spot like that. I just thought that by giving you the grand tour I could bribe you into showing me how to stand up for myself and take charge of my life. I'm sick of always taking the path of least resistance because I'm too busy trembling in a corner to fight for the right to be happy."

If anything, Pat seemed to be having trouble getting her breath. "A *mouse*? Where in the hell did you ever get that idea about yourself?"

Hope's face heated a few more degrees. This was a mistake, a dreadful one. But she might as well see it out. The alternative was to say nothing and let a miserable silence make the situation even more awkward. So she ticked her flaws off on her fingers. "I'm a coward, completely spineless. I wouldn't know how to assert myself if my life—"

"Spineless?" Pat interrupted. "You can't be serious!"

That stopped her. Was her friend as outraged by the notion as she looked?

"Hope, you are one of the most kind-hearted, diplomatic and strongest people I ever met. When that client reamed *me* out because the bank turned down his loan, I wanted to punch his lights out. You stepped in and, by the time he left, he was all smiles. I'm not strong, Hope. I'm a hothead. Big difference."

She couldn't have heard right. "If I'm so together, why can't I stand up for myself?"

"You can. You do! You just don't recognize it. Bravery isn't Joan of Arc with PMS." Pat shook her head as if she couldn't quite believe this entire conversation. "Let's back up and start over. I assume this has to do with that sleazebag you're married to?"

Hope writhed inside in humiliation. Unable to sit still, she got up and paced, her shoes silent against the rag rug. "I have a right to live out my dreams. Just because I fell for a good-looking jerk with a line as long as his arm doesn't mean I should have to pay for that mistake with the rest of my life." Her thoughts were jumbled, and she didn't know if she was making sense or not. "I never wanted to be Cathy Career Woman. I just wanted a good man to love. I wanted to stay home and raise kids and bake bread and"—she stopped and gazed fondly at the room around her, at the freshly waxed cedar walls that glowed in the lamplight—"restore the rest of this house."

From Pat's startled expression, Hope knew she needed to pull herself together better. "I waited a long time to marry, mostly because I don't trust my judgment where men are concerned. Too many of the ones I was attracted to bore too much similarity to my father and grandfather—both hard-core alcoholics. They love me, and they're good people, but they have problems. Even as careful as I was to avoid the generational trap, I fell into it anyway. Richard isn't just an alcoholic. He's an addict, too, and he's getting mean."

Pat shuddered.

"Once I figure out how to get out of this mess, I'm swearing off love—at least the romantic kind. I'll adopt kids, be a working mom and return Hawkings House to what it was a hundred years ago. This will be my dream castle. I just have to find a backbone first so I can evict the resident sleazebag.''

From the pensive expression on Pat's face, Hope was thoroughly convinced she'd just ruined a perfectly good friendship. That fear deepened when the other woman blinked slowly, then gave her a pointed look.

''For a coward, that sure sounded like a battle cry.''

Now it was Hope's turn to blink. ''It did?''

''Kiddo, apparently your childhood wasn't easy, and you've got some self-confidence issues. Being married to Superjerk probably hasn't helped. You don't need a new spine. The one you own is perfectly good. Just give yourself permission to draw a line in the sand. Then refuse to let Richard cross it.'' The fierceness in her eyes took on an intent sparkle. ''Now what is your deepest worry? Give me the worst-case scenario.''

Hope took a moment before she answered. She felt like she'd negotiated the first step on a long, painful journey, one she had to take if she was going to survive. ''I'm afraid that after I throw him out, he'll ask to come back, and I'll cave. He can be pretty convincing when he wants to be.''

''You won't cave.''

''How can you be sure?''

''Because I know you. Besides, you've got *me* for moral support. Next question. Do you want me here when you kick his sorry ass out into the street or do you want to handle that pleasure all by yourself?''

Chapter Two

Britt hadn't seen the house Nestor had built for Lucinda and the children in 111 years, not since Katherine's wedding in the gazebo out back in '88. Before that, he'd given his widow and his best friend their privacy, but he'd also desperately needed to watch his children as they suffered the joys and pains of growing up. Nestor had been a good stepfather, and back then, this house had been a happy place. Now, he stood on the modern, concrete sidewalk in front of the paved circular driveway, feeling more condemned than usual.

The house reeked of the malignant self-indulgence typical of everything connected to Richard Brittain McLean, one of Britt's direct descendants. When Richard's parents had given him Britt's first name as a middle name, Britt had swelled with pleasure. As the child grew into a deceitful, immoral scoundrel, it rapidly turned to shame.

Knowing he needed to take up residence here disturbed him nearly as much as the situation that required it. He didn't want to live where Lucinda had found happiness in the arms of another man, didn't want to hear the echoes of his children calling Nestor "Papa." But he had no choice. Shoving the old pain to the back of his mind, he tried to look at this move like any other he'd made in the 127 years

since his death. But that didn't mean he liked it. Then
again, he hadn't found *anything* particularly appealing
about being dead.

A man and woman's angry voices rose from somewhere
in the back of the first floor. Britt presumed it was Richard
and his wife. A living man couldn't have heard the quarrel
from here, but unnaturally acute hearing came with the territory.

Groaning, Britt pulled his hat low over his eyes and let
the warm, night breeze sweep him up to a second-floor
window. Maybe he could find one part of the house, that
wasn't contaminated. But as he circled the outside, he
couldn't escape the truth. All three floors as well as the
attic of his new home were permeated with the echoes of
a marriage that had never truly had a chance and of a self-
absorption that destroyed everything it touched.

"Better get this over with." Resigned, he slipped
through the roof into the attic and looked around.

Access to it was still as he remembered it, a door leading
from the back of a third-floor hall closet. As best as he
could gauge, only about two years' worth of dust covered
the floor. No footprints. If appearances could be trusted, no
one had been up here in a long time. The attic was roomy
with a nice accent window looking out over the street. He
doubted this place would ever compare to the dignified
peace of the museum where he'd lived since 1946, but with
the exception of the stench of discontent radiating from the
combatants downstairs, he could be comfortable here. Richard screamed a drunken accusation, while the woman tried
to reason with him.

Britt groaned as the meager hope crumbled. "Then
again, probably not."

He knew Richard had married three years before. Keeping track of his ever-growing numbers of descendants gave
him a pleasant distraction from the tedium of having nothing to do. A surprising number of McLeans still lived here
in Manzanita, and that pleased him.

Glass shattered downstairs, and Britt grimaced, casting a
futile wish for mortal ears with their limited range. His
journal lay somewhere within this house, and he needed to
find it. He made a quick inspection of the top floor, then

sank down to the next one. In his mind's eye, he could still see which of his children had slept where. A twinge of an old jealousy surfaced, and he squashed it. Nestor had provided far better for them and their mother than Britt ever could have. But after all this time, he doubted the wound from that failure would heal any more than it already had.

Sensing the journal somewhere beneath him, Britt dropped to the first floor and into the music room. What he found shocked him. He didn't think anyone in the current generation cared that much about family history. Someone here did, though, and cared deeply. Who? It certainly wasn't Richard.

A hulking mass of lead and steel in the corner caught his eye. Startled, he moved closer, unable to imagine what the old bank vault was doing here. It was dented and scarred from its many years in service, but no one had ever stolen a dime from it other than Tyler Carbow. He slipped easily through the reinforced lead and steel door, then settled into the leather-bound pages of the old journal. Soaking up badly needed peace and a sense of homecoming felt better than a hot bath after a week on the trail.

Since death hadn't come with instructions, he didn't know why he needed to remain near people and possessions that meant something to him in life. His best assumption was that by going against the natural order of life, he'd accidentally chained himself to objects like his journal. Whatever the reason, the bottom line was if he got too far away for too long, a cloying restlessness ate at him until he thought he'd lose his mind.

Since his murder, the years had crawled by. Even his children's grandchildren were gone now. Still, Britt remained, and thanks to a museum fire, his dwindling possessions had been destroyed—all but this one.

Richard's wife raised her voice, fracturing Britt's meager peace. On the heels of it came worry. What would he do if living here really did prove intolerable? With the quarrel in the next room fueling his concerns, he moved through the walls from room to room until he reached a bright-yellow kitchen. A typically twentieth-century man and woman faced each other on opposite sides of a work island, their combative stances well-established.

At six feet, Richard was far taller than Britt had been in life. But his dark hair, deep-set eyes and high cheekbones bore a strong family resemblance. The arrogant set to his jaw was identical to men Britt had known in life, none of whom he'd ever called friend. Richard was dressed in rumpled designer slacks and a polo shirt. The bloodshot eyes and seedy air about him made Britt want to turn away in disgust. Most of his descendants were honest, hard-working people. Some had done quite well for themselves. Not this one.

Britt had long ago learned to block out the emotions of the living whenever he needed to. He had no reason now, and what he found was far worse than what he'd expected. Not since Tyler Carbow had he sensed such a fundamental evil. Knowing that such filth had crept into his descendants' bloodlines infuriated him.

The woman came as another surprise, this time a pleasant one. Britt had expected someone of the same ilk as Richard, and he'd unconsciously prepared himself to dismiss her as such. Instead, she was fine-boned with violet eyes and shoulder-length, soft brown hair that glowed in the harsh electric lights. Her pale lavender slacks and sweater were expensive and well cared for. Her crossed arms and delicate, lifted chin presented a picture of hard determination. But her pounding pulse and hidden heartbreak told the real story. What touched him most was the gentle vulnerability and loving nature about her. She was a true lady, one who deserved better than the man she'd married. Instant protectiveness wrapped itself around his heart.

Richard spat obscenities at her, and Britt nearly backhanded him. Over the endless decades, he'd learned much about moving solid objects and communicating with the living. Even if he dared interfere with this quarrel, it would accomplish nothing. Richard's moral bankruptcy would take God Himself to redeem. Still, he was tempted to grab his miscreant descendant by the ear and haul him to the old carriage house for a lesson in manners.

What was a woman like this doing with a hellspawn like that? Britt had to do *something*. But what? Virtually every time he tried to help the living, he brought disaster down on their heads. At the very least, he complicated their lives beyond all excuse. Keeping himself out of their affairs was best for everyone. Yet how could he just turn his back on this innocent? She was a lamb in the lion's den, completely unaware of how deep her husband's corruption ran.

"Richard, you can't keep on this way." The turmoil of confronting him had Hope's heart pounding so hard in her chest that it hurt to breathe.

After a lifetime of being programmed to avoid creating a scene, doing just that was one of the hardest things she'd ever faced, and her mother's voice echoed loudly in her ears. *Mustn't disturb Daddy when he's drinking, sweetheart. It just creates upset for everyone, and we don't want that, do we?* Hope would obediently shake her head "no" then tiptoe to her room to wait until her father had passed out on the sofa. Mom had meant well, but she didn't have any idea that she'd been the perfect enabler for an alcoholic and trained her only child to follow in her footsteps.

Hope shook off the memories. Her knees trembled, but she stood her ground. For the first time in the two years since Richard's drinking and recreational drug use had gotten out of hand, she didn't feel helpless.

Thanks to Pat's insistence that she was tougher than she thought, plus the Al-Anon meetings she'd attended for the last three weeks, a whole new perspective had opened up for her. She didn't have to endure whatever life threw at her and only dream about being a take-charge kind of person. *She could make herself into one.* The prospect of turning her life around made her light-headed, but why did the process have to be so frightening? And why hadn't she discovered this *years* ago?

"Richard, the sooner you admit you have a problem, the sooner you can deal with it." Each word sounded wonderful coming from her mouth. But was she being selfish? That's what her mother would say. No, she decided. She had to stop listening to the old programming and start hanging on to the truth—that she had a *right* to live her life and that no one could fix an alcoholic or addict except themselves and God.

"My only problem is you." He yanked a beer from the

refrigerator, his glower an open dare to make an issue of it.

His midnight eyes were glazed from the chemical stew he'd ingested, but she could still see traces of the devastatingly handsome man she'd once known. His dark-brown hair still had an enticing hint of copper, but it now hung in dirty waves past his collar. Instead of his features looking lean and aristocratic, they'd grown gaunt, his skin sallow. Even his once well-toned muscles had softened from disuse.

At one time, love had been a given, and the passion had felt endless. How could she have been so blind to his true nature? Had her years-long infatuation with Britt caused her to see only what she'd wanted to see—a man who bore the McLean name, a man who had McLean blood running in his veins? Because of that had she convinced herself that Richard must also bear his ancestor's character and heart? So it seemed. The questions no longer mattered. The horror show was ending, and she would rebuild her life and her dreams—this time maybe with a few less stars in her eyes.

"Besides," he added, "if I had a little support around here instead of your endless bitching, maybe I wouldn't need to drink."

"Bitching? I've bent over backwards to—"

"What is this really about, Hope? Some sort of power play because you're the breadwinner now, and I'm nothing but a lowly house husband?"

The self-pitying backspin he put on everything used to pound her into the ground. Not anymore.

"Richard, I'm not responsible for your addictions." The iron in her voice pleased her. Maybe she really *did* have a backbone! "I refuse to spend the rest of my life married to an alcoholic and addict. You'd better think about how important our marriage is, because you're on borrowed time. Good night." Giving him one more chance made her newly found backbone feel a little less strained, even though she knew the gesture was pointless. She left the kitchen and walked through the dining room to the stairs in the hall. Her legs trembled so hard she could barely walk, but she'd drawn her line in the sand. If he didn't believe she meant business, that was his problem.

"Oh, stop acting like Miss Holier Than Thou," he yelled after her.

Hope stopped the flinch before it took hold, curious at the sensation of cleansing that trickled through her soul. Standing on the threshold of breaking free from a prison was a nice place to be—even if the process of escape did scare the stuffing out of her. A tiny smile began to form, and the trembling eased.

As her foot touched the bottom step, she changed her mind about her direction and walked to the music room, her haven.

A well-used notepad sat on her desk. Two new clients wanted to look at property early tomorrow, and she needed to prepare. Somehow, though, going through the real estate listings required more focus than she could muster right now. Instead, she opened the antique bank vault for her closest link to the man she'd fantasized about for years.

Ever since that high-school history paper, she'd been fascinated by the hardy frontier lawman who'd demanded civilized behavior from an uncivilized land. Few such men had kept a record of their hopes, dreams and adventures—most died in obscurity after a lifetime of hardships. Some of them had worse criminal records than the outlaws they'd sworn to hunt down. In this, too, Britt had been different. Honest, hard-working and better educated than most, he'd made a permanent mark in Manzanita. And his twenty-year-long personal accounting of events was a primary source of history for the entire region.

Gingerly lifting the brittle, leather-bound volume from the vault, she settled into Evie's love seat. As fragile as the journal was, she knew it belonged sealed behind glass where nothing could harm it. The published version of his writings were easier to read than the faded, flowing script of the original. But nights like tonight, when life seemed endlessly complicated and lonely, she needed to run her fingers across the pages he'd once touched, needed the tactile closeness to a simpler time when choices were easy, and men like Britt McLean never questioned the lines between right and wrong.

This one surviving journal contained his final entries before his murder in 1872, and the empty pages in the back grieved her. As she opened to a favorite section, an unearthly chill brushed past her, then vanished. Her skin crinkled with gooseflesh, and she shuddered. The whole reaction was as bizarre as the chill itself. Worse, though, was the sudden sensation of being watched.

Nervous and half expecting to find someone lurking in the shadows, she scanned the room. "Oh, stop imagining things," she muttered. "You're overtired and stressed from the argument." The voice of reason should have banished her case of the willies, but it didn't.

Britt sensed his journal move the moment someone picked it up. Having his belongings touched by anyone had always been a rare occurrence. Not even the curator of the museum had done so in years. Worried for the journal's safety, he'd shot from the kitchen to the music room, misjudged his distance and practically collided with Hope. He winced as she recoiled from the chill of death that marked his presence. Then he tipped his hat in silent apology, annoyed by his carelessness. She couldn't see him, but being invisible didn't give him license to be rude.

She was curled up on the love seat that Evie's husband had built, one foot tucked beneath her, his journal cradled in her lap. After a moment's puzzlement, she went back to his scribblings, savoring all the words as if they were part of a love letter written just for her. The situation startled him so badly, he didn't know what to make of it.

Intrigued, he peered over her shoulder to see what exactly held such interest. It was nothing, just a tirade on a miner's reluctance to move on after his claim had gone bust.

> *Dreams are as important to life as food and drink, often more. They flavor the plainest bread and give water the quality of a fine wine. It's only when we fail to lay them down at the proper time that they ruin us.*

Why was that so meaningful to her? Then he opened himself more deeply to her feelings. What he found stunned him. It made no sense. Crouching down to see her face, he discovered a tenderness shining in her eyes that confirmed the impossible. She not only respected him, she was sweet on him and had been for many years!

"Well, Britt," she murmured to the page, "I can't say I hadn't read that before. I just didn't recognize how much your advice to your friend also pertained to me, at least not until tonight."

He felt himself gape. The ever-present loneliness rose up with a shattering strength. Out of self-preservation, he moved away, not stopping until he began to drift through the opposite wall. *I died nearly a century before she was born. How could she possibly hold so much in her heart for . . . ME?*

Reverently, she turned another page. Longing and affection radiated from her like a comforting fire. For over twelve decades he'd been cut off from God and humanity. Suddenly learning that a living, breathing human cared about him was a priceless gift he'd never thought to experience again.

Making his presence known would be simple enough. He'd become quite adept at appearing solid after 127 years of practice, but a gentleman didn't just materialize in a lady's house. In the first place, it would frighten her. Most importantly, it violated ethics he'd formed from bitter mistakes. Still, he was tempted. He felt like a man dying of thirst who'd unexpectedly found himself at a cool stream. Only in his case, he dared not drink from it. And what about the danger she was in? Lord, he wished he knew what to do.

"For right now, she's just a troubled lady who found solace in a fantasy," he told himself. "Leave her be." An insidious voice in the back of his head wondered if he wasn't entitled to a few fantasies of his own—like having someone to talk to.

Hope looked around the room and frowned. He knew she hadn't heard him, but it was possible she'd felt his presence. Some mortals were better at that than others. Keeping his distance and his mouth shut would be a good idea while he lived here.

Britt tried to make himself leave the room, but couldn't. After a quick debate—one in which common sense lost— he settled into her desk chair to watch as she read and then reread passages that held particular significance to her. Did she know how incredible her violet eyes were?

His conscience prodded at him that this was worse than peeping at keyholes as a child. His father had introduced him to the business end of a willow switch at age ten and long ago ended such tomfoolery. But would a few minutes hurt? This beautiful, gentle woman cared about him, and he'd been starved for human contact for so long. To suddenly find himself with a tiny morsel within his grasp was too much to walk away from.

"What did I ever do in life to deserve your notice now?" he asked deliberately below the normal range of human hearing. So much for keeping his mouth shut.

This time when she glanced up, she looked right at him and frowned. Had she heard his question, or just a whisper of nothingness? Shaking her head in dismissal, she tucked a strand of shoulder-length brown hair behind her ear, checked her watch, then slowly closed the journal. With great care, she placed it in the old bank vault, gave it one final caress and bolted the lock.

From down the hall came the sound of shattering glass. He sensed Hope cringe inside. Britt had long ago come to a place where he'd accepted his ability to read other people's emotions. In the context of what he was, it was no different than sight or hearing. He tried to be respectful of the living's privacy but not to the point of denying himself needed insights as occasion warranted.

Hope's valiant determination to ignore Richard made him nervous. Under normal circumstances, it would have been fine, if he correctly understood the modern view of such matters. Which he was fairly sure he did. The problem came from what Britt sensed as Richard's true nature—bad to the bone. The protectiveness solidified into commitment to her safety.

"McLean, if you think you're getting involved, then you're a bigger fool than you were in life." He slammed his mouth shut. Had common sense deserted him completely? So it would seem.

She looked around again, this time in fear. "Is there anyone here?" she asked. Abruptly, she felt foolish, and Britt decided that if he didn't pull himself together, he'd create problems that neither of them needed.

Her mortal ears couldn't have picked up much, but his carelessness still irritated him. Afraid he might do something worse—like materialize and introduce himself—he drifted up through the ceiling.

A living, breathing human being cared about him! Awe and wonder filled him as nothing had since the birth of his grandchildren. Sixty years had gone by since Evie—his firstborn and the one to outlive the others—had died. At her passing, no one remained on earth who'd known him as a living man. It was then that he'd truly learned what it meant to be alone.

For whatever reason, he'd suddenly been given a priceless gift, a respite from the torment of his endless isolation, and he didn't know what to do with it.

Overwhelmed, he slipped through the layers of the house and sat on the roof. For hours, he savored the joy of discovery and let his thoughts drift. Needing an outlet for the energy it created, he returned to the attic and set about the task of settling in.

Perhaps if he found some wood, he could build a simple desk, chair and bookcase. The small room might be rather homey, and it would give him something to do. He didn't actually need furniture, but "feathering a nest" made him feel like he belonged somewhere and soothed the aching need to pretend he was still a little bit human. Sneaking supplies up here and working while the occupants were gone or asleep would be a nuisance but worth it. After making a mental list of tools and building materials, he went to the town's lumberyard and rummaged through their scrap pile.

Hope shut her bedroom door and changed into her pajamas. As always, reading Britt's words had quieted her. His sometimes poetic, often blunt observations of a bygone era had such relevance to her life. If only she could make sense out of what had come over her tonight. Why had she felt watched? Why had she thought she'd heard someone asking her a question?

"Battle fatigue?" She walked into the bathroom and drew a brush through her hair.

Richard dropped something else downstairs. Somehow she knew he'd never change. As she slid into bed and tucked the covers around herself, she braced for tomorrow. Unless a miracle happened, it would be D-Day for evicting the sleazebag.

The next morning, Hope found Richard passed out on the couch in the den, one arm flung above his head, his legs propped on the coffee table. She took a moment to study him. She remembered how his smile used to make her weak in the knees.

At one time, Richard McLean had been the center of her universe. Now she felt only pity, disgust and an unshakable desire to get him out of her life. Thank God they'd never had any children.

Bending down, she shook his arm. The stench of body odor and stale booze made her pull back. "Richard, wake up."

He didn't stir.

"Wake up!"

Not even his eyelids flickered.

Looking at him, she knew her instincts last night had been right. She'd hit the point of no return.

On the drive to work, she debated her options. She just wasn't up to the emotional trauma of a divorce. On the other hand, most of her exhaustion was caused from not solving the problem in the first place.

"That and being a lifelong coward," she muttered as she opened the door to the real estate office.

Pat was at her desk, rummaging through her morning mail.

"The spineless wonder has reformed," Hope chirped.

Pat looked up, a broad smile curving her lips. "Did you kick him out?"

"Not yet. That little party comes down tonight."

Pat's brows lowered in an intrigued frown. "You don't sound like yourself."

Hope did a pirouette. "You're looking at the new and

improved version. Of course, by the time I have to actually get tough, I'll be back to shaking in my boots, but no more Ms. Doormat for me.''

''Oh, yeah?''

Hope opened her mouth to fire off something self-deprecating but stopped herself. Her sponsor at Al-Anon told her you are what you believe. No more putting herself down. ''My only real fear is that I'm so far in debt because of him, I may have to sell Hawkings House. There's no way I can come up with the money to buy out his half interest.'' She teared up. ''That would be a hard blow, but as Britt once said, sometimes a dream has to be laid down.''

At the speech, Pat's jaw sagged, and her eyes rounded. ''Can you do that?''

''I may not have a choice.'' Suddenly, it all seemed so overwhelming. But telling her plans to Pat was like making a promise to herself. She'd hold firm to it or die trying.

Pat leapt from her chair, threw her arms around Hope and spun her around. ''I am so proud of you! Tell me all about it.''

''I don't know where to start.''

''How about the beginning?''

To give herself a moment to collect her thoughts, Hope wandered over to the refreshment table and poured herself a cup of coffee. Brian, their boss and owner of the office, must have been experimenting with different blends again because it was rich with a hint of spice. ''Richard knew when we were dating how I felt about drinking to excess. I think he knew if I ever saw him drink, I wouldn't marry him.''

''Smart girl.''

''No,'' Hope sighed. ''Gullible girl. All he did was hide it. By the time I found out, we'd been married almost a year. I nearly divorced him then, but he was . . . I don't know . . .''

''Come on. Don't hold back on me now. Give!''

''I came to Manzanita three-and-a-half years ago to do some research on Britt McLean. My hero worship thing you already know a little about, so I won't bore you with it again.''

"Fair enough." Pat winked to soften the teasing comment.

"The local librarian showed me the phone book with the numbers and addresses for several of his descendants. The idea of actually meeting people who had a tangible connection to him was like a dream come true. They were charming and more helpful than I had ever hoped for. My first thought when I saw Richard was how could a man who looked that good still be single."

"Yeah," Pat conceded. "He's a major stud-muffin. Too bad he's such a creep."

"Anyway, I thought I saw some of Britt's character in him." Hope shrugged. "I wanted to believe it so badly. I don't think I looked very hard for the truth." Turning away, she shook her head. "Pretty juvenile."

"No, just overly romantic."

She saw no pity in her friend's face when she looked back, just compassion. Taking another deep swallow of coffee, she continued, "Then it all crashed down around me when we'd been married about a year. I fell into the same trap my mother did—love a little more, try a little harder."

"It never works."

"I know, but he was so remorseful, and he promised to quit. Then he let me buy Hawkings House, even though he hated it and wanted something that had a better investment potential."

"Ahhh, the ol' guilt gift routine, huh?"

"Yeah, but it seemed like something else at the time."

It still appalled her that she'd been that naive. But at least she had the house. If she could find a way to keep it, one day it would *sing* instead of sitting there looking neglected and unloved. Hope cringed inside at what an incurable romantic she still was. Hadn't experience taught her *anything?*

"I know a really good attorney." Pat's eyes glittered, giving Hope a vision of a barracuda with a briefcase.

The legal battle loomed largely before her, and she sagged into her chair. "I hate this. Why couldn't things have worked out the way they were supposed to?" It was a rhetorical question, and she wasn't surprised when her friend didn't answer.

"Every time my mother gets sick of Dad and threatens to divorce him, he sobers right up. It never lasts long. Promise me something, Pat," she continued, meeting the other woman's eyes. "If Richard pulls the same stunt and I'm tempted to take him back, don't let me do it. Yell. Kick. Scream. Do whatever it takes. But don't let me cave like Mom does."

"You got it, but you sound as if believing in people is a dreaded disease to be expunged at all costs."

Hope opened her mouth to protest, but Pat waved her off.

"In this case, that's the right choice, but your ability to see the good in people is a gift, Hope. Don't let Richard the Wonder Slug damage that. The world needs people like you."

An uncomfortable self-consciousness made her squirm. "I don't want to be nice. I want to be rough and tough and write people off if they annoy me."

Pat choked on her coffee. "Wicked Bitch of the West?"

The image tickled her. "Yeah!"

Pat's lips twitched into a self-indulgent smile. "I promise I won't let you get that far out of hand, but if you want a hothead in your face to help get you started, you've got it."

"Thank you." Hope prayed that the good guys might win one for a change.

"Hope! Where in the hell are you?"

Hours after she left for work, Britt watched from a corner of the den as Richard woke, then stumbled to the bathroom. When the idiot finished emptying his stomach of assorted toxins, he trudged into the kitchen. With shaking fingers, he opened the fridge and grabbed a beer.

"She's my wife, for God's sake. I shouldn't have to put up with this shit." Richard leaned out the back door. "Hope! Answer me, damn it! The house looks like hell. When are you gonna do something about it?" When she didn't answer, he slammed the door.

Britt—generally slow to anger—bristled. As the hours passed, he watched his descendant crawl back into a chemically-induced stupor that started with a beer, then progressed to a dissolved powder injected into his veins.

The more Britt saw, the more it repulsed him. Five generations separated him from Richard, but he felt a certain responsibility for his family's conduct. That and leaving the living to their own damnation created an irritating internal conflict that he still didn't know how to resolve.

It had been twenty-six years since his last disastrous interaction with a living person. But a perfect picture of Hope formed in his mind. Anger at Richard built. Violating his "no contact" rule on her behalf tempted him like nothing ever had. He knew his conscience wouldn't tolerate him standing idly by and watching her get hurt. If events proceeded along the course he expected, he might not have a choice. Or was that just what he wanted to believe? Then he remembered the gentleness of her heart. Temptation won.

"Your wife is at work," he drawled loud enough to be heard. After so long, the clear ring of his own voice sounded odd, but not unpleasant. "Isn't that someplace you should be?"

Richard whirled around his drug-glazed eyes huge. In the bright light of midafternoon, Britt couldn't be seen even if he'd wanted to be, but invisibility suited his purpose. He didn't want Richard to know what he looked like,—the ghost of a man of average height—short for this century—whose harsh life had aged him beyond his thirty-seven years. Certainly nothing intimidating. In this instance, Richard's imagination could be a lot more effective than the truth.

"Who's there!"

Britt said nothing.

"Answer me! Who's there!" Fear ignited.

"Let me ask you a question first," he drawled again, leaning against the kitchen island and crossing his feet at the ankles. He didn't have physical sensations, but the habits he'd found comfortable during life had carried over into death. He drew his pipe from his shirt pocket and lit it with a thought.

Lucinda had tucked his favorite pipe into his shirt pocket at the funeral. Consequently, he had its afterlife counterpart with him, just like the rest of the clothing he'd been buried with: his favorite boots, best brown trousers, lucky red shirt and his new hat. Seconds later, wisps of smoke only he could see floated in the air around his face as he drew on the stem.

Richard sniffed the air, undoubtedly able to smell it—another phenomenon Britt didn't understand but had long ago accepted. Richard turned around a few times, then faced Britt squarely. "Where are you?"

"How can you do this to yourself?" he demanded. "To your wife? Where's your self-respect? You're a McLean!"

Richard jumped. "Whoever you are, this isn't funny!" The eyes tried to focus. Probably suspecting a practical joke of some type, he walked from the kitchen through the dining room down the hall and into the ladies' parlor. "Come out before I call the cops!"

Britt shook his head, pulled his hat low and followed. "Hope's a good woman. If you won't take hold of yourself for your own sake, maybe you need to for hers."

"That's it," Richard snapped, heading for the phone on an end table by the sofa. "I'm tired of this game."

"No game," he said around the pipestem. "You need a change of direction before you hurt Hope and land yourself in jail. I believe the modern expression is 'clean and sober.'"

Richard gave the area where Britt stood a suspicious look. Walking gingerly, he approached, shoulders hunched, hand extended experimentally. Britt held his ground. The moment Richard got too close, the blistering cold hit him, and he stumbled back with a yelp.

"What the hell was that?" he shrieked.

"Just me," Britt muttered, taking another draw on his pipe. "Now, put down the beer and go clean up."

Richard glanced at his latest can, then gave Britt a sidelong look. "Show yourself, you son of a bi—"

"Listen, boy, you can call me whatever names you like. Believe me, I've heard worse than anything you can dream up. Now, for the second and last time, put down the beer and take a shower."

Belligerent, Richard lifted the can to his lips. Sighing in

disgust, Britt reached out and took it. From the perspective of mortal eyes, the can left Richard's fingers on its own, floated into the kitchen, then emptied itself into the sink. The chill of death couldn't have been real pleasant. Terror clotted the air, and Richard lost what little skin color he still possessed. That suited Britt fine. Fear had its uses.

He blew smoke into Richard's face, then dropped a lethal dose of menace into his voice. "Now, do you plan to acquaint yourself with that soap, or would you like my help?" The basso rumble he put into the last two words made them echo off the walls. The theatrics weren't necessary. The man was already scared spitless. But compassion didn't rate particularly high on Britt's list of priorities at the moment. Results did.

He couldn't comprehend why anyone would treat his body with such casual disregard. Didn't he understand how precious life was? Envy swept through him with sadistic fervor. He desperately craved to feel a heart beating in his chest once more, to feel the sun warm against his face, to know the tenderness of a woman's touch. Instead, all he had was this horrible in-between state that, from all evidence, would last forever. He'd had his chance to move on to the afterlife and had ruined it. Shutting his mind to the misery, he held himself motionless until he gained control over the worst of it.

Richard stumbled backward and flopped onto the couch. "I'm hallucinating." He dug the heals of his hands into his eyes, then blinked as if to clear his vision. "Got hold of some bad stuff is all."

Britt grabbed him by the shirtfront and hauled him to his feet. Richard shrieked like an old woman with a mouse up her skirts. The cold probably numbed the man's brain, but Britt didn't care and propelled him up the stairs and down the hall to the bathroom.

"Turn on the water."

Whimpering, Richard complied.

"Strip." Britt didn't stay to see if he'd been obeyed. Standing over a drunkard's naked, reeking body was about as revolting a thought as he could imagine. Instead, he went to find some clothes from the master bedroom.

Personally, Britt liked modern fashions. Briefs, for example, had to be a lot more comfortable than long johns. The soft, stretchy fabric looked like it would feel wonderful against a man's skin.

Unfortunately, he no longer owned skin. Nor did he have a sense of touch. He moved things around. End of subject. The loss of all mortal sensations except sight, hearing and smell had bothered him from the beginning, but he'd resigned himself to it years ago. As if he'd had a choice.

Brushing aside longings that could never be fulfilled, he dropped Richard's clean clothes by the bathroom door, went into the kitchen and poured out every can and bottle of booze in the place. The empties he tossed into the plastic boxes with the appropriate recycle symbol on it.

He'd kept in touch with the changing times. In some respects, he knew the culture better than the people born to it. When one had nothing but time to study, that wasn't so surprising.

When Richard emerged from the bathroom, he'd put on the same filthy clothes he'd worn for days.

"Didn't you see the fresh ones I laid out?" Britt asked.

Richard shrieked again. The noise was getting tiresome, and Britt swallowed a groan.

"I hallucinated you!" He looked wildly around the room. "I did! You're not real."

"Afraid you got that wrong, too, boy." He put out the pipe with another thought and tucked it into his pocket. "Now, go change, then fix yourself a decent meal before I lose my temper."

"But I—"

"Move!"

Richard cooked burnt eggs, toast and coffee. Britt didn't think the man's stomach could keep it down, but apparently terror served as a great motivator.

"All right, now to the next item on the list."

Richard tried to make himself look smaller in the chair at the table. "What now?"

"Your stash. Get it."

His already pasty skin became cadaverous. "I don't do drugs."

Britt floated above him, then bent to his ear. "Would you like to see me angry?"

Richard shot off the chair and headed for the china hutch. He jerked open a top drawer and reached behind it. After a moment's fumbling, he pulled out a clear bag with a syringe and a bunch of things Britt wasn't sure he could identify. He took it, and Richard's dark eyes widened.

"Okay, that's one. But that's not where you got your poisons from earlier. I guess we're playing scavenger hunt today."

Richard backed toward the front door, fear replaced by blind panic.

"Stop right there, boy," Britt snarled. "We have a house to go through."

Chapter
Three

Hope finished with her last client at eight. That meant there was very little chance Richard would be sober enough to remember anything she said tonight. She braced herself for the worst and went home. Ending her marriage would have to wait until morning. The disappointment seemed almost more than she could bear.

When she pulled into the circular driveway beside Richard's sedan, something about the front yard didn't look the same. Then she spotted what was out of place, and her jaw sagged open. The grass had been cut, the hedge trimmed and debris raked from the flowerbed. Walking into the house, she had no idea what to expect. Then came another shock. Someone had cleaned the gentlemen's parlor. No assorted piles of beer cans littered the floor or were stuffed between couch cushions. For a moment, she suspected she'd walked into the wrong house. Then another idea came to her. What if he'd taken her seriously last night and decided to sober up?

That gave her a few mixed emotions. Yes, she wanted him to be sober for his own sake, but it was just too late for their marriage. In her heart, she'd already closed that door. Nothing would make her want to go back. She pursed her lips, determined to follow through. Her future depended on it.

"You can't run with the big dogs if you pee like a puppy," she murmured under breath. "Richard?" she called out.

Silence. Had he moved out on his own?

Cautiously, she tread down the hallway, checking each room in turn. If he was drunk and in one of his darker moods, she wanted to find him before he found *her*. It didn't take long. He was huddled on the floor in her office, his back wedged into the far corner beside the vault. He looked up at her, stone-cold sober and wild-eyed with terror.

The unease she'd felt upon discovering the yard and clean house paled in comparison to the full claxon alarms that now rang in her ears. Hope took a wary step toward him. "What are you doing down there?"

His eyes narrowed as if deciding whether or not he could trust what he saw.

"Richard, what's wrong?"

A soul-deep shudder rolled through him, and he swallowed hard. "A demon. Or maybe Satan himself. I don't know. He wouldn't tell me."

This surprised her. Hallucinogens weren't his normal style. Then she had another thought. DTs, maybe? "What are you talking about?"

"A demon! When he touched me, it was like touching death."

Hope drew in a long breath and forced herself to hide her pity and disgust. The truth of what she felt toward him would only antagonize him.

"You don't believe me." His eyes flashed in anger. "I didn't believe it either until after my shower."

"Your shower?"

He glowered up at her. "Do I have to repeat *every damned word*?"

Hope mentally collected herself, swallowed hard, then cleared her throat. "Richard, why don't you start from the beginning?"

"He's been after me all day. Just when I think he's gone

and I can leave, he shows up and starts bossing me around.''

She stared at him, trying to think of a reply that wouldn't make a bad situation worse.

''Go ahead, Hope. Say it. You think I'm having DTs or got hold of some bad shit.''

Hope tried not to stare, but it was like finding a wreck on the freeway. She couldn't tear her gaze away. ''What I think is that you need help.''

''Figured you'd say that,'' he snapped. He reached out and shoved her to the side. ''Get out of the way so I can see him coming!''

Hope needed to put some distance between her and the unbalanced man on the floor. She made great show of smoothing her skirt and adjusting her blazer, praying it masked the step she took toward the hallway. ''Is the demon here now?'' She tried for a conversational tone, but her voice cracked and faltered.

His gaze flicked to her face, darkened in irritation and moved on. ''Stop looking at me like that. I'm not crazy. He's here. In this house. He took my beer. My stash. Everything. It's gone.''

Hope gauged the distance to the phone on her desk. Too far, considering she had to reach past him to get it. The next closest phone was in the kitchen. Old houses were often built like a maze—this one included. To reach the phone, she had to get down the hall and through the dining room. For the first time, she didn't think the layout was quaint. ''Satan took your beer?''

He nodded vigorously. ''The Scotch, too. Poured it all out. Won't let me leave the house so I can buy more.''

Her mind raced. She had to get help. Fast. ''Richard, you should talk to someone who knows more about this than I do.'' Clumsy, she knew, but it was the best she could come up with under fire.

His gaze riveted onto her face. ''No! They'll think I'm crazy.'' He lurched to his feet. Tremors overtook him. ''Bet you'd like that, wouldn't you!''

Hope wanted to run for her life, but she dared not make any sudden moves. *Calm*, she told herself. *I must stay calm.*

''If that worries you, don't mention the demon. Just say you need to get a handle on things again. Besides, at the hospital, maybe the demon can't get at you.''

''He can, too.'' His gaze became wild-eyed again as it darted all over the room, searching. ''He can go anywhere. He was with me every step when he made me mow the damned lawn.''

Hope blinked at that one. ''He forced you to do that?''

''Said I needed hard work and fresh air to clean me out. Said what I really needed was a field to plow or some wood to chop, but the yard and house would do. Thought he'd work me to death.''

Hope stared. She'd never heard of hallucinations so complex. This would take an expert to untangle.

''You don't believe me!'' Richard shoved away from the wall. Hope took two more steps back while he steadied himself. ''I'll prove it to you.'' He turned in a slow circle, staring into space. ''Hey, Satan! Say something!''

Drawing back, Hope took a deep breath, wondering if she would survive the next few minutes.

''Say something, damn you!'' Richard continued his wanderings, his head cocked, listening. There was only silence. ''Damn you to hell!''

Before she could react, he rushed past her, knocking her off balance. She grabbed the doorjamb to keep from falling again. He tore down the hall screaming obscenities at the air, and it occurred to her that he probably was no longer even aware of her presence. Not daring to waste time gathering her wits, she walked casually to the kitchen and lifted the receiver off the wall phone. She'd just punched in the first digit of the emergency code when Richard's arm snaked over her shoulder.

''You can't get rid of me that easy!'' He ripped the cord from the wall.

Heart-pounding terror overwhelmed her, and she tried to scoot past him. His fingers threaded into her hair and closed into a fist.

''You're my wife!'' He yanked her head back. ''I deserve some loyalty.''

The pain was horrific. Hope screamed, then clawed at his

hand. With a bellow of rage, he turned loose and shoved her from him.

Free, Hope inched toward the backdoor, not daring to take her eyes off of him. "Richard, think about what you're doing!"

Advancing on her, he pulled his fist back to strike. But his arm stopped in midair as suddenly as if it had slammed into a wall. "He's still here!" he shrieked, stumbling backward. "Oh, God, keep him away from me!"

Hope froze. There was no reasoning with someone who'd fried his brain. Forcing the panic from her mind, she eased to the backdoor. Richard turned toward her. A chilly breeze passed between them, and she sucked in her breath at the harshness of it. Before Hope could take another step toward the door, he lunged for her again. Then suddenly Richard doubled over, his breath driven from him.

"Leave me alone!" he wheezed. "I have the right to do what I want in my own home."

The whole tableau shifted into slow motion. The air crackled with fingers of blue lightning that seemed to come from nowhere. They hit Richard full force, and he flew across the room, slamming hard against the wall. With a shake of his head, he regained his bearings and glowered at her. He took half a step. But that was as far as he got before his head snapped to the side. Then his eyes rolled back in his head, and he fell to the floor unmoving, arms and legs sprawled like a rag doll. Blood trickled from the corner of his mouth. The air stank of ozone.

Terror like nothing Hope had ever experienced wrapped around her. Frozen in place, she stared, afraid even to breathe. Adrenaline's fire surged so hard through her veins that her hands and arms burned with it.

In the silence of the kitchen, her mind raced. What she'd just seen couldn't have been real. Yet the evidence lay unconscious ten feet in front of her. Her lungs burned from lack of air. The pit of her stomach knotted tighter and tighter. The sense of being watched sprang to life, then became overwhelming. Had he been right? Was there an otherworldly being here?

A whimper hovered at her lips, and she wanted to run

screaming into the night. Oddly, something Britt wrote echoed faintly in her ears. *When a man runs from a fight, the enemy's behind him, and he can't see what's coming.* Hope dragged in a long breath and marshalled what courage she could find.

With what little rational thought remained, she struggled to find a more plausible explanation than the supernatural, but every avenue came up blank. Keeping her back to the wall, she reached behind her for the doorknob and closed her fingers around the cool metal. The knob held fast when she tried to turn it. Locked! The whimper did escape then. Her heart pounded against her ribs with bruising force. She wanted to whirl around and unbolt the door but was too terrified to turn her back on the room. Instead, she found herself crab-walking along the wall toward the dining room, the closest route to the front door.

At the bottom range of her hearing she half felt, half heard a low, tortured "damn it to hell."

Hope gasped. The room swam, and she thought she might faint. "Who's there?" she croaked out.

Again the muttering. This time it was followed by a defeated sigh. "It's all right, ma'am." The masculine voice was honey-soft and pitched to invite trust. "You're in no danger from me."

Her knees started to buckle. She willed herself to remain standing, afraid that if she passed out, whoever had invaded her house would kill her while she lay helpless. Survival depended on staying alert and in control.

Her gaze darted everywhere, unable to land on anything out of place. The dishwasher and tile counters hadn't mutated into something sinister. Her country-mouse cookie jar still sat in its usual spot, its happy, blank stare the same as always. Only Richard's unmoving form was out of place. Hope took another step toward the dining room. She needed to get out of here.

"My word on it, ma'am. I won't hurt you." The disembodied voice came from between the kitchen island and the dishwasher. *But there was* nothing *there.*

A logical explanation had to be just a thought away, but she couldn't find one. Lifting her chin, she said, "Mind if I judge that for myself?" She'd intended to come across as brave and confident, but the words came halting and wracked with fear.

The voice sighed. "Ma'am, I'm truly sorry I'm frightening you. Your husband was bent on murder, and I didn't have time to stop him any other way. I rid the house of his liquor and drugs, and I tried to get through to him. But he's not the sort to listen to anyone but himself."

The speech shocked her. Yet, at the same time, she believed Richard really had wanted to kill her. Was this demon some sort of otherworldly protector? No, the rational side of her countered. Demons never did that kind of thing—not ever. Which left the other side of the fence.

"Are you an angel?" she rasped.

The voice sputtered and choked. "No, ma'am. I'm just . . . me."

She checked the doorway to the living room, making sure she still had an escape route. Maybe she'd watched too many horror movies as a teenager, and this was a delayed reaction. Maybe the voice was actually inside her own head, and this whole thing was one massive hallucination. She found it odd, though, that she'd never before noticed any mental problems. Didn't the insane usually at least *suspect* they weren't normal?

"It's my usual practice to tend to my own business," he continued, "but I couldn't sit back and watch while he . . ." The voice trailed off miserably.

Hope continued to stare, her heart still racing. Her eye muscles had begun to cramp from straining so hard to see something that apparently couldn't be seen.

"Ma'am, why don't you go on into the parlor . . . er . . . family room," he corrected, "and sit down. You're very pale."

An odd calm settled in, and she wondered if she was skirting the edges of a nervous breakdown. "This isn't happening. I'm stressed out and hallucinating. That's all. In a little while, I'll relax, and everything will make perfect sense."

"There's nothing wrong with you," he assured her. "I'd leave if I could, but . . . Oh, hell, I knew better than to . . ." After a short pause and a few more muttered imprecations, he loosed a miserable sigh so heart-rending that it blunted some of her terror. "Ma'am, would you please sit down before you fall over?"

The overwhelmed exasperation lent the impression of someone as off-balance with this situation as she. A fraction more of the fear eased.

Her eyes burned and began to water, but she dared not close them. "What are you?"

"Will you sit down first?"

Was he out of his mind? Or was she? "Not until you answer me!"

The voice paused. In the silence, she heard her adrenaline-driven pulse pound in her ears and felt it throb through her veins.

He sighed again, this time with resignation. "I'm someone who won a battle but lost the war."

"I don't understand." That was the biggest understatement of her life.

"I don't either, not entirely," he murmured.

"Could you *try* to explain?"

"In simple terms, I'm a ghost."

For a stunned moment, Hope was tempted to give him the benefit of the doubt. But logic won out. She shook her head, then rubbed her eyes. "A what?"

This couldn't be happening. Please let this be some sort of elaborate prank. The alternatives appalled her. Her home was either haunted or her mental faculties had disintegrated. "For the sake of argument, the ghost of whom?"

He groaned. "Mrs. McLean, ma'am, I'd just as soon you'd put your feet up until you're feeling like yourself again." His concern came through so strongly she had to glance at Richard to remind herself of the danger. Her soon-to-be ex lay oblivious on the floor like a discarded toy. At least the bleeding at the corner of his mouth had stopped. Without taking her gaze from the room, she knelt beside him and pressed her fingers to the pulse point at his neck. His heartbeat throbbed steady and strong.

"Your husband is fine. He'll come around soon enough. When he does, I'll have another talk with him . . . with words," he added quickly, "not my fists."

The voice seemed so worried about giving her a wrong

impression that her heart rate slowed a notch. "I don't believe in ghosts."

"I never did, either."

That surprised her. Then again, if her own mind was inventing all of this, nothing should surprise her. "Who are you?"

There was a long pause. "Britt McLean."

His answer echoed in her head, becoming louder with each drumbeat of her pulse. Blistering rage erupted with volcano force. If this was a hoax, the joker could have said anything else but that, and it would have only earned him her ire. But *this* ridiculed her on a level that was cruel, making it inexcusable.

Britt McLean was more special to her than anyone could understand. Something about him drew her uncontrollably. Even though they were separated by more than a hundred years and connected only by his writings, it was as if they saw the world through the same eyes. In her heart, he seemed no further away than an old friend she just hadn't seen in a while. When Richard had found out how she felt, his reaction had been predictable. He'd laughed uproariously and never really stopped.

Beneath the fury, though, she recognized that if she were to conjure up a rescuer, who else would it be but Britt McLean? Fighting through the confusion, she tried to analyze the events of the past few minutes, not knowing if she could trust her senses at all.

From all appearances, Richard hadn't been playacting. He'd tried to kill her. Then there was the blue lightning— electricity without a source. Impossible. But she'd seen it. Then someone—or something—had knocked him out. Haunted, crazy or victimized. They weren't pretty choices. The mental whiplash of jumping between the three options made it hard to think.

As an act of faith, she opted for the practical joke theory. She crept to the dining room, pulled a chair from the table and sat with her back to the wall. "I'm not sure how you rigged all of this, but the practical joke is over. When Richard comes to, he'll probably try to sue you just because it would make his day. I suggest you quit now before you make it any worse for yourself."

"This isn't a joke, ma'am."

"Well, it's a safe bet the ghost of Britt McLean is not in my house, and he did not just punch out my husband." In the quiet of the room, the words sounded fine. Any normal, rational person would believe them without question. But Richard, lying unconscious on her kitchen floor, spoke another truth.

Through the doorway, she watched Richard stir. With a pain-filled groan, he levered himself upright and gingerly explored his battered mouth. "You hit me!"

"No, I didn't." *At least, I don't think it was me. Dear Lord, how would I know?* "There's something weird going on here."

He blinked to clear his vision, then ran his tongue across his blood-smeared teeth, still taking inventory of the damage. Awkwardly he got to his feet and stood, glowering at her. "What do you mean? That somebody else did this?"

"I don't have any explanation for it, but you attacked me. Then something attacked you." Not knowing whether to battle rage over being the butt end of a practical joke or scared to death over an invasion from the supernatural world, she only partly noticed that she was functioning quite well. No mouse. No spineless wonder. "I want you out of this house—permanently."

"I'm not going anywhere," he snarled.

"Richard, you need help!" She couldn't believe any of this.

His anger began building again. She could see it in the tight muscles across his shoulders, in the swollen line that his mouth had become and the glitter in his dark eyes. The thought occurred to her that maybe she should leave for her own safety, then fight out in court who'd claim Hawkings House. But that was too much like defeat. This was *her* house. She'd been the one who'd fallen in love with it as much as if it were a cherished pet. It needed her!

She was learning to stand up for herself, and no way in Hades was she backing down, not even in the face of a haunted house or the most involved hoax she'd ever heard of. If it was insanity, she'd be locked up soon anyway, so it wouldn't matter. "I've tried to help you every way I know how. It's over. Go!"

"No." He crossed his arms in a silent dare to push the issue.

She started to panic. How would she back up her demand?

"The lady asked you nicely," drawled a familiar, honey-soft, masculine voice.

Hope gasped. Richard shrieked, pressing himself hard into a corner. "Satan."

Was Richard really hearing the voice, too, or was it all part of the hallucination? How would she know?

"If you're a real, smart fellow, you'll respect her wishes." A steel edge replaced all hint of softness.

If Hope's senses could be believed, the voice emanated from the air between herself and Richard. But there was nothing there. Absolutely *nothing!*

Richard's face turned a pasty gray. His gaze darted from place to place as if looking for a sanctuary.

"Get away from me!" he yelled.

The voice started muttering under his breath. After a moment of what sounded like swearing, it—he?—refocused on Richard. "Son, I didn't want to come here in the first place because I knew what manner of man you are." The undercurrents churned ominously. "The lady has had enough of your abuse. I've had enough of your sniveling. Now you have until I count to three to remove yourself, or I'll do it for you."

"But—"

"One." The iron in that one syllable rattled Hope's bones.

"You can't—"

"Two." The voice moved toward Richard's corner.

"But I—"

"Don't make me say three, boy." The words rolled like thunder.

Richard whirled and grabbed the backdoor. He yanked it open but misjudged his proximity and plowed the edge into his cheek. He grunted in pain, then scrambled around the door and out into the night.

"Wisdom came a little late," the voice observed sourly as the door—from all appearances—swung shut by itself. "But it did arrive."

Hope tried to shrink into the wall behind her. This couldn't be happening! But it *was!*

"Sorry again about all this, ma'am." He truly did sound remorseful. "Something had to be done. I only intended to keep him from hurting you, not scare you half to death."

Too frightened to move, she didn't even try.

"I think the kindest thing would be for me to leave you alone to collect yourself. Good night." There was a slight pause. "Again, ma'am, I'm truly sorry about all this. Maybe if I'd had a little more time, I could have found a way to be more discreet. But I didn't."

Beyond rational thought, she nodded.

"Oh, by the way, on your behalf, I took his wallet earlier. It's in the freezer behind the ice cubes. Without his ATM and charge cards to withdraw cash, he'll have a harder time buying more drugs. I suggest you close those accounts in the morning."

"Thank you," she squeaked. "I'll do that."

It could have been minutes or hours in the ensuing silence before Hope was able to get up off the dining room chair. Even then, her legs shook. So did her arms and her teeth. She crossed her arms tightly, seeking what little comfort they offered. It didn't help.

Cautiously, she went to the kitchen and looked around. Then she peeked in all the corners of every downstairs room, needing to find some evidence of a diabolically clever hoax, but found nothing.

"There's a logical explanation. I'm not crazy. My house isn't haunted, and no one is trying to get into the *Guinness Book of World Records* for perpetrating the most elaborate hoax." Hearing herself say that over and over should have helped, but it didn't.

A ghost? Even if she believed in them, weren't they supposedly obsessed with resolving a piece of unfinished business before they could move on? In theory, her house was certainly old enough to have a resident ghost, but Britt McLean had died five months before Nestor Hawkings began constructing it. No tragedies happened here that would warrant a haunting, particularly by someone who had never lived here. Had Britt come to haunt this place in protest over his widow marrying his best friend so soon after his death? No, a man like him would have understood that marriage to Manzanita's wealthiest bachelor was Lucinda's best means to keep herself and the children fed and clothed.

"What else could it be?" she murmured to herself. "The idea of Britt McLean's ghost is out. Too far-fetched." Yet she'd heard the voice, seen what it could do. The ghost option wouldn't go away. If this had been a practical joke, how had it been rigged? Who would go to the trouble and expense? The whole concept was just as far-fetched as the others. But at least she could easily prove or disprove it.

Pulling herself together, she searched more carefully for wires, speakers and microphones. Room by room, she unscrewed light bulbs, checked under and inside furniture cushions. She felt along the edge of the carpet by the baseboard. The second floor with its four bedrooms and one bath got the same treatment. She even checked for evidence of disturbed dust in the closed-off third floor. Nothing.

"Someone of flesh and blood had to be responsible for this," she murmured as she came back downstairs. Glancing around the living room, she raised her voice. "Joke's over, people. You can come out now."

The answering silence made her skin crawl.

Hope eased over to the couch, trying to convince herself of the ridiculousness of the only other two conclusions left to her—that her house was haunted—and by *Britt McLean, no less*—or she'd unknowingly slipped into mental illness. The whole concept was so bizarre that none of this could possibly be true—could it? For hours, she analyzed the events as she remembered them, but came up empty.

Exhaustion finally drove her to bed. She crawled—clothes and all—beneath the covers, pulled them up to her chin, but couldn't bring herself to shut off the light. She lay like a board, moving nothing except her eyes.

The house creaked and groaned as it, too, settled for the night. For two years, she'd found the sounds comforting, like Hawkings House had been saying good night to her. Now, the same sounds had a sinister pitch. Hours ticked by. Her body ached with fatigue. Still, she couldn't sleep. Who could possibly be behind this? Who would have reason to play such an elaborate mind game?

As each avenue of thought came to a dead end, the idea of taking the incident at face value tempted her. But the concept of her home being haunted was just too ridiculous, and entertaining the idea—no matter how briefly—made her feel gullible and stupid.

For hours her mind whirled through the endless circle—picking up each of the three possibilities, turning them over, then discarding them as illogical, then picking up the next one in the loop. Shortly after four, her body's demand for sleep overrode the fear and confusion, and she drifted off.

A short three and a half hours later, the radio alarm blared with Elton John's "Crocodile Rock." Hope woke with a start. She must have bumped the station setting. Waking to oldies instead of adult contemporary was notably harsh, especially after the night she'd just endured.

Her muscles complained from a fitful night of sleeping in her clothes. Mercifully, her usual morning mental fogginess was absent as the events of the previous night began their endless merry-go-round in her head again. Somehow, she'd half expected to have all the answers the moment she opened her eyes, sort of a "things look brighter in the morning" logic. Well, it didn't happen, and she was more confused than ever.

Nervously, she selected an outfit for the day, wondering if there were hidden cameras in her room. The thought occurred to her to dress by the bed as usual. It would make for a nice act of defiance against spying eyes. This was her house, and she wasn't going to knuckle under to a bogeyman mentality. Moreover, she needed a shower. Would unseen eyes watch?

"I think that's about enough paranoia, Hope," she muttered. The self-rebuke didn't come out as defiant as she would have liked. A picture of a cowering mouse formed in her mind, and she grabbed a towel.

A previous owner had built a master bath by taking out the adjoining bedroom wall and completely remodeling this section of the second story. The fixtures were forties era and in need of replacing. It was just one more item on the list of restorations she hadn't gotten to because Richard drank away every dime she earned.

She unscrewed the bathroom ceiling light and checked for tampering. Finding nothing, she peeled out of her wrinkled suit, then broke a personal speed record for showering and dressing.

Going downstairs proved to be another test of will. She'd never noticed that the stairs popped and creaked with each step. They did—loudly—and her heart rose higher in her throat at each one. She made a quick walk through the downstairs rooms, giving each a quick once-over for anything different from last night. Nothing was out of place, no dusty shoe prints on the carpet, no Richard passed out in one room or another. In fact, she saw no sign of him at all.

Defiance finally gained an upper hand against anger and fear. She was *not* crazy, and her house was *not* haunted. Hope threw back her shoulders.

"Hello?" she called out. To her ears, her voice sounded a bit more controlled than the night before, but not by much. It was a start, and she'd take it. "Anybody here? How about practical jokers? Or ghosts of all stripes and places of origin?" The smart-aleck remark didn't change anything, but it made her feel a little more in control. Maybe whoever had orchestrated last night's performance was still listening and would be open to admitting it if they thought she'd be a good sport about being suckered.

She hoped so, because more than anything in the world, she wanted the chance to give a flesh-and-blood human being a large chunk of her mind. But part of her didn't expect an answer and wasn't surprised not to get one.

As she toasted a blueberry bagel and nuked a cup of milk for hot cocoa, she noticed a feeling of being watched, but it was the nervous, self-created type, not the intense *knowing* of last night. That had been far too real, and she doubted she'd ever forget it.

Rather than eat at the table, she stood at the sink, looking out into the backyard. At one time, Hawkings House had been surrounded by four hundred acres of cattle land. Developers had carved it up parcel by parcel until just barely over one acre remained, and that mostly overgrown with weeds. Three walls of the beautiful, old, stone carriage house still stood, but the roof had long since collapsed. The gazebo in the middle of what had once been formal gardens was a fallen-down wreck. The termite-infested boards needed to be cleared away and burned.

In her mind's eye, she imagined how the old home had once looked with Britt's five children and the three more that Lucinda and Nestor had added later. There must have been laughter and endless upheaval. Thinking about it warmed her.

Once the dust of her divorce settled and she got on her feet financially, she'd see about adopting a house full of kids. People lined up for years for the chance to adopt a baby, but the older kids were in desperate need of families and she intended to be there.

She tried to keep her mind on the modified version of her dream, but echoes of the disembodied voice kept circling through her mind. Was the ghost of the man she'd been infatuated with since high school actually living in her house? A tiny part of her soul leapt at the prospect of meeting him. But the whole idea was simply too far-fetched. Ghosts weren't real. If her rational mind thought it had heard one, then it had a problem.

Hope set her jaw, then refocused her attention on the house. A tiny smile formed. "One day, I'll figure out how to make Hawkings House and my life into what they were meant to be." She put her cup and plate into the antique-fronted dishwasher, patted the counter as if saying good-bye, then left for work.

Just being out in the early spring air lifted her mood and distanced her from the previous night's events. Refusing to think about them helped, too. At five minutes to nine she opened the door to the realty office.

As usual, Pat was already there and going through the mail. The small office consisted of three desks spread artfully about a room decorated with posters advertising different financial programs. An artificial ficus tree adorned one corner. In another stood a narrow table with a coffeepot, assorted cups and creamers and a large, covered plate of breakfast rolls.

"Good morning," Hope chirped. She headed to the coffeepot and pulled a mug from the shelf.

Pat rose from behind her desk and followed her to the table. "What's wrong?"

Hope didn't turn around. Instead, she poured herself a cup of coffee and stirred in a large spoonful of the instant, gourmet hot cocoa she kept there. She didn't mind coffee as long it was properly flavored. "You wouldn't believe me."

Glancing at the empty desk, she asked, "Where's Brian?" Their boss was almost always the first one in every morning and the last to leave.

"Running late." Pat was not to be sidetracked, and Hope felt her friend's gaze boring into her back the moment before Pat took hold of Hope's arm and turned her around. "What did that creep do now?" Her bright blue eyes blazed with fury.

"Richard left," she said. That was true enough and didn't require any details.

Pat blinked. "You got him out?"

She nodded but didn't elaborate.

"For good?"

Hope suspected that Pat would demand details down to a microscopic level, especially after all the times she'd cried on her shoulder. She might as well start talking. Truthfully, she wanted nothing more than to tell Pat every gory detail and see if her ghost buff friend had any theories. But it sounded so ridiculous that she didn't want to risk it. "In all honesty, I don't know."

"Sit. You look awful." Pat took her by the arm as if Hope were five, not thirty-five, and steered her to a chair.

Obediently, she sat, then remembered the "ghost's" admonition of the night before that she needed to sit down before she fell over. Discreetly she fought down a shudder.

"You're shaking," Pat accused.

"I didn't sleep well last night."

Pat blinked again. "You look like you've been hit by an oncoming freight. Whatever happened must have been really bad. I want to know *everything*."

Sure, Hope thought. *I'll give you the short version. Richard got violent, and the frontier sheriff I've obsessed over for years—the same one who died before my great-great-*

grandparents were born—rescued me. He's a ghost now, and living in my house. He knocked Richard out cold, apologized for upsetting me, then politely retired to parts unknown. Voices. Hallucinations. Just your everyday basic psychosis. Out loud, she said, "I don't know. What little I remember couldn't have happened, so I'm opting for hysterical amnesia."

"Not funny and far too evasive." Her brows pinched. "Try again."

"When I got home last night, he was having DTs. At least, I think that's what it was. He claimed a demon had been after him. He became violent, stopped in his tracks"—*boy, did he stop*—"then ran out of the house. I went to bed, then jumped at shadows all night. I'm so tired I can't see straight. He was still gone when I left for work this morning. End of story." Hope took a long sip. Definitely needed more chocolate.

Pat trailed behind her as she dumped in another spoonful of cocoa and returned to her desk. "So you think he's gone for good or just until he comes down off whatever he used to get rid of the DTs?"

"Your guess is as good as mine," she answered honestly. "For right now, he's gone, and I'm trying to concentrate on just that." Hope grabbed the phone book from her desk drawer and flipped through the Yellow Pages. "I need to make an appointment with that attorney you told me about and begin divorce proceedings. I also need to call a locksmith and the bank." She hadn't checked to see if Richard's wallet was really in the freezer where the voice had said it would be, but closing all their joint accounts made sense.

Pat's expressive eyes softened. "I don't know what to say."

"How about one of your pep talks? I could use a 'Hope, you're a mouse with muscle. You dumped that loser all by yourself, and the rest of your life will come up roses.'"

Dutifully, Pat repeated it back, then added, "I'm so sorry you're going through this."

Hope put the phone book down and gave her friend as chipper a smile as she could muster. "Beats the alternative. From now on, I plan to remake my life into exactly what

I want it to be—quiet, simple and addict-free.'' Firmly, she put in her mind her mental picture of Hawkings House loaded with kids and laughter. Today, it didn't seem like it would ever happen, but nothing felt real at the moment, so she hung on to the dream by faith.

Pat just stared for once, speechless.

"Enough sitting around and talking about all this." Hope forced a smile. This one was easier. "I've got to stay busy. If I think too much, I'll worry myself to death."

Chapter Four

Britt tried to concentrate on his book, but he kept finding himself rereading the same page. Hope's mental state worried him. She was a strong woman, but last night—most of which was his own doing—was enough to make *anyone* feel unsure of themselves. He'd respected her privacy and stayed out of her bedroom, but that didn't mean he'd been unaware of her difficulty in sleeping.

As much as he'd love nothing more than to sit down and talk with her, he knew indulging his own needs was not in her best interests. He had to find a way to give her the logical explanation she needed so her life would return to normal. His involvement had shown all the finesse of a bull in a china shop.

True, he'd had to do *something*. She never could have stopped Richard herself. And his conscience couldn't have tolerated standing by while Richard had beaten her to death—which was exactly what the man had intended. Yet Britt suspected that somewhere deep inside he'd been selfishly looking for an excuse to make his presence known to her.

He didn't want to believe he was that self-absorbed, but discovering otherwise wouldn't surprise him. Twenty-six years was a long time to go without talking to anyone. The whole subject was moot, though. The damage was done, and he had to find a way to repair it.

Maybe he ought to check on her. Finding Hope's office would be no problem. He had a passing knowledge of where most businesses were in Manzanita. He'd certainly had enough years of watching it grow from a rough, gold camp to a respectable town of twenty thousand.

A few minutes later, he drew into a far corner of the real estate office and floated above an artificial ficus tree. Room corners weren't high-traffic areas, so they were generally safe places for him to observe people unnoticed. Hope sat at her desk, riffling through papers and talking with a man and a woman he assumed worked there. They both had that settled feel about them, as if this building was a familiar place. Employees instead of customers, he surmised. Outwardly, Hope appeared calm and collected, but on the inside, her emotions had a fractured quality that made him nervous.

"Brian, you've lived in Manzanita most of your life," she said. "I visited a lot during the six months Richard and I dated, but I didn't actually move here until we married three years ago. Does this town claim any hauntings? Something connected to the McLeans?"

How could you have been so stupid? Britt chastized himself. *You could have gotten Richard out without a word. But no, you had to talk out loud, pretend you're still human.*

Pat gave her a hopeful look. "Did stuff start going bump in the night?"

He felt Hope grapple with panic for a moment, then control it. In a convincing show of calm, she rolled her eyes. "No bumps. No moaning. No glowing people wandering the halls."

Brian chuckled. "About the turn of the century, Jonah McLean, a farmer, claimed to have tried to burn his father's journals in a garbage fire he had going." He shook his head. "God, what a waste that would have been. Britt McLean's journals contain more detailed documentation for twenty years of Manzanita's history than any other source we have."

"What happened?" Hope asked in a small voice.

"He insisted they rose from the fire, then danced above the flames while his father's ghost told him beware the vengeance of the dead." Brian dropped his voice into vampirish tones. Britt had seen enough movies over the years to recognize a bad parody of Bela Lugosi when he heard one. "The journals are a sacred trust and to be protected at all costs."

I did not say that! Britt couldn't believe he was still irked over a lie told almost ninety years ago. Then again, he'd never handled being lied about very well.

He remembered the incident quite well. One of his sons decided no one would ever be interested in the journals of a father who'd died when he was still in short pants. At that point, they didn't have any historical significance. Not enough time had passed. Britt had snatched the volumes from midair as Jonah dropped them into the flames. He'd just begun to master moving objects and communicating with people, and his efforts were clumsy at best. Looking back, he should have put the fire out in such a way to appear that the journals had smothered it. Getting his son away from the cold ashes would have been simple enough. Any of a number of distractions would have done it. Then he could have taken the journals to safety and been done with it.

Instead, he'd grabbed the journals and carried them to the back porch of Jonah's farmhouse. Jonah had started screaming and told the story to everyone who'd listen. Britt then compounded his mistake by pleading with him to keep quiet. People who believed in ghosts weren't well thought of back then, and no matter what Britt would have done to verify the story for him, there would be those who didn't believe. But the man wouldn't listen, and the story got more elaborate with each telling. As curiosity seekers came to hold séances, he fleeced them for everything he could get. Eventually, he lost his friends and his business. It took him years to regain his senses and rebuild his life. Nestor and Lucinda—both getting on in years—had been mortified.

He felt Hope's heart leap in her chest, and he cringed at the implication.

"The general consensus after everything was said and done," Brian concluded, "was that it had been a simple scam to separate the gullible from their money."

Britt shook his head in resignation over the old mistakes. He cast a glance at Hope and wondered how much harm his blatant intrusion into her life would ultimately cost her.

"Then there was old Jessup out at the museum."

Britt writhed with grief and shame.

"He claimed to talk to Britt McLean all the time. Then again, he talked to his mop bucket, too."

In the seventies, Britt had struck up a conversation with the janitor at the museum. Old Jessup already had a reputation as an eccentric, and Britt figured it was safe. Unfortunately, Jessup didn't keep their talks private, and one day he just stopped coming to work. Britt tried to find him, but he had less skills in that area than a living man because he couldn't ask anyone. He'd still tried, though.

"Jessup's McLean stories were the final straw for the old man's daughter who lived back East. She dragged him to Pennsylvania and had him committed to a mental facility. He died about six years later."

Britt had eventually learned of Jessup's fate years too late to do anything about it. The old man had already passed away. Every time he got involved with the living, even discreetly, he ended up either scaring them half to death, interfering with their religious beliefs or worse. *And now you've risked all that again!*

"That's awful," Hope exclaimed. He felt her sudden worry. Was she afraid the same thing would happen to her? "Do all the stories have to do with Britt McLean?"

Britt came very close to despising himself.

"Oh, no," Brian replied. "When I was a kid, there was a big flap involving Howard McLean. He swore a ghost moved the walls around in his house three nights in a row, always putting them back every morning. He was a well-respected member of the city council, and there was a lot of hoopla over it."

"What happened?" Hope leaned forward, hanging on every word.

"Turned out that he'd recently painted his bedroom, and the fumes caused hallucinations. He was lucky that's all they did. Confined like that, they could have killed him.

That was years before consumer safety laws, and there were a lot of dangerous paints out there.''

For Britt, people's emotions were as easy to read as signboards, but specific thoughts remained hidden. Even so, he knew Hope was floundering, desperate for an explanation that would make sense to her. He wished he could read her specific thoughts to give him a clue which direction to take this.

Please, Hope, he thought to himself. *I'll arrange things so you can have your logical explanation, but you need to give me someplace to start. What's logical to one person isn't to another.*

With a shudder, she took a long pull on her coffee. ''Paint fumes,'' she said thoughtfully. ''I don't imagine he would have thought about that no matter how hard he looked for the cause.''

''I know I wouldn't have,'' Pat chimed in. ''Why all the questions?''

Temptation to confide in her friends literally boiled from her.

Hope, please don't. Your life will never be the same if the story of last night gets out. Some people will believe you, but others will brand you with the reputation of being peculiar. At the very least, they'll say you have an overactive imagination and are a crackpot.

She took a small breath. ''Nothing. Your remarks the night you came over got me to thinking about it. And one thing led to another. I started hearing things last night. Probably from suddenly being alone in that big house and worrying whether or not Richard was coming back.''

''That would do it,'' Brian said, nodding.

She forced a credible smile. ''Maybe if I *did* have a resident ghost, I could rent out my living room to anyone who wants to hold a séance. Given the bills Richard has run up, the only other alternative is to win the lottery.''

Brian and Pat both gave her compassionate looks. ''Well, kiddo, you got him out,'' he said. ''That's step one. And if I hear of any ghosts looking for employment, I'll give them your number.''

Hope went pale—inside and out—but she broadened her smile. ''Sounds like a plan. We'll form a partnership and sell tickets. They can rattle pipes, and I'll talk to the mop buckets. Works for me.''

''That's the ... *spirit*,'' Pat added, giving them a mock superior smile at her wit.

Brian and Hope both groaned. The phone rang, and Hope picked it up, relieved over the tidy end to the subject. From her churning emotions, the situation was still very much on her mind, though.

Britt stayed close by in case last night came up in conversation again, but it didn't. Occasionally, she looked up, frowned and stared hard where he stood in the corner. Britt closed his eyes and grimaced. It would be so much simpler if she wasn't so sensitive to his presence. She couldn't know how accurate her instincts were. With luck, she'd never find out.

At two-fifteen, Hope met the locksmith at the house. ''Thanks for squeezing me in today,'' she said.

''No problem.'' He smiled. ''You only have the two doors in the house?''

''And one on the garage.''

He nodded and went to work recoding the locks. Richard's car wasn't parked in the circular drive out front when she'd arrived, and at this hour it was a safe assumption he was out with Chris and Eddie, his primary drinking and using buddies.

''That'll do it,'' the locksmith said, handing her a couple of keys.

''Thank you.'' She wrote him a check and waved as he drove away. The shiny keys in her hand struck her as symbolic of the new life she'd begun. Freedom. ''You have a lot of rough road still ahead of you,'' she said to herself. ''But this is day one. You're a survivor, and you're going to be okay.''

She stepped out onto the sidewalk to get a good look at the home she and Richard had bought back when she'd been full of dreams of what their lives together would hold. Buying the old place had been a terrible financial investment. But Hawkings House had spoken to her. Walking away had felt too much like abandoning an orphaned child.

Feeling the inexplicable need to try out the new key, Hope smiled as she went inside.

The house was quiet. No matter what she thought she remembered about last night, she knew one thing to be true. With Richard gone, Hawkings House felt 100 percent cleaner.

Then the feeling of being watched permeated the room. Fear clawed through her again. Now that she thought about it, she'd felt the same way at the office.

"You're okay, Hope," she assured herself. "File the incident under 'W' for weird, then move on."

She didn't have any clients scheduled for the rest of the afternoon, no prospects to check with, and both Pat and Brian planned to be in the office. In the highly unlikely event she was needed, they'd call. It was time to take some action. She grabbed the box of leaf bags from under the sink and proceeded to stuff every article of clothing Richard owned into them.

Then she toted them out to the garage. It had been built in the sixties on the spot where the stable had once stood and was the only structure on the whole place that needed nothing more than a new coat of paint. Because of its relative newness, it held no special interest.

Trip after trip, she carried out bags of clothing and other belongings and dropped them on the concrete floor. She had no way of contacting Richard, but whenever he next surfaced, she'd give him a week to get his garbage off of *her* property.

Britt watched her try to pretend everything was normal. Each time she looked up from her work, she scanned the air, searching for what she felt but couldn't explain. He cursed himself with all the fluency he could muster.

For hours, he watched her try to scrub down the house, ridding her surroundings of every trace of the man she'd once loved. Her mop spared nothing. At first he was worried about the emotional energy she expended as she worked herself into a state of exhaustion. Then he realized how cathartic the labor was for her. Gradually, her emotions lost the raw edges, then began to mellow. Britt breathed a mental sigh of relief.

God help him, but Hope was the type of woman he would have chosen for himself in life. Gentle. Kind. Strong-spirited with an infinite capacity for love. Unlike Lucinda, she understood his need to write down his thoughts.

His Lucinda had been a good woman, and they'd learned to love each other. But she wouldn't have been his first choice if he'd had any other prospects. Their personalities were just too different. Single women had been scarce in Manzanita back then, and he'd met her through his cousin in St. Louis. Geoffrey thought they'd get on well and helped begin a correspondence. After two years, Britt proposed in a letter, and she came to California for the express purpose of marrying him. Their lives had proceeded uneventfully through eight years and five children, ending abruptly when Carbow murdered him.

All that was so long ago, and Lucinda had later found a deep and abiding passion with Nestor. At first Britt had been consumed by jealousy, but eventually he resigned himself to their love. His best friend and his widow had the rest of their lives ahead of them. They had a right to happiness.

As he watched Hope finally put her cleaning supplies away, he became acutely aware of how much he noticed her as a woman. The whimsical mental image formed of him arriving on her front porch with a bouquet of flowers and nervously asking her out for a buggy ride. The concept was so ludicrous that he nearly laughed out loud. *She's married to your great great great grandson, and you're dead.* He pulled his hat down low and tried not to think about the fact that death was forever, and he had no way out.

The last thought stabbed deeply. Normally, he guarded against allowing the loneliness and despair to eat at him. But he meant something to Hope. For whatever reason, he was special to her. She wanted to know him, and that made his usual common sense seem very expendable. A deep yearning wrapped itself around his heart and squeezed.

Bone-weary from her labors, Hope settled at the dining room table with a sandwich and a diet soda, too tired to do more than look at them.

"Ma'am, it's three in the morning," he whispered. "Go to bed. Get some sleep."

At his words, her head snapped up as if she'd heard him. He cringed. He'd never been around anyone this sensitive to him before. Temptation and guilt hit with equal force.

"Is anyone here?" she asked, her gaze timidly darting from place to place. Her heart pounded. Hawkings House was a big place, and he felt her awareness of that fact increase tenfold. Being alone and afraid had a tendency to do that. "If this is some sort of prank, it's not funny, okay?"

Britt held himself motionless. It wasn't necessary, but it made him feel like he had a better hold on the urge to answer.

She clutched her arms to her body. The distress in her violet eyes paled compared to the fear roiling through her. "I don't believe in ghosts," she muttered. Then she said it again—louder, as if the volume would make it more real to her.

Britt said nothing.

"Oh, this is so stupid. I'm jumping at shadows." She glanced at her watch and groaned. "Sleep deprivation. That would cause all sorts of problems. I'd feel better about it if I'd recently painted my bedroom with toxic paint, though."

Then she remembered Richard's wallet. The voice had clearly told her where it would be. Gathering her courage and not sure whether she wanted the wallet to be there or not, she opened the freezer. She felt around behind the ice maker, at first finding nothing. When her fingers closed over the leather billfold, her heart slammed against her ribs and stayed there.

"I'm not going to deal with this tonight," she half whimpered. "I just can't." With that, she snapped off the lights, went upstairs and dropped the billfold in her bureau drawer.

Good night, ma'am. Remorse rode Britt's conscience hard, and he wondered how many years it would stay that way. *Sleep well. Maybe by morning, I'll have some idea of how to return your life to normal.*

• • •

All through the next day, Hope was plagued by the certainty that she'd heard someone telling her to go to bed. And, she still had no explanation for the wallet. She thought about mentioning it to Pat and Brian. After all, Pat believed in ghosts, a concept that Hope just couldn't swallow. Which *again* left the other alternative—that her mind had slipped its leash. If so, would she end up like the old janitor from the museum? She tried not to dwell on it. Instead, she turned her energies toward work. By day's end, she'd sold an executive home in the Quail Ridge area, and she practically danced on air on the way home. The commission would take a few big bites out of some bills.

Late the next afternoon, Richard was waiting for her when she came home from work. He sat on the porch swing, his sallow skin dark with anger.

"What are you doing here?" she demanded, trying to quell the internal shaking.

"I live here," he snapped. He got to his feet, posturing as usual with legs spread and arms folded, his version of military parade rest. Not all that long ago, that same body language had intimidated her into agreeing to anything to keep the peace. Calm still eluded her, but that didn't mean she felt in danger of caving.

Almost as an aside, she noticed the total effect of how much weight he'd lost. His short-sleeved shirt and wrinkled slacks hung on him like a burlap bag.

"Not anymore you don't," she replied, mentally drawing a line in the sand.

"My key doesn't work. What did you do?"

"Figure it out." After slinging her purse strap onto her shoulder, she motioned for him to follow her around back, then tapped the button on the electric garage door opener. The door rose smoothly and slid out of sight. "Get an attorney. He'll explain it to you."

Richard gaped at the piles of bags, haphazard stacks of boxes and loose stuff covering most of the garage floor. "What's all this?"

"I want it out of here within a week. If you won't have enough room where you're living now, storage units don't cost much." She doubted he had money for a cup of coffee, much less rent on an apartment, but that was his problem. He'd probably been staying with Eddie and Chris, happily getting wasted.

"You can't do this." He took a step toward her.

Discreetly, she reached into her purse and threaded her keys between her fingers—points out. The prickly self-defense weapon wouldn't stop him, but it should slow him down enough to give her a fighting chance to get back into her car and lock the doors. "Leave now, and I won't call the police."

"You still want me, you know," he said, a cocky sneer twisting his face.

Even in his run-down condition, he was an incredibly handsome man. But on the inside where it mattered, a cancer of self-indulgence had eaten away his soul. Not all that long ago, she'd thought she loved him. Shuddering in revulsion, Hope pointed toward his car.

"Leave now, and I won't call the police. Your choice."

He took another step toward her, and she lifted her other hand from her purse, the one sporting the makeshift version of brass knuckles. He gave her a considering look. Was his vanity still strong enough to make him think twice before risking a set of ugly scratches across his face?

"You wouldn't." His voice had more confidence than his eyes.

"Last month, no. Today?" Squaring her shoulders, she told herself that given enough provocation, even a mouse could bite. "I don't think it would be a problem."

Richard stood a full head taller than she, but she stared up at him, unflinching. He shifted his weight as if debating how far he could push her without getting hurt. Hope hardened her expression. She still didn't know how she'd really gotten him out of the house the other night. But she had to find a way to do it again.

His expression became more appraising and a little uneasy. He glanced at the house.

"Worried about your demon coming after you?" she asked.

"Not funny."

"I didn't intend it to be. Call it a day, Richard."

"You're my wife!"

"Not for much longer." It sounded cold and unfeeling, exactly as she'd meant it. The mouse had muscle.

That idea died when his sneer deepened, and he took a menacing step forward. Murder glittered in his eyes. Panic rushed through her, but she held her ground.

Suddenly, he spasmed as if something startled him. The skin on his bare arms broke out in gooseflesh, and he began to shiver. She'd seen him high on a lot of different drugs, but never anything that did *that* to him.

"Okay! I'll go!" he snapped suddenly, eyes fearful. He turned toward the garage and began carrying bags out toward his car.

On his third trip, Hope couldn't stand the confusion any more. "Richard, who were you talking to a moment ago? I don't think it was me."

He glowered at her. "I'm your husband, Hope. I deserve better than the mind games you're playing. I don't know how you're rigging all this, but . . ." His voice choked off, and he suddenly nodded his head furiously. "All right. I'm going. I'm going!" He gave Hope a pleading look. "Just quit, okay?" He shivered again, then finished loading his car with as many of his belongings as would fit.

Bewildered, she watched him lay rubber as he drove away. She turned to what remained of his clothes and personal items. He'd made a shambles of her neat stacks and piles. She thought about leaving it as it was, but she bent to the half-emptied bags and clothes strewn all over the concrete. As she worked, she knew the task was more than a little symbolic. Picking up after Richard was something she'd been doing for a long time. This would be the last.

Later, as she ate her solitary meal in the dining room, she again listened to every creak and groan in the old house as it settled for the night. She flipped on the radio to a soft rock station and turned it up loud enough to drown out the sounds that used to give her comfort.

"You picked a wonderful time to lose your grip, Hope," she murmured to herself as she took another bite of meat loaf.

She still hadn't abandoned her hoax theory, even though innumerable searches had turned up nothing. The idea that anyone had invaded Hawkings House made her feel vulnerable to attack.

Exhaustion burned through her body, and all she wanted was peace, quiet and a soft pillow. But she couldn't stop worrying. Had someone played a horrible prank on her, or was Hawkings House really haunted? Tired of worrying and tired of feeling foolish, she once more methodically searched, starting with the first story and working up. She even checked the three rooms on the top story. But the coating of dust on the bare floors was disturbed only by her own footprints.

A new thought came to her. The attic.

It was the only place she hadn't looked. Access was through a door in the back of the hall closet. But she'd loaded that closet with boxes of keepsakes from her childhood as well as books she would probably never read again but couldn't bring herself to give away.

As she lifted out each box in turn, she made herself a promise. If nothing turned up here, she'd spend the rest of her energies putting the inexplicable incidents behind her.

When she reached for the closet doorknob, Britt panicked. If he had any chance of convincing her that the other night had been a bad dream—not that he was any closer to figuring out how to do that—he had to stop her from invading his room. His home decorating was about to cause a big problem. If he hadn't indulged in the stupid need to feign humanity, the attic would be as empty as the rest of the third floor.

He glanced around at the homemade desk, chair and half-filled bookcase. Hell, he'd even indulged himself in a hurricane lantern, a rug and an ashtray for a pipe that never needed emptying. Granted, he was quite adept at moving things, but he had no place to hide them. The ability to move solid objects through walls hadn't come with his condition, and the only window was much too small to shove furniture through.

He could speed up his relationship to time and matter—an interesting trick he'd stumbled across about twenty years ago—but he still had no place to hide anything. And she stood outside the only door *now*. Damn!

If she saw this, he'd never be able to return her life to normal. That meant he had to prevent her from coming in here, no matter what the cost. That left him with one option—resorting to a skill that had left him feeling dirty every other time he'd been forced to use it. With a heavy sigh of defeat, he decided that after everything else, why should he be squeamish about invading her mind?

Chapter Five

A lethargic sense of well-being crept through Hope as she dragged out the last of the boxes. Finding answers didn't seem particularly important anymore. She yawned. Nothing sounded better than a good night's sleep. What on earth was she doing up here chasing shadows? There were no hoaxes, no hauntings, no great mysteries to solve. Richard was gone, and everything would be fine from now on.

Yawning again, she dragged one hand through her hair, then slid the first box in the stack back into place against the attic door. A faint whiff of pipe tobacco came to her. At first the implication didn't register, and she picked up another box. Then the odor came to her again. Why could she smell a pipe? The question didn't seem important, but it wouldn't go away, niggling at the back of her mind, slowly crowding out the fatigue. She sniffed. There was no mistaking it. Someone was in her attic smoking a pipe!

Reality slapped her hard in the face. Oh, God, she really *did* have an intruder! The fatigue returned twice as strong as before. The dueling set of emotions made it hard to think straight. Was she truly safe and just needed to go to bed? Or should she call the police? Then Hope noticed something strange about wanting to go to sleep. Those weren't her feelings! It was as if someone had planted them. But how could that be?

"Hope, you really have lost it," she whispered to herself.

She pulled the boxes out of the closet again. Then, before her courage gave out, she unbolted the slide lock on the door in the back and grabbed the tiny, brass knob.

"Leave it be," came a voice so soft, she couldn't tell if it was inside her head or if someone had truly spoken.

The pounding of her heart became erratic as the fear intensified. Her legs shook so badly that she could barely stand. The adrenaline burned. She wanted to run into the night, but resisted.

"Leave it be." Again the whisper might have been wind in the trees. But she was inside the house. No wind. No trees. A cloying sense of danger smothered the final traces of lethargy.

"Buck up, Hope," she murmured sternly. "And stop inventing things to be afraid of—like your own attic." The door had been bolted from the outside, but as she jerked it open, she caught the much stronger, earthy scent of pipe tobacco.

The room should have been pitch-black, but instead a soft, yellow glow greeted her. The bulk of the attic was to the right, and she would have to poke her head inside the doorway to see anything. She wanted to believe sunlight or a streetlamp shone through the accent window, but it was long after dark and the flickering light was far too bright to originate from anywhere except inside the attic itself.

"Get on with it," she murmured under her breath. Every muscle in her body locked up in protest. "I am *not* a coward."

Then another whisper came, this one at the far lower range of her hearing. It sounded like a muttered "damn it to hell."

Desperate to master the fear, she concentrated on her breathing and trying to get her heart to beat in her chest where it belonged, rather than in her throat and ears. Adrenaline roared through her veins. Prepared to run if necessary, she peeked inside.

Her mouth fell open, and a whimper escaped. The six-

by eight-foot attic—the same one she'd swept clean two
years before—was filled with a small secretary-style desk,
ladder-back chair, rag rug and a bookshelf half filled with
books. A paperback lay facedown on the desk next to a *lit*
hurricane lamp, the flame swaying slowly. Someone had
built a beggar's library.

But who?

Between one breath and the next, her throat went dry.
That intense *knowing* that she was being watched in the
small room invaded every cell in her body. She couldn't
even swallow, much less talk, but she tried both. "Who's
here?" The question came out raspy and forlorn.

For long moments, nothing broke the silence but the uneven shudder of her own breathing.

"Please. I need to know."

The silence drew out unbearably. Drawing in a fortifying
breath she waited.

"You have a stronger mind and will than I expected,"
came the now-familiar male voice, regretfully. It sounded
as if it originated from the chair, but no one sat there.

Hope's knees buckled, and she grabbed the doorjamb.

"I thought I could get you to turn away so you wouldn't
have to go through this. In a few more days, you'd have
dismissed the assorted events as unexplainable and not
worth worrying over, just as you'd planned. At least, that's
what I wanted for you." He sighed, a mournful sound, as
if a tremendous weight rested on his shoulders.

"You're real," she croaked.

"I'm sorry." The apology sounded as sincere as the one
he'd offered downstairs.

"You're a ghost?"

"Unfortunately." There was such melancholy in that
voice that through her terror, she felt a twinge of pity.

"A *real* one?" she asked, belatedly realizing how stupid
that question was.

"Believe me, ma'am, I'm a lot more unhappy about it
than you are. I've just had a while longer to adjust."

Hope couldn't move. Desperately her gaze darted from
place to place, trying to find some sign of a hiding place.
But there was none.

"If you want to talk about this," he said, "I'll oblige,

but I'd rather we do so downstairs where you can be comfortable and have a cool drink to settle your nerves."

She nodded, convinced she'd lost the rest of her mind. "Sure, why not." Sounding calm was much easier when insanity was now a given.

"You're not crazy," he assured her.

"Of course not," she said drily, retracing her steps to the hallway. She pointed over her shoulder to the door in the back of the closet. "Would you mind closing and locking that for me?" As far as tests went, it wasn't much, but it was the best she could come up with on short notice.

"Certainly, ma'am." The door swung shut, and the bolt slid into place—without the benefit of human hands.

Hope nearly fainted.

Just relax, she told herself. *The nice men with the one-size-fits-all rubber suit will come soon. Then you won't have to worry about anything except your next shot.* She headed away from the closet. It beat looking at it. *I wonder what kind of happy juice they have for this sort of thing?*

Hope didn't have any particular direction in mind, but found herself wandering down to her office. The room looked the same as usual. No one had tampered with her desk or the love seat or her bookcases or the grandfather clock. Nor were any of those aforementioned objects walking around on their own.

"Or is my form of insanity confined to voices only?" she wondered out loud. Crazy people talked to themselves all the time, didn't they? If that was a criterion, then she'd lost it years ago. "No, wait. I saw Richard fly across the room and splatter against the wall." She nodded. "My hallucinations are definitely in the full sensory range."

"Ma'am?"

She gasped. Even though she half expected to hear something, the voice shocked her. Hope turned to the doorway where the voice had come from. Clearing her throat to prime her vocal chords, she said, "Yes?"

"I feel badly about this. All I wanted was to straighten out that . . . that hellspawn Charles and Ruth raised up, but I wanted to do it without hurting you, without you ever finding out about me." Self-reproach came through as sharp as glass. "It didn't work out that way, I'm afraid."

Having Richard described as a hellspawn didn't sound like anything her own mind would invent.

"Who are you?" She threw her shoulders back and laced her fingers in front of her. It made for a courageous, dignified front, but that's all it was.

"I told you, ma'am. I'm Britt McLean."

"No, you're not," she shot back defensively. "I think I could accept anything or anyone else, but not that. It's too . . . too . . . *Freudian*."

"Would it help if you could see me?"

No! She swallowed hard. "Thanks for offering, but no thank you. The last thing that interests me is to add another hallucination to the list. A voice is bad enough. Besides, since no photographs of Britt McLean survived, nobody knows what he looked like." The level of civility in the conversation only added to its weirdness. Then again, when one's mind was a few cards shy of a deck, the standards were different. But what if this wasn't insanity? What if she truly was talking to Britt McLean? No!

He groaned again. "Ma'am, you're not having a mental breakdown."

"Mental breakdown," she repeated thoughtfully. "Isn't that too modern of a term for the ghost of a nineteenth-century frontier sheriff? Wouldn't you use 'madness'?"

"Do you talk the same as you did even twenty years ago?"

"I was a teenager!"

"I've changed over time, too," he explained patiently. "Despite my being on the outside of life looking in."

Neither spoke for several minutes. Maybe she should test reality again. "Are you still here?" she asked.

"Yes, ma'am."

Again, she jumped.

"You're more relaxed than you were, but I'm not sure I like the direction it's taking."

Her eyes widened, and her pulse doubled. "You . . . you can read my mind?"

He sighed. He did that a lot. "Your thoughts are private. It's just your emotions I can read."

"You know what I . . . feel?"

"Yes, ma'am."

A distant part of her mind noticed his old-world manners. Odd how little details jumped out at her while the important information—like what was truly happening here—escaped her.

"Everything?" She rubbed her arms.

"I can't always decipher meanings and what different emotions connect to, but yes. I wish you'd believe me. You're perfectly sane. I'm the one who has a problem."

That was a new twist on an old theme.

"Please don't be afraid," he said. "I won't hurt you. My word on it." He sounded as if making her believe it was the most important thing in the world to him.

"I'm trying."

"Thank you."

Was it her imagination, or had a note of relief entered his voice at her concession? That helped stiffen her backbone a little. "Okay, why don't we try letting me get a look at you."

"I don't think you're up for that," he said.

"That makes two of us, but I need to do it anyway."

She felt him study her. It was the same sense of being watched that she'd experienced before, an odd sensation when she still didn't quite believe she wasn't alone in the first place.

"I have to lower the lights. There won't be anything . . . supernatural about it. I'm just turning down the dimmer switch on the wall. All right?" He'd pitched his tone to a soothing level, as if he were reassuring an injured child, not calming a reasonably intelligent adult—or at least that's how she'd perceived herself until now.

"Any particular reason we need to turn down the lights?" she asked, feeling strangely calm, like the lull before the storm. "Beyond the ambience, I mean. Dark is spookier, after all."

"I can only appear solid in subdued lighting." Apparently he didn't feel inclined toward acknowledging her sarcasm.

"Oh, of course. I should have thought of that."

"I'm serious. I can appear quite solid, but only—"

"In shadows."

"That's right."

Hope's gaze snapped to the switch by the door. Sure enough, it began a slow counterclockwise rotation. Her heart thumped once and lodged itself in her throat. The lights went down to near-darkness.

"Take a breath, Mrs. McLean," he instructed kindly. "You're about to faint on me."

She complied obediently.

"It took me sixty years to learn this. I'm fairly adept now."

"Just not at high noon at the O.K. Corral."

He sighed at her half-hysterical humor. "Exactly." After a timeless pause, he asked, "Ready?"

"I appreciate your consideration of my feelings," she replied, not trusting any of this, but civility worked fine as a vehicle to keep from falling apart. "That's very kind of you."

A long and frustrated sigh eased from him, but he said nothing more.

By the wall switch where there had been nothing, a hazy, translucent impression of something human slowly came into focus. Hope's heart began to pound again. The form took on more details, that of a man about her height who wore old-style trousers, a long-sleeved shirt, boots and a wide-brimmed hat with a rounded crown.

Gradually, features came into focus. They were weathered in a roundish face. The eyes watched her with a gentle compassion. Dark hair hung in shaggy waves around his ears, brushing the collar of his shirt in the back.

As the image resolved itself, color became more vivid, and she had a harder time seeing the wall behind him. His eyes were a pale sky blue, his shirt a badly faded red, the trousers tan. Still watching her, he drew his hat from his head and held it before him in both hands. With each passing heartbeat, he looked more solid, more real. If she hadn't watched this with her own eyes she would have sworn she stood face-to-face with a living, breathing man. He watched her, saying nothing. Was he waiting for something? If so, what? For her to finish her inspection? For her to regain her composure?

"You're very brave, ma'am," he whispered. His mouth moved normally, adding to the illusion. "The women in my day would have had the vapors straight off."

She flinched. Somehow the voice had been easier to accept when it hadn't been connected to someone who'd just materialized from nothing. She hadn't realized until then that a tiny part of her mind still clung to the theory of this being a sick practical joke. "I don't feel brave. I keep waiting for someone to jump out of the woodwork and yell 'gotcha.' To be honest, I wish they would."

He gave her a lopsided, apologetic smile.

"Any chance you're a projected hologram?"

"No, ma'am."

"You're a man?"

"Used to be. I haven't been one in a hundred and twenty-seven years." It was a simple, unadorned statement of fact.

To her straining eyes, he looked absolutely, flesh-and-blood real. "Can you prove you're a ghost?"

He turned his hat in his hand in what struck her as a nervous gesture. "No one has ever asked me to do that before."

Hope's mind-numbing fear eased a little. "If you're some sort of fancy camera projection, you can't go where equipment isn't set up. Right?"

He looked thoughtful a moment. "Sounds like a reasonable assumption."

She pointed to the space between her desk and the vault. "Would you walk over there, please?"

Without a word, he crossed the room. No sound of footsteps marked his passage as he walked by and stood where she'd indicated. His expression was attentive but uneasy, like a lonely kid desperate for acceptance but afraid to dream.

The whole situation was too much to take in, and she felt the blood drain from her face and hands.

"Thank you," she said as calmly as possible. If he could be polite, so could she. "That was very kind of you to humor me."

He groaned. He was also turning his hat in his hands

with entirely too much force. "You really don't have anything to be afraid of, ma'am. I swear it."

"You're going to ruin your hat if you keep mashing on the brim like that," she quipped, determined to keep the hysteria from overtaking her. She forced her chin up and her shoulders back.

His gaze dipped as he inspected the article of clothing in question. "It's okay. These are the clothes they buried me in. They're sort of like me. Indestructible. Or at least I think I am."

Unlike the ghosts in horror movies or books, he didn't seem consumed by pathos. Nor did he project an aura of being all-powerful or malevolent. He just seemed like an ordinary man slogging through life, trying to figure out why it wasn't working.

Mentally she frowned. "Do something else."

He cocked his head. "Ma'am?"

"Something dramatic."

"All right. What?"

She thought for a moment. "Lift all the furniture in this room. I don't think anyone would think to rig something like that. Besides, I would have found the wires by now."

He glanced around the room, his gaze studying each piece. A distant light hardened his eyes, and a blue sheen rippled across him. Then the furniture—everything, including the bank vault—lifted from the floor in unison. The curio cabinets and bookcases turned end over end, the contents staying in perfect position. He swept everything into a circle in the air in a dance of perfect weightlessness. The whole tableau was accompanied by a faint whisper of something resembling static electricity.

Hope gripped the wall behind her. He looked stricken and carefully set everything down. Not one stick of furniture was in its right place, but at least they were back on the floor.

"That was too much for you."

She tried to force a reassuring smile. God only knew if she succeeded or not. "The practical joke theory is pretty much history. That leaves me with two options. You're either real, or I'm crazy. Since for the moment I have a choice, I'll take real."

He made a hesitant step, as if he'd considered approaching her then changed his mind. "You don't believe that, though," he said.

"Not really. If ghosts were real, someone would have proven it by now."

Lowering his gaze to the floor, he plunked his hat back on his head. "Lucinda always told me I was a hopeless meddler." His shoulders slumped. "You'd think I'd have learned by now."

"I don't understand."

He squared his shoulders and lifted his gaze like a man owning up to his actions. "I may have handled the situation badly, but if I hadn't stopped Richard, you'd probably be dead now. No matter what the consequences, I couldn't let that happen." He gave her a look of implacable conviction. "I was like this before I died. Always thought I should help other people. With my job, it usually worked out. Ever since my death, though, when I get involved, I make the situation worse."

If he'd been confident and in control, she probably would have continued to be afraid, but he was floundering as badly as she was, and she nearly smiled. "You're really Britt McLean?"

"Yes, ma'am."

She still had trouble with the concept, and she was going to have to take his word on faith. He didn't look at all like he had in her dreams. This man was neither handsome nor plain. His was an honest face with weathered skin, clear eyes and a kind mouth. She knew much of his life from memory. If ever someone was Britt McLean, this had to be him. "What are you doing here? Isn't there supposed to be some sort of eternal reward?"

He moved as if to take his hat off again but changed his mind as he mulled over his answer. "I passed up the opportunity. Thought I'd have another one after I finished up some business. Sort of like catching the next train. I was wrong. There was no next train."

She didn't understand what he was talking about, and she got the impression that whatever had happened, the trauma still bothered him. "But why *here*? Why me? Why

Hawkings House? You died before it was built.''

"You have my journal." He glanced toward the vault and back as if that settled the matter.

"I'm sorry, but I don't understand."

"The museum had the remainder of my belongings since 1946. There wasn't much, the other journals, a set of my clothes and a gun belt. When it burned down two months ago, the only thing of mine left was the journal you have. I tried staying away, but by the end of another month, I couldn't stand the restlessness anymore."

She nodded, not entirely following what he was saying. "So you've been here four weeks."

"Roughly," he said, then gave her a hesitant frown. "May I ask you something?"

Hope nodded again.

His face—weathered though it was—took on a boyish vulnerability. "I've watched you read my scribblings."

She blushed clear to her feet. Had he heard her comments as she'd pretended she was talking to him? Oh, Lord, if so, how could she stand the humiliation?

He looked stricken. "I didn't mean to embarrass you."

She started to deny that he had, but changed her mind. If he really could read her emotions, lying served no purpose. "I've survived worse."

He looked as uncomfortable as she felt. His gaze dipped then rose. "I know. I saw."

Richard. She blushed in embarrassment that she knew wasn't hers to feel, but let it go without comment.

"When you read what I wrote all those years ago, you feel as if you . . ." He glanced away, then back. When he finally spoke, it was punctuated with hesitations and breaks. "You feel as if you know me. As if you want to ask me questions about my day. As if you . . . care."

Having someone reading her emotions unnerved her. "I do," she admitted slowly. "Your writings told me a lot about you as a person. They weren't just a chronicle of events." Now it was her turn to feel unsure of the subject matter. Was she really talking to the man she'd fantasized over since her teen years? It just didn't seem possible. "Many of your entries struck me as if written by a man who wished he'd had someone to share the events with but didn't, at least not on the level you wanted.''

"But why is that important to you?'' he asked. His features became pinched with intensity over whatever turmoil ate at him. "There's nothing there but the musings of a fool.''

Anger flashed to life so quickly that she nearly laughed over the emotional whiplash. "Don't you dare put yourself down or denigrate the importance of something that has meant so much to me for so long.''

"What?'' He was shaking his head in bewilderment.

"You wrote about the way all of nature fits together for the good of the whole. It makes me feel like I belong to something, that I'm not a nothing little person, living a nothing little existence with no value beyond my family and friends. I'm an important part of life itself.''

He drew back, clearly shocked.

"It's true. You made me realize that just because I'm adopted and don't know my family history, doesn't mean I'm worthless or don't belong where I am. Even with all the problems my adopted family has, there is still good there.''

"I don't remember writing anything like that,'' he breathed, his eyes widening.

"Maybe you didn't consciously. But it's there nonetheless.''

His weathered features went slack as if she'd rendered him speechless. She hoped so. Turn about was fair play.

Then she thought of another problem. How did one address a hero? She didn't want to be too familiar and offend his nineteenth-century sensibilities. In her heart, she'd always thought of him as Britt. He'd been friend, dream lover and maybe even a mentor of sorts. A lot of teenagers developed crushes on rock stars. She'd had him. "Do I call you Mr. McLean—or do you prefer Sheriff, or . . . Britt?''

"I haven't been a sheriff for a long time,'' he whispered, apparently still thunderstruck by her speech. "Times have changed since my day. Some of the differences suit me fine. But I'm not comfortable with strangers calling each other by their given names. It's just too familiar.''

But you're not a stranger, she thought. "Then Mr. Mc-

Lean, it is." She sat on the edge of the love seat. "What does your journal have to do with you being here?"

"I need to stay near my belongings that were important to me."

"Why?"

"I don't know. It just is. My best guess is that I somehow chained myself to them. Punishment, maybe for not moving on when I was supposed to. I don't know. But if I get too far away for too long, I experience a grating restlessness that's very close to pain. When the museum burned, I had a choice. Come here or go to the cemetery where I'm buried."

"I take it you're not into graveyards."

He grimaced. "No, ma'am. I'm not."

Hope could only blink at that point.

"After the fire, I stayed with the ashes," he continued, "hoping it would be enough. It wasn't, but it was better than nothing. Then the staff finally got to clearing out the basement. With one sweep of a broom, what little peace I'd managed to hang on to was gone."

"You found yourself at loose ends and came here."

"That's about it."

Hope sank back into Evie's love seat. "This whole thing feels like *The Ghost and Mrs. Muir.*"

He frowned. *"Who?"*

"It was an old TV show and an even older movie. A lady and her young son moved into a seaside house haunted by the ghost of the original owner, a very dashing sea captain."

Britt's frown deepened and he looked down at himself, at his worn, humble clothing of another century. An endearing display of vulnerability came into his eyes.

"I'm afraid 'dashing' doesn't describe me very well," he said.

Hope studied his features. He wasn't an unattractive man, just aged beyond his years by the harsh life he'd led. Mostly, he looked tired.

She kept her observations to herself, uncomfortable with letting him know that her mental picture of him all these years had been very dashing indeed.

"You need some time alone to absorb this," he pronounced. "You also need some sleep."

"How do you know that?"

He looked guilty.

"Sorry," she said. "I forgot."

"That's okay, ma'am. I understand. Good night." He touched the brim of his hat and vanished.

Hope sat blinking in surprise. There had been no slow fade out. Just poof and gone. She wanted to call him back, but wasn't sure she ought to. One thing was certain—he was right. She did need time to absorb all this. For a long time Hope kept her place on the love seat, staring at the room that he'd completely rearranged.

Chapter
Six

A giddy euphoria flooded Britt as he blasted through the assorted layers of the house and into the attic. Not paying attention, he misjudged his trajectory and found himself hanging partway through the roof and into the night air. It didn't matter. *Nothing* mattered at the moment. For a precious few minutes, he'd actually had a real conversation with a living, breathing person! That hadn't happened since Jessup at the museum. Had that really been twenty-six years ago?

"Please, God, don't let this end the same way." He'd been cut off from God and humanity for so long, he didn't know if his prayers were heard or not, but he still made the effort.

The worst part of his death was the staggering isolation. The world and all its people marched on completely oblivious to his presence. He frequently spent his days sitting in the oak tree at the corner of McLean and Peterson Drives just watching humanity *live*.

During his own life, he'd enjoyed solitude. A week on the trail hunting down one outlaw or another had been restorative, a reconnection of who he was and how he fit into the greater whole of life. Back then, he hadn't looked at it in quite those terms but, as Hope pointed out, she'd seen his observations more clearly than he.

Through a miracle he refused to question, he had Hope, a woman who—against all odds—cared about him. He sighed in contentment, pulled out his pipe and lit it. Smoke curled around his face as he puffed on it. Absently, he watched the gray swirls dissipate.

She'd compared their situation to *The Ghost and Mrs. Muir.* Maybe one night after the main library in Sacramento or San Francisco closed, he'd run down there and see if they had the video in the archives. He'd been borrowing books from assorted libraries for decades. A movie would be a first. Was the story a pleasant one? Had the sea captain and the lady been friends? Had they talked on a regular basis?

Please, God, let it happen.

Britt extended his senses down to the first floor where Hope still sat on the love seat, trying desperately to absorb all this. In the past few days, he'd turned her world upside down. He still wasn't comfortable with having taken such direct action against Richard. Maybe if he hadn't pushed so hard earlier, that vermin wouldn't have become violent. Then again, maybe he'd only hurried along the inevitable. He wished foretelling the future had come with being dead, but it hadn't. Either way, he'd made the best decision he could at the time, and the results were his responsibility.

Floating back down into the attic, he settled into his chair, put his feet on his desk and closed his eyes. He was still dead, and he still hated it. But for a few minutes tonight, it hadn't been so bad.

Britt savored the warmth of contentment as he sensed her finally heading to her room. "Good night, ma'am. If you ever need me, I'll never be very far away."

Hope closed up the house for the night, then went into her bedroom to change. The old place was quiet without Richard downstairs destroying himself and blaming her for it. She was alone. Sort of. But what did one do after finding out one's house was haunted by the dream lover of her adolescent years? The mixed emotions the situation created were ones she'd never considered having to face. She didn't know whether to be happy at the chance she'd been given to meet him or to ask him to leave. After the hell Richard had put her through, she needed absolute peace and quiet so she could clean out all the internal wounds. The last thing she needed was any extreme emotional upheaval—good or not. She couldn't think straight.

Hope snatched her pajamas from the bureau drawer and started to pull her sweater over her head. What if her resident ghost was in the room? Watching her? Had he watched her all along? A cloying sense of violation permeated her skin.

"Don't be ridiculous," she muttered. "Richard hurt you a lot more than your ghost has." Her ghost. Britt. If he was the man she believed him to be, he'd never stoop to voyeurism.

As a teenager, she'd often lose herself in daydreams of having lived in the Old West. Her favorite was the one where she moved to Manzanita, stepped off the stage and had Britt fall hopelessly in love with her at first sight. He'd been gallant and kind, a simple man who'd courted her with old-fashioned grace and charm. He'd put so much of himself in his writings, she felt as if she knew him better than any of her flesh-and-blood friends.

She couldn't begin to sort through the turmoil. He'd stepped from twenty-year-old daydreams into the here and now to save her life. Part of her acknowledged that if she wasn't so raw from two years of being beaten down, she would probably be euphoric. She'd probably still be in the music room trying every trick she could think of to get him to talk to her. As it was, she stood shivering in her bedroom, clutching her pajamas to her chest and feeling like Alice falling down the rabbit hole.

Trying to dismiss the whole subject, she picked up the TV remote and flipped through the movie channels. Nothing appealed to her, and she finished getting ready for bed.

The nightmares began almost immediately. She jerked awake, half expecting to find Richard coming after her with fists clenched. It seemed as if she'd barely closed her eyes again when flames cropped up all over the walls like malevolent leprechauns. She raced from room to room, trying to pat out the fires, but the walls crumbled to ash beneath her hands. No matter how hard she tried, she couldn't save her beloved Hawkings House. Britt pleaded with her to forget the old hulk and rescue his journal. It was all so real, she could hear the crackle of burning wood.

Waking with a start, she sat up, ready to do battle. But no smoke hung in the air, and the walls looked as solid and strong as they had for over a hundred years. Groggy, she climbed from bed and ran her hand along the ugly floral wallpaper that someone had put up in the sixties. Replacing it was just one more task she hadn't gotten to. Finally, she got her mind awake and functioning enough to accept that Hawkings House was still standing and that she'd been dreaming.

The shakes took longer to control. The thought of going back to sleep and risking more nightmares held no appeal at all, so she went down to the kitchen for a cup of hot cocoa.

As she sat at the dining room table, her hands wrapped around the soothing heat of the mug, she began to wonder. The conversation with Britt had the same clarity as the dreams. Could that whole conversation have been merely the first of a series of nightmares? Cautiously, she crept into the music room. All the furniture was in its proper place. She saw no indication that any of it had ever been moved—by a ghost or anyone else. Had all that been real, or was it just a hallucination? Could she have been dreaming she was awake?

"You look like a poster child for the wrath of God," Pat observed as she came into the office at about ten. She'd had early clients and been out all morning.

"Didn't sleep well," Hope answered, without looking up from the contract she was filling out.

Pat walked over to her. "Are you sure that's all?"

She nodded, feeling her friend's speculative gaze on her. Then she realized she had the perfect research source right here. She looked up. "I had one nightmare after another last night. The kind where it's hard to shake off even after you wake up."

"Is that normal for you?"

"Last night was a first. It could be the last, too, and I wouldn't object any."

"Do you need to talk about it?" Pat perched on the corner of Hope's desk.

Might as well test the waters. "I dreamt that a ghost is living in my attic. He moved all the furniture around the music room to prove he was real, then told me I needed some sleep."

Pat burst out laughing. "And it was a nightmare? That sounds like something out of a Hollywood comedy."

"Well, it wasn't very funny at the time."

Pat smothered the laughter, and had to purse her lips to keep them from twitching.

"You're a ghost nut. Have there ever been any cases where a ghost talked to people and answered questions? That type of thing?"

"You mean like two people chitchatting over coffee? That scenario is a ghost hunter's dream." Pat sighed. "Dramatic stories like those always turn out to be a con job. Some of them are pretty convincing, though."

"That's what I thought. But I could have sworn Britt McLean stood right in front of me. I even smelled his pipe, saw the remorse in his eyes that he'd upset me."

Pat brushed her long, pale hair behind her shoulder. "You dreamt Britt McLean just popped in for a quick 'hi, how are you'?"

Logic told Hope one thing, but her senses screamed another. "Yeah." She loosed a small laugh. "He was a very nice man, too."

"If you had an encounter with a ghost and it spoke to you the same way you and I are talking now, then it probably was a dream."

"I suppose. He even rescued me from Richard at one point."

"Ahhh," Pat said, as if everything made perfect sense. "The white knight syndrome invaded your sleep."

"The what?"

"The perfect hero comes along and sweeps the overwhelmed heroine off her feet, magically solving all her problems."

Worded like that, it sounded so ridiculous that she didn't dare tell Pat she didn't think it had been a dream.

"Hey, what's wrong?" Pat asked, her features pinched with concern. "You look like you're going to cry."

"Emotional overload. Divorcing a drunken addict has maxed me out. Britt looked at me with the bluest eyes I've ever seen and called me 'ma'am.' So real."

Pat gave her a big hug. "I know what you need. My special stress reliever."

"Your what?" Hope asked cautiously.

"A girls' party night. My hubby will watch the kids, and we'll go play."

"I don't know," she hedged.

"Come on. Do you still want to be an up-front, in-your-face kind of person? Then go forth and conquer something."

Hope grinned. From the twinkle in Pat's eyes, tonight could be memorable. "No, thanks. With Richard gone, I feel like working on the house."

"Eww. Attacking disintegrating wallpaper and dry rot is not my idea of a good time."

"Well, it's *mine*. How's this for symbolism?" She laid her hand across her heart in great theatrical drama. "Ripping out wallpaper is ripping away the memories and pain of everything Richard did."

Pat snickered. "If you're sure."

"Yeah, I am. But thanks for inviting me."

Then they both turned to the task of making a living. Many times during the day, Hope nearly broke down and told Pat the whole story. But Pat knew that Hope had more than a casual interest in Britt McLean's writings. Any amateur psychologist would have had a field day with it.

Once home that night, she put the key in the lock and entered cautiously. The silence in the old house felt bottomless, especially since she couldn't trust that she was alone. Who did she fear being here the most now? Richard, or Britt? With her ears straining for any hint of sound, she went to the music room and stared at those places where she thought she remembered seeing Britt. Lack of sleep and a hard workday made for aching muscles and a weary mind. She slumped into Evie's love seat.

''Sheriff McLean?'' she called out, belatedly remembering that he preferred just plain ''mister.'' For years in her mind, his title had been as inseparable from him as the values he'd lived by. ''Are you still in the house? Or have you gone on to other haunts?''

She'd talked to herself for years, and it didn't bother her. But calling out to a ghost who might or might not be there made her feel extremely silly. A sad chuckle rolled from her lips as her gaze drifted to the floor. It really was past time for her to get a grip.

''Good evening, ma'am. Did you need something?''

Her gaze snapped up. Standing in the middle of the room was the man she remembered from last night. With hat again in hand, he smiled at her in what appeared to be pleased surprise. That was the last thing Hope remembered.

Britt stood gaping as Hope slid from the love seat to the floor in a dead faint.

''Ma'am?'' he called, distressed. ''Please wake up. I didn't mean to scare you. But you called me. I don't understand. . . .''

She didn't stir, and he paced around the room, helpless. He slapped his hat against his leg and hovered. ''Ma'am?'' Finally he knelt beside her and fanned his hat just close enough to her cheek that she'd pick up the chill.

Moaning as she came around, she frowned and drew away from the cold. Britt stepped back to give her room. Her gaze settled on him. Not a muscle moved except her eyes, and they widened alarmingly.

''Feeling better?'' he asked tentatively. He knew she wasn't, but it was the polite thing to ask. Besides, he couldn't think of anything else to say.

''You're real,'' she said. There was a numb quality to it that made him wince.

''Yes, ma'am.'' He frowned, backing further away to make himself as nonthreatening as possible. ''Why did you call me if you didn't think I was . . .?'' He sighed. ''Oh. Another test.''

She nodded. Her eyes were like liquid violet moons. He'd never had a woman stare at him quite like that before. He still had enough vanity to want the sea of negative emotions flowing through her to be because he was a ghost as opposed to his being ugly. Oh, he knew that he'd never been one to turn a lady's head, not like some of his descendants—Richard more than most—but women had never fainted at the sight of him, either.

"I'm not asleep. So you're real," she repeated.

"Yes, ma'am. Would you like me to get you a glass of water?"

Speaking took too much effort, so she merely nodded.

Britt almost slipped through the wall, but caught himself. Granted, it was the quickest route to the kitchen, but he decided she'd had enough shocks. He turned around and walked through the doorway as if he were any other living man. The illusion had taken years to perfect. Until now, no one but Jessup had seen it, but learning how had given him something to do, a hobby of sorts.

Once out of sight, he did revert to the quick method, though. In the kitchen he stuffed a glass under the ice dispenser of her refrigerator door, then under the tap beside it. Back in his day, he'd never dreamt of anything more lofty than a good ice house. The unending stream of inventions in this century delighted him.

"Here. This should make you feel better," he said, walking back into her office. Hope now sat behind her desk, her face exceptionally pale. He wanted to hand her the glass, but he really didn't want her to faint again. "Why don't I set it down within reach, and you can pick it up whenever you want."

She watched him owl-eyed and without comment as he put the glass on her blotter, then retreated a step.

Tension and confusion radiated from her like a bonfire. Britt waited her out. He didn't have much choice. There was nothing else he could do.

Trembling, she reached for the glass. He felt her surprise when her fingers closed around it. Had she thought it wasn't real? Experimentally, she took a sip. A greater level of surprise filled her. Then she looked squarely at him. "Say something."

"Like what?"

"Anything. I just need to hear your voice, so I don't talk myself out of believing I'm awake."

"My name is Britt McLean." He decided to stick to the basics, so there was less chance of him frightening her worse. "In life, I was the first sheriff Manzanita hired. I also worked for some of the smaller towns and gold camps in the surrounding area along the American River. The residents pooled resources to pay my salary of ten dollars a week. That was good money back then, and I tried to do right by everyone. I never once took a bribe or looked the other way when I saw someone breaking the law."

She blinked a couple of times. Her eyes came into sharper focus and the raw edges of her emotions smoothed a little. Britt felt himself smile.

"The townspeople also threw in a cottage owned by a man who'd died and left no kin. They didn't know what else to do with it. It made a nice place to live for me and Lucinda. The children, too, once they started coming along. I lived a good life and wish I could have died an old man with my children and grandchildren beside me."

"You're real. I'm not a candidate for a sanity hearing," she said, standing up. "And you're here because I have your only remaining possession that meant anything to you when you were alive."

"Yes, ma'am." He smiled as he felt her relax.

She frowned. "I thought only vampires needed their own things. Or is that just their home dirt?"

"I wouldn't know," he said, amused. "I never met one."

"Are they real, too?"

"I rather doubt it."

"But ghosts are real."

"Not usually. If it's not trickery or overreacting to something otherwise explainable, it's usually a demon of one type or another. They masquerade as all sorts of things." He'd met up with a couple of them over the years. Not something a wise ghost messed with.

Without quite taking her eyes off of him, she reached with trembling fingers for the glass. Several drops spilled before she got it to her lips. "I'm not sure I like having a ghost in my house, especially you."

The remark would have hurt if he hadn't been able to read what she felt. As it was, he understood. "Freudian."

"You know about him?"

"I've been around a long time. I also read a lot."

"Oh." This whole situation struck her as so bizarre, she didn't have the emotional reserves to explore his base of knowledge. She entreated him with her eyes. "Don't get me wrong. I'm grateful for your help in getting Richard out of here, but I need things to be normal. I don't even know how to go about figuring out how I feel about you being here. My marriage just ended, and I have too much to sort through right now."

Disappointment clawed deep. He'd so hoped he could have found a friend. Maybe later, when she wasn't so close to emotional collapse. His need for human contact had always been strong, more so now when he had it within his grasp. He so very much needed someone to talk to now and then. The risks made it an act of pure selfishness, but he couldn't seem to help himself. He'd lived his life. She deserved to live hers. "Give me the journal, ma'am, and I'll be on my way."

The thought horrified her.

"I'm deeply touched that owning the handwritten journal has meant so much to you and that you don't want to lose it. But I also know how much my presence unnerves you."

With a groan, she curled the fingers of both hands around the glass and hunched over it in misery. "You saved my life. Booting you out wouldn't be very nice, and I won't do that. But I need to be alone."

The appeal of knowing that someone wanted to read his actual handwriting because it gave her a stronger connection to him made the thought of walking away unbearable.

"You have no idea how many years I wished I could have met you." She shook her head in amazement. "The fantasies I had as a teenager."

"You did?" He hung on to her every word, every emotion that pulsed from her. Savoring them, he smiled. Who knew when he'd have another chance to experience the affection of another human being?

"You were my hero. My one true love. I learned a big part of my values from you."

That stunned him. "From me?" Finding his words took a moment. "Why not someone from your family?"

"Them, too, but my family has problems." She shrugged. "I don't know. You spoke to me."

The honesty that flowed from her confirmed the impossible. She meant every word. Knowing he'd had such a profound effect on another person so long after his death humbled him. "How did you find out about me?"

Hope explained about the high school history assignment, and how the more she studied, the more she wanted to know. She read everything she could find, finally locating an unabridged version of his journals in college. "Three and a half years ago I came to Manzanita to do research on you and to experience for myself the area where you'd lived. I fell in love with the town on sight. The librarian told me how many of your descendants still lived here . . . and . . . well . . . the opportunity was too great to pass up. I called a few of the telephone listings. Richard was the first McLean I caught at home. I think part of what I did was believe there was a little piece of you in him. Even his middle name. Brittain. It's your name. That's the only reason I can find to explain why I was so blinded. I saw what I wanted to see, I guess."

Britt was dumbfounded by what he was hearing. He knew she cared about him, but he could scarcely comprehend that she'd changed the entire direction of her life for him, married a man because he was a descendant. "Six months later, you and he were married," he said.

She nodded, and he felt her pull into herself. Deliberately, she met his gaze. "The first year was . . . a disappointment, but okay. The last two have been hell."

He knew how badly scarred she was. She didn't need to explain the details. But if she chose to, he'd listen.

"I no longer have only scraps of you. I have the whole you. But you're dead. I'm an emotional basket case, and I can't handle any of this. Maybe if you'd come here a year from now . . ." Tears dripped down her cheeks. Her delicate face looked drawn from the strain. "The worst part is, I don't think I could bear to find out you're less than I've always imagined. Heros never live up to their images. They can't. I've lost so much. I can't lose that, too."

Britt was thunderstruck. "Ma'am, I don't know what to say. It has been a long time since anyone felt anything for me. And for damn sure, no one ever called me their"—he could hardly say the word—"hero."

"It's the truth, though."

He nodded, speechless. They stared at each other as he tried to absorb at all. "My being here is tearing you apart at a time when you're least able to handle it."

"Then I haven't offended you?"

"No, ma'am." He wasn't offended, just surprised at what he'd learned. During his life he hadn't realized how important human affection was until it had been ripped away from him. Now, for the first time in over a century and a quarter, he had the chance to taste it again. Only he had to turn away.

Her hero.

What he was about to suggest grieved him, but honor demanded that he put her needs before his own. "If you don't want to give up the journal, I'll still have to live here, but I won't contact you anymore. We can each come and go as we please, and I'll make sure you never suspect my presence."

"You mean, ignore each other?"

"It's the only way you can keep the journal in this house. Over time, there's the chance you'll be able to convince yourself our conversations hadn't been real, that it was a product of stress from throwing Richard out. The mind can rearrange memories to make them easier to live with."

"I don't think I can delude myself to that degree."

Yes, you can. With help. "You'll be surprised how much this will fade in your memory. I'm sure of it."

"How can you know what I'll feel in the future when I can't even think straight now!" She clasped her hands to the sides of her head and curled into herself.

"I just know." He touched the brim of his hat. "I'll be going now, then. Good night, ma'am."

As he vanished, he felt her mixed emotions and heard her broken voice telling him good night.

Nothing had hurt Britt this badly since he'd helplessly stood by while Nestor took over his family. He craved hu-

man contact so much that sometimes he thought the loneliness would drive him insane. To have a morsel within his
reach, then have it yanked away, had been worse than none
at all. Now, unless a great deal changed, he was going to
be living in a house with someone who cared about him
and he'd never be able to talk to her.

Was simple human contact asking too much? Why was
it every time he tried, something disasterous happened? He
would always carry with him the guilt over what had happened to Jessup. At least this time, he'd saved a life. Hope
was forever changed, but she was alive.

He lifted his anguished gaze and prayed. ''God, I made
a mistake in not moving on when my time came. I know
that! But how much longer will I have to pay for it? I
always believed You were just and loving. That nothing
happened without a reason. That You could even make our
mistakes come out right. Was what I did so unforgiveable
that this is my hell for all time? Or do You have a way out
for me—even after all these years?''

As always, no answer came—at least none that he could
hear. Decades ago, he'd accepted that he'd never find the
answers or a path of deliverance. Still, a tiny piece of him
couldn't give up. He drifted outside, lit his pipe and let the
breeze carry him through the hills for a while.

At one A.M., Hope's eyes flew open. It was pitch-black,
and she didn't know what had wakened her, but something
definitely had. Then she heard a soft rattle and thunk from
downstairs. Someone was in the house. At first, fear stabbed
into her. Then she remembered Britt. It was probably just
him doing whatever ghosts did at night. Refusing to be
afraid, she settled back into the blankets and forced her eyes
closed. Then she remembered that Britt had been absolutely
silent. If not for those times he'd deliberately allowed his
presence to be known, she'd never have suspected a thing.
What had changed? The fear came back.

Cautiously, she slipped out of bed, pulled on her robe
and tiptoed downstairs. The lights were on. Richard and
Chris—one of his drug buddies—were carrying the TV
from the living room. Anger ignited.

''What are you doing!'' she yelled.

They jumped and nearly dropped the set.

"God, Hope, don't scare me like that," Richard snapped.

"Me scare *you*?" The man's gall was incredible. "Put my television back where you got it."

He signaled to his friend with a jerk of his head, and they resumed their trek around the corner into the hallway.

"I said put it down!" They had no intention of listening to her.

"Ma'am, I can't seem to mind my own business these days," came Britt's whisper soft voice from behind her, "especially when you're in trouble. Those fools are drunk and high."

She gasped, and a shot of adrenaline slammed into her veins. In her opinion, having to cope with two addicts and a ghost at one o'clock in the morning really was a little much to ask of a person. Her heart pounded for a moment before she got it under control.

"Sorry, ma'am. Don't mean to keep startling you."

"That's okay," she whispered back, trying to sound as unruffled as if this were an everyday occurrence.

Richard watched her strangely as he and his friend wres-- tled with the front door.

"Thank you for the offer, Mr. McLean, but I can manage." The reply sounded oh so civil.

"What are you talking about?" Richard sneered. "I didn't make you any offer." The overall seedy air about him had worsened tremendously. He didn't look as if he'd shaved or bathed once in the three days since Britt had thrown him out.

She moved from the stairs to the doorway into the living room. A quick glance inside showed an empty entertainment center. "Where's my stereo and VCR?"

The two men shared a look. From the loose-limbed way they moved, Britt was right about them being under the influence. They probably intended to pawn her stuff to buy more drugs. She didn't know what Richard was using these days, but *how* he destroyed himself was no longer any of her business.

"The TV is mine, too." Richard glared at her, challenging her to stop him. "Community property laws and all that."

He had a point, but she wasn't in the mood to be generous. "Put them back before I call the police."

The chill settled in front of her, a little to the left. "Ma'am, if I hadn't been at the library when they arrived," he whispered, "they wouldn't have gotten this far."

"You were where?" The dual subjects taxed her more than she could spare. "Never mind. Times have changed since your day," she added. "Women take care of themselves now." That made for a nice speech, but the truth remained that she was in over her head. If he really could tell what she felt at any given time, then he knew it, too. And she didn't want him rescuing her again. "I can handle these two."

"There's three of them," Britt corrected. "Someone called Eddie is putting the stereo into Richard's trunk. The VCR is already there."

She groaned.

Chris shot Richard a nervous look. "Who's she talking to?"

"I'm talking to *you*," she snapped, trying to pretend she felt invincible. In her mind's eye, she had a perfect picture of a poster she'd seen once of an eagle diving for the kill on a defenseless mouse. The mouse was flipping off the eagle, and the caption read, "The Last Great Act of Defiance." At the time she'd thought it was funny. Right now, the humor eluded her. "Put that TV back and get out of this house!"

"Ma'am, I understand what you're trying to—"

She turned toward his disembodied voice. "I can take care of myself, Mr. McLean. Thank you."

Chris stared at Richard, who blinked in bleary-eyed confusion.

"Not against three drugged and liquored-up vermin, one of whom tried to kill you," Britt whispered back, indignant. She could almost see him standing with shoulders squared, arms crossed and lips pursed.

As much as she hated to admit it, he had a point. Still, she needed to learn to fight her own battles, or she'd never become the self-confident woman she wanted to be. "Thank you, but I'm fine." She turned her attention back to Richard and Chris, who finally had the door open. *Think brave,* she told herself. "Put that back, or I'll call the police."

"Call whoever you want," Richard sneered. "This is my stuff, too."

"The restraining order I took out against you says that's a negotiable point." Hope brushed past them, jogged to his sedan parked on the street, trunk open.

Eddie was walking toward the house. He grinned when he saw her. "Hi ya, Hope! How ya been?"

His eyes weren't tracking right. High as a kite, she surmised, looking away in disgust. How anyone could do that to themselves was beyond her understanding.

She stacked the stereo components and VCR, then tried to lift them out. As far as dead weight went, the pile wasn't bad, but the CD player slid and she nearly dropped the entire stack.

"Ohhhhh, don't do that," Eddie whined. "We need those." The other two men set down the TV and ran outside. All three bore down on her.

Fear spasmed through her, and she turned toward the house. Britt stood behind them in the doorway, translucent in the harsh light of the entry and porch. His feet were spread, hands low on his hips, expression hard with anger. Overall, it was not the picture of a happy ghost.

Despite her insistence that she needed her independence, there was no physical way she could wrestle her electronic equipment from three "drugged and liquored-up vermin," as he'd called them. She again glanced at Britt, who was still watching her. Every line in his translucent body screamed that he wanted to take over. In fact, from his sour expression, staying out of it took considerable willpower.

Richard jerked the stereo components from her hands and clumsily dumped them back into the trunk.

"Careful!" Chris snapped.

"They're mine!" she countered, trying to work her way back to the trunk.

Eddie chortled. "Not anymore."

She spared him a hot glower, then swung her gaze back to Richard. His dark eyes were so glazed over, she wondered how he could see at all. From the menace in his expression, she'd crossed the line. He reached for the front of her robe. Britt took a step forward. Richard needed a scapegoat for his problems, and he'd once again elected her for the job.

Independence was one thing. Foolhardiness was quite another. "If you won't listen to me," she said loudly, "would you listen to your demon?"

Richard recoiled, drawing his hand back. "That's not funny, Hope."

She glanced nervously at the house. Britt had moved onto the walk. "I wasn't intending to be funny." Then she raised her voice to just below a yell. "If there are any supernatural types hanging around who would like to help me carry a sound system back into the house, I would be very grateful."

Richard tensed. Chris and Eddie just looked confused.

Britt blurred into a moving streak, vanished and was beside her before she could blink. Just how fast could a ghost move? He didn't rematerialize, but she felt a chill, and knew it was him. Goose bumps raced along her skin. She fought back a shudder.

"You made the right choice," came his relieved voice in her ear.

She gave him a chagrined smile over her shoulder where she thought he stood and tried not to feel defeated.

"Don't be so hard on yourself, ma'am. You haven't failed. Everyone needs help now and then. That's different than being rescued."

The words came just at the bottom edge of her normal range of hearing, and she couldn't tell if she'd heard them with her ears or in her head. Either way, it was an unnerving experience. She swallowed hard and nodded.

Britt dropped his voice into a basso rumble guaranteed to scare the pants off a sober man. "Delighted to be of service."

Richard screamed and scrambled across the lawn. "It's back!"

Chris and Eddie backed away, their gazes glancing wildly between Richard and Hope. Various pieces of electronic equipment appeared to stack themselves, then floated from the trunk and headed toward the house.

"Don't let it come near me!" Richard shrieked, stumbling backward.

From the equipment's steady pace to the house, Britt apparently had no intention of allowing the drunken men on the lawn see him. Moreover, he seemed to be ignoring them entirely. His choice, she supposed. Without another word, she followed Britt into the house, then shut and locked the door.

"How did they get in?" she asked, dimming the light.

Britt went solid, a courtesy probably, and set her belongings on the top shelf of the entertainment center in the ladies' parlor. Then he gave a pointed nod to the window hanging open.

"I must have forgotten to lock it," she observed. Manzanita wasn't known for its high crime, but it did have its share. Anything could have happened tonight. She'd been lucky.

"I'll be right back," he said. He touched a fingertip to the front of his hat brim, then vanished.

A moment later, three men screamed. She resisted the urge to look through the window to see what Britt was doing to them. A full minute passed before she heard the front door open and shut. Britt walked around the corner, looking as normal as anyone else, and holding four spark-plug wires. She wondered why he didn't just come through the walls. Maybe he couldn't carry objects with him if he did.

"They shouldn't be driving. They might hurt someone. Besides, the walk will sober them up a little. Unfortunately, that means one of them will return for the car tomorrow." His expression pinched with worry, and she got the distinct impression that he was concerned about her approval.

Hope smiled at him. "No, they won't."

He cocked a brow. "Ma'am?"

She picked up the phone and called a tow truck. After she'd made the arrangements, she turned back to Britt. Boyish pleasure crinkled his eyes, softening his harshly weathered features.

"You're very handy to have around," she said.

"Thank you, ma'am." His lips widened into a cautious

smile. "I've always tried to earn my keep."

They stood in the living room a moment longer, looking at each other. She needed to make amends and wasn't quite sure how to go about it. What did one say to a ghost she'd all but thrown out after he'd saved her life, and who was still willing to help her whenever she needed him?

Chapter
Seven

He frowned. "You were happy a moment ago. Now you're upset. Why?"

She was barely used to the concept of Britt McLean's ghost living in her house. She wondered how much longer it would take before she got used to him—or anyone else—being able to read her emotions. It made her feel naked.

"About the other night," she began, "I didn't mean to be so unfeeling about your situation. You've gone out of your way to be considerate, and I haven't been a particularly sympathetic host. Ever since we talked, I've strained to hear any evidence of you being here, but I haven't heard a thing. Staying that quiet can't have been easy."

"I've had a lot of practice." Then he cocked his head. "You're really upset about this."

"Yeah, I am." How did one make amends to a ghost? "Mr. McLean, would you like some coffee? I don't think I can sleep anymore tonight anyway."

His smile saddened. "Thanks for the offer, but I don't eat or drink. I can hang on to things, but things don't hang on to me. So unless you want to watch me pour perfectly good coffee on to your carpet, I think I'll pass."

That embarrassed her. He looked so *real*. In this light, there was nothing hazy or ghostlike about him. He looked like any other normal person. "I see." She tried to think of something else she could offer, but he didn't seem to need anything beyond his journal. "Then would you be interested in keeping me company while I make myself a cup?"

His eyes lit up as if she'd unexpectedly offered him the world on a plate. "Something has changed," he said. "You're not afraid like you were. You're not resentful, either."

"Let's go into the kitchen." She looked over her shoulder as she walked to make sure he followed. "It's kind of hard to describe what I feel," she said as she set up the coffeemaker.

"It's okay," he soothed. "I understand."

Hope blushed. "Oh, that's right."

"I remember making a lot of coffee in a plain can on a campfire," he said, tactfully changing the subject.

They both stilled, listening to the raucous machine.

"Never dreamed making coffee could get so fancy," he said. "Smells the same, though."

He seemed like such a pleasant person, a true old-fashioned gentleman, a friend she'd known for years. Just as she'd always imagined him to be. "I wish you could share a cup with me."

His expression became pained. "I never get hungry or thirsty. Never get sick or hurt."

"You don't sound happy about it. Do you miss those things?"

"I shouldn't after all this time, but I do. I miss feeling the sun on my face. I even miss the cold in the winter. The worst, though, is not being able to touch anyone."

There was such sadness in his voice and on his face that Hope ached for him. This was such a psychologically dangerous situation, she didn't know which way to jump. In her raw state, she could develop an unhealthy attachment to him. Pat's phrase—"white knight syndrome"—echoed loudly in her ears. She needed to heal, to learn to stand on her own two feet and rebuild her life. How could she do that when she was living with the ghost of a man she'd always been infatuated with, a ghost who had already saved her life and rescued her property?

"Is being dead really that bad?" she asked.

"For most people, I don't know. What few other ghosts I've found are a strange bunch. They keep themselves locked in houses or other buildings, obsessed with a problem that has long since resolved itself one way or another. They don't think or talk about anything else." He shook his head. "They don't make good company, ma'am. Not at all."

"Call me Hope."

His eyes glowed with pleasure. He pulled off his hat as if only belatedly remembering he had it on his head. "I'd like that." His dark hair hung in tousled shaggy waves that brushed his collar. It gave him an appealing, boyish quality.

Her own smile widened as she filled a coffee cup and stirred in a spoonful of gourmet hazelnut hot chocolate.

He seemed to be searching for something to say. "Where would you like me to put these?" He indicated the spark-plug wires in his hand.

It was as safe a topic as any as they floundered through the attempts at beginning a conversation.

"How about in the garage on the workbench?"

He gave a polite nod, opened the backdoor as anyone else would have, then carried them outside.

Hope didn't realize she held her breath until the door closed behind him. Against all odds, Britt McLean was in her house. The thrill of it warred with the apprehension of where it would lead.

More quickly than a mortal man could have made it to the garage and back, Britt returned. She deliberately tried to project feelings of welcome.

"You don't need to try so hard," he said gently.

She blushed again and bent to stirring her coffee. "This is so awkward." Suddenly she knew how to thank him. Taking a sip first to steady her nerves, she looked at him. "It's not right that after everything you've done for me that you're living in the attic. This is a big house. Would you please take one of the upper bedrooms? Actually, the entire third floor is closed off. You're welcome to it. That will give you all the privacy you need, plus room to spread out."

His mouth sagged open. "You're serious."

"Of course. I don't need that space for anything. And if you've been living in attics, museum basements and the like for the last hundred and twenty-seven years, I imagine a place of your own might sound pretty good."

Apparently rendered speechless, he continued to stare.

"Is that a problem?" she asked hesitantly, half convinced she'd made another blunder like she had when offering him coffee.

"Please, ma'am—Hope. That's very generous, but I don't need that much room."

"What else am I going to do with it?" The whole idea felt right.

"You could rent it out to boarders or turn this place into one of those bed-and-breakfast things."

She wasn't surprised at his suggestion. From what she knew of history, it wasn't uncommon for women alone to rent out parts of their homes. It brought in extra income, and he had to know how badly she needed the money right now. "I don't think having strangers parading in and out of Hawkings House is right for me."

He nodded in understanding.

"Is there something I *can* offer you?"

His eyes lit, even though he seemed to be trying to hide it.

"What?" she asked.

"Well, if you don't mind, I would like to talk whenever you have time. I've come to realize just how valuable companionship is."

Hope felt as if he was giving her a dream on a plate while acting as if it were the biggest gift she could give *him*. "I'd really like that," she said shyly. "Anything else?"

He looked chagrined. "The chance to be useful would be nice. Idleness really is a form of hell all by itself."

There was such banked emotion in his plea that she was sure it was a monumental understatement. The concept of having all the time in the world but nothing to do filled her with compassion. "If that's the case, what do you know about hooking up stereos?"

The grin came back.

"Are you serious? You know that stuff?"

"I know a little about a lot of twentieth-century inventions. Like cars and how to keep one from operating," he said, referring to the spark-plug wires.

Hope analyzed the situation for a moment. Britt McLean could do anything he wanted without fear of reprisal. Vandalize someone's car. Throw them out of a house. The victim could hardly complain to the police. But based on what she knew of the life he'd lived, she had no fear that he'd abuse that ability. The knowledge made her feel safe—too safe—and not nearly so empty. The potential for emotional disaster loomed large in her mind.

Shaking it off, she asked, "It sounds like you've tried to keep up with the times."

"I think I've done a fairly good job. Except the roaring twenties." He actually shuddered. "I found little to like about it and kept to myself."

"Why? What was wrong with the twenties?" She found that she and Britt had wandered into the dining room. Then, as comfortable as if they'd both been doing so for years, they sat across from each other at the table.

"The attitude was one of self-indulgent recklessness. Little caution. No sense."

"Everyone?"

"No," he admitted on a growl. "But one of my granddaughters had more money than sense. Because she had the old trunk filled with my journals—except for the one you have—and my clothes and whatnot, I lived with it in her attic and saw more than I cared to. Orgies and drunken excess were a regular occurrence. She finally woke up and realized what she was doing to herself, but it took losing everything in the stock market crash to make her change her ways."

Hope was enthralled. With very little coaxing, she had Britt telling her all manner of his experiences. In addition to his personal observations, he was remarkably well-read. Then again, he didn't have much else to do with his time. She got his perspective on both world wars, Korea, Vietnam and the Gulf War as well as space travel and the changes in society. Hope hung on his every word.

"You've seen so much," she said, her voice hardly more than an awed whisper.

He shrugged. "Between thirty-seven years as a living man and the hundred and twenty-seven years afterward, I've had a lot of time."

And most of it alone, she thought. Comparing the years against the historical events he'd witnessed made her grieve for him. How had he born up under the isolation?

At some point during the discussion, they moved into the living room and he reconnected her stereo, TV and VCR.

Hope blinked. "Is there anything you don't know how to do?"

The corner of his lips lost their contented curve. "Yeah. Figure out how to move on to the afterlife."

"What exactly happened?"

He told her, and her eyes welled up with tears.

"At the time, my only thoughts were to stop Carbow. It never occurred to me that I'd only have one chance to move on."

"Do you regret what you did?"

"Yes and no." He answered so quickly that she knew it was an old subject for him. "I've had a lot of time to get all philosophical about it and wonder whether what I did was worth the price I paid. I'll never know if the shot would have gone wide anyway and Nestor would still have saved my family or not. Maybe Carbow would have killed Nestor first just to get him out of the way. Lucinda and the children were next on the list. It all comes down to whether or not I could have left them knowing they might die. And the answer is no."

"You had no trouble communicating with Richard. Why were you so helpless back then?"

He was shaking his head even before she finished. "Decades passed before I figured out what I know now."

"How was it that Nestor Hawkings married your widow so soon after your death? Wasn't that hard for you?"

He groaned and lowered his gaze. "It was agony to watch, but at the same time, I knew it was her only way to support herself and the children. In life, I did the best I could for my family, but I wasn't a wealthy man like Nestor."

"What happened?"

He was a long time in answering. She suspected it wasn't because of not remembering, but because of the depth of pain associated with dredging up events that had happened more than a century ago.

"It took Nestor and five search parties three days to find my body. I hovered close, trying to let them know I was there, but other than making everyone flinch and curse the foul winter weather, I didn't accomplish anything.

"Then, despite the continuing rain and muddy roads, almost all the residents of Manzanita and the three other towns I served turned out for my funeral. I never suspected how people felt about me." His gaze briefly landed on hers, still awestruck after all these years.

"Amanda Abrams, the mayor's wife, loaned Lucinda a black dress, and I stood by unable to do a damned thing while she grieved. I couldn't even tell her one more time that I loved her.

"Watching Nestor and Lucinda prepare my body for burial was a horrifying experience." He looked down at his clothes. "This wasn't what I wore the day Carbow murdered me. At the funeral, I sort of changed into what they put on me."

Hope ached for him, discreetly blinking away the moisture in her eyes.

"I remember Nestor asking her if she was going to be okay. Lucinda looked up at him, struggling to find the words. Six-year-old Robert and five-year-old Bradley clung to her skirts, confused. Two-year-old Jonah and eight-month-old Katherine were too young to know or care what was going on, content to let neighbors hold them. The worst was Evie. At seven, she knew I wasn't coming home, and she stood there rooted in a deeper shock than any of the adults suspected. Her and Lucinda's grief and fear pounded at me, but I couldn't do a damned thing to help either one of them." He paused a moment to collect himself.

Even though she didn't have his ability to read emotions, Hope saw how little the wounds had healed.

"I watched Lucinda blink back tears and tell Nestor she didn't know how they were going to make it. Nestor folded those long, bony fingers of his around her delicate hands. Then he shrugged sheepishly and told her he'd take care of everything.''

"He was a millionaire, wasn't he?" Hope asked softly.

"Not yet, but damn close. He raised cattle for the miners. That and a few other ventures made him one of the wealthier men in the area. I'd never paid much attention to that fact before Lucinda needed someone to provide for her and the children." His expression turned inward. "I still don't know what I'd done to earn that kind of loyalty, but I was sure grateful for it."

"You're a special person, Britt. He was probably glad to be there," she said, her voice hoarse. "I imagine feeling your family's grief was hideous."

"No one should have to watch that," he pronounced. "Lucinda and Evie walked around in a daze, both crying without warning. It upset the little ones, so they tried to be brave."

"Evie was just a baby herself."

"Yes, and she was such a little mother." He gave Hope a bittersweet smile. "I wanted to hold them all, tell them I was all right. But everything I tried failed. Finally, a week after the funeral, I decided Nestor had everything well in hand, and it was time to go. I waited until Lucinda seated everyone at the table for breakfast. That was always a special time for us, and I wanted to see it once more. I told them I loved them—not that they could hear me—then I left."

It was all Hope could do not to break into tears herself. "When did you realize you were trapped?"

"About a week after. I went back to the stream where I died, hoping to find the tunnel of light, but it never came again. I hunted everywhere."

"I can't imagine how frightened you must have been."

He looked up at her, the memory swam in his eyes, the horror of it beyond her comprehension. "I don't think anyone can," he said softly.

As they talked, a bond began forming between them the likes of which she'd never experienced. One subject led to another, and time lost all meaning. When the phone rang, it struck her as a jarring intrusion. "Hello?" she said irritably.

"Hope, are you okay?" Pat asked.

"Sure, why?"

"It's ten o'clock. A client has been waiting for fifteen minutes."

Hope spun around and pulled back the heavy drapes. Daylight flooded the darkened room. "Oh, my," she groaned. "I'll be right there."

"What happened? Did you oversleep?"

"Something like that." She turned back toward Britt, but in the harsh morning light streaming through the window, she couldn't find him.

"That's not like you," Pat said.

Britt moved to a shadowed corner. It was still too bright for him to be seen beyond a fuzzy impression of a silhouette, but at least she knew where to look. Somehow during the night, she'd forgotten he was a ghost. The reminder jarred her far worse than the phone had.

"She's afraid for you," he whispered. "Probably because of Richard."

"Of course," she said, warmed by the realization.

"What?" Pat asked.

"Nothing. Late night last night. I got involved with a good book."

"Is that all?"

"No, Richard showed up about one this morning, but—"

Britt gave a warning shake of his head—or at least she thought that's what he did.

"I got him to leave. I couldn't sleep after that."

"As long as you're okay."

"Never better. I'll be there in fifteen minutes." Then she looked down at her robe. "Make it thirty." She hung up and broke the speed record for dressing for success.

As she snatched up her purse and sprinted for the front door, she noticed Britt had drawn the dining room curtains again and stood in the slightly darkened doorway. He was translucent, but recognizable, his expression content, his pipe nestled in one hand. Distantly, she wondered how she could ever have thought his face looked anything but charming and attractive.

"Is there anything I can get for you while I'm out?" she asked.

His generous lips spread into an indulgent grin. "I've been taking care of myself for a good long while now."

Hope's cheeks burned. "Can I bring you something to do? I feel like I'm deserting you."

The smile widened, and he chuckled. "I went to the library last night. Remember? I have plenty of books upstairs."

"How do you check out . . . Never mind. We'll talk when I get home." Still, she hesitated. "Are you sure you're all right here?"

He actually laughed then, the sound of a man who'd discovered paradise and knew it. "I go to movies if there's a film I want to see. Some days I just sit in a tree at the park and watch people live out their lives. I'm fine."

She paused. "It sounds lonely."

All the amusement leached from his face. "Yes, ma'am, it was."

Past tense. It said so much. They'd talked for hours, yet she wanted more. Her friend Pat was a whirlwind who made her tired, and Hope could only take so much. She had the strangest feeling that in a few short hours Britt had become a friend she could never live without. But would it stay at that nice safe level, or would she get sucked into something damaging?

"Go on," he urged, and she wondered how much of her thoughts he actually knew. "Stop worrying. I'll be fine."

Okay, so he knew the feeling but didn't always interpret it correctly. She could live with that.

"You have work that needs you. I'll keep that ne'er-do-well descendant of mine from robbing you blind while you do it."

"I'd appreciate that." She smiled at him again, then left.

Britt simply could not believe his good fortune. This wonderful lady not only cared about him, she actually enjoyed his company! The hours crawled by as he waited for her to come home. He couldn't remember time ever passing so slowly. Finally, a few minutes before seven, he heard her car pull up. He wanted to rush outside to greet her, but he didn't know her well enough to predict how she'd respond. As she turned the key in the lock, he forced himself to remain in the gentleman's parlor.

Her own hesitant eagerness as she stepped into the entry made him feel a little less foolish. With the drapes pulled, the house was dark enough for him to appear solid. So he materialized in the middle of the room where she wouldn't miss him.

"You're really here," she breathed. Pleasure tinged with a little awe radiated from her like a warm fire.

"Yes, ma'am," he said.

In an attack of sudden shyness, her incredible violet gaze darted away then back.

During the long hours she'd been gone, he'd thought of a thousand different things he wanted to talk about. Now that the opportunity was at hand, he could only smile and stare at her, tongue-tied. He had a friend! After all this time, someone in the living world knew about him, thought about him, wanted to interact with him.

She opened her mouth, questions in her eyes. A sea of emotions threatened to drown her. Their complexity made it hard to sort out specific ones, and Britt feared the worst.

"You've had another whole day to think about me being here," he said cautiously. "Am I still welcome?"

"If I wasn't so raw from my marriage falling apart, I'd never have had second thoughts in the first place." She smiled at him, fighting and conquering the seething mass of emotions that ebbed and flowed through her like the tide. "But I really am glad you're here." The last came through uncluttered and honest.

Each day after that, Britt found himself counting the hours as he waited for her to return to Hawkings House. He sat across from her while she ate, sharing the events of her day or old memories. Heaven itself couldn't have been sweeter. Even so, he could sense something bothering her about his presence—but she wouldn't tell him what. He tried to stay watchful and not examine the worry too closely. It made for an interesting juggling act.

• • •

For most of her next day off, Hope stood on a ladder, coaxing decades worth of paint and wallpaper off the walls of
the high-ceilinged entry. As she worked on the upper
moulding, Britt floated beside her, laughing and talking,
periodically refilling her glass of diet soda. Being this
happy seemed like a dream come true.

"I wish stripping would go faster," she said, troweling
on another layer of goo that was supposed to dissolve old
paint. "This is the one part of restoration that I don't care
for."

"Why didn't you say something before? I can take that
off much easier. I thought you were enjoying yourself."
He frowned at her as if puzzled by how he could have
misread something as basic as pleasure.

"It's the project I love, not paint stripping in particular."
She pressed a fingertip into one of several depressions
spaced at regular intervals in the moulding. "This stuff is
so thick that I can't even tell the original shape of these
mouldings. From the indentations, this looks as if it's
carved, but there's no telling. If you can do a better job
than I can, please feel free."

Drifting closer to the wall, he took a look. His gaze
turned strangely introspective. Then the paint began to rise
up in blisters that bubbled and ran, one into another. It
looked like special effects from a premier horror movie.
The smell was like the one surrounding huge generators—
ozone.

Hope sucked in her breath and watched in fascination as
a three-foot-long sheet of multilayered paint lifted from the
moulding and fell to the floor. Britt floated down the central
hallway, effortlessly freeing the wood and littering the floor
with the debris.

What remained was far from a pristine surface, but she
was still amazed at what he'd uncovered. An incredible
acorn and leaf pattern had been revealed, a design worthy
of a master carver. "Whoever painted over this ought to
be shot," she grumbled.

"I can't get the old paint that soaked into the wood itself.
It will need to be sanded down."

The idea of sandpaper further desecrating this gorgeous

workmanship appalled her, but if she took great care, it could be managed.

"Would you like me to get started?" he asked, a restrained hopefulness in his voice.

At first she wanted to decline his offer, to explain that restoring Hawkings House was something she needed to do. It was a monstrous job, but her sense of independence needed to accomplish something grand, even if it took years. On the other hand, Britt had been active his entire life. A hundred and twenty-seven years of uselessness had to have been hell. Hope was amazed that his mind hadn't snapped. Maybe he needed to help more than she needed to go it alone.

"Thank you." She smiled at him.

His entire face beamed with pleasure as he took a piece of sandpaper from the package. He glanced at it, and a narrow strip tore away with the precision of a scalpel. Then, again using only the power of his mind, he pressed it into the intricate curves, bending the corner to mold around the delicate carvings. The procedure was eerie to watch, but his contentment was so pronounced, the air surrounding him crackled with it.

Hiding a smile, she loaded the power sander with a fresh belt and went to work on the flat surface of the wall. A few minutes later, she turned the machine off and looked up at Britt. He was happily chewing on his pipestem and quietly humming a tuneless melody.

A deeper contentment settled in. This type of companionship was what she'd always craved. She wanted to share the simple activities of life, curling up in a spouse's arms in front of a fireplace on a cold night and enjoying quiet conversation, walks in the park on a warm summer afternoon, the joys and pains of raising a family. If Britt were alive, maybe their friendship would have progressed in that direction. It certainly had all the right ingredients. But several immutable facts remained. He was a ghost. Nothing could ever change that. And she was in serious danger of falling in love with him.

He stopped humming, turned to her and frowned. The sandpaper he manipulated stopped in midstroke. "Something just upset you. You're almost in tears. What are you thinking about?''

That brought her up short, and she jerked her emotions under control. Taking care with her thoughts wasn't something she had much experience with, and she needed to learn some caution. ''What-ifs and regrets intruded. That's all. I'm fine. Really.''

''Richard?''

It occurred to her to lie and tell him yes, but what would be the point? He'd know instantly that she wasn't being truthful. ''Can I weasel out and claim 'woman stuff'?''

He blinked, surprised. Then his expressive face darkened in self-reproach. ''I normally respect people's privacy better than this. I don't know what's wrong with me lately.''

She and Britt quite literally existed in two separate worlds. Blending them would take compromises, not just consideration. ''Reading emotions is a natural ability for you, Britt. Use it. I'll adapt.''

He gave her a considering look, then nodded his head in gratitude. Without further comment, they went back to their tasks.

Britt had enjoyed their day together so much he hated for it to be over. But the living needed sleep. What touched him, though, was that Hope felt genuine reluctance to go to bed as well as to work the next day. The lost contact while she tended to her life meant time snailed by for him. He couldn't concentrate on any of the books in his room. He replastered the entry walls and covered the wooden mouldings and wainscoting with a modern wood finish he'd picked up from the pile of cans behind the home improvement store. It was discontinued stock intended for toxic waste disposal and didn't qualify in his mind as theft. But the work didn't have the same pleasure without her beside him.

''You've been distracted all morning,'' Pat observed as she and Hope took their lunches to the park. It was still too early in the season to be warm enough to enjoy being outside, but the long, rainy winter was over, and Hope craved some open spaces.

"I'm afraid I may be getting myself into another mess," she explained cautiously, wondering how far she could skirt the truth and keep Pat from getting suspicious that she wasn't hearing the whole story.

"What kind?"

They picked a table by the duck pond. Most of the resident water fowl were pestering a young mother and her kids who were throwing crackers for them. Hope figured the demanding little beggars would leave her alone.

"I have a friend helping me with Hawkings House. He's unemployed and just looking for something to do until he gets work." She wondered if her nose would grow from the whopper she was telling. "He knows I can't pay him anything, and he's just being neighborly."

"Unemployed but not asking to be paid. Neighborly, hmmmm?" Pat unwrapped her sandwich. "Do I see an opportunist on the prowl in your parlor?"

Hope blushed. "He's not a masher, if that's what you think. He's considerate, charming and so appealing that I'm scared to death I'll do something stupid."

"Rebound romance doomed to failure?"

"How do I keep that from happening?"

Pat gave her a firm look. "The dust hasn't even settled from your separation yet. Your judgement is probably raw and bloody enough to qualify as hamburger. If you want any possibility of something developing with him when you're ready, I'd tell him, 'thanks for the help, but adios. I'll see you in about six months.' "

"That's what I thought," she said, turning her apple over and over in her hands.

"So, tell me. Who is this wonder boy?" Pat purred.

Oh, dear. Hope wilted. She'd known talking to her would be a mistake. So why had she done it?

"Any realistic chance you can put him on hold?" Her best friend was nothing if not persistent.

Hope gave her a telling look—or at least, she prayed that's how it came across. "No chance it would ever work. He's gay."

"Oh." Pat looked crestfallen. "Bummer. Once you're on your feet, I gotta get you out and circulating. The hunk

of your dreams is out there someplace. All we have to do
is find him.''

Hope felt nauseous.

The moment Hope came home, she and Britt chattered like
a couple of young lovers, delighting in sharing the smallest
detail of their day. Just seeing him again filled the empty
place in her heart.

Then she noticed the entry hall. Her mouth sagged in
wonder at the progress he'd made. ''How did you get the
new plaster to dry this fast?'' She glanced at his face, which
beamed with an almost innocent pleasure. ''Do you use
your ghostly''—she hated to use the word ''powers''; it
sounded so overblown—''smoke and mirrors stuff?'' Comparing his abilities to a magician's trick was far from accurate, but the tag served its purpose.

''My what?'' He chuckled.

''You know, your hocus-pocus powers, like you did to
remove the paint and stuff in the first place.''

He thought about that a moment. His eyes sparkled.
''Yeah, I suppose I did.''

The conversation swirled through one subject after the
next as she cooked dinner. She even told him about planning to one day fill Hawkings House with kids. Britt agreed
that it would make good use of all the bedrooms, but she'd
have to be careful not to let the children find out about him.
He made it clear he wouldn't appear to any of them, deem-
ing it too damaging.

''Richard came by while you were gone,'' he told her as
she took her plate to the dining room. They both settled
into what had become their ''usual'' places across from
each other. ''I don't think he'll bother you anymore after
today.''

''Do I want to know?'' she asked. The twinkle in her
eyes matched the one in her heart. Both pleased him im-
mensely.

He tried not to be affected by it, but that was like expecting the sun not to rise. He needed love as much as any
living man, more given how starved he'd been for human
contact. What made this situation doubly tempting was

knowing that if he were a living man, he'd be actively courting her.

Hope needed someone to care for her. It was an outdated concept, but that part of his thinking never changed with the times. His heart turned over. Maybe when she was ready, he'd see if he could find her a good man with proper values, one who didn't mind having a ghost for a houseguest. In the meantime, he'd watch over her himself.

"Richard was just his usual charming self," he answered. "I carry a respectable electrical charge."

"I thought that's what you were using to move things, but wasn't sure. What did you do to him?"

"He didn't find grabbing on to the doorknob very comfortable, particularly when I held on to the other side."

She actually laughed. The sound pleased him. Far too much, in fact. He wanted to run the backs of his fingers along her cheek to see if it was as soft as it looked. Was her mouth as kissable as he imagined? Disturbed by the pointless direction his thoughts had turned, he tried to concentrate on accepting the gift that he'd been given—her friendship. But greed for more had crept in, and he wanted what death had denied him. Somehow, he had to be content with the boundaries of this reprieve. Because that's all it was. He'd watched several generations live out their lives and die. Hope would eventually pass on in her time, and he had no reason to believe he wouldn't continue on as he had for almost thirteen decades. He didn't think he could stand it. But he had no way to break the cycle.

Chapter
Eight

The next night, tension boiled from her as she walked into the house, the day's mail clutched in her hand. She didn't call out to him the moment she opened the door as had become her habit. Britt went as solid as he could in the late afternoon light. He was little more than a gray haze, but she'd still know he was there. With trembling hands, she opened two envelopes. Quickly, she scanned the contents. Her heart raced, and he sensed a sick despair overtake her.

"What is it?" he asked.

When she looked up at him, her eyes were haunted. "Both charge card companies are threatening to send my accounts to collection. The bank that carried the note on a personal loan probably will, too. I knew this was about to happen, but I simply don't have the kind of money I owe."

Hope was not the type to live beyond her means.

"Richard?" he asked.

Lowering her gaze to the notices, she nodded heavily. Sadness and defeat poured from her. When she looked up again, she glanced around the room, her eyes distant. "All I have is my house. If I sell it, I can . . ."

The thought of selling Hawkings House grieved her beyond what Britt thought it should. After all, it was only a building. *He* was the one with the love-hate attachment here. Personally he would be content to live elsewhere. "Why is this place so important to you?"

"I don't know. Probably because it's old. Being a part of it makes me feel as if I have a history, too." She explained about being adopted by a family who loved her but had so many problems that no one was ever really connected. Her eyes glistened with moisture. "If I can't get a home equity loan to pay off the bills, the house will be just one more thing Richard has taken from me."

Now Britt understood. Moreover, the idea that she couldn't pay her bills because of Richard's excesses bothered him nearly as much as the notion of a woman paying her own bills at all. "I wish I could help."

His offer had warmed her, and she gave him a sad smile. "What? No hidden caches of gold? No secret diamond mine?" she teased. "What kind of ghost are you, anyway?"

"You've been reading too many penny novels." He tried to grin, but it felt like an abysmal failure.

She laughed at his comment, obviously trying to be cheerful, but it carried the same mournful cry she felt on the inside.

With everything in him, Britt wished he could do something. "Are the amounts so high that you really have to sell your home?"

"I have to come up with almost forty thousand dollars within thirty days just to avoid collection. That's not all the bills he ran up. That's just the minimum the companies will accept."

The figure Hope quoted stunned Britt. "In my day, only the wealthiest of men made that kind of money. I earned ten dollars a week and considered myself blessed."

"If I put this place on the market at below value so it'll move quickly, I can avoid legal proceedings."

She blinked a few times, trying to swallow back the tears. She was a brave woman. No weepy eyes for her. Lord, he wished he could put his arms around her and pull a pot of gold from his back pocket. But he could offer neither. "I understand what an equity loan is. Why do I get the impression you think that's an impossibility?"

She closed her eyes. "Because my credit rating is horrible."

"Richard." Britt's great, great, great grandson gave his helplessness a focus. Anger flooded through him, and he gave it free rein. That man needed to be horsewhipped.

"Enough talk about money," Hope injected into the silence. "Tell me something to keep my mind off of it. Something happy. Like . . . I know! Tell me about the first dangerous criminal you brought to justice."

Startled, Britt drew back. Worded like that, his job sounded rather lofty. In reality, it had been hot, sweaty, frustrating and dangerous enough to have finally gotten him killed. Maybe he could embellish a little.

Over the next few days, Britt went with Hope as she showed houses to prospective clients. Each one filled her with an ocean of tension. She needed a frightening amount of money.

"Why is the owner selling it so cheap?" one man asked as she showed him an executive home in an exclusive area of town. Britt disliked the pompous money-grubber on sight.

"The owner has been transferred and needs a quick sale."

"I'd have to win the lottery to afford this place," he said.

Britt manipulated her cell phone so it would ring.

Hope picked it up.

"Don't be afraid," he said through the line. "It's just me."

She gasped, and her pulse leapt.

Britt muttered under his breath in irritation with himself. "I need to figure out a way to contact you in new situations without scaring you half to death."

"We're making progress," she said drily, her heart rate returning to normal. "Half to death is a solid improvement over passing out cold—which was my last option." She projected her good humor into the room as her racing heart calmed, and he chuckled. "Is there a problem?"

"He wants this house badly. I'm picking up a lot of predatory greed from him. I suspect that taking financial

advantage of people is a game with him. Hold your ground
on the price.''

Hope laughed. He liked that sound. A lot.

''Thanks,'' she said softly. ''I'll handle the situation ac-
cordingly. Anything else?''

''Since you asked, yes. I don't like you doing business
with his sort. Not at all.''

The riverlets of pleasure that coursed through her puzzled
him. He wasn't sure what he'd said that caused her reaction,
but Hope was obviously pleased with him.

''I wish I could have your input more often,'' she said.

''That can be arranged.''

''Really? If that's the case, then I accept.'' Her worry
cut in half.

Hope hung up and made a searching glance around the
brightly lit, opulent room. The best he could do was appear
as an out-of-place shadow. When she spotted him, her eyes
sparkled and her contentment increased. Affection poured
from her, and Britt clung to it like a lifeline. If God was
merciful, maybe he'd have her caring for the rest of her
mortal days. The thought of ever losing it made him sick.

''Would you like to go through the house again?'' she
asked, returning her attention to her client.

The man gave a negligent wave, his expression sour.
''No, I've seen enough. This isn't quite what I'm looking
for. It would do, but it's just not . . .'' He let his voice trail
off as he preceded her out the door.

Britt eased up behind her and pitched his voice low
enough that only she could hear. ''He's lying.''

Hope smiled again and nodded. Message received.

She showed him out to her car. Britt moved into the
backseat as she drove away. Throughout the afternoon, he
called her cell phone at appropriate times to let her know
who was wasting her time and who was actually interested.
By the end of the day, two people seriously considered
making an offer on two separate properties.

Exhaustion made even blinking painful as Hope trudged out
into the backyard the next night. She was too tired to cook,
and probably wouldn't eat anything if she fixed it. Kicking

her shoes off first, she stretched out in one of the lounge chairs.

"Do you know how much help you were to me?" she asked, letting her eyes drift closed.

"I hope I was," he said.

The sun hadn't gone down yet, and he couldn't be seen in the bright light. Still, she could see a faint impression of movement as he sat on the other lounger.

"When you're with me I don't have to rely on nearly so much guesswork on what a client wants. You let me know who's serious and who isn't. Knowing what feature in a house appeals to them when they're not really sure themselves is a tremendous time saver."

"I enjoy it."

She couldn't imagine what it must have been like to have no one to talk to for decades at a time. If a living, breathing human had been subjected to solitary confinement for even a fraction of that time, his or her mind would have crumbled. Maybe insanity was one more type of illness ghosts avoided since they didn't have a body.

They sat in silence, watching the sun wane. He seemed a little tense, but she couldn't place why. "Are you upset with me?"

"Not with you."

"Who?"

"I arrived at the office this morning just before you did, and Pat was telling Brian you have a 'hunky gay guy' helping you with restorations, and you're in danger of having a 'rebound thing' for him." Britt gave her a bewildered look. "Does she normally make up tales like that? I can't say I think much of her as a result."

Hope groaned, blushed crimson and prayed that the ground would swallow her. "I, ah, mentioned that I had a friend helping me, and the subject came up of whether or not he'd be a good candidate for future romance." She swallowed hard. Britt was a walking lie detector, and she couldn't bear for him to to learn what she'd really said. "I got out of the conversation by telling her you were a homosexual."

It was finally dark enough to see him clearly. His expression hardened, and she wanted to cringe. His translu-

cent body took on a faint blue sheen, crackling with a
leashed electrical charge. He was so modern in so many
ways, but on this subject apparently was still very nineteenth century. Right now, he was very *offended* nineteenth
century.

"You're not telling me quite the whole truth," he pronounced finally.

Okay, she hadn't fooled him as well as she'd hoped to.
"True. But the less said about that conversation the better.
Please?"

The electrical sheen faded, and the expression in his eyes
softened. "Your life is your own, Hope. You don't owe
me any explanations. I was just concerned about someone
lying about you."

She smiled at him. "Thanks." Then she sat up. "By the
way, I bought you a present today."

His expressive face smoothed in shock, and he stared at
her openmouthed. "You what?"

"A present." She stood up. "I wanted to thank you with
more than words. I still need to win the lottery to pay off
Richard's bills, but I don't feel so defeated."

"You bought me something?" The concept so obviously
boggled his mind that she laughed.

"I left it in the car. Since you can see through walls and
whatnot, I didn't want you peeking through the gift wrap."
She waited for him to answer, but she only got continued
openmouthed staring. Laughter bubbled from her. She
couldn't remember the last time she felt this good. Her
fatigue melted away. "Do you promise not to peek when
I bring it out here?"

"I promise," he rasped.

If he'd been a living man, she'd have thrown her arms
around him. Instead, she gave him her best smile and retrieved the flat, rectangular package from the front seat of
her car.

His eyes glowed with reverence as he took it from her.
Their hands brushed close, and she felt the painful chill of
death that surrounded him. For long moments, his gaze
darted from the package to her face and back again as if
he expected the box to vanish or for her to tell him it was
a mistake.

"Open it," she encouraged, hardly able to contain her excitement.

His gaze settled on the package. The paper slid away as if it had a life of its own, revealing a white, shirt box. More of his smoke and mirrors stuff. He lifted the lid. Tucked inside was a leather-look, vinyl-covered journal, a black pen and two ink refills.

"I couldn't afford the fancy set, but I wanted you to have something."

"I don't understand."

Her heart melted. "You need to return to your writing," she said softly. "It gave you great pleasure in life. There's no reason it can't now, too."

"Hope, I don't know what to say." From the luminous cast to his eyes, she'd touched him more deeply than anyone had in a long time.

"Tell me you'll fill it up with one hundred and twenty-seven years' worth of memories." Her eyes filled with moisture, and she blinked it away. "Then when you're finished with the past, write down your observations on day-to-day modern life as you see it."

"I'd never considered . . . Thank you. I will." His shock-slackened mouth curved into a smile. "You shouldn't have spent any money on me, though. You have bills to pay."

Hope shrugged. "Given the amount of money I have to come up with, your present won't make any difference one way or the other."

"Your whole situation is an abomination. Richard should have to pay for his own indulgences."

Hope warmed at his concern for her. "I don't think it's fair, either, but as long as they were incurred during the marriage, he and I are equally liable for them. Since I'm working and he's not, the creditors have no choice but to come after me." She leaned back and closed her eyes. The sun hadn't set yet, and in the late afternoon light, he couldn't appear solid. With her eyes closed, though, it made it easier to imagine that Britt was a flesh-and-blood man beside her, not a ghost. "Maybe I should buy a stack of lottery tickets. You never can tell."

Britt didn't answer right away, and she opened her eyes. The tension on his face was odd, different than anything she'd yet seen in him. Thoughts appeared to churn behind his pale blue eyes.

"You gamble?" he asked.

"No. It was just a pleasant what-if. A daydream."

"I used to play poker once in a while. It passed the time. I think I was only in a handful of honest games my whole life."

Smiling, she said, "I wouldn't know a decent poker hand if I fell over one."

His eyes took on an intensity she didn't know how to interpret. "Would you consider buying a lottery ticket for me?"

Hope laughed at the idea of throwing away a perfectly good dollar. "Can you predict which numbers will hit?"

"Well, no, but I still might win. I hate to ask for a favor after what you just bought me, but . . ."

"Are you serious?"

He looked like he wanted to argue the last point but stopped himself. "I occasionally need funds when there's a book I want that the library doesn't have. I don't like stealing. Would you buy a ticket for me? If we win, I'll split it with you."

"You *are* serious."

"Yes, ma'am." Conviction rang in his voice.

Hope didn't like this reckless side to him. But this was the first favor he'd asked of her, and she really did owe him more than she could repay. Besides, it was only a dollar. "When did you want to do this?"

"Why not in the morning? The weekly drawing is to-morrow night, and I'm feeling lucky."

"You are, are you?"

"Yes, ma'am." He gave her a sideways look that struck her as boyish and appealing. "I have some lucky numbers and want to see if they still work."

The next night, Britt blew into the TV studio where the drawing was held. He was so unused to needing to keep track of time that he'd misjudged the hour. He was late, and one of the little white numbered balls had already been sucked up into the tube.

The balls whirled in the tank, and he sped up his relationship to time and matter. The world around him began to move exceedingly slow. He checked on the ball that the machine had already caught. Its number wasn't on his list. The idea of cheating bothered his conscience, but it was the only chance he had to stop her creditors from taking her home. Besides, from his experience, anyone dumb enough to gamble with their hard-earned money deserved whatever they got.

Discreetly, he deflected ball after ball, only allowing those on his list to hit. The last two he nudged into position, and they were promptly sucked up in turn. He stepped back, disappointed. Five out of six wouldn't get her anywhere near as much as she could have had. He'd hoped to set her up for life. He knew part of his reason was his outdated notion that a woman needed a man to protect her from life's harder edges. In the back of his mind, he knew there was more to it than that, but he refused to think about it.

By the time he returned to Hawkings House, Hope was on the phone with Pat. He felt her euphoria long before he opened the backdoor and walked inside.

"No, I don't know how much I won. I'll call the lottery people tomorrow. But five out of six numbers can't be too bad." She waved enthusiastically at him.

It wasn't that Britt disliked Pat or that he found anything wrong with the woman. He just didn't care for her. Too brash for his sensibilities. He sat on the couch, soaking up Hope's joy and trying to look innocent.

When she hung up, she whirled around and faced him. "Where have you been!"

"Watching people at the park." Not quite a lie. He'd been there first. "Why?"

"We won!"

"Really?" Her joy made it easy to looked pleased.

"Not the jackpot, but five out of six. This is incredible! I've called everybody. Those really *were* lucky numbers." Suspicion drove away her smile. Her eyes narrowed. "You didn't do any of your smoke and mirrors stuff, did you?"

He tried to look insulted. It was hard when he was guilty as hell, but he was afraid she wouldn't take the money if she knew how he'd gotten it. "Me?" He gave her his best arch look. "Are you asking if I cheated?"

Doubt crowded out some of her mistrust.

"We really won?" he asked before she had a chance to examine the subject any more closely than she already had. He leaned forward and plastered on an enthusiastic smile. "How much?"

"I don't know yet," she said, her attention diverted. "It'll depend on how many other winners I have to share it with." The suspicion crept back. Even without reading her emotions, he could see it in her eyes. "Are you sure you didn't . . ." She shook her head. Mentally, she retreated from the entire question. She didn't really want to know. He probed a little deeper and discovered relief.

"Do you think the winnings will be enough to pay off some of your bills?"

She gave him a haunted look. "I hope so. I really do."

Over a week later, she was unusually quiet as she fixed her dinner. Britt sensed a turmoil that hadn't been there before.

"Did you claim our winnings today?" he asked while she fixed dinner. "A hundred thousand dollars is quite a sum."

"Yes, and I wanted to talk to you about that."

She turned from the stove, switched off the kitchen overhead light and crossed her arms. The stance looked a lot like Lucinda's just before she flayed him over one infraction or another. With the room lit only by the low-wattage stove light, he lost all traces of translucence. She apparently wanted to get a good look at his face while she had her say.

"You were a poker player, right?" she asked.

Uh-oh.

"That was the only gambling you did, right?"

Oh, Lord, he was in deep. "Yes, why?"

"I've had a lot of time to think about this. What possible use would you have for six lucky numbers back in 1872? Are you sure you had nothing to do with me winning?" she demanded.

A stew of emotions ripped through him, not the least of

which was guilt. He reacted like he always had when caught red-handed. He got mad. "Hope, you need the money. I don't think how I got it should worry you all that much."

"Britt!" Wounded betrayal covered her face. "How could you! You really cheated?"

"Yes, I did." He squared his shoulders. "It's not something I'm proud of, but the situation made it necessary."

"What did you do?" She pulled back, her expression pinched. "Never mind. You're a ghost. That probably explains all of it."

He braced himself. He'd been married long enough to know when a woman got this wound up, she wouldn't stop until she let it all out. And Hope was just getting started.

"I don't want money I didn't win honestly. Why didn't you tell me up front?"

His gut churned with things he hadn't wanted to think about, not even now. It blunted his anger. "I knew how you'd react. I couldn't let you end up like Lucinda!" The words shocked him as they tumbled out.

They shocked her, too. Her anger fled. "What are you talking about?" she asked softly, confusion and compassion overriding all else.

"Nothing. I'm a fool. That's all."

"You're a lot of things, Britt. A fool isn't one of them. Now tell me what's eating you."

Anger flared again. "You don't know what it was like to watch the wife I loved marry another man because I'd left her and the children with nothing."

"Cut yourself some slack, Britt," she fired back. "You made the best living you could."

"It wasn't enough!" His image rippled, going translucent in places. Electrical energy pulsed through him. Having become so agitated that he couldn't maintain the illusion of being solid or control the amount of charge he produced made him even angrier.

The desire to offer him comfort radiated from Hope like heat from a fire. She reached for him, but the blistering cold hit her when her hand hovered a good six inches from his arm, and she drew back.

"What's bothering you?" she asked in a small voice.

He took a heavy breath, probably an affectation left over from life. Ghosts certainly didn't need air. "Nestor was gentle about it, but he insisted Lucinda marry him so there wouldn't be talk about him giving her money. People would be more likely to understand a marriage for practical reasons so soon after my death than they would something that looked like she was his mistress. He didn't even press her on their wedding night." Britt paused. "Eventually, she came to love him. They had a long and happy life together. Jonah and Katherine were too young to remember me. All their lives, they called Nestor 'Papa.'"

"Sounds like your friend was quite a man."

"He was." The translucent, bluish ripple shuddered through him again. Hope waited him out until he controlled himself enough to become solid again.

"Can I fill in the blanks here?" she asked softly, doing her best to project feelings of warmth and comfort. "I'm a woman alone in big financial trouble. No matter what it took, you were going to help me. It's the best you can do to make up for not being there for your own family."

He stared into the distance and gave a terse nod. "I want you to have the money—all of it. Don't do something noble like give it to charity."

"If you'd given me any other reason for cheating, I wouldn't accept a dime. But this has eaten at you for more years than I can comprehend." She interlaced her fingers in front of her. "So, all things considered, thank you. I accept."

Again, the terse nod. "If you wouldn't mind, I need to be alone for a while."

"I understand. You probably revealed things you never told anyone. Men, in general, aren't inclined toward baring their souls. I imagine that was even more true in the 1800s."

How did she hit on that with such accuracy? It made him want to squirm. "I have a new book I want to read."

She smiled, letting him have his face-saving excuse. "Good night, then."

He touched a fingertip to his hat brim and vanished.

• • •

Britt knew nothing about selling houses, but he and Hope fell into a comfortable routine as he helped her with clients whenever she needed him. It had been a long time since he'd actually held a job, and he savored taste of purpose and long-denied humanity. Best of all, he talked to Hope throughout the day.

Sometimes at night, a sadness would overtake her, and she needed to talk about the death of her marriage. Britt was glad to be there for her. Then, once he got used to "baring his soul," as she called it, he shared his own griefs and joys of watching his children grow up without him, as well as watching his wife fall more deeply in love with Nestor. Until now, he hadn't believed anything could ease the pain, but he'd been wrong. With each discussion while they worked on one room or another of Hawkings House, the grief, heartache and regrets eased a little further away.

One night she came running into the house, more excited than he'd ever seen her. "Britt! Do you remember that jerk you said could afford the executive home but just wanted to take advantage of someone else's misfortune?"

"Yeah." He'd spent the day pulling down the old plaster on the ceiling in the lady's parlor and replacing a few boards that had succumbed to dry rot.

"He got into a bidding war on the property and ended up having to pay thirty thousand more than the asking price." Her violet eyes glowed with excitement, then dampened. "I have to ask. Did you have anything to do with it?"

"Of course not!" Would she wonder that every time something good happened to her? "Your bills are paid off. You have money tucked away. And you're content—like you should be."

"So you're back to living your version of *Star Trek*'s noninterference directive?"

He'd seen his share of television over the years, too, and smiled at the reference. "The producers of that show had the right idea."

"So I did this on my own?"

He nodded. Hope came to him in a rush of motion, and he was convinced that if he'd been a living man she would have thrown herself into his arms. As it was, she barely

stopped herself in time. Longing and regret hollowed out
her eyes and face, a perfect match of what he felt inside.

He no longer owned a body that could become aroused,
but he suspected if he did, he'd have his work cut out for
him to stop himself from making love to her. Even without
that, the need for human touch became more torturous with
each passing day.

Hope was bright and charming, and she was truly interested in whatever he had to say. More than anything in the
world, he wanted to hold her. He wanted a flesh-and-blood
body that could know her touch, know the feel of her skin
against his.

Fighting down the wave of despair, he vowed never to
burden her with knowing how he felt. "So what does this
mean for your divorce?" he asked, forcing cheer into his
voice.

"My attorney called Richard. Typical of an addict, he
wants money now rather than wait until I can buy out his
half interest in the house. If escrow on that sale closes on
time, he'll accept a minimal amount for a property settlement."

Britt would never tell her about his "chat" with the man
to encourage that decision. "So you'll be divorced then?"

"Depends on the judge. He may give a several month
delay where we can change our minds." She shuddered.

Something turned over within him, and he realized how
close he was to falling in love with her. He didn't know
when it started, but he couldn't deny that's what he felt.

*And when you find a living man to love, I'll remain as I
have been for the last hundred and twenty-seven years, a
ghost who has no idea how to fill the endless prison sentence I condemned myself to. And when you do move on in
death or just with a new direction in your life, how will I
ever be able to let you go?*

He asked her another couple of leading questions so she
could expound upon the details, but he couldn't shake what
it would mean for him when she was free and began dating
again.

"You look sad." Her delicate brow furrowed in concern.
"Are you all right?"

"It's nothing."

"You're lying through your teeth," she said unexpectedly.

"I don't have teeth anymore. What you think you see is just part of how I appear. The real ones are buried with the rest of my body." The blunt reminder had been deliberate. He suspected that they both needed a reality check. He knew *he* did. "Now come into the parlor so I can show you the dry rot that I pulled out."

"Okay, Hope," Pat muttered good-naturedly. "What gives? You won a ton of money on the lottery, and you're closing houses left and right. Do you have a guardian angel?"

Hope didn't dare tell her. "It looks like it."

"No magic formulas, huh?"

"I wish." Hope shrugged. "If I had one, I'd bottle it and make a fortune."

Pat rolled her eyes.

After writing checks for over eighty thousand dollars to cover Richard's bills, and with escrow closing on three houses at the beginning of next month, Hope felt that life was finally turning her way—thanks not to a guardian angel, but to her guardian ghost.

"Hope," Pat whined at the end of another long day. "All you've done since you threw Richard out is show property and work on the restoration. All work and no play makes a person very dull."

"I'm having a wonderful time."

"Yeah, just living an addict-free life is probably making you feel like you found paradise."

"Very true." Hope beamed inside.

"I am in bad need of a Mom's night out," Pat said. "Why don't I pick you up at six-thirty, and we'll party."

"I don't know," Hope hedged. She really just wanted to go home and be with Britt.

"Great," Pat said, apparently only hearing what she wanted to hear. "How does that male stripper place in Sacramento sound? They've got some real cuties down there. A little on the young side, but great pecks. Abs to die for."

Hope gasped and blushed purple. "Thank you, but can

we go out for pie instead? I'm not into that kind of—''

Pat cut her off with a wave of her hand. "Nope. The mouse has reformed. Remember? Live a little! Get rowdy!"

"Yeah, but—"

"No buts. I'll pick you up at six-thirty. That way we won't miss the early show."

Hope was infinitely glad she'd planned to catch up on paperwork. Britt wasn't needed and had stayed home to finish that ceiling. How would she ever explain this to him?

When she got home, she still hadn't thought of anything plausible. Consequently, she wimped out and volunteered nothing.

"Well, I suppose it isn't my business," he said.

She winced at the hurt he wasn't able to hide. "It's just a girl thing," she hedged, taking her own angle on Pat's words.

Britt nodded, obviously pretending it didn't matter to him what she did. Feeling rotten, Hope went upstairs to change.

Thirty minutes later, Pat gave a rapid-fire doubled-fisted knock on the door. When Hope opened, her friend enveloped her in a fierce hug. "I am so proud of you. You're actually getting out where real people live." She leaned back to look into Hope's face. "Does Richard still have a pair of his underwear here?"

"Why?"

"We can start off the evening by burning them. We'll lay them out on the barbecue and pretend he's wearing them."

Hope gasped. "My, that does paint a graphic picture, doesn't it," she offered weakly.

Pat howled with glee. "Thought that would get your attention. Come on, future party animal. Let's blow this joint."

Hope braced herself to be towed along, focusing on Pat's chatter. She didn't really want to watch a bunch of men ten years her junior prancing around on a stage. But she didn't want to be a spoilsport, either. Maybe Pat had a point. Maybe she needed a radical change of pace. Her life revolved around Britt and Hawkings House. The house isolated her, and her deepening feelings for Britt could go nowhere.

Since it was so soon after the breakup of her marriage, she knew part of what she felt for him was a rebound thing. The rest had been around for too long to question its reality. It was the latter that scared her. She had to do *something* to wake herself up. A mental picture of his soft blue eyes and gentle smile tinged with regret was never far away. But he was *dead*! At the rate her heart was going, she was ready to try anything to break out of this downward spiral toward love.

Forty-five minutes later, she and Pat pulled into the crowded parking lot of a chrome and glass establishment. The flashing marquis proclaimed it "Buns and Roses."

Hope groaned. "Shock therapy. If I look at it like that instead of the dumbest, most embarrassing thing I've ever done in my life, maybe I can get through the evening."

Pat chortled with glee, tossed her car keys to the valet attendant and dragged Hope inside.

Chapter Nine

Britt's reaction to being shut out of Hope's plans for the evening irritated him. She had the right to do whatever she wanted without explanation or justification. Still, seeing her assert those rights had pricked him to the core. No matter how firmly he told himself his attitude was selfish and a hundred years out of date, he wanted to be with her during all her free time. What did he expect? For her to live her life as a recluse? He couldn't exactly escort her anywhere.

Beyond battling his own questionable emotions, he was aware of Hope's disquiet as she dressed in a black evening dress and took extra care with her makeup. His own disquiet slid into full apprehension when Pat arrived and spirited her away. Hope's friend was far too cocky, even for her. She was a woman on a mission, and Britt's protectiveness flared.

As Pat's minivan sped down the street, the temptation to follow overpowered the intelligent choice of letting Hope live her own life. Until he understood what was bothering her, he planned to stay close.

Everything about the gaudy exterior of the building marked "Buns and Roses" repelled him, from its pink-and-purple blinking lights on the marquis to the tuxedo-clad doorman. Britt slipped inside and floated near the ceiling to keep anyone from touching him. The pink-and-purple draperied walls reminded him of a bordello. Booths and tables by a curtained stage were packed with several dozen raucous women and only a couple of men. The mood unnerved him. Some of the women were just there to have a good time, but the rest frightened him. Their attitudes were rebellious, predatory and vengeful. Why? What was this place? And what was a lady like Hope doing in such a crowd? He'd just decided to go backstage and find out what manner of show was being prepared when Pat jumped to her feet.

"My friend is celebrating. She threw out her deadbeat husband. It's party time!"

The crowd cheered and shouted their congratulations as Hope shrank into herself in abject mortification. Outwardly, her only reaction was a horrified widening of her eyes and a weak smile. Then she huddled over her drink and devoted an undo amount of energy on chopping up the ice with a plastic straw.

Britt had the sinking sensation that he'd just found a glaring hole in his twentieth-century education. Every instinct within him screamed to rescue Hope from this viper's den as fast as he could.

At that moment, a tuxedo-clad announcer introduced someone named Darling Dan. Music blared, and a man wearing a Zorro costume—complete with mask, sword and cape—leapt from behind a curtain. The women screamed lewd comments at him as he gyrated on the stage, peeling off one layer of clothing after another. Not since the orgies of the Roaring Twenties had Britt seen such openly bawdy behavior. The predatory mood from the female audience choked him with its intensity. Symbolic revenge. Now he understood the mood. They were treating the dancer as they had been treated, like a piece of meat, a sex object. From what Britt could tell, only a couple questioned what they really felt.

Britt felt Hope's mortification and her unwilling fascination with the sordid proceedings. She slid further down in her seat and covered her eyes. His relief at discovering she wasn't an active participant fled as she then peaked through her fingers. As Darling Dan slithered over the stage, now only wearing a...covering...that barely stretched over his privates, Britt turned away in revulsion. Then he shot backstage. Several other men were finishing up their equally provocative preparations.

He extended his senses to check on Hope. As much as he wanted to shield her from this spectacle, Britt kept his overactive protective instincts under control. Hope was a grown woman. He had no right to interfere, but she was *his* woman and that made it—

The realization of how far he'd fallen for her stopped him in his tracks. Keeping his senses trained on her, he floated through the ceiling and out into the night air.

How could he possibly have let his heart get in this deep? Was his love for her new enough that he might have a chance of pushing it away? The temptation to hang on to it as hard as he could wailed to be heard. He had the chance to love someone again—however briefly. Which would hurt less in the long run?

"What chance?" he railed at the night sky. "She's a flesh-and-blood woman. She deserves a living man who can raise up a family with her, grow old with her. I can give her nothing."

Well into the third dancer's performance, Britt sensed Hope leaving her seat. He went back inside and watched her head toward the ladies' room. It was empty, and as she walked toward the row of stalls, he materialized in front of her, making himself as solid as he could in the strange fluorescent lighting.

"Britt!" she gasped, placing her hand to her throat. "What are you doing here?" she whispered, then peeked around the corner to see if anyone stood at the row of sinks. No one did.

"What am I doing here? Come home!" Inside, he cringed. He'd intended to convince her rationally and calmly that she had no business here.

Her face smoothed in surprise. "Why? What's the matter? Did Richard do something to the house?"

"Of course not. But you need to get out of this... this..."

"Male strip joint?" she offered.

Part of him realized how badly he was sabotaging his

goal, but he couldn't seem to gain control over his mouth.

Hope looked as confused as she felt. "Britt, I'm with Pat. I can't just leave, especially if you won't tell me what's wrong. Besides, how would I get home? Manzanita is sixty miles from here."

"I'll find a chair, sit you on it and carry you."

From her glazed look, he knew she needed a moment to absorb that one. "Britt, I don't know what this is all about, but I think we can talk when I get home." Pointedly, she laid her hand against a stall door and pushed it open. "Now, unless you're suddenly into voyeurism, you need to leave." Locking the door behind her, she added, "Bye, Britt."

Britt seethed. How could he have bungled this so badly? How could she have decided to stay? Afraid he'd make a bigger fool of himself than he already had, he returned to Manzanita. The trip took only seconds, and he regretted that, too. What he really needed was some extended physical exertion to bleed off his anger. But not owning a body made that impossible.

Once back at Hawkings House, he slipped inside the vault and absorbed the soothing effects of being wrapped in his journal. He tried to clear his mind and just drift in that amorphous state that was as close as he ever came to sleep, but as time slipped past, he only became angrier.

"Shock therapy," Hope muttered, flipping on the light just inside her front door. The entry blossomed into the warm hues of refinished wood and freshly plastered walls, the latter painted in soft peach. She and Britt had accomplished so much together. Hawkings House had begun to take on the look of a much-loved home. If only one day she could fill it with kids, she'd be happy.

For the moment, though, she needed to figure out Britt's problem.

As if summoned, he went solid in front of her. It was such a common occurence these days, she barely reacted. Hope started to smile but noticed his thunderous expression, crossed arms and adversarial stance.

"Is everything all right?" she asked cautiously.

"No, it isn't." He shifted, looking too agitated to contain himself. "That place you went tonight."

"What about it?"

"You have no business being party to that kind of a . . . a . . . display! You sat through the entire performance, humiliated and wanting to be anywhere else but there. Yet you didn't do one thing to remove yourself. Not even when I easily could have taken you home."

"And you're upset about that." Over the course of the evening, she'd laughed, cried and left the real world behind for a while. She also decided that no power on earth would ever drag her back into one of those "displays," as he'd called it.

"Of course, I'm upset about it! What man wouldn't be!"

For the last two years of her marriage to Richard, she'd put up with having to be accountable for every minute she didn't spend toting and fetching for him. She'd despised it, but that had been back in her spineless mouse days. Hope knew she'd grown a lot since then. Her temper bristled, but she held it in check.

"So what are you saying?" she asked. Maybe she'd misunderstood something and needed to hear him out. If not, then he'd better be prepared to get blasted with a piece of her mind.

"How could you lower yourself to that kind of . . . of . . ."

"I am not answerable to you, Britt," she said in a low, warning voice. If he read the building anger, he gave no indication of it.

"What were you thinking!" he fired back, apparently locked into a storm that nothing could penetrate.

"I'm thinking that where I go isn't subject to your approval. Apparently, you don't agree."

"No, that's not—"

"Then what exactly is it!" The grip on her temper slipped. She knew she was reacting as much from embarrassment and from the old scars as to Britt's highhandedness, but that didn't help.

"I never witnessed anything so repulsive in my life. Or afterward, come to think of it! Women stuffing money into those men's . . . into their . . . their . . ."

He was fumbling so badly, that right in the middle of being furious with him, Hope started to snicker. "It's called a G-string."

"You even know what it's called?" His nineteenth-century outrage suddenly struck her as hilarious.

A giggle escaped, and his eyes widened in shock. That struck her as even funnier. A guffaw followed, and Hope knew she was lost. Laughing at someone locked in the middle of a towering rage wasn't the smartest thing she could imagine, but she couldn't help it and she laughed harder. It was obvious now that his reaction wasn't the manipulative garbage Richard had subjected her to. The situation had blown his unusually enlightened nineteenth-century mind, and he didn't know how to handle it.

"You are so sweet, Britt," she said, trying to pull herself together. "Yes, I know what it's called." An ornery imp of a thought captured her. She cocked her head and gave him a deliberate once over. "In fact, I think you'd look rather cute in one. You've got a great-looking body—well, I suppose 'shape' is a more appropriate term."

He gasped, appalled, and Hope turned crimson. She'd never in her life made such a suggestive comment to a man. The spineless mouse had reformed. But had she gone too far in the other direction?

Britt gawked at her, sputtering, completely unable to say a word. He shoved his hat down on his head and vanished.

Hope went into the gentleman's parlor, sank onto the couch and laughed until her face hurt.

When she sobered a little, she realized her reaction had probably hurt his feelings. After all, he'd only had her best interests at heart. Given that his ethics had been formed during a childhood begun 164 years ago, he was surprisingly liberal in his outlook.

The more she thought about it, the guiltier she felt. An apology really was in order. Groaning in remorse, she took herself up to the third floor. When she got to the landing at the top of the stairs, she called to him.

"Britt?" She knew she couldn't have sneaked up on him even if she'd wanted to, but announcing her presence was the polite thing to do.

The door to the room he'd claimed as his own was closed. She knocked on it, but he didn't answer. Maybe he'd left for a while, but she felt that the more likely reason was he'd decided to ignore her. "Britt, can we talk?"

Still there was no answer.

She opened the door and peeked inside. In addition to his desk, chair and bookcase, he had added an old, over-stuffed couch and coffee table. Two electric lamps flanked the couch. From the looks of them, he'd scrounged them from a junk pile and made repairs. Only one lamp was lit, and he sat beneath its light on the far end of the couch, semitranslucent, a book in his hands. The scene under-scored how badly he wanted to be a living man again. She ached for him.

"Can we talk?" she asked.

"Can you stop laughing at me?" he retorted archly with-out looking up from his reading.

He sounded so prissy she nearly giggled again. He glared at her and vanished. The book stayed suspended in midair, so she knew he hadn't left.

She stepped inside, her humor replaced with guilt. "Friends laugh with friends, not at them," she said. "I'm sorry. I understand you reacted the way you did because you care. I should have been more respectful of your con-cerns. If I had, we could have worked this out and avoided harsh words."

The light snapped off, leaving the room darkened except for the glow of the streetlamp through the windows that lined one wall. The book closed, then dropped onto the table as if tossed. A second later, he materialized, standing in the middle of the room, remorse in his eyes. In the dim-ness, he looked as real as any flesh-and-blood man. Those times she could see through him, it was easy to remember what he was, but not now, not when she saw every weath-ered line in his beloved face, the slight cleft in his chin and his work-roughened hands.

"I'm sorry, too," he said finally. "You're not my wife. Even if you were, times are different now than in my day. Sometimes I forget."

A silence descended as they stared at each other, both weighed down by their respective regrets.

Unable to stand the strain of the quiet, Hope spoke first. "If I'd thought the incident through, I wouldn't have exploded. Actually, your reaction made me feel protected, not smothered. I've never had that before. It's nice."

His heart shone in his eyes, and she held her breath at what she saw there.

"Hope, I . . . do care about you," he said slowly. "More than is wise."

The air between them ignited.

Without a word, she knew they'd crossed the line. Her heart swelled, and her throat closed up as she acknowledged the love and the impossibility of the situation. Pain tightened his features, and she felt him mentally retreat from her.

Deliberately, she projected everything in her own heart.

"I love you, Britt McLean," she whispered. The words weren't necessary, not when he could read her emotions in their pure form. But she needed to say them out loud to give them life and make them real.

The pain on his face twisted into agony. "Don't," he said, his voice ragged with emotion. "You can't. It isn't right."

Her breath puffed out sadly, and her gaze dipped to the floor. "Since when has that ever stopped people?"

"But that's it," he said, anguished. "I'm not human anymore. You need a man who can . . ." Again his voice trailed off.

Not since she'd given him the new journal had she heard him at such a loss for words. Then again, she'd never seen him vulnerable and looking as if his heart were on his sleeve, either.

"Who can do what, Britt? Share with me the joy of restoring Hawkings House? Who better than you who saw it during every phase of construction? You watched your children grow to adulthood here."

"Don't make it sound so—"

She cut him off. "What do I need, Britt? Someone who understands me. Who better than you who can read everything I feel?" She gave a soft laugh. "What man wouldn't give his right arm to be able to figure out women's emotions?"

"I'm a ghost! I'm dead! If you have any doubts, go look at my headstone at the cemetery."

He meant the image to be repelling, a reminder that his body had long ago rotted to bone and dust, but all Hope did was smile. "I visited your grave several times," she whispered. "I even put flowers on it during my first trip to Manzanita."

From his stunned immobility, she was convinced if he'd been a living man, his knees would have collapsed and dropped him to the floor. "You did what?" he breathed. "Why?"

"Over the years, I've felt many things for you—hero worship, infatuation, even an adolescent crush complete with pretend conversations. That last part never really quit—as you probably found out before I knew you were here." At one time, his knowing that had embarrassed her. Not anymore. It lent credence to what she needed to get across. Having the freedom to express what was in her heart like this gave her a quiet sense of satisfaction. "Most teenage girls go crazy over rock stars. I had you. But all that was fantasy. The real you is far better."

His mouth opened and closed several times, and she smiled as she realized that she'd rendered him far beyond speechlessness. She'd completely upended his world.

"I love you, Britt McLean. I always will."

No, he mouthed, shaking his head before any sound came out. "Don't say that. Don't even think it."

"Why not? It's the truth."

"That doesn't make it right." He couldn't even look at her. "Eventually you'll find a mortal man who can hold you, give you children, grow old and die with you, as it should be."

The air between them shimmered with new life and unfulfilled need. Tears glistened in her eyes. "I'd give anything for you to be that man. But we'll settle for what we have."

"No," he snapped. "We can't touch. We can't . . ." He deliberately went translucent and drifted toward the ceiling to emphasize their differences. "Hope, you need a man who can walk in the sun with you, someone you can share friendships with. Build a life together. You'd eventually long for what others have in normal relationships.''

"We'll cross that bridge if and when the time comes.'' A single tear fell. "For now, I only want you, and I can't see that ever changing.''

"No.'' Even as he denied it, he knew it to be true.

"If things go well between us, we'll live out my days here in Hawkings House. Then when I'm old and wrinkled, if you still want me when I'm dead, I'll do what you did. Stay here. Then we'll be together in death. It'll work just fine.''

Britt slid backward without appearing to move, his expression a study in horror. "I forbid it!''

"I don't think you can stop me.'' She extended a hand toward him in a silent plea.

He began shaking his head. "Hope, I won't allow you to throw your life away as you wait to die.''

"I don't plan to. I'm just saying I intend to live differently than most.'' She took a step closer to him. "In love with a wonderful man named Britt McLean.'' She wiped at her eyes and smiled at him. She didn't need to project her feelings. Her heart was so full, it overflowed.

She took another step closer. But Britt, again without appearing to move at all, retreated an equal distance.

"What are you doing?'' she asked.

"You want to touch me. You can't.''

"I didn't think you could read my mind.''

His lips pursed in exasperation. "I didn't need to!''

"Okay, you're right. I want to touch you. What's wrong with that?''

Exasperation turned to despair. "You wouldn't like it. Don't you remember what Richard said about touching me? Don't you remember how you shiver whenever I get too close?''

"I've decided it can't be that bad, and I'm going to get used to it.''

"That's your heart talking, Hope,'' he said incredulous. "I'm dead, and I'm every bit as cold as you'd expect. The living can't tolerate it.''

She was shaking her head before he finished and began walking toward him again. "Let me try.''

"No!"

As before, Britt was just suddenly further away. When he had the wall at his back, he vanished, reappearing behind her.

"How long do you plan to keep this up?" he demanded, his desperation clear.

"Until you let me touch you." But rather than move after him again, she kept her place. "Tell me you love me, Britt."

His eyes drifted closed in torment. "I can't."

"I know that's what you feel. I need to hear the words."

"No, you don't."

"Why is that?"

"It serves no purpose!"

The words were cold, but his expression wasn't. This time when she moved toward him, he held his place but turned his face away, jaw clenched. She reached to his cheek. Within a foot, she felt the chill that surrounded him. He looked so real that the cold was disconcerting. Slowly she moved even closer. The temperature of the air became glacial, uncomfortable but not intolerable. When her fingers were four inches from his cheek, the death chill intensified, the discomfort crossing into pain. But she'd expected it and didn't give in to the urge to pull back.

"Had enough yet?" he snarled, his voice punishing in his agony.

His isolation and heartache pushed her onward. The extreme cold made her skin feel as if it were burning, and the fire traveled up her arm as she closed the final inches. Her fingertips brushed where his cheek appeared to be, then passed through as if trying to capture vapor. Her arm burned clear to her shoulder. Agony collapsed her resolve, and she jerked backward.

Britt's gaze swung to her, his eyes glittering with loneliness and anger. "Have you worked that out of your system now?"

Hope refused to be hurt by the punishing tone. His tormented expression made it clear this was just as hard on him—probably harder, because he'd had to exist this way for so long. Shaking his head, he gave her one last longing look, then vanished. This time he didn't reappear.

Hope sagged onto his couch. The tears refused to be dissuaded. It wasn't fair!

She woke the next morning to the discordant sounds of a radio commercial. At first she tried to roll over and ignore it, but the bed felt all wrong. Forcing open her tear-swollen, sleepy eyes, she looked around. She wasn't in her bed at all, but stretched out on Britt's couch. Some time during the night, he'd thrown a quilt over her, set her radio alarm on the coffee table and stretched the cord across the room to a wall socket.

Mornings weren't something she did well on the best of days. To realize she'd fallen asleep in his room and that he'd taken care of her after their disastrous encounter last night, made her self-conscious—not a good way to start the day. But it also made her feel very loved.

He had made a valid point, though. Could she give up having the big family she'd wanted in exchange for living an arm's length life with a ghost? Could she be satisfied with conversation and companionship but no warm embraces? She really didn't know. Maybe time would help with the answers. Sitting up, she glanced around at the large, sparsely furnished room.

"Britt?" Her voice had its typical morning rasp. Clearing her throat, she tried again. "Please, don't play invisible games. It's too early. If you're home, please say something."

The only sound came from the radio announcer as he gave the day's weather report. Sunny and hot. She punched it off, wrapped the quilt around herself and went downstairs to the kitchen. A cup of freshly brewed coffee was on the counter beside her canister of hazelnut cocoa.

Even half awake, she smiled. He'd refused to break down and tell her he loved her, but he hadn't been able to stop himself from showing her.

"You're a good man, Britt McLean," she said into the silence.

At noon, she had the office to herself and risked calling the house. After the beep, she said, "Britt, it's me. Please, pick up."

"Hello," he said. The defensiveness in his voice nearly broke her heart.

"Thanks for the coffee this morning," she said. The awkwardness wasn't what she'd expected. "And the other stuff."

The strained pause on the other end of the line made it worse. "You're welcome."

Not exactly a giant lead-in to declarations of love, but she'd take it. "I have two new clients scheduled for this afternoon. Can I have your help?"

"What time?" The blunt replies did a credible job of keeping the conversation from swinging into dangerous territory.

"Two?"

"I'll be there."

Hope wanted to cry, to scream, to wail in frustration. She wanted to shake him until his ghostly teeth rattled. Why the stubborn refusal to acknowledge what he felt, at least? "I meant what I said last night."

He said nothing, and she let the silence hang.

"Hope, don't do this. To either of us. Nothing can come of it." His voice lost its detached edge, and his own heartache once again came through.

Never in her life had she experienced a cold that hurt as badly as when she'd tried to touch him the night before. The phrase "chill of death" echoed in her mind, and she could think of no more apt description.

"We can't hold hands, much less make love," he continued. "Why are you willing to settle for so little?"

Suddenly, she had the answer. There was nothing she wouldn't sacrifice to have him in her life. If ever she had to get her words just right, it was now. "Because you're everything I want in a man. An imperfect relationship with you is better than physical closeness with anyone else."

"You can't mean that," he wheezed.

She let her breath ease out slowly. "You read emotions as clearly as I read a newspaper. You know exactly how serious I am."

This time the pause on the other end sounded defeated, but she couldn't quite say how she knew that.

"I'll be there at two," he said, then hung up.

Hope propped her elbows on her desk and buried her face in her hands.

Just before two, a gentle chill drifted behind her, and she projected feelings of love and welcome. Thanks to last night, she knew exactly how far away he stood from her. But Brian had returned, so neither spoke.

That afternoon, she showed the listings to a couple who wanted to move to the area. As usual, Britt helped her zero in on what they were looking for, but he kept an emotional distance that made her want to scream out her love, even if it meant making her clients think she was crazy.

She settled for nurturing an inner glow of love and determination. By late afternoon, she envisioned him with a physical body and daydreamed of them making love. She wasn't sure how the latter translated into something he could read, but she gave her best efforts into immersing herself—and him—in the sensual fantasy of such a moment. Surely, he'd get tired of the bombardment and tell her what she needed to hear. But he said nothing apart from helping her make a living, and she didn't know if she'd succeeded or not.

That night when she cleared the door, she had her speech all written. The mouse was at war. "Okay, Britt, we're going to talk now." She slammed the door behind her. "Britt!"

He didn't answer.

"I know you're here." She stormed from room to room, calling for him. When she went into her office, she found the drapes pulled tightly closed, the vault open and Britt sitting behind her desk. The old journal lay on her blotter. She'd seen his expressive face indicate a great many things, but she'd never seen it this grim. Apprehension crawled up her spine.

"What are you doing?" she asked.

"Asking you one more time to stop this," he said. "If you don't, I'll take the journal and leave. You'll never find me. I won't allow it."

Hope's knees buckled, and she grabbed for the doorjamb to keep from falling. "You'd leave me?"

His normally soft, blue eyes glittered with merciless intent. "If that's what it takes to keep you from throwing the rest of your life away on me, yes."

"Throw it away? That's not how I see—"

"I know you don't. That's the problem. It occurred to me that you were looking at your life as some sort of trial to get through so we can be together. Or worse, how perfect it would be 'if only.' We can't be together, Hope." The harshness fractured under the weight of his own pain, leaving his voice with raw edges. "Not in life or in death. Can't you see that? The light will come for you, and you'll go."

"No, I won't. I'll fight with everything I have to stay, or I'll drag you with me."

He tipped his head back, and the walls echoed from his agonized groan.

"I've watched other people try to stay. They couldn't. The light took them anyway, no matter what they did. I seem to be the only one who ended up like this. From what I can determine, the few other ghosts I've met are mentally ill, locked into circumstances and events that happened before their deaths. That's all they know. As far as I can tell, I'm a fluke."

"Then I'll take you with me, and we'll both move on."

The hard set to his shoulders wilted, and he glanced away. "I was with four of my children when they died, as well as with Nestor and Lucinda. Nestor was the first to go. After he got over his shock of seeing me standing beside his body, he refused to leave me behind. We clung to each other with everything we had. The light ripped us apart. The electrical current that flashed between us and between me and the tunnel was the most terrifying, painful thing I've ever experienced. I blacked out. When I came to, three days had passed, and Nestor was long gone."

Each word battered holes into her dreams.

"Lucinda was too surprised to do much but stare at me. After all those years, I finally got to tell her one more time that I loved her. Then the light swept her away."

Hope found the strength to walk to the love seat and sit. It was either that or fall down.

"For whatever reason, Evie, my firstborn, was also the last of my children to pass away. She was seventy-four and had lived a full and happy life. She still recognized me." His expression became distant, bittersweet. "She threw her arms around my neck and burst into tears. Kept crying out 'Papa' over and over and wouldn't let go. The light came a little later than usual—it does that sometimes—and we made the most of the few minutes we'd been granted."

"Did she try to take you with her, too?"

He nodded. "The result was the same as with Nestor." He seemed to be locked into those old memories so deeply that the present world disappeared for him. Eventually, his eyes refocused on her. "You have one chance to move on. When your time comes, you'll go. You won't have a choice or say in it." He stood. "And I will not allow you to try to stay. I'll throw you into the light if I have to."

Hope reeled from the blows he delivered. "You don't leave much for a person to fight back with, do you."

He picked up the journal. "Every time I involve myself with the living, I end up bitterly regretting the damage I do."

"You haven't hurt me. You saved my life!"

"And now you want to throw the rest of it away!"

"That's not how I see it."

He ignored her. "We either pretend last night never happened, or I leave now. Which will it be? Choose."

Heartbreak pulsed from him, and Hope knew with every fiber of her being that he'd return to his existence of absolute isolation rather than allow her to commit the rest of her life to loving him.

Forming her answer took forever. "I don't know what you're talking about. I went out with Pat last night. Maybe I had too much to drink. If I made a fool of myself over you when I got home, I'm sorry. Odd, though, I don't remember a thing."

Primly, she turned on her heel and went out to the carriage house. She picked out a fallen section of stone wall, sat down and cried.

Chapter
Ten

Hope admitted defeat, and not once during the next three months did she bring up the subject. She knew what they both felt, and she forced herself to accept that not hearing him say the words was enough.

One night they sat in front of the fireplace in the fully restored ladies' parlor. Cold November rain beat down outside, emphasizing the warmth of the fire in the old marble fireplace. They sat on either end of the long sofa, a solid two feet between them. It was as close as they could get without his death chill bothering her.

The flames made Britt's image fade in an out, but she'd grown so accustomed to the effects of different lighting on his appearance that she paid little attention to it.

The man he had proven to be was so much more wonderful than the one she'd been infatuated with for years. She couldn't imagine her life without him.

He sat with his new journal in his lap, ballpoint pen in hand, quietly making another entry. She knew he held both items by force of will rather than actually resting them on his lap or in his hand. But the illusion was so complete, she had to remind herself forcibly of what she truly saw—a ghost who was extremely good at appearing mortal.

A loud pounding at the front door broke the aching si-

lence. Hope gave Britt a questioning look. She rarely had
company, and at half past ten, no one should be visiting.

His expression took on a faraway cast as he extended his
senses. A moment later, he scowled. "Richard."

Her stomach clenched into a knot. "What does he want?
I paid him off. The divorce will be final just before Christmas."

Britt cocked his head, looking more distant. "I don't like
what I'm picking up from him. He's high and spoiling for
a fight. Don't answer the door," he said. "I'll get rid of
him for you."

The proprietary air was pure nineteenth-century male,
and Hope bit back a smile. "Thank you, but I need to
find out what he wants. If there's a problem with the
divorce—"

"Then your attorney will let you know."

"I'm not a mouse anymore, Britt. I stand up for myself
quite well now."

"In my day—" He cut himself off, and gave her a chagrined half smile. "I know. This isn't the 1870s."

"Well, I still think your protectiveness is sweet. Your
Lucinda was a lucky woman."

He rolled his eyes.

"If I'd been born a century and a half ago," she said,
heading for the door, "I'd have given that lady a run for
her money." She didn't wait for him to fire off a warning,
but slid back the dead bolt and opened the door.

Richard stood on the porch, swaying, his feet spread to
brace himself. All traces of the devastatingly handsome
man she'd once known had been destroyed by the booze
and the drugs. He looked ill. Hope sighed.

"Well, it took you long enough to answer the door," he
snapped. "Thought I'd have to break it down."

Hope glanced over her shoulder. Not surprisingly, Britt
had vanished, but she was sure he'd moved into the hallway
and stood behind her. The air felt inexplicably different,
charged.

"What do you want, Richard?" she demanded.

"I need more money. It's gone."

She gaped at him. "You signed the property settlement, saying that would be enough."

He gave her a bland look. "So? I need more."

"Get into treatment, then get a job." She started to close the door in his face, but he grabbed it and levered it open. A ribbon of fear slithered up her spine. But Britt was near. No matter what, she knew he wouldn't let anything happen to her.

"You owe me."

"For what?"

"Kicking me when I was down."

Hope snorted. "That won't work. I no longer buy into your addictions." She gave him a hard look. "It's your monkey, and you're the only one who can get it off your back."

"That's you," he sneered. "Ms. Compassion."

"Get into treatment, Richard. Good-bye."

"Well, it doesn't matter now anyway. I just came by to tell you it's over. You won."

Something about the undercurrent set off alarms. A new game? It certainly wasn't the old one. "Won what?"

"You were never there for me, Hope," he snarled. "And you'll have to figure a way to live with your guilt."

"What are you talking about? On second thought, don't tell me, I don't want to know. Just let go of the door and leave." She shoved against it. Even as wasted as he was, she couldn't budge it. The "poor me" speech had taken a new twist. She wanted to ask Britt what he made of it, but she studied Richard instead.

"You don't know what I've taken," he whispered in a singsong voice.

The tone made the hair on the back of her neck stand on end.

"So, you can't do anything but sit back and watch me die."

Stunned, Hope's grip on the door slipped. Richard's weight shoved it open. He tried to catch himself but couldn't get his legs under him. Hope leapt out of his way as he fell on his face on the tiled entry.

"His heart isn't beating right," Britt said.

"Who said that?" Richard demanded. "Satan, is that you?"

Surprised that Britt had spoken at all, Hope turned toward him. "Do you think he needs medical attention?"

"I don't know. I'm not a doctor." Anger and disgust lay heavy in each word he spit out. "But I don't like what his heart is doing. Of course, if he is dying, he did it to himself."

Hope felt no sympathy for Richard, but she was startled by the vehemence in Britt. She turned back to Richard, who was making an uncoordinated attempt to roll onto his back. When he finally succeeded, he lay there laughing as if privy to the greatest joke of all time.

"Got your attention, didn't I?" The singsong took on an ominous undertone.

Something had changed in the manipulative games he liked to play, but she didn't know what. Turning to Britt, she headed to the gentleman's parlor and the nearest phone. "I'm calling an ambulance. Please, don't let him come in any farther."

"I'd rather throw him out onto the lawn and let them pick him up from there." The flat iron in his voice left no doubt as to his opinion of her being involved any further than shutting the door in the man's face.

Fear clouded the victory in the gaunt lines of Richard's mouth. He cleared his throat and tried to slough it off. "So, Satan, you're still here, huh?"

Hope ignored him and called 9-1-1.

"What are you up to now?" Britt demanded.

"Already told you. She's going to watch me die. Afterward, she can spend the rest of her life blaming herself for not treating me right."

Hope returned. "The ambulance will be here in five to ten minutes. How is he?"

Britt didn't answer right away. "His brain is becoming more and more . . ." He paused as if trying to come up with the right words. "Wrong."

"Fine. The county will take care of him. What about you? I've never heard this tone in your voice." She wished he'd materialize so she could get a good look at his face.

Richard giggled. The sound grated on her ears. "Aren't you even going to ask what I took?"

Hope glared down at him. "Would you tell me if I did?"

"Nope."

"That's what I thought." She turned back to Britt. The air tingled with his quiet fury, and she didn't know what to make of it. "Why are you letting him get to you?"

Richard looked up at her. The giggling became almost maniacal. "You are such a stupid bitch. I don't know what I ever saw in you."

At one time, a remark like that would have crushed her. Now, she brushed it aside without a ripple of concern. Britt's agitation rose. Hope wasn't psychic, but she could feel the electrical energy in Britt build with each taunt Richard made. The air crackled with it, and the hair on her arms stood up. She lifted a calming hand to let him know she could handle this. Turning to Richard, she said, "Your problems are your own."

In a heartbeat, Richard's mood snapped from crazed to lethal. "You were supposed to be there for me!"

"She owes you nothing," Britt ground out.

The blue sheen roiled through him, and the air hissed. So this was what a ghost looked like just before erupting into full-blown rage, she observed distantly.

"If you choose to die, boy, that's your business. But you have no call to drag her into it."

"What would you know about life, Satan?" he whined.

Hope flinched. Britt knew more about living than any man she'd ever known. As deeply as he craved to be alive again, the remark had to inflame him.

Britt's voice moved closer to Richard and lowered as if he'd crouched beside the prone man. "If you do one more thing to hurt Hope, I . . . will . . . kill . . . you." The quiet promise echoed off the walls in the long hallway.

Richard drew into himself, but the hate never left his eyes. Hope gaped.

"Do I make myself clear?" Britt whispered in a low rumble.

The last was spoken so softly, she had to strain to hear it. Backing into the ladies' parlor, she whispered to him to

follow. A moment later, he went solid. The firelight gave
him translucent patches, making the rage more ominous.

"Britt, he's not worth getting worked up over," she said.
"Don't let him provoke you into even *toying* with the idea
of doing something foolish."

"Hope, I won't risk your life. In my day, I could have
shot him, and no one would have raised an eyebrow."

She thought about that a moment. That was probably true
if she and Britt had been married and Richard had been
harassing her. But that wasn't the situation. "This isn't the
1870s, and you can't gun down a man unless it's life or
death. Take a deep breath or whatever it is you do to relax.
Okay?"

A brooding silence descended. "He already tried to kill
you once. He won't leave you alone, and if this posturing
tonight doesn't work, he'll try something else. He isn't just
an addict, Hope. He's evil, and I will not risk him hurting
you anymore."

The concern warmed her as much as the deadly light in
his eyes worried her. "Britt, you won't tell me you love
me because you're so locked into the mindset of leaving
the living alone. How would you forgive yourself if you
killed him?"

Resolve swirled around them. Richard stumbled around
the corner into the parlor, hate twisting his features into a
mask that only vaguely resembled something human. Before Hope had the chance to draw in a breath, Britt extended an arm. Tongues of blue lightning shot from his
fingertips and slammed Richard back into the hallway. Britt
followed him, vanishing in the brightly lit hallway. He
loosed another charge that blasted Richard out onto the
porch. Richard hit the wooden planking with a thud and a
groan.

Hope gaped. Britt carried quite an electrical charge. She
just never expected to see it again. And from appearances,
this hadn't required much effort. She wondered what he
could do if pressed. She felt the chill as he headed toward
the door.

"Britt, don't!"

"Moving him didn't hurt him," he ground out.

In the distance she heard a siren wail. "Please, Britt. I

love you. Don't do anything rash. Help is on the way.''

''He's a rabid dog that should be shot.''

''Maybe, but he's not our problem anymore,'' she pleaded. ''Let it go.''

He didn't answer. She was tempted to stand between the two. But keeping someone who can walk through walls away from something would have been an act of total futility.

Projecting all the love in her heart, she looked at the place where she thought he stood. If he'd let her, she'd promise him her entire world. But since he wouldn't, the best she could do was keep him distracted until he calmed down.

A couple of minutes later, paramedics were swarming over Richard.

''What are you on, man?'' demanded one of them. He was a grim-looking black man in his mid thirties who was crouching beside Richard, hooking him up to assorted pieces of equipment.

''Ask my devoted wife,'' Richard drawled, his speech slurred almost beyond recognition. ''Satan's in there, too.''

The paramedic scanned the readouts. ''Listen up. I need to know what you're on.''

''Guess.'' Richard sounded like a petulant three-year-old.

''He arrived here like this,'' Hope said, stepping onto the porch. ''I don't know what he's using now, but in addition to alcohol, his drugs of choice are usually cocaine and heroin.''

The paramedic nodded, then signaled to the two other men with him. They picked up the collapsible gurney and walked off the porch to the waiting ambulance. He turned to her. ''Can you follow us to the hospital?''

How often had she believed if she could have just tried a little harder that maybe it would have made a difference? All that seemed like a lifetime ago. Had it really only been five months? ''We're separated.''

The man's eyes widened.

''Our divorce will be final in about six weeks. He's trying to get me to take him back so my paycheck can underwrite his drug habit. No way.''

He nodded in compassion and approval. "If more people made addicts stand accountable instead of covering for them or trying to 'help' them, they'd kick their habits a lot quicker."

"You sound like my Al-Anon group. Thanks for understanding."

Giving her a tight smile, he said, "Call a friend. Unload. It'll do you good." He and the other two members of the crew loaded Richard into the ambulance and left.

Hope didn't realize she was shaking until Britt closed the front door and she found herself staring at it. Then he turned off the hall lights, leaving the house lit only by the flickering fire from the ladies' parlor. He went solid.

"Come and sit down." Despite the tender tone, the undercurrent of rage in him hadn't abated any.

Hope would have sold her soul if it would make Britt a living man. He was gentle and kind and loving and caring. In her adult life, she'd looked for someone like him—a copy. Now that she'd found the original, she couldn't even put her arms around him and have him hold her. The weight of what could never be descended on her. A heartache to match her own claimed his face. He met her gaze with his own, the only way they could ever touch.

Hope couldn't take any more. Tears erupted with wrenching force. She reached for him, but his flickering form lurched back.

"No," he moaned. "Nothing has changed." He looked away.

Hope knew he was right, but her arms felt so empty. It was as if they'd never be full again. She stood suspended, desperate for human touch—the one thing Britt could never give. Again, she reached for him. He flowed across the room. As before, she couldn't call it a step. He simply became farther away. She closed her eyes and imagined him as she'd seen him so many times in dim light, then moved toward him, solid and real and human, a man she could love forever. His months-old ultimatum about leaving her rang loudly in her ears. It made no difference.

"Please, Hope. Don't," he pleaded. From the lines of torment on his beloved face, he needed touch as much as she. From the horrible way he'd existed for over twelve decades, he probably needed it more.

Deliberately . . . she closed the distance, her extended hand and arm engulfed in the mind-numbing cold four inches from his chest. The death chill took her breath away. Even as she recoiled, his voice became a grieved caress.

"I told you nothing had changed."

The hopeless heartache of their situation reverberated through the room. Neither spoke for long moments. They didn't need to. The words had been said. Maybe he'd been right. Repeating them only made the hurt worse.

"Hope, the paramedic was right. Call your parents or Pat, someone alive who can be with you tonight." The sadness had disappeared, buried deep in the anger.

She drew in a long, pain-filled breath to help pull herself together. Then she wiped away the tears. "Why? Are you going somewhere?"

"To the hospital." Flat. Cold. Dangerous.

"No!"

"Hope, I need to check on him. When he's sober, he and I will talk." Britt's eyes hardened. "He will not keep doing this to you."

"Stay. He won't be coherent for hours—if not days." Something was going on in Britt's head, and she had the horrible feeling that his control was only on the surface. If she didn't stop him, their relationship would be changed forever. "Don't do anything foolish. Given your circumstances, you'll be living with it a long time."

"Call Pat," he whispered. "You need a human tonight. Not me."

"You are human, and I only need you," she protested. Even as she spoke the words, she knew they weren't true. She *did* need the human-to-human contact of an embrace from someone warm with life.

"I'll be back soon."

"Wait until tomorrow. Then decide what you need to do. Don't do *anything* when you're this angry."

A profound longing covered his face. He blew her a kiss, the first concession to his love. Then he vanished so fast, she felt as if the air from the room had been ripped away.

"Britt! Come back!" she yelled into the silence. Instinctively, she knew he was gone, and she hadn't slowed him down at all. She called again anyway, hoping his extraordinary hearing was tuned to her.

Desperately, she prayed he'd regain control of his temper before he arrived at the hospital. From his writings, she'd learned that Britt was slow to anger, but once provoked past his limits, he held nothing back. Was it within him to commit what amounted to an execution? Was she reading him right? After a few moments of panicky reflection, she decided the answer had to be no.

"He'll be fine," she said, squaring her shoulders in confidence. "His honor and sense of justice will win out." She settled on the couch in the parlor to wait. He promised to be back soon. They'd talk more then. "As for *you*," she muttered at herself. "You really need to reevaluate your taste in men. The last one was a manipulative alcoholic-addict. This one's *dead*." The gallows humor made her shudder.

Thirty minutes later, Hope's worry had returned. She had absolute confidence in Britt. But as time continued to pass, a flurry of niggling unknowns crawled through her veins. Where was he? If he'd decided to have a final talk with Richard, he'd have to wait until Richard's system rid itself of the toxins. That would take hours if not days, and Britt would have opted to come home. So why wasn't he here? After another thirty minutes, Hope began to pace.

Finally, she picked up the phone and called Richard's parents' house. If they could tell her something about their son's condition, it might give her a clue as to Britt's plans. Charles picked up on the second ring.

"I hate to bother you," she said, "but did you know Richard was taken to the hospital tonight?"

"Yes, a nurse phoned," he answered. "Did they call you, too?" Disgust at his son rode heavy in his voice. Charles McLean was a decent sort, but he'd assumed that children raised themselves and had put his career ahead of spending time with his son. He'd wakened too late to make a difference.

"He came here high as a kite, and I called an ambulance.

He claimed to have deliberately taken an overdose."

"Why would he go to you?" Now the man was wary.

Hope sighed. "He wanted me to take him back."

Charles swore. "I take it you said no?"

"There was nothing else to say."

"Well, I'm not pandering to him, either. I haven't told Ruth about the call. She'll only charge down to the hospital and make it worse. Besides, until he crashes from this high, he won't remember anything I say."

Richard's mother had spoiled Richard from birth. She still made excuses for him, always trying to find an extenuating circumstance or someone else to blame for his misbehavior.

"Did the hospital say anything about his condition?" she asked.

"Nothing other than someone recognized him and thought we'd like to know he was there. Why?"

So much for Charles being a source of information. "This whole situation is just very strange. Sorry to have bothered you. Good night."

After she hung up, she returned to pacing. Britt could have popped to the hospital, checked on Richard's condition and popped back home in a couple of seconds. He was also quite adept at using the phone. "So why haven't I heard anything?" she said out loud.

With each passing minute, her sense of impending doom escalated. Feeling foolish, but unable to help herself, she drove to the hospital. As she located the information desk, she didn't know whether to give Britt a piece of her mind when she found him or work on an excuse for being there that wouldn't make her look stupid. She certainly couldn't say she'd been worried about something happening to him.

A clerk smiled expectantly at her as she stopped at the desk. "Excuse me, I'm looking for my . . . for Richard McLean."

The woman's expression froze, then slid into a professional mask that revealed nothing. "Why don't you take a seat in the waiting room, and I'll get Dr. Marin. He'll be with you in just a moment."

"Thank you." The rapid change in the woman's mood

gave Hope the shakes, but she smiled and went into the beige-colored room across the hall. It was empty, and Hope peeked back out the door to see if anyone was coming before she lifted her chin. "Britt," she whispered furiously. "Where are you?"

No answer.

"Britt?" she whispered so loud it make her throat scratchy.

The doctor undoubtedly wanted a medical history. She'd give them that, but her entire reason for being here was for Britt to sense her presence. Her skin crawled with foreboding. Something was horribly wrong. Nothing would please her more than to feel the brutal cold of his presence and hear his tenderly amused laughter over her worry.

She still didn't understand her nerves. Britt was dead, for crying out loud, and had been looking after himself in that state since 1872. What could happen to him in a hospital?

A short, thin man with a manic stride zoomed into the waiting room, then took a short breath to collect himself. "Mrs. McLean?" he asked.

She nodded cautiously, and he stuck out his hand. Oddly, when she took it, he didn't let go.

"I'm Dr. Marin, and I have some difficult news for you. Can we sit down?"

A strange crackling tore the length of the wall behind them as she sat beside the doctor.

Marin glanced at the wall and frowned. "What on earth was that?"

It happened again. The sound bore an odd similarity to Britt releasing an electrical charge. Then she caught an odor, the kind one finds around huge pieces of electrical equipment. Ozone. Britt!

Above her head, jagged forks of blue light flashed along the wall. It was a dozen times stronger than anything she'd seen Britt unleash. A malevolent pall fell over the room.

Marin turned full circle, a bewildered frown creasing his face. More crackling, but further away. Fluorescent lights up and down the corridor exploded. Someone down the hall screamed. The lights in the waiting room flickered. Hope and the doctor shared a look, and they both leaned through the doorway.

Overhead lights were exploding one after another all over the emergency room. Shards of glass rained onto the floor, and the building went black. A male voice from one of the trauma rooms bellowed for emergency power. Through the huge, picture window and the automatic doors, Hope saw the parking lot lights glow. Whatever was going on, it affected only the hospital itself.

An explosion from the next room made her jump. Both computer monitors at the information desk blew up. Sparks rained from smoking light fixtures. One woman ran outside. Others milled closer to the door, clearly torn between personal safety and abandoning their loved ones deep in the rabbit warren of the hospital.

Smoke filtered into the hall from a dozen doorways, and someone punched the fire alarm. Emergency lights snapped on but glowed dimly in the darkening haze. As she leapt back into the waiting room, a double shadow roiled on the far wall close to the ceiling. The blue sheen flickered and rippled through it like lightning inside thunderclouds. It oozed back through the wall the way it had come, then vanished.

''Britt?'' she asked, mindless of what the dumbfounded doctor beside her might think of her talking to herself. She strained to detect the slightest whisper in her ear, but she heard nothing.

Another explosion. This time, people poured from assorted rooms and out the exit. The acrid stench of burning wires filled the air. Walls burst into flame at irregular intervals. Security guards herded visitors out, some with patients in tow. The hospital staff began evacuating the rest.

The emergency lighting went down.

''Britt!'' Even with all the mayhem, she knew he could pick her voice out from the others and would come to her. But no comforting chill touched her. No quiet voice whispered in her ear.

Several people rushed past the guards to get into the ER to rescue their loved ones. A few made it, but the guards sent the others out. Between the explosions, the cries of terror and the crackle of lightning, the noise was deafening.

''Britt!'' she screamed again. A twisting shadow erupted

from a wall, leaving a trail of smoke in its wake. The wall burst into flame. The shadow was formless, without color, just an unearthly darkness shot through with blue. Britt! It had to be. But it was twice the size she'd ever seen him.

She opened her mouth to call out again.

"Hope, run!" Britt barked out. "Get out of here! Don't look back!"

Never had she heard him afraid. She did now, and a matching fear claimed her heart. Adrenaline sent its own fire through her veins. "What? Why?"

"No matter what happens," he called, his voice strained as if from a great exertion, "know that I love you. Now go!"

As if her life depended upon it, she ran toward the exit. A crush of people crowded through the automatic doors. To the left, the picture window had broken. Only a few shards of glass remained. Taking care where she placed her hands, Hope vaulted through the opening and into the parking lot. When she reached the far sidewalk, she stopped and turned to face the hospital.

People were still racing through the exits through clouds of smoke. Deep inside she saw flickers of orange. The fire was growing. Soon it would begin claiming the second and third floors.

"Britt? What's wrong?" With his extraordinary hearing, he could have heard her a block away if not more. There was no answer. "Britt, where are you?"

Firemen arrived. Some rushed into the building. Others manned hoses, the rest helped the hospital staff evacuate patients. Hope paced the parking lot and fretted for what felt like hours, but it couldn't have been more than minutes.

Time snailed by. She checked her watch, but she couldn't remember what time it had been the last time she'd looked, so it did no good.

"Britt?" Something had happened to him. She couldn't imagine what, but deep in her heart, she knew it was catastrophic. "Britt, please answer me. Where are you?"

A nurse grabbed her arm. "Here, hold this! She stuffed an IV bottle into Hope's hands and went back to work on her patient.

When Hope was no longer needed there, she noticed a frightened old man wandering in a daze. She snatched a blanket from the stack by an ambulance, wrapped it around his shoulders, then guided him to the curb to sit with a group of ambulatory patients who were being triaged. Every few minutes, she looked toward the burning building and called to Britt. Then she returned to hunting for ways to be helpful.

Smoke and flames billowed from the broken windows and doors of the ground floor, turning the white stucco an ever-darkening gray. Hope moved from gurney to gurney, adjusting a blanket or holding a hand, praying for a chill to brush against her shoulder or for a quiet voice to whisper in her ear.

Had he known the hospital was about to catch fire? Was his fear only for her? She wanted to believe that. But logic complained that she was only deluding herself. Britt would have contacted her as soon as she'd gotten out safely.

Ambulances began loading patients to transport them to other hospitals. Families not content to wait for the next wave put their loved ones in cars and drove them. Over time, the deafening chaos eased to a less impossible level.

In the shadow of a fire truck, a man lay on a gurney, no one near him. One arm rested limply on his chest, and an oxygen mask covered the lower half of his face. She didn't know what drew her to the man so apart from everyone else, but something did and on a level so deep she couldn't identify it. But with each breath she took keeping her distance became less and less of an option. Cautiously she walked to his side.

Richard! Why had he sparked such a strong reaction in her? She hadn't even recognized him at first! Bewildered anger ignited. His eyes were closed, and he breathed deeply and easily. Passed out, she surmised.

Hope turned to walk away, but that same instinct that had drawn her to him wouldn't let her leave. Before he passed out, had Britt spoken to him? If so, had Britt said anything that would give her a clue as to what was going on now? She had to know.

"Richard, are you all right?" she asked.

He didn't stir. With the fire truck blocking most of the light, his face lay in deep shadow, and she couldn't see it well.

She touched his arm. "Richard?"

His eyelids trembled, then opened. He stared straight up at the night sky, seemingly unaware of her presence. Puzzlement drew his brows down.

"Can you hear me?"

Turning his head toward her, he focused on her face. She saw no evidence of recognition, just a blank nothing. Something about his eyes struck her as odd, but in the poor lighting she couldn't tell what. The stillness in him unnerved her. Normally at this stage—if he was conscious at all—his eyes jerked or rolled, and he couldn't focus on anything.

"It's me. Hope." She wasn't sure what made her identify herself, but for all the reaction she got from him, she might as well have been a stranger.

The frown deepened. His mouth moved from behind the fogged-up oxygen mask, but all she heard was a garbled rasp. His eyes widened as if her voice had startled him. She glanced around, foolishly worried that someone might yell at her if she tampered with the equipment. Then she lifted the mask from his face, the elastic band stretching easily.

"What did you say?"

He took a deep breath. His mouth worked experimentally, and he forced out a mishmash of sound. Puzzled fear tightened his too-thin features.

"Can you talk, Richard?"

Seeing him too drunk or high to speak clearly was nothing new, but this was different. *He* was different. Again, he tried to talk, but got no better results. Then he moved an arm. She didn't have any idea what he was trying to do, but it flailed in the air, then flopped onto his stomach. Lack of coordination was common, but this too was different. Oddly, he seemed as aware of it as she. Again he tried to control his arm enough to lift it. It swung to the side and banged hard against the fire truck, then dropped to his chest. The whole picture reminded her of an infant who didn't know how his body worked. The fear on his face gave way to panic. His breathing came in shallow, rapid gasps.

A white-coated hospital employee rushed over. "Hi, I'm Dr. Marin. Who do we have here?" It was the same doctor who'd started to talk to her in the waiting room.

He jerked a handlight from his lab coat and checked Richard's pupils. Hope's mouth sagged open. Dear God, how was this possible!

Denial of what she saw made her want to run away, but her feet had taken root in the asphalt.

Richard's eyes. They were *blue*! How could that be?

"Ma'am?" Dr. Marin glanced over his shoulder at her. "Things are a madhouse here. The records are inside. We're having to triage everyone from scratch. Who's this and what's the problem?" He reached for the ID band on Richard's wrist.

Hope couldn't think straight. She checked Richard's other features. No mistakes. This was definitely him. But how could his eyes have changed from brown to blue? Maybe she'd made a mistake about his identity. In the bad light anything was possible. "Shine the light on him again."

The harried doctor glowered at her, but held the light over Richard's face, this time a little further a way so she could clearly see all of it at once.

"Ma'am! I don't have time for this! You either know him or you don't."

That jolted her from her stupor. "This is my estranged husband, Richard McLean," she choked out.

If she'd clubbed him, he wouldn't have stared at her any more shocked. Marin blinked. "Who?"

"Richard Brittain McLean. He was here for a drug overdose suicide attempt." Hope had no idea how she got that many words out in her condition.

The doctor's head jerked toward his patient so fast she thought his neck would snap off at the shoulders. Richard's confused gaze darted from the doctor to Hope and back. A look of horror came over the doctor's face. Then he shined the light into her face as if to identify her.

"This can't be," he breathed. Marin stuffed the end of the penlight between his teeth, and examined the ID bracelet around Richard's wrist.

"What's the problem?" she asked.

"I declared this man dead about three minutes before

everything went to hell.'' Then he caught himself and realized what he'd just said to a patient's wife. Even in the shadows, she saw him flush. "Mrs. McLean, I'm sorry. I have no explanation for my outburst other than I'm obviously mistaken and remembered a name incorrectly.'' He took hold of her arm. "I'm truly sorry. What's he here for?''

"I told you. Drug overdose. Attempted suicide.''

Marin froze. Then he whipped back to Richard. The man didn't need to say a word. The truth was written all over his face. At some point that evening, Richard had died and this doctor had been right there.

"Mr. McLean, can you tell me how you're feeling?''

Richard gave him a confused and pleading look. He forced sound from his throat, but it was no clearer than before. Marin gave him a quick examination, checking heart rate, breathing and the very-blue eyes. The pupils contracted normally against the bright light. As wasted as Richard had been, how could that be?

"Mr. McLean, I'm not picking up any problems other than your pulse is a little elevated. Not surprising, considering the circumstances.'' He waved in the general direction of the burning hospital. Then he turned to Hope. "He appears stable. Come get me if anything happens, okay?''

He jogged away, frowning over his shoulder twice before he reached the next patient. What in God's name was going on here! What had kept Britt at the hospital in the first place? Why had he sounded so terrified when he'd told her to run? Why had he told her not to look back? Why had his declaration of love sounded like a good-bye? Where was he! How could Richard be staring at her so sober? The human body couldn't rid itself of that garbage this fast! Could it? Had Britt done something? The foreboding grew, smothering her.

Again she lifted Richard's oxygen mask. "Do you know where your demon is? Do you know where he went?''

He tried to talk but couldn't produce a single recognizable sound. His lips tightened, and his eyes rounded into a wild-eyed stare. She'd seen a great many emotions from him before, but never mind-bending terror.

Was she looking at brain damage brought on by unbridled use of drugs and alcohol? His confusion reminded her of a stroke victim. Would this state be permanent? Or just temporary, while his body worked out the remainder of his overdose? She mentally cursed the selfish arrogance that had been the root of his downfall.

Overwhelmed, she shouted at him, "Why are your eyes blue!"

He suddenly went very still. Was he worried about not provoking a crazy person? His gaze never wavered. Whatever he'd taken, he was past the high. What could have altered the effects so rapidly?

She put the mask back in place over his nose and mouth. "I need to find someone."

Hope backed away from the gurney, too fascinated and repelled to break eye contact until she was ten feet away. She walked all through the parking lot, calling for Britt.

With all the shouting and crying in the milling crowd, no one paid any attention to her. In every puff of night air, she tried to find the chill of death, but it never came. Periodically, she retreated into a far corner where he could answer her without anyone overhearing. Nothing. Worry churned in her stomach. With his ultrasensitive hearing and ability to read emotions, he should have picked her out from the crowd and come to her long before this.

Maybe he'd returned to the house. "Oh, come on," she grumbled to herself. "After the warning he gave me? That doesn't even make sense."

She reached into her purse for her cell phone just to put her mind at rest, but the unit wasn't there. Then she remembered she'd left it on the recharging stand. The only other option was the pay phone at the nearby convenience store. At least thirty people stood in line, waiting for a turn.

Hope brought up the rear. Time felt as if it had stopped altogether. Her stomach churned with worry and fear. Finally, when it was her turn, she dropped a quarter into the slot and punched buttons. Her fingers shook.

The machine picked up on the third ring. "Hi, this is Hope McLean of Manzanita Realty. I'm not available right now to take your call. If you leave . . ." She squirmed with impatience as her message played itself out. Finally the beep came. "Britt, are you there? Britt, pick up." She prayed. "Come on. If you're there, please answer. Britt?"

Again, she waited. The lady behind her gave her a word-less plea to hurry. "Britt! Pick up!" Nothing. She took a breath. "Okay, I don't know if you'd think to check the machine when you get back from wherever you are, but if you do, I'm still at the hospital. Please try to find me." She couldn't think of anything else to say. Reluctantly, she hung up and stepped away.

For another hour, she alternately watched Richard from a discreet distance and called the house. Richard drifted to sleep shortly before his turn for an ambulance to take him to the hospital in Breford, twenty miles away. As they loaded him up and shut the doors, she had the horrible intuition that her only link to finding out what had happened to Britt was an addict she never wanted to speak to again.

Chapter
Eleven

Hope wandered the parking lot, waiting and praying. By four, the fire department had the fire out and was methodically conducting their mop-up work. The emergency wing's windows and doors had deep scorch marks. Water ran like a river from the ER's main entrance, but the rest of the small hospital appeared intact. She called for Britt one final time then climbed into her car.

The moment she pulled in front of Hawkings House, she called to him again, but he didn't answer. She ran to the third floor and checked his room. A book lay on his desk, one of those "tough love" things for families of loved ones with addictions. A bookmark rested in page 229.

"Well, he'd said he'd been reading up." The volume had been one of the last things he'd touched. Holding it against her chest gave meager comfort, but it was better than none. She searched the rest of the house, including the attic, and found nothing.

"Reality-check time, Hope," she told herself, aggravated. "He's a ghost, not a mortal. It's not as if he could have gotten mugged or collapsed from a heart attack." It sounded perfectly reasonable until she remembered the fear in his voice when he'd told her to run and not look back.

Why now—of all times—had he finally told her he loved her?

She checked her watch. Ten after five. She had a full workday scheduled, and it would begin in just a couple of hours. Sleeping would be pointless. She retrieved a blanket from her bed and curled up on his couch to wait. Despite everything, she dozed off, waking with a jolt at seven. The dark sense of knowing something bad had happened to Britt hung in the air around her more strongly than ever.

Before she left for work, she cleared her machine of the countless messages she'd left from the hospital and wrote out a note for him to call her. Even as she laid it on his desk beside his new journal and pen, she feared the gesture was wasted.

"Morning," Brian called out from his desk as Hope walked in and headed to the coffeepot. Fortunately, he didn't look up. Pat gave her a distracted wave. November had proven unusually busy, burying the small office under an avalanche of paper.

"Morning." Hope's eyes felt like someone had kicked sand into them. She doubted her face looked any better than it had in the mirror thirty minutes before when she'd applied her makeup. "Any coffee left?" she asked. She knew the moment the words were out, she'd sounded like death warmed over. As if on cue, Pat and Brian left their respective desks and converged on where she stood at the refreshment table.

"What's the matter?" they chorused. Brian turned her to face him. He was a nice guy to work for, and the gesture came across as caring rather than authoritarian.

"Richard's back! Right?" Pat snapped. "Damn!"

Hope flinched, suddenly feeling a lot like the mouse she'd once been. "He tried to commit suicide last night and chose my house to do it. Did you hear about the hospital fire? I was right in the middle of it."

Brian grabbed the paper. On the front page was a photo of Manzanita Community Hospital with smoke and flames billowing from the emergency wing. He began to read. "At press time, investigators still aren't sure of the cause or point of origin. Eyewitness accounts vary but seem to point toward a series of massive electrical surges. Captain Mike Challis of the Manzanita Fire Department says, 'I've been fighting fires for twenty-three years, and I've ever seen anything like this. It'll be a while before we have answers.' ''

Electrical surges. Britt. He'd obviously been at the heart of the disaster, but she'd never seen him generate that much. What had he been doing? ''When they transferred Richard to the hospital in Breford, I came home.'' Sort of the truth. ''I assume he's doing fine.''

''You poor thing.'' Pat folded her into a hard embrace. ''You need to unload. Start at the beginning.''

Hope selectively edited the sordid details, avoiding any reference of her resident ghost. Talking it out only made her feel marginally better.

''I thought the divorce was done except for the shouting,'' Brian said with a frown.

Hope looked up. ''It is. Why?''

''You're worried sick about him,'' Pat observed.

Hope recoiled. She was worried, all right, but not about her soon-to-be ex-husband. ''If I could take Richard out and shoot him, I'd do it. What you're seeing is emotional overload and exhaustion.''

She caught Pat and Brian sharing identical disbelieving looks over her head.

''It's the truth,'' she protested. It was hard to pull off a convincing indignation when she couldn't tell them about Britt.

''Yeah, sure, honey,'' Pat said. ''Why don't we go out to dinner later? A girls' night out. It'll help you relax.''

Hope shook her head. ''No, thanks. I've got my Al-Anon meeting tonight. I think that's where I need to be.''

''Good idea,'' Brian chimed in. ''It'll help you refocus.''

He and Pat shared another look. Hope wanted to scream at them to stop it, but dared not protest any further. It would only worsen their suspicions.

She poured herself a cup of coffee—black—then gave them the best smile she could manufacture. It felt awful. ''For now, I plan to give myself a major infusion of caffeine, then get busy.''

Their return smiles were equally strained. But what else

could they do? Tie her up and beat a confession out of her? On her way to the bathroom to recheck her makeup, the phone rang.

Pat picked it up. "It's Mercy Hospital in Breford. How do you want me to handle it?"

Hope debated what to do. If she took the call, would it lead to a clue about what happened to Britt? Or would she be opening herself to another attempt by Richard to drag her back into his life? The blue eyes haunted her.

"I'll take it." As she put the receiver to her ear, she braced herself to be ruthless. "Hello?"

"This is Dr. Marin. I'm following up on some of my patients who were transferred last night. I was wondering if you'd come down this morning to talk about your husband's condition." He sounded only marginally less confused than he had last night.

"We're going through a divorce, doctor. I don't even know where he's living. How did you get this number?"

"From the paramedics who brought him here. Apparently one of them knew you from your picture on the realty signs around town."

Hope groaned.

"Your husband's records were among the few that were saved from the fire, and nothing is matching up."

If Richard truly had died, Hope imagined the records were creating a *nightmare* for the man.

"We have him in the neurology ward. He's experiencing some problems that we can't find a cause for. So far, all the tests, including an MRI, have come up normal."

"Doctor, I appreciate your desire to be thorough, but the marriage is over, and I do not wish to be involved. I suggest you try to reach his father, Charles McLean. He's in the phone book. Good-bye."

"No, wait!" Marin's insistence startled her, and she didn't hang up. "Mrs. McLean, has he ever had any motor dysfunction?"

"Any what?"

"Problems with coordination in his arms and legs. What about speech difficulties?"

"No." Eerily, she remembered him trying to move his arm last night.

"His motor control is on par with a newborn. Reflexes are normal for an adult, but . . . I need a full medical history." He sounded at the end of his rope. "This isn't consistent with substance abuse, and that's what I saw when he was first brought in."

Hope didn't want to sound cold-blooded, but she had to ask, "Could he be faking? I wouldn't put it past him as a bid for attention."

"No." It was unequivocal. "He's too frightened for that. I gave him a mild sedative, but since no one knows what he took last night, I can't do much for him."

To her knowledge, only Britt had ever frightened Richard. An uneasiness crawled along her backbone and settled between her shoulder blades. "I need to ask you a question. It's rather bizarre."

"Anything." He sounded like he'd concede any point to get her to the hospital.

"What color are his eyes?" She braced herself for the doctor's reaction. Surely, he'd think she was nuts. What woman didn't know her husband's eye color?

"I don't think I noticed," he replied guardedly. "Why?"

"Nothing." Hope pulled herself together. "It's a thirty-minute drive to Breford from here. I'll be there as soon as I can." She hung up.

"Hope, you can't be serious," Pat complained. "Let his family take care of him."

"This is something I have to do. I can't explain."

Brian reached for her hand, but she kept out of reach. "Hope, he'll suck you back into his life."

"No, he won't. That doctor isn't the only one who needs answers." She took a long pull on her coffee before she set the mug on her desk and headed out the door.

The nurses and the doctor called him Mr. McLean. It sounded right. Everything else was a blank, like someone had pulled a blanket over his brain.

Several times he tried to ask them why he was in a hospital. But he couldn't form the words. He knew he used to know how to speak, but it was as if the memory had been lost over many years. Actually, nothing worked. Touching his fingertip to the end of his nose as the doctors had asked this morning should have been easy, but he hadn't even been able to reach his face, much less connect with his nose.

That was another thing. His hands looked all wrong. The fingers were long and slim, not short and calloused. Yet part of him recognized them as looking exactly as they should. His face—once he finally figured out how to get his hands to it—felt like it belonged to someone else. Why wasn't it more round, with a slight cleft in his chin? He remembered the cleft because of the nuisance it had been to shave around. But as with his hands, part of him found a solid familiarity with the too-thin, sharply defined features. How could a man be confused about the shape of his face and hands? The concept unsettled him, to say the least.

For hours he lay in the hospital bed, one arm flopped on his chest, just enjoying the beat of his heart beneath his fingertips and the simple act of drawing air into his lungs. Somewhere he'd heard that breathing was the rhythm of life. For the first time—at least he thought it was the first time—he believed it.

A lady with violet eyes and soft brown hair peeked around the corner to his room. She watched him nervously for a moment, then squared her shoulders and walked in.

He knew this lady. His wife! He clearly remembered the heat of her satin skin beneath him as they'd made love. Hope was a good woman. He loved her. No, he despised her! Blamed her!

He took a calming breath to keep the panic at bay. The last thing he needed was more contradictory answers for each question he posed to himself. Hope loved him without reservation. Maybe she'd help him sort through the confusion.

First, though, he needed to find a way to say hello. Concentrating on moving his mouth around sound, he formed a single word. "Hi," he breathed. Intelligible! Good. Why was this so hard?

"Hello, Richard." The coldness in her voice startled him. It didn't invite conversation; neither did the increasingly hard set to her shoulders.

Had they quarreled recently? He needed to ask her so

much. Why was he here? Why was his mind clouded and dark, relieved only by the occasional blur of disjointed images? He needed to hold her, but the words came out a garbled mess. *Keep it simple,* he told himself. *Start with one-syllable words.*

She approached the bed, but stayed out of reach. "You really did it to yourself this time." Hatred came through loud and unmistakable.

That scared him. What had he done? He gathered what few mental faculties he could find, then enunciated carefully. "Love . . . you."

Her eyes widened, then narrowed with loathing. After a moment, she seemed to conquer it. Still, her expression wasn't friendly. "Your eyes aren't brown anymore. They're blue."

It was such an odd thing for her to say that he wondered if *she* was the one who needed to be in a hospital.

Her expressive features tightened in pain. "They're like Britt's."

He didn't remember a Britt. For that matter, he didn't remember a Richard, either. The latter was just something attached to McLean, the only name that felt connected to him even a little. It wasn't enough. "Help . . . me."

She recoiled from him. He wanted to weep. But he had to be strong for her, like always.

"I talked to your doctors. They don't know what to make of your condition. I couldn't help any."

Flashes of memory assaulted him. He had made love with this woman. She was his wife. Yet, he'd *never* touched her. One night, she'd needed his comfort. She'd reached for him, but the attempt had hurt her. He remembered his angry grief that she'd insisted on trying. What was going on here? Confusion and contradictions set off the full-blown panic again.

Clumsily, he extended his hand in a plea for her to take it, but she pretended not to see. More discordant thoughts crowded his brain. What had he done to her?

He needed to speak, but he still couldn't remember how. Gathering what wisps of memory he could find, he formed a single word. It needed to say so much. If he succeeded, would she understand? "Hope."

''What's wrong with your eyes?'' she asked.

He nearly wept with frustration. Why was she fixated on his eyes? They felt fine. He frowned a question at her.

She opened up his bedside table and tilted out the mirror. Once she lined it up, he saw himself for the first time.

Not his face! His hands hadn't lied. The shape *was* wrong, the features sunken and gray. Horrified, he whipped his gaze back to Hope, his one constant in a world gone mad. ''Me?''

Shuddering, she hugged herself and took a backward step toward the door. ''They said you have some memory loss. Do you know who you are?''

He needed answers, not more questions! As he shook his head no, he felt like a drowning man having to beg for a life raft.

''Your name is Richard Brittain McLean,'' she said. ''You tried to kill yourself on my front porch last night, and now you're in the neurology ward at a hospital twenty miles from Manzanita. Our divorce will be final just before Christmas.''

Each word plunged like a knife blade into his heart. None of it could be true. Suicide? Him? *Never!* How had he lost Hope? How could he exist without her? Having been served up more hell than he could swallow in one bite, he sagged back into the mattress. He studied her face and bearing, trying to find answers there. Her normally soft mouth was pinched tight from the force of keeping him from seeing what she felt, her eyes bleak with accusation. She'd spoken the truth. How could he accept such ugliness?

''No.'' The single-syllable denial tore from his throat. From the way she pulled her head up, she'd taken it as a contradiction.

''I won't argue with you,'' she said. ''I just came here to see if my brain had slipped a cog. Your face is Richard's. But your eyes are Britt's. I don't understand it, but that's what I see.''

She had mentioned that second name before. It hadn't sounded familiar, but now . . . Yes, he knew it! Britt Mc-Lean was an ancestor from the 1800s. Hope was a fanatic about the man. It had always made him jealous as hell.

''Hate . . . Rich . . . ard,'' he snarled. He didn't even

know where that thought had come from, but the garbled sentiment ran soul deep. He hated . . . *himself*?

Her eyes widened at his outburst.

"Help," he pleaded. "Me."

Fear clouded her eyes. "You need more than I can give. Talk to the professionals." She started to back out of the room.

If she left, it would throw him headlong into the crushing isolation he'd known since . . . He couldn't acknowledge the rest. Too bizarre. "Hope," he groaned. "Need . . . you . . . Alone . . . So . . . alone."

Hope stopped just short of the doorway. "Who are you!"

He desperately needed an answer. But he had none. "Don't . . . *know*."

He tried to sit up, but it was like he was drunk. Why couldn't he do such a simple thing? Brain damage? He didn't want to believe it, but what else could it be? One thing he knew, he couldn't let her go. Again reaching for her, he leaned forward. His body overbalanced and started to topple. He grabbed for the bars at the side of his bed, but couldn't make his hands work well enough to catch himself.

Hope rushed to his side and pressed her hands against his shoulders to keep him from falling to the floor. "Be careful!" The admonition was not made kindly.

Her touch warmed him as she gently eased him back onto the mattress. When she moved to pull away, he flopped one arm in the general direction of her hand. Miraculously, he connected with it. Groaning in relief, he closed his fingers around hers and clung to them. Survival depended on not losing her.

She stiffened and tried to yank her hand free. In desperation, he tightened his grip. Something deep inside reacted to their connected hands. Sexual awareness pulsed around them. Her face pinched in confusion, making her look as bewildered as he felt.

She managed to free her hand. Standing by the bed, she rubbed at her fingers. A shudder went through her. "Tell me about being alone. You said you were so alone."

Thank you, God. She's not leaving me! "Apart." He shook his head, trying to clear it of the useless flashes and sparkles.

Her pinched expression became more tortured. "Richard, drug addiction isolates people, and you've been an alcoholic and addict for a long time now. As for being apart, you drove everyone away, including me."

No! "Love . . . you!" he cried out in agony. If he didn't have her, he had no one. "Hope. Mine!"

Sighing, she stepped out of reach. "At one time, I loved you, too. Or thought I did. Not anymore. Maybe your drug buddies Eddie and Chris will come by later."

The names triggered something in his head. She was right. He had no friends anymore, especially not Chris and Eddie. He didn't even like them, but Chris was his supplier. Like every other piece of information, he didn't know how he knew that. He just did. *Oh, God. No!* He groaned in shame and self-hatred.

Pity smoothed the soft lines of her face, and she shook her head. He knew that this time when she backed toward the door, no power on earth would stop her from leaving. In grieved defeat, he watched her go.

Brian was out with a client when Hope returned, and Pat was manning the office by herself. She rushed from behind her desk to fold Hope into a hug.

"*Please* tell me you aren't getting involved with him again," she begged.

Hope leaned back and gave her a level look. "Did Hell freeze over yet?"

"Does that mean no?"

"Yes, that means no," she said drily.

"Thank God," Pat breathed. "I've been worried sick."

Hope tried to give her a reassuring smile, but she couldn't get past the memory of Britt's eyes in Richard's face. The concept of Richard suddenly having anything in common with Britt was obscene. But moreover, the impossibility of such a change boggled her mind. "Pat, I told you if I ever let him back into my life, that you were to get in my face. Right?"

She nodded.

"Well, that hasn't happened, so you're off the hook."

Pat grinned, part in relief, part in victory. "Then let's get back to work."

For the rest of the day, Hope couldn't get Richard's eye color out of her mind. Twice that afternoon she had the office to herself and called the house. Britt still didn't answer. Despite her better judgment, she called the hospital to check on Richard. Locked in his drug-fried brain could be the answer to what happened to the man she loved. The nurse in neurology transferred her to the chemical dependency unit.

"He started going through withdrawals about three hours ago," explained a nurse. "So we moved him here."

Hope shuddered. "Is he hallucinating?"

"Doesn't appear to be. And he still has all the other problems, too."

"Is the amnesia because of what he took?"

"Probably."

"Will the effects be permanent?"

"Not likely. Our records are pretty skimpy. Can you tell us what he uses?"

"A little of everything, but he leaned toward cocaine and heroin, last I knew." She needed to ask something that would probably make the nurse think *she* was the one who needed detox. But it was the only way she could think of to find out if Richard was seeing Britt and if the staff had noticed him talking to an "empty" room. "Sometimes when he's high he sees demons who won't let him drink."

"Won't *let* him?" The nurse snorted. "That's a new one."

"So he's not talking to Satan or anything today?"

"No," she drawled. "He just seems thoroughly bewildered as to why he's hurting like hell. We keep telling him, and he stares at us like it makes no sense at all. But when an addict is coming down the hard way, the brain does all kinds of weird things. We'll see how lucid he is in a day or two. That's when we'll have a better idea about any permanent damage."

Hope didn't know what to make of it, but she had the irrational urge to run back to the man in the hospital bed.

In her mind's eye, she still saw Britt's blue eyes pleading with her not to go and heard Richard's voice telling her he was so alone. The wrongness of it scared her. Badly.

The moment she arrived home that night, she checked Britt's room. His book and her note lay undisturbed.

"Where are you?" she cried out into the depths of the old house. The echoes of her mournful voice in the empty rooms of the third floor taunted her. For timeless minutes, she strained to hear an answer that never came.

For three days, the relentness worry gnawed at her. Finally, she headed toward the Manzanita hospital after work. A big sign painted on a sheet of plywood announced that all emergencies needed to go to the neighboring town of Breford. She parked the car and got out. The cleanup crew had made remarkable progress. The smoke had been sand-blasted off the exterior of the upper floors. They'd swept away glass and debris. A gaping hole stood where the ER's main entrance had once stood.

Trying to look casual, she strolled up to a couple of workers sitting on a truck's tailgate and pouring coffee from a thermos.

"You guys are working late," she said with a smile.

They looked up. The taller of the pair grinned. "Overtime until the job's done."

"Has anyone figured out exactly what happened yet?"

The shorter man lowered his brows in a heavy frown. "Are you a reporter or something?"

"No," she said with feeling. "I was here that night. Can't get it out of my mind."

"Really weird shit in there," replied the other. "Forget what they tell you in the papers, I heard an investigator say the only way to explain the damage was if electricity bounced around the ER like a volleyball. Fifteen separate areas of origin on the fire. Fifteen! You can even track some of them from room to room as it went through the walls in a straight line."

Based on what she remembered from that night, she believed it. "Do they have any idea what would cause something like that?" She did, but couldn't exactly tell them.

"*Nada*. Zip. They don't know nothin' and they're spouting a bunch of jibberish to keep from looking stupid to the public.''

The shorter man chimed in. ''The city and hospital authorities are pressuring them to come up with answers.''

A third man, this one wearing an orange hard hat, peeked around the corner and bellowed at them to get back to work. Hope turned as if she were leaving. But the moment they turned their backs, she sneaked inside to see for herself.

Even in the waning daylight, she could see quite a bit. One of the many burned-through places on the walls was close to the ceiling, exactly where the strange double shadow had been. It was also where she'd heard Britt's impassioned scream for her to run and the only time he'd ever said he loved her.

''Britt?'' she called out as she went through the remains of the emergency wing. She didn't care if anyone heard her. It would never occur to them she wasn't hunting for a normal flesh-and-blood human being.

Within moments, a security guard spotted her and made long strides in her direction. ''Can I help you, ma'am?'' His tone was decidedly unhelpful.

''No, thank you,'' she said with a smile. ''I'm just leaving.'' She turned on her heel, aware that he followed to make sure she headed back the way she'd come.

When she got into her car, she intended to go home, but headed down the road toward Breford instead. The entire thirty-minute drive, she cursed herself for being a masochistic idiot.

The nurse at the chemical dependency unit's front desk looked up when Hope stepped off the elevator.

''I'm sorry, ma'am,'' she said when Hope explained who she wanted to see. ''This is a no-visitors ward. Too many people try to sneak their friends a little something to get them through. No visitors. No exceptions.''

Oddly, that made Hope feel better. Nothing like hospital rules to help her keep from being totally stupid. ''Can you tell me if he's progressing normally?''

''Given that we don't know what all he's addicted to, we can't say specifically. He appears to be in the worst of it already. Mostly, he's confused. Drying out is hard enough without not knowing who you are."

"So his memory hasn't cleared?"

She shook her head. "No."

"No demons or devils talking to him?"

"If they are, he's not letting us know about it."

Hope thanked her then left.

Four days later, a nurse handed McLean a pen and a Refusal of Treatment form to sign. He took the pen in his right hand. It felt wrong. Transferring it to his left didn't feel any better. After switching it back and forth several times, he finally scrawled out his name with his right.

"We wish you'd reconsider the counseling sessions, Mr. McLean," she said. "You've only cleaned out your body. Without counseling, you won't stay clean and sober on your own. The psychological predispositions that set you up for addictive behavior in the first place are still there. Your body is just an innocent victim of where the brain took it."

Richard McLean. He had to start thinking of himself as "Richard," not just "McLean." But "McLean" was the only name that felt as if it belonged to him. Calling himself "Richard" felt like wearing someone else's clothes.

"Thanks for the concern," he said. "But I can't stay here any longer. If I can't remember all that, then I shouldn't have any problems—at least until my memory returns. For now, my body is cleaned out, and I intend to keep it that way."

"If you walk out of here you will fail," she pronounced in a tone designed to make a patient think twice.

He rose to his feet and smiled at her. "If the cravings come back, I'll be on your doorstep, but for now, I'm leaving."

Her eyes got huge. "You can't just walk out the door. You have discharge forms to fill out!"

He wasn't about to tell her he didn't dare wait another minute. If he did, he might start telling the doctors about the things in his head. Then they'd lock him in a madhouse for sure. He needed to find Hope. The fact that he didn't have any idea in hell where to look was a bridge he'd cross after he got some wide-open spaces around him.

"I'll be fine, ma'am."

"Didn't those withdrawals teach you anything?"

The reminder sent aftershocks of the tremors through him. Never in his life had he experienced pain like that. Never. And with God as his judge, he vowed never to experience it again. "Thanks for everything."

He reached up to tip his hat, then realized he was bareheaded. Where was his . . . He had to get out of here—now. Ignoring the nurse's protests, he strode out the sliding doors and into blessed fresh air.

Crisp sunlight and raw November air enveloped him, and he paused to take it all in. Lifting his face to the life-giving sun, he closed his eyes and soaked up the warmth against his eyelids and face. How could he *ever* have preferred a life of drugged-up shadows and illusions? He drew in deep breaths. Without a coat, only thin cotton shirtsleeves stood between him and the biting yet invigorating cold. Even the hardness of the pavement beneath his feet felt strangely wonderful as he walked without direction from the hospital. The sound of his own footsteps pleased him. The raw physical sensations made him feel more alive than he could remember in a long, long time.

Eventually, he came to a four-lane road. "I've driven this road," he murmured to himself. "Not every day, but often."

He looked left and right, unsure which way to go. Instinct said left was out of town and toward the town of Manzanita. Hope lived there. It wasn't a memory. Just a knowing. Desperate to find her, he headed left.

As he walked, the sheer joy of motion brought a smile to his face, and he broke into a run. Almost immediately, muscle fatigue complained. His breath grew short. God, how could he have let himself get so weak? No more! Gritting his teeth, he ran onward. Pain was good.

Within a few yards, the pain in his side threatened to drop him to his knees. Every muscle trembled from the impossible demands he'd made of them. Shaking, he sank onto a corner fire hydrant to catch his breath. Goose bumps rose up beneath the perspiration. Alive! He loved it!

The doctors said he'd nearly died. In fact, Dr. Marin said he'd pronounced him dead just before the fires broke out at the other hospital. Maybe coming that close to death had finally gotten through to him. Whatever happened didn't matter. Today was the most incredible day of his life.

Need formed in his belly. At first he couldn't identify it. Then it came to him. Thirst, with a trace of hunger. He checked his pockets, but had no money to buy food. Forcing himself to his feet, he again headed north toward Manzanita—and Hope.

Traffic on the four-lane winding, mountain road was brisk. The thought occurred to him that he should hitch a ride before exhaustion did him in. Instead, he rested under a tree for a while. Then began again.

By the end of two hours, his progress had slowed to a crawl. Long unused leg muscles screamed from fatigue. Setting his jaw, he pushed on.

A twenty-mile walk—which, by his calculations, shouldn't have taken more than five hours—took all day and most of the evening. Hours after dark, he found himself in front of Hawkings House, the home he and Hope had bought two years before. Her blue sedan sat in the driveway. Normally she parked in back by the garage. Unless she was very tired, he added. She must have had a rough day today. He latched on to the fragments of knowledge, knowing they were true just as surely as he knew his name was McLean.

Chapter Twelve

Five days had passed since the night of Britt's disappearance, and Hope had long since run out of places to search. He'd simply vanished. She couldn't sleep. Constant worry ate at her, overpowering everything else and making it nearly impossible to concentrate at work. To relax, she tried to finish staining the wood trim in the gentlemens' parlor she and Britt had worked so hard on. Restoring Hawkings House had once provided such satisfaction. Now the task only called attention to Britt's absence. Over and over she replayed in her mind the raw terror in his voice as he'd told her to run. He'd been afraid for her. Had there been fear for himself as well? Or had she imagined that part? Had he told her of his love because he'd feared he'd never have another chance?

"Oh, Britt what was happening to you?" she asked under her breath, clearing away a meal she'd known she wouldn't eat even before she'd cooked it. "What were you doing?"

Why had the lights exploded? Fire investigators still hadn't come up with a cause for the electrical surges that had spawned over a dozen fires. From what little she'd seen of Britt's abilities, she had no doubt he had the power.

Blasting Richard onto the porch that night had been effort-
less.

Maybe if she fully understood his existence and the rules
that governed it, she could lay some of the unknowns to
rest. As it was, though, the more she worried, the more
possibilities she found to worry over.

Could a ghost be killed? Could the essence that was Britt
McLean simply cease to exist? Before he'd left the house
that night, he'd decreed that Richard would never bother
her again. The anger in his voice had worried her. What
had he ultimately decided to do? Had those plans gone
terribly wrong? Then there was Richard. Beyond the
change in eye color, she'd sensed serious differences between the man she'd been married to and the one who lay
in the hospital bed. Britt had accomplished something, at
least. But what? And at what cost?

She struggled to believe that nothing sinister had happened. Maybe Britt had been trapped on the earth until he'd
done a particular good deed. Maybe whatever he'd done to
Richard qualified—whether it burned down part of a hospital or not—and he'd been freed to move on to his final
reward.

He'd missed his proper chance. Maybe if he'd been
given a second one, he hadn't dared risk taking the time to
come home to tell her good-bye. Maybe he'd had no
choice. After 127 years, he deserved an end to that hellish
in-between state. If that was true, she'd had no opportunity
to tell him one more time that she loved him.

Crushing grief made it hurt to breathe. To counter the
debilitating lethargy that accompanied it, she tried to plant
in her mind a peaceful image of Britt in heaven, reunited
with his family and best friend. But she couldn't believe it,
not for a minute. A tear rolled down her cheek, a tiny reflection of a heartache too great to hold inside.

Hope curled up on Evie's love seat, cradling Britt's new
journal in her lap and praying he'd come to her. She'd
taken strength from his words long before she'd met him
and tried to do the same now. But after a taste of the man
himself, the few entries felt like crumbs. She spent hours
staring at the vibrant, swirling script, the fresh ink of the
new journal bold and clear and as familiar as only a lover's

hand can be. Not many pages had been filled in. And like
the final journal he'd written as a living man, the entries
ended without warning.

She read about different people he'd seen on his way to
or from the library, and different conversations he'd had
with her. She read of his awestruck wonder that against all
odds, he'd found love again and of how this was as close
to being restored to humanity as he dared dream. Each
word, each sentence flowed onto the page as decisive as
the man himself.

The tears that ran down Hope's face were unable to ease
the cloying agony. She projected her feelings toward the
ceiling. "How can I help you when I don't know where to
look? Are you all right? What do I do if I find you and
you're not okay?" Without conscious intent, she clutched
the journal more tightly.

Someone knocked on her front door. Reluctantly, she
laid the journal on her desk, snagged a couple of tissues
and repaired her face the best she could as she walked to
the door. She checked her watch. It was nearly ten and
pitch-black outside. Cautiously, she swung open the door.
Anger and surprise ripped through her in equal parts. Richard stood on her porch, looking uncharacteristically ill at
ease.

Blue eyes. Britt's eyes.

Despite knowing who he was, all she saw was the impossible—a shadow of the man she loved. She shuddered.
"What are you doing out of the hospital?" It came out flat,
accusatory, exactly as she'd meant it.

"The withdrawals are over," he said hesitantly, as if not
quite having his speech prepared. "The rest didn't seem to
be relevant to me, so I left. I needed to"—he fought for
his words for a moment—"get out."

"Spoken like a true addict. The rules apply to everyone
but you."

His expression tightened in barely perceptible anxiety.
But he didn't fire a retort back at her. That alone struck her
as very odd.

"You're talking better."

He nodded. "Been working on it."

"Richard, what will it take to get it through your head?

Our marriage is over. Don't come back here anymore.''

He flinched. ''I don't have much recollection of anything, Hope, but I got the impression during your visit that I must have . . . hurt you very badly. I'm sorry.''

That flabbergasted her. ''Hurt me? You tried to kill me!''

For a frozen moment, not a muscle moved in his gaunt frame. Thoughts seemed to churn behind his eyes. She sensed more than saw the moment he found what he was searching for. ''I have a faint memory of wanting you dead. I had hoped it was a nightmare. I don't remember much of anything. None of what I do remember seems connected to me. It's just . . . in my head.''

''How convenient.''

''I remember we were in the kitchen.'' His gaze dipped to his hands and he turned them over and over as if trying to divine a great mystery. ''I wanted to strangle you. I could practically feel your throat beneath my fingers. I was going to enjoy it. Why?'' A desperate cast darkened his eyes. Did he want her to tell him it wasn't true? When she didn't, he collected himself. ''I am truly sorry.''

''Thanks for the sentiments, but no thanks,'' she said. ''I've had too much experience with alcoholics to buy any of this. You all excel at begging for forgiveness and promising to make amends, but it never lasts long. I came to the hospital for one reason—to find out if you knew what happened to a friend of mine.''

His gaze dipped to the porch, then rose to meet her eyes reluctantly. ''Who?''

This whole conversation had the strained edge of two friends who'd had a bad quarrel and didn't know how to mend the fences. But that wasn't her situation at all. So why did this feel that way? Time to set Richard back on his heels. ''I was looking for your demon. You were apparently the last one to see him.''

He blinked. ''My what?'' From anyone else, his bewildered expression would have been charmingly endearing. But she knew him too well to be fooled ever again.

''Don't you remember your demon?'' she asked, knowing that in part, she was deliberately baiting him. ''The one who poured out all your beer one day and made you shower and eat?''

"No," he said cautiously.

"Before I threw you out, the ghost of one of your ancestors moved into the attic. It's a long story, but Britt didn't take kindly to you destroying yourself and hurting me in the process. He chose not to identify himself to you, and you thought he was a demon or Satan himself. He has become a very good friend over the last few months, and he's missing."

Richard held unnaturally still. His words—when he finally spoke at all—were chosen with care. "Well, this obviously wasn't a good time to bother you."

Hope burst out laughing. "I can't believe it. The shoe is on the other foot. I thought you were nuts at first, too." She shook off the irony and focused on the problem at hand. "What are you doing here?"

He frowned. "I don't really know."

His audacity flabbergasted her. "After everything you've done, did you think I might take you back?"

"This is home." The frown deepened, turning into confusion. "No," he added, his expression taking on a faraway look. Then he refocused on her face. "*You* are home."

Terror burned up her spine and down her arms. Hope had never seen him like this. Something had happened to him. "What did Britt *do* to you?"

He gave her a blank look.

"Never mind. Just get out of here."

"And go where?" The forlorn and slightly panicked tone in his voice made him sound completely lost.

"Try your parents' house. I'm sure your mother will give you your old room back."

"I have parents?"

Long experience with him made Hope very suspicious. "If this is a new game you're trying out, play it on your mother first. She swallows your every word. For myself, I've smartened up a lot lately. Now go!" Before he could reply, she slammed the door and bolted it.

Then she went to the ladies' parlor window. The room was dark, and she could see him quite well by the glow of the streetlight as he walked down the steps, rubbing the cold from his bare arms. For a long moment, he stood in the circular drive, looking so out of his element that she felt a twinge of guilt at sending a half-naked amnesiac out to fend for himself.

He quietly studied the house, then went to the lawn and turned on the hose. He downed the water in long gulps that seemed to go on forever before he reached his fill. After shutting off the hose, he turned on his heel and strode down the walk.

Gone was the arrogant, self-important swagger. In its place was a rolling gate more in keeping with a man who'd spent most of his life on a horse—exactly the way Britt moved. Spellbound, she couldn't tear her eyes away until he was long out of sight. Something was horribly, horribly wrong with this picture.

"Oh, Britt," she moaned. "What did you do?"

McLean found himself wandering aimlessly through the streets of Manzanita. The cold and fatigue had long since ceased to be a joy. Without a coat, a place to stay or any idea where to go, that worried him—a lot. So did the gnawing hunger in his belly. He tried to ignore it all, but that approach didn't help much. By morning, the temperature would be dangerous. He needed food, shelter and a place to sleep.

Despite the crushing fatigue, he kept moving, hoping something he saw along the way would jog his memory, but nothing did. He even went inside stores at the shopping center near Hope's house. Surely he'd been in one of them. Nothing registered. At least they were warm.

After the grocery store closed at eleven, he pulled up the collar on his shirt and again braved the cold. This time, it hit him like a wall. The street glistened with forming frost. An inescapable truth also hit him. In his weakened condition, he'd be dead from exposure by morning.

He noticed a lighted phone booth at the gas station on the corner. An idea struck. He hurried across the street and lifted the thin phone book chained to the pole. Shivering, he thumbed through the white pages until he hit the M section. Then he drew his finger down the column. There it was. McLean. The list startled him. There had to be at least two dozen names there. Surely in a town this small, there had to be a connection. None of the first names sounded familiar. So, what was he going to do? Call every name there and say, "Good evening, I'm told my name is Richard. Do you know me?"

Toward the bottom, he found his own listing. McLean, Richard and Hope, 143 Whispering Oaks Dr., 555–4492. It meant nothing more than words on a page.

The temperature had already fallen well below freezing. It could drop farther still. He had no choice but to call people at random. When faced with the alternative, pride wasn't an option.

As he reached into his pocket, pride took another beating. He had no money for a call. None at all. A quick check of his remaining pockets showed all of them equally empty except for the papers he'd signed at the hospital. What happened to his wallet? In the absence of any clues, he stacked the question in his mind with the rest. Now what? Groaning, he leaned his head against the wall of the phone booth and tried to come up with a plan.

When he'd left the hospital, he'd had two goals—to get outside and to find Hope. Nothing else had mattered, certainly not long-range plans. Now he was in trouble. Sure, he could make it through missing a few meals, but he couldn't keep that up for long, not as depleted as his system was. Moreover, he was fresh out of detox, and he'd walked over twenty miles that day. His mind was still willing, but his flesh had definitely exceeded its limits. He needed food and a warm place to sleep. And until his memory returned, he needed help.

He carefully studied the McLean listings again. One of them had to be his parents. But which ones were they?

With a mother like her, no wonder Richard grew up to be such a . . .

That stopped him. Why did some of his thoughts feel as if Richard was another person, separate yet the same as himself? Was this normal with amnesia?

Looking up, he studied his reflection in the phone booth's glass. No matter how many times he saw it, the strangeness of the face brought him up short. Yet it belonged to him. Shaving it in the hospital had brought back

a forgotten familiarity. So why did it look wrong? To keep
the threatening panic at bay, he mentally listed everything
he knew to be true.

He was an addict and an alcoholic. The withdrawals he
remembered vividly. But why didn't he have any cravings?
His name was Richard. No, that wasn't knowledge of his
own. It was what others had told him. Hope had called him
Richard. He could trust her. She was the only one who had
cared for him since his daughter died in 1939.

McLean recoiled as if having been hit with a sledgehammer. "Oh, God," he said, backing away from the booth.
Panic flooded him with punishing force. His heart pounded
hard enough to hurt. Each breath came ragged and choppy.
"Oh, God. Oh, God. What kind of mental case am I?"

Trembling, he hunched down in his shirt and started
walking. He tried not to think about anything, not who he
was, not where he was going. Nothing!

After Richard left, Hope fretted for an hour. She wasn't
worried about him. He'd pushed her far past that point. The
man had other family, and as far as she was concerned,
they could take care of their own. But one thought wouldn't
go away. Locked in his head could be the answer to what
happened to Britt. The chance was slim, but it beat nothing.
She had to find out.

With mixed emotions, she picked up the phone and di-
aled a number she swore never to call again. His mother
answered after the first ring.

"McLean residence."

Hope swallowed back her distaste. "Hello, Ruth."

A decided chill fell over the line. "What do you want?"

"Is Richard there?"

"No," she said in that singsong voice of hers that set
Hope's teeth on edge. "Why? What have you done to him
now?"

Hope remembered her pre-Al-Anon days when she
would have rushed to her own defense. Now she was comfortable enough with herself to know she didn't owe the
woman an explanation for anything. Ruth had ruined her
son all by herself, and Richard had completed the process
as an adult by refusing to take responsibility for his life.

"Ruth, I'm not interested in arguing with you. I just need to know if you have talked with him since he let himself out of the hospital this morning."

"What was he doing in the hospital!" she shrieked. "What's wrong with him? Why didn't he call me?"

So, Charles hadn't told her about Richard's overdose— probably to keep her from interfering. Hope groaned. "If you haven't spoken with him, then I'm sorry I bothered you."

She pulled the phone from her ear to hang up.

"Don't hang up on me!" Ruth screeched. "What's wrong with my son!"

"If I find him, I'll have him call you."

"But—"

Hope hung up. Her next call was to Eddie and Chris. They hadn't seen him either. Then she called every member of the McLean family who lived in Manzanita, and no one had seen him. Not even the cousin who ran the local rescue mission. By midnight, she was climbing the walls. The one person who had even a remote chance of helping her find Britt was missing.

"You're being a victim, Hope," she chastized herself as she gathered up her purse and car keys. Her Al-Anon meeting was the next evening. "I can hear them now. Hope, did you inventory that out first? Are you enabling again? Then my sponsor will offer to help me rework step four—the one where the twelve stepper makes a fearless moral inventory of their life."

Glancing at the ceiling, she called to Britt. "If you're here, and if something happened to you that weakened you too much to contact me, I'm still trying to find you. Don't give up." Then more quietly, she added, "I love you."

The empty silence brought a lump to her throat. Forcing it down, she headed out into the night.

For more than an hour, she drove around Manzanita, looking for Richard. Stores had long since closed and only the subdued lights of a city asleep glowed. Even the twenty-four hour gas station looked abandoned.

"This is really stupid," she muttered, turning into the parking lot of the city park. "You're out in the middle of

the night trying to track down a man who tried to kill you.''
Not even that sobering fact dented the need to find him.

Manzanita was a quiet town, and the police department
did a good job of keeping the park safe for the residents.
Even so, the heavily wooded area was popular among the
homeless, and a few of them had mental problems. As she
climbed from her car and locked it, she pulled her coat
more tightly around herself and tried to think warm
thoughts.

At the picnic tables, a couple sat across from each other,
holding gloved hands, heads bent toward each other, the
air between them fogged with the heat of their mingled
breath.

Scrunching farther down into her coat, Hope followed
the path through the deserted playground and around the
groupings of bushes and trees. Every place where someone
could burrow in for protection from the cold, she stopped
and looked. Nothing.

The pond loomed into sight, the moonlight looking frigid
on the wind-kissed water. Ducks slept on the stone retaining
wall surrounding the three-acre body of water. A few more
dozed in the pond itself, their heads tucked comfortably
into their backs.

Hope nearly ran as she followed the concrete trail. Heavy
frost had formed on the walk and shimmered on the grass
and on the patches of dirt where constant foot traffic had
worn the lawn through to the bare ground.

More picnic tables were scattered by the retaining wall,
but they weren't anchored, so people routinely moved them
into the bushes for shade or privacy. With nothing but the
moonlight to guide her, she could easily miss him in the
deep shadows.

The cold seeped through her coat, and she picked up her
pace. This was nuts. Halfway around, she saw a lone figure
in shirtsleeves sitting on top of a table under a cedar tree,
his feet resting on the bench. He was hunched into himself,
staring at the ground, unmoving. Everything about him
screamed a picture of misery. It had to be him. Getting
close enough to be sure took another few seconds. Yes!

She trotted the last few yards. "Richard?"

He didn't look up. His arms were crossed tightly over

his chest, apparently to hoard what scraps of body heat he could. He had to be freezing.

She stopped in front of him. Still, he didn't glance up at her. "Richard?"

Then it hit her. What if he was high? *Oh, great.* Before she had the chance to analyze that possibility too much, he lifted his eyes. If the moonlight could be trusted, they were pale and clear, but she'd never seen anything so bleak. Not even her first encounter with Britt.

For lack of a better question, she asked, "Are you okay?"

He frowned at her. "What are you doing here?" His teeth chattered.

"Looking for you."

His brows dipped lower, giving his eyes a flattened look. "Isn't that a rather strange thing for a woman to do? Poke around in a deserted park after midnight for the man who tried to kill her?" The undercurrents were dark, self-punishing, the speech pattern pure Britt. "I remember that night now. Oh, God, what I remember."

"There's something not . . . right with you. I don't know what it is, but . . ." Her voice trailed off. What could she say? She didn't know herself what she was seeing yet still missing. How could she explain it to anyone else?

"I tried to murder you. I don't remember what stopped me. But something did. Doesn't matter," he added in a tortured whisper. "Only that you're safe."

She said nothing, waiting him out.

His features twisted in pained anguish. "I cornered you in the kitchen," he murmured low. "Go away!"

"Why?"

"You're not safe around me."

"Why is that? You're as sober as I've seen you in two years. You're not angry or blaming me for the mess you made of your life. I don't see anything to fear." The depths of how much she believed that surprised her.

"Well, you should." The shivering was so bad that she could hardly understand him. He raised his face just enough to glower at her. He'd probably meant to make himself look vicious so that she'd want to run, but it only made him look like a wounded and hunted animal.

"You didn't answer my question. Why should I be afraid of you now?"

"I'm an addict, an alcoholic, an attempted murderer, an amnesiac, and I think I'm insane. That's the short list. Would you like the long one?"

Hope sensed within him the same loneliness and isolation she'd seen in Britt. Again, her better judgment took a backseat to instinct. She climbed onto the table and sat beside him. At this point, she needed a really good opening line, something to get the conversation rolling. Her mind went blank.

Richard's stomach growled.

"Have you eaten?" she asked, pleased that a topic presented itself with such loud insistence.

"No money." Flat. Unequivocal.

"Given any thought to where to spend the night?"

"No idea where a hotel is." Flatter. "Even if I did, how would I pay for it? I asked someone on the street if there was a rescue mission in this town. He called me a bum and told me to get lost."

"Can I buy you dinner?"

"Don't be a fool," he snapped, finally straightening up to look at her. "I don't want you anywhere near me." His voice cracked. "What if I can't tell if I'm in danger of . . . of . . . Go away!"

In the dark, she had to angle her watch toward the moonlight to check the time. Twenty after one. "All the restaurants are closed. The only thing still open is the Pioneer Club."

"You want to take me to a bar?" He gaped at her as much as his chattering teeth allowed.

"Good, you remember it. And, no, I thought I'd leave you in the car, run in and get a burger and fries. After you eat, I'll drop you off at your parents' house."

Something flickered in his eyes. The man was really hungry, but something kept him from accepting the offer.

"You have a problem with that?" she asked.

"Yes, I do." The words were ground out. "Have I ever attacked my parents?"

"No, just offended your father to the point he wants

nothing to do with you until you get serious about your recovery.''

He winced and groaned. "I can't even trust what I'm thinking.''

"Why not?''

"Because of the *things* running through my head. I'm delusional or something.''

"What makes you say that?''

He jerked around to face her so abruptly that she jumped. "What are you doing, Hope? Badgering the headcase as an act of revenge?''

Hope realized with absolute certainty that she'd never met this man at all. *Oh, God, Britt what did you do?* "I'll admit you have a serious substance abuse problem and you're a mean, spoiled, self-centered creep. But you're not insane.''

"Thanks,'' he muttered, his lip curled into an attempt at a sneer that didn't quite make it.

Seeing him like this was like watching a lost puppy wander in traffic, unable to rescue itself.

Rescue. Enable. Caretake. All of those lovely spouse-of-alcoholic terms came flooding back. Before she thought it through and changed her mind, she hopped off the table. "I wouldn't leave my worst enemy out here tonight. You have two choices. Come with me and get something to eat and a place to sleep or stay here and be frozen to death by morning.''

He said nothing.

"Something tells me you're as desperate for answers as I am. Now what's it going to be?'' She turned her back on him and headed down the path. At first she heard nothing, no matter how hard she strained. Then came the creak of the wooden bench and the muffled thud of his sneakered feet landing softly on the frost-hardened grass. A moment later, he was beside her.

When he climbed into the car, she turned the heater up on high and started to drive. As the hot air blasted him, he closed his eyes and moaned with relief. His hands were so cold, he could hardly bend his fingers as he held them by the vents.

"What kind of things are running through your mind?" she asked, trying to sound casual. In truth, the tension was tearing her apart. "Anything from the night of your overdose?"

From the corner of her vision she watched him stare into the distance. "If I told you that, then you'd know I'm insane."

"Not necessarily. Try me."

Still, he hesitated. "I remember hovering in the air above my body at the hospital. But I was also coming *out* of my body at the same time. There was a big argument."

Dizziness engulfed her. "An argument between whom?"

He gave her a tortured look. "Myself and myself. I think."

Hope digested that a moment. "Could have been a hallucination caused by whatever you took that night. I wouldn't take that one too seriously."

He gave her a wary look.

"Do you remember lying on a gurney in the parking lot by a fire truck and me talking to you?"

"No."

"What else do you remember that's making you question your sanity?" She felt like a cop interrogating a suspect.

He opened and closed his mouth several times before any sound came out. "My birthday." He still shivered so badly that each syllable came out clipped and broken. "I remember it as September twelfth, 1962."

"What's odd about that?"

His eyes became even more intense. "Because I remember my friends buying me a drink in the Gold Saloon to celebrate it on June ninth 1862, the year Manzanita elected me sheriff."

Hope nearly drove into a tree. She slammed on the brakes and laid rubber for yards. *Sheriff! June 9th!* "The Gold Saloon burned down in 1871," she said as calmly as she could. "Britt wrote about the fire in one of his journals. Eight boarders upstairs died. Maybe you read about it."

He shook his head. "If I'd read it, then how can I picture that day in my head as clearly as if it happened last week? I even remember how bad Jack Hergoff's breath was. God, he had bad teeth."

Her knuckles whitened as she tightened her grip on the wheel and she stared at him unblinking. "Your aunt used to talk about various ancestors a lot. Maybe you took a bit of something she'd said, and it manifested itself in a dream or something." The feeble attempt to find an explanation sounded worse out loud than it had in her head.

He snorted and tipped his head back. "Nice try, Hope, but that won't wash and you know it."

Hope couldn't tear her eyes away. She couldn't think, couldn't breathe. Time passed, but she couldn't tell how much. Reality seemed to have fallen into a hole of monstrous proportions. Finally . . . she found her voice. "I want you to come home so we can figure this out. Something happened between you and Britt the night you tried to commit suicide. We both need to know what."

He shuddered, then visibly brought himself under control. "Don't you think I might try to . . . kill you again?"

Swallowing hard, she shook her head. Only because she loved Britt so completely would she risk so much. "When you're clean and sober you're obnoxious, not violent."

His expression turned inward. "I remember . . ." Never had she seen such torment on a man's face as he fought to make sense of the images in his head. "Money." The word came out with conviction, then more softly, "You needed what we had left for the house payment, and I took it anyway. Eddie was running a little low so I bought for both of us." He cringed. "You were so hurt. I didn't care."

Every time he opened his mouth, Hope thought she could handle it, but each statement was like a fresh blow. No wonder he thought he was losing his mind. "That happened about the time the museum burned down, one month before Britt moved in."

"I have several such memories—at least I think that's what they are. But they're pictures, stills, like a movie in freeze-frame." He trembled. This time it wasn't from the cold. "The things I did . . . they shame me, Hope. The way I treated you." He swallowed hard, debate raging on his face. "Are you sure you want me to come home?"

She nodded, not at all sure, but if she let him know that, she might never get the answers she needed. "Maybe between the two of us, we can put the pieces together.''

"Why are you doing this?''

His questions seemed to be multiplying by the minute. What few answers she had couldn't satisfy even the little ones. She chose her words carefully, mostly because she wasn't even sure of her ground. All caution fell apart when she gazed into his eyes. "Britt, are you in there?''

Richard visibly paled. "Your ghost? Oh, God, Hope. Don't even think that!''

She took her foot from the brake and headed to Hawkings House. They made the remainder of the drive in silence.

Once home, she took some leftover meat loaf from the fridge. Still silent, Richard watched, eyes avid, as she put it in the microwave. While it heated, she made a salad. The hunger on his face as she set the plate in front of him at the dining room table told her this would never fill him up.

"Thank you.'' The radiant gratitude softened the sharp edges of his features, revealing a faint impression of Britt. Or was that what she wanted to see?

Was Britt inside Richard? The concept horrified her. She could only imagine how appalled Britt would be by the idea. There had to be another answer.

Richard attacked the meager meal with gusto.

"I can't remember Richard thanking me for anything,'' she said. The questions within played over and over, demanding answers she didn't have.

Then she noticed something. "Richard is left-handed. You're holding the fork with your right.''

He stopped, a bite midway to his mouth. "Are we making a list of everything that's out of place with me?'' It could have been sarcastic, but she didn't think that's how he meant it.

"We can if you want.''

"Good. Add something else to it. My hair is the wrong texture. This is . . . softer, a little straighter. I don't know.'' He ran a hand through the collar-length mess. "It's just wrong.''

Unable to speak, she nodded, then went to nuke the rest of the meat loaf. From the way he'd mowed through the first plateful of food, she suspected she had her work cut out for her if she wanted to fill him up. While the meat warmed, she heated a can of green beans and toasted some sourdough bread.

When he looked up and saw the heavily laden plate, his shoulders sagged in grateful pleasure. "Thank you again."

She nodded, watching him eat. She'd never seen him consume that much at one time. He was still too thin, but his skin color was better. If he'd been eating like this the last day or two at the hospital, it would account for a lot.

"Hope?" he asked when he finally began to slow down. "I need to ask a question."

"A full stomach can make one a little braver."

He twitched a brief smile, but the determination would not be swayed. "Did I ever smoke a pipe?"

She was braced for something off the wall and managed to flinch only a little. "No, but Britt did. Lucinda buried him with it. The afterlife version went with him, I guess. I miss the smell of it."

He stared at her a long time. "None of this makes any sense. I am Richard McLean. I remember enough to know I can't escape that." He looked down at his hands and rubbed the fingers together. "Britt had calluses. I don't." His face was pale with strain. "How do I know a dead man had calluses? Why do I keep pawing at my shirt pocket for a pipe? What do you know about the night of my overdose?"

The rapid-fire barrage took a moment to recover from. She took a long breath and tried not to read too much into what he'd revealed. "Britt was determined to make sure you never bothered me again."

"I can't believe I'm discussing a ghost in the first place, much less one that I'm supposedly connected to somehow." He grimaced.

"Believe it." She gave him a level look. "My turn for a question. What if the only way he could straighten you out"—short of murder, she added to herself—"was to give you a piece of himself? Could he have somehow impressed into you some of who he was, sort of a reprogramming of the brain? If so, did he misjudge his abilities and destroy himself?"

The expression on his face reminded her of someone who'd just been told they had a deadly virus. "Provided the ghost is real," he hedged. "Would that be possible?"

Hope leaned back into her chair, trying to remember how many nights she and Britt had sat across from each other while she'd eaten her meal for one. The whole situation was too much to comprehend. "I don't know. He was the only ghost I ever met. I don't know what all he could do. He didn't like talking about being dead."

A hollow silence fell in the room.

"Whatever he was doing at the hospital, he was expending a tremendous amount of energy. I wish to God I knew what. Maybe he's here and just weakened too much to communicate."

When Richard didn't reply, she dared a quick glance. His tightly pursed lips and bleak blue eyes spoke volumes. He had less of an idea than she did. Until his memory came back in more than snatches and blurs, there wasn't much point pursuing this. Besides, she'd had enough for one day.

"I keep the bed in the downstairs guest room made up all the time," she said with more calm than she felt. "Why don't you sleep in there tonight?"

His jaw dropped. "You can't be serious."

"You're my only link to Britt, and I don't want you wandering too far out of my sight."

The appraising look he gave her was long and level. "Inasmuch as I can trust myself, I swear, Hope, you're in no danger from me."

A tiny bark of sad laughter filled the silence. "That's very similar to something Britt told me after he saved my life." She walked into the hallway without looking back. "Good night."

"Hope?"

She didn't turn around.

"Lock your bedroom door. Brace it with something. Whatever it takes."

She tried to hold her expression neutral, but she felt it crumple under the strain.

"Just in case."

Nodding, she headed for the stairs. "I had planned on it."

Chapter
Thirteen

McLean's body burned with exhaustion as he closed himself into the downstairs guest room. The twin bed was made up with an inexpensive floral-print comforter, sheets to match and a fluffy pillow. The promise of rest in that feminine-looking setup managed what nothing else had so far—it temporarily stilled the terrifying unknowns that had plagued him since he'd wakened in the Breford hospital five days before.

Warm and with a full stomach, what little energy he had left drained away. He needed a shower, but he just couldn't force his body to remain standing that long. Besides, a shower hadn't been offered. Sitting on the edge of the bed, he dragged his clothes from his body, then left them on the floor where they fell.

When he settled between the covers, the sheer comfort of a decent mattress beneath his back and clean sheets against his skin elicited a soul-deep groan of pleasure. Nothing could be closer to heaven. Again he asked himself why he had ever traded the simple joys of living for an alcoholic stupor.

He had two thoughts as sleep overtook him. One, how amazing Hope was to offer him food and shelter after everything he'd done, and two, disgust that he'd been fool-

ish enough to mistreat the woman he cherished more than
his own life.

Before the sun rose the next morning, he took the liberty
of showering and borrowing a disposable razor from the
medicine cabinet. The mundane activities brought him a
staggering amount of peace, but he didn't know why. Was
it because he'd survived the overdose and been given a
second chance? Or did the reason lie behind the black wall
in his head that kept the past hidden? Deliberately, he set
aside the unanswerable for a while and just soaked everything else in. By the time Hope stumbled into the kitchen,
he had found the coffee and brewed up a pot.

Her eyes were bleary from sleep, but she still gave him
a sidelong glance as if she expected the worst and was
second-guessing her decision to let him stay the night. The
first item on his things-to-do list was to appear as inoffen-
sive as possible.

"Good morning," he said with a smile. "Did you sleep
well?"

Her normally sleek, brown hair looked as if it had tangled with a cyclone, and she ran a hand through it to
smooth down some of the snarls. "I finally dozed off about
three."

He grimaced. "How much of it was because of me?"

"About half." She fumbled for a mug, dumped in a
spoonful of chocolate hazelnut cocoa, then poured coffee
into it, stirring the customized brew longer than needed.
Was she always this groggy in the mornings, or was today
different because she'd gotten so little sleep?

"The rest was . . . Britt?" he asked.

Nodding her head, she wrapped both hands around the
steaming mug. "I haven't slept right since he disappeared."

He knew Hope's motives for helping him went no further
than the friendship she claimed to have with a ghost. He
wasn't sure how he felt about ghosts or haunted houses,
but the images that flashed in his head scared him. They
bore too much resemblance to memories, and they were of
things that could only be known by an ancestor who'd died
over a hundred years ago. He prayed they were pieces of
things he'd read, but made to seem real by all the drugs

he'd taken. That appealed to him far more than the idea of
a ghost tampering with his mind.

By the time she had two good swallows down her throat,
her violet eyes focused. Oh, how he loved her. How could
he have treated her so badly when all she'd ever tried to
do was love him? The images of what he'd done to her
appeared static, unmoving, photolike. Why? A gallery of
his sins? For a man with gaping holes in his memory, he
felt uncomfortable making judgments about *anything,* but
he was pretty sure that type of recall wasn't normal.

"Is your head any clearer today?" she asked, her speech
sleep-slurred.

"You're not a morning person."

"Not on four hours of sleep, no." She yawned, then gave
him a level look. "Was that statement a memory or an
observation?"

The answer was just one more that eluded him. "Probably both. It feels very familiar."

She put a bagel in the toaster. "It hasn't been that long
since both Richard and Britt saw me when I first woke up."
She drew her shoulders back and seemed to be deliberately
pulling herself into more focus. "So which list do you think
we ought to put it on?"

"List?"

"The one we're making of thoughts and impressions.
Does my being a zombie until midmorning belong to the
Britt-knows-this column or the Richard-knows-this col-
umn?"

A mental picture formed of a long, narrow piece of paper
with a line drawn down the middle and a series of check
marks on either side.

He thought long and hard before answering. "I can't
tell." He wished he could give her a better answer, but not
knowing was at least honest.

Heartache and speculation swam in the changing tension
lines in her face. It made him feel as if she were trying to
see inside him. Part of him wished she could. Maybe she'd
have better luck.

As he watched her gaze drift to the toaster in defeat, he
wished he *were* her ghost. Real or imagined, Britt had so

much of her love. Jealousy stabbed him with enough power
to make him suck in a breath.

She dragged her fingers through her hair, still trying to
put it into a semblance of order. How often had he watched
her go from zombie to human in the mornings? He hadn't
a clue. Was it as familiar as it felt? Or did he just want it
to be?

"Did Britt have breakfast with you every morning?"

Her gaze snapped to him. "Why? Do you remember it?"

"No," he said, feeling overwhelmed by all he had to
conquer. "Just a question."

"He didn't eat, but yes, we always made a point to spend
a few minutes together before I left for work." She gazed
down into her mug. "Sometimes he went with me."

That surprised him. "Why?"

"We made a good team." She didn't elaborate. The
toaster popped, and he watched her smear cream cheese on
the bagel as he tried to think of something else to say.
"Richard, I—"

"Please don't call me that. It makes me feel . . . I don't
know . . . contaminated."

Her eyes widened. "You have something better?"

He didn't. Not really. He just couldn't tolerate being
called that hellspawn's name. "What about McLean?" he
offered. "It feels . . . right."

She mulled that over, then nodded. "I think I can be
comfortable with that." Handing him half of the bagel, she
took her breakfast into the dining room.

Without comment, he followed her, staring at the
strange-looking object in his hand. He wasn't sure he'd ever
held one before, much less eaten one. He thought about
asking her if he liked them or not, but he assumed he did
or she wouldn't have handed it to him.

When he sat across from her, she looked up, her eyes
flashing hostility. Just as fast, her gaze darted away, turning
into pain. Then he remembered what she'd said.

"Am I in Britt's chair again?"

She nodded. He didn't know what to say, so he moved
one seat over and focused on his meal. The bagel tasted
incredible—then again, everything did—and the speed with
which he downed it embarrassed him a little.

"There's a whole package in there if you want more. You need the calories."

"Thank you." He got up to head back to the kitchen, when the doorbell rang. "I'll get it."

At her quizzical expression, he added, "I'm dressed."

He walked down the hallway and had the door open before Hope could swallow her bite of bagel and object.

On the porch stood a tall, willowy blonde. He didn't think he knew her. Then again, how could he be sure?

Her baby-blue eyes snapped with pure loathing. "What are you doing here?" she demanded.

McLean sighed. Was this someone else he'd wronged? God, how he wished he could remember. As it was, he couldn't even defend himself.

"Not even going to say anything?" she ground out.

"To what? The obvious? Yes, I'm here. We can both see that." He probably could have come up with something less inflammatory if he'd thought about it first, but frustration made him short on charm for the moment.

"Come on in, Pat," Hope groaned from behind him.

McLean turned at the resignation in her voice. She pulled her robe more tightly around her and made another attempt with her fingers to tame her hair. She got better results this time, and it fell into a soft ripple to her shoulders.

The blonde swept past him as if he were a dead cockroach. McLean bristled but kept the reaction to himself. At this point, he didn't know when he had a right to respect and when he didn't.

"Oh, God, Hope, please tell me this isn't what it looks like." The other woman enveloped her into a fiercely possessive hug.

Hope peeked over her shoulder at him. "McLean, this is my best friend, Pat Collins."

Pat stepped back and gave her an incredulous stare, a silent demand for an explanation.

"He has amnesia."

She snorted. "Oh, sure he does. And I'm the king of France."

Definitely someone he'd offended.

"Even if he does, what's he doing here?" Pat turned her back on him and kept it that way.

The insult rankled. No matter how vile he'd been, surely he deserved basic courtesy.

"Pat, it's not what it seems. Honest." Hope stepped away from the door and motioned her friend inside. "He slept in the guest room."

"He slept in . . . " she echoed faintly. Then she groaned out loud. "Have you lost your mind? Last night the guest room. Tonight, you know where he'll be."

"Don't presume to know my intentions," he said. "Talking about me as if I were invisible won't help this situation, either." Overhearing people talk *about* him and not *to* him hurt like a remembered toothache. He wished he knew why.

Hope made a "let me handle this" gesture. Her expression warmed as she looked at Pat, but her eyes glittered with a defensive edge. "I'm not doing anything stupid."

"Oh, Hope, letting him within ten miles of you is stupid. You can't do this to yourself."

A blind man could see the raw worry flooding from Pat. Strangely, it comforted him to know that Hope had someone so protective of her.

McLean's hands clenched at his sides. Being the cause of so much grief for so many shamed him. How could he make amends without the memories of exactly what he'd done? From the looks of things, his brain was taking its own sweet time in straightening itself out. Until it did, he was at the mercy of people whose negative opinion of him had been formed for a long time.

He swung the door shut and squared his shoulders. "I'm not trying for a reconciliation. Hope was kind enough to give me a place to stay until I can make other arrangements."

Pat glowered at him over her shoulder. "Nice speech, dirtbag, but I know you better than that."

"It's true," Hope added, stepping in. "Also, there's a situation you know nothing about. He's the only one who can help me with it."

Pat crossed her arms. "Like what?"

"You'd think I was nuts, and I'd just as soon avoid that."

"Try me."

Firmly, Hope shook her head.

Half turning, Pat shot him an acid glance. "You have family in this town. They can take care of you. Whatever Hope needs, she can count on her *friends.*"

McLean stood firm in the face of the hatred boiling toward him. "I don't remember any of . . . my relatives. Hope is—"

"Not going to be your doormat any longer!" The blonde's face was darkening, her anger and fear building. McLean admired her loyalty but wondered at the vehemence.

"Pat, I'd rather he stay here for now," Hope insisted.

"Why?" she breathed, writhing where she stood. "You made me swear to get in your face if you ever let him back into your life. You said it yourself. Alcoholics are very convincing with their promises of sobriety. You're caving big-time, just like you were afraid you would."

"Pat, please." She squeezed her friend's hands.

"You're a compassionate person, Hope, and an easy mark for someone who wants to weasel his way into your life. What did he say to convince you he's the only one who can help you with that situation you won't tell me about?"

Hope stood a little straighter. "Nothing. I went after *him.*"

"You *what?*"

"This isn't getting us anywhere." Hope gave her a quick hug, then stepped back. "Now, what did you come here for?"

The other woman stared at her feet for a moment, collecting herself. "I wanted to surprise you and take you out to breakfast. Thought you needed a pick-me-up."

Hope smiled, her face lighting with pleasure. "We just ate. How about I get dressed, and we can go out for a morning capuccino?"

"Anything to get you away from him long enough for me to talk some sense into you."

"I'll be dressed and ready in ten minutes." As she trotted upstairs, she added, "No talking until I get back, you two!"

"Like hell," Pat muttered under her breath. The moment Hope was out of sight, she turned on him. "Amnesia? Oh, that's rich. She doesn't know how many times you've propositioned me, buster, and I don't want to be the one to tell her. If you hurt her this time—even a little," she warned, stabbing her finger into his chest, "I'll send the cops after you anytime I even *suspect* you're using again. They'll nail you for possession so fast, you'll be in jail before you can blink."

He bent toward her. "You'd be a poor friend if you didn't."

That set her back, and she gaped at him.

"My drinking and using days are over. I don't know why I'm so sure of it, but I am." He didn't know what to think about the womanizing she'd accused him of. "I have a debt to pay here, and I will pay it."

"Rather confident talk for an amnesia victim, wouldn't you say?"

"I don't go back on my word."

Pat stared for a full two seconds before she burst out laughing. "Give me a break. I can't remember one time you *kept* your word."

The only person he knew at all was the man he felt like today, and that person didn't make promises lightly. He took a slow breath. "Time will tell, Pat."

"Okay, you two. That's enough," Hope said, rushing down the stairs. She turned Pat toward the door and steered her outside. Then she turned back to McLean.

"Will you be okay here all by yourself for the day?"

He nodded. "I don't know how to thank you for taking me in and trusting me." He left the remainder unsaid.

"You're not the same person." She gave him a sad smile. "I don't know who you are, but you're not Richard." She lifted her chin. "Even if you were, I'd deal with the devil himself to find Britt."

"What are you going to tell Pat?"

"I don't know. She's too good of a friend to keep out of the loop. But Britt didn't want anyone else to know about him." Tears glistened in her eyes.

"You're in love with him, aren't you?" The question came out flat, resigned. He knew the answer, but he needed to hear her say it, so he couldn't delude himself into believing he was mistaken.

She glanced away and blinked a couple of times. "More than I ever thought I could love anyone." When she looked back at him, she was clear-eyed. "Do you believe he's real?"

McLean suppressed a shudder. He would give anything to have her that worried about him. "You believe. That's enough for me." He took a breath, then plowed onward. "What if Britt did destroy himself trying to straighten me out?" The idea that another person—living or not—would make such a sacrifice for him made him ill. "Will you blame me for it?" He didn't think he could stand another taste of her hatred.

Hope paled and began to shake. The denial in her violet eyes told him she hadn't truly dealt with that possibility. "I'm choosing to believe that whatever happened just weakened him. Wherever he is, as soon as he regains his strength, he'll contact me." She swallowed hard. "Either that, or he was finally granted a path to the afterlife."

She sounded so fragile and alone, he wanted to reach out and comfort her. But he kept his place. "I'm sorry, Hope."

She gave him a helpless shrug. "It's all speculation." Her breath puffed out in sad amusement. "I will say, though, it's nice hearing you concerned about another person for a change."

Had he really been that selfish? Most of the disjointed images in his mind supported that idea. How could he have considered himself the center of everyone's universe, their attention his just due? "No matter what happens, Hope, I promise I will make up for the past."

"We're not reconciling, Richard."

"I'm McLean, not Richard. Remember? There's no reconciliation to try for." Inside, he grieved. *How can I let you go now that part of me realizes what I threw away? Oh, God, when is this going to start making sense?* "Like I told Pat, I have a lot of debts to repay. Helping you find your . . . ghost is one way to do it." Jealousy roared its protests, and he battered it down.

Her brow knitted as if she were staring at a stranger and didn't know what to say.

"Is there anything I can do to hunt for Britt?" he offered. "Maybe something you haven't had time for?"

She blinked, clearly stunned. "I don't know how one effectively searches for a missing ghost. Do you?"

All he wanted was to hold her. "I'll think about it."

"By the way, your wallet is in my night-table drawer. The credit card and ATM card are no longer valid, but I thought you'd want your driver's license back." Without waiting for him to answer, she reopened the door and hurried out.

Pat sat behind the wheel of her minivan, hands clenched on the wheel. She rolled down the window at Hope's approach.

"Please don't do this to yourself, Hope. He's trouble."

"This isn't what it looks like."

"The mouse is back." She slammed her mouth shut as if biting back a tirade before it got loose. "Sorry," she said subdued. "This isn't any of my business."

"Was that Joan of Arc with PMS?" Hope quipped. "You told me about her once." She put a smile in her voice to lighten the mood.

Pat sighed, her shoulders sagging. "Yeah. Ms. Butt-in Hothead strikes again."

Hope punched her on the shoulder in a mock macho gesture of friendship. "You still haven't taught me how to do that. We'll call today lesson one."

Pat gave her a resigned smile. "I'll meet you at the coffeehouse."

Thankful to be alone with her thoughts on the drive over, Hope wondered if Pat's concerns were valid. Had she worked enough bats out of her belfry to recognize an unhealthy relationship brewing? Falling in love with a ghost couldn't be indicative of great strides in that area.

What about the man who called himself McLean? Who was he? *What* was he? Without a memory, Richard had a fairly good chance of staying clean and sober. But what would happen as those memories returned and all the emotional glitches that created the addictive personality came back into play? The thought that he might not regain the memory at all sent acid ribbons of dread coursing through her body. He had to remember. He just had to.

When she and Pat were seated at a table in the busy restaurant, Hope unloaded, telling her everything. Pat stared in wide-eyed silence.

"I've studied ghosts for years," Pat complained, her expression pinched with hurt. "What you're describing is more like a Hollywood script than anything anyone has ever documented."

"You don't believe me."

"I didn't say that. I just wish you had let me try to talk to him—whether he wanted you to or not. It just seems so odd that the ghost of the one person in history you obsessed over is the one who showed up."

"Not if you take into account how close I am to everything important to him. The town. His family. His possessions."

Pat nodded, still skeptical. "Richard could be playing on your worry to—"

Hope shook her head. "He didn't know anything about Britt until I told him."

"If Britt shows up, I get to meet him. Right?"

If, she echoed in her heart. Then she forcibly replaced it with the word "when." "I may throw a party."

McLean went upstairs to Hope's bedroom for his wallet. An impression of knowledge rather than an actual memory overcame him when he walked into the spacious room and saw the queen-sized bed with its plain headboard. He'd slept in that bed with Hope, held her in his arms. Yet something else told him he'd always made it a point never to come in here. Hope's privacy was part of the reason, but it had started with a woman named Lucinda. Frowning, he made quick strides out, opening his wallet on the way down to the gentleman's parlor. The TV was in there, and he needed to watch the news. Maybe one story or another would jog loose a memory or two.

As he walked, he pulled out his driver's license, an ATM card, a charge card and a couple of dog-eared business cards. He scanned the DMV photo, half hoping it would provide concrete proof of who he was and banish this strange sense of duality that plagued him. The idea of placing that much faith in DMV struck him as lame, but desperation had begun to make grabbing at straws sound less outrageous. How long could someone live without an identity before they had a mental collapse?

The signature on the bottom of the license caught his eye. There was something odd about it and he gave it a closer look. Foreboding crawled through him. The handwriting was a sloppy, blockish-looking scribble. Frowning, he reached into his back pocket for his copy of the Refusal of Treatment papers he'd signed at the hospital. Then he compared the signatures. Fear burned through his veins as he stared at the elegant flowing script he'd written in the hospital.

The flourish he'd put on the letter R in Richard and the M and L in McLean had an Old World style to them. The tail of the N tucked back under both words in a loose figure eight. People hadn't written like that since the last century.

"I am Richard Brittain McLean!" he snarled defiantly into the silence. "I am my own person! A ghost hasn't tampered with my mind!"

It was a long day.

Hope came home that night braced for the worst. Richard had been alone in her house all day. At noon she'd remembered the hundred dollars she'd tucked in her desk drawer. Or at least she prayed it was still there. She couldn't begin to guess how much money he'd stolen from her over the last two years. The more she thought about the possible ramifications of bringing him home, the more she doubted her judgment.

"Hello?" she called.

"I'm in here," came his voice from down the hall. Her office.

She sucked in a breath and went in search of him. He had rolled her desk's chair over to the antique bank vault and was leaning forward in the seat. His bemused expression was locked on to the vault.

"Is there a story behind this?" he asked, his brows drawing low. "This isn't normal home decor for most people."

Hope almost told him the vault's history, but kept her

mouth shut in favor of a better idea. "Why don't you tell me what *you* know about it?"

He gave her a sharp look, one that changed to defensive insecurity as he scrutinized her face.

"It's all right, McLean. I'm not setting you up."

A fraction of the tension leached from his body. "Sorry. I guess I'm not very trusting these days." He lifted his hands in a gesture of helplessness, then dropped them into his lap. "I can't help but feel I'm the victim of a hoax, that any minute someone will jump out and give me a perfectly logical explanation for all this. They'll restore my memory, and I can get on with my life."

Hope burst into half-hysterical laughter. "That's exactly what I felt like when Britt showed up. It had to be a hoax. Either that, or I was losing my mind. Having a haunted house was just too outlandish to accept."

"At least it's not just me."

"The vault," she said, bringing the subject back around. Maybe her judgment hadn't been so bad after all. "Britt guarded it against several attempted bank robberies. If something ever happened to his last journal, I think he'd planned to see if staying close to the vault would accomplish the same thing, give him a measure of peace. It certainly beat the only other option—hanging around his body at the cemetery."

At his morbidly puzzled frown, she explained what had happened to Britt after he'd died and how he'd spent the last 127 years.

"Poor bastard," McLean said.

His compassion touched her. "What does the vault mean to you?" she asked.

He opened his mouth, then closed it, eyes flashing wildly. Then he put a damper on it all. "Nothing."

"You're lying."

"Not exactly. What's in my head isn't pleasant."

"Tell me anyway."

Staring at the vault, he rose from the chair almost in a trance as he traced the scars in the metal with the fingertips of one hand. His expression became more troubled with each passing second.

"This isn't a test," she said. "Honest. Just tell me what you remember."

He patted at his shirt pocket, frowning at finding it empty. She didn't comment, but watching him hunt for Britt's pipe was very disconcerting.

"I remember that you paid too much for this 'hunk of junk,' as I'd called it. I was furious and called you . . . some foul names." He cast her an apologetic look, then went on. "To get it in here, we had to install French doors and re-inforce the floor." His gaze flicked to the double doors on the far wall. "All that happened. Right?"

She nodded. "What do you find so unbelievable about it? Anger and name-calling was very typical of you."

"Apparently."

"So what's not real?" she asked.

"Other things. Dreams, maybe. I don't know."

When he tried to leave the room, she took his arm. Heat penetrated skin and muscle. An irrational desire to draw closer to him swept through her, and she wanted to feel his arms around her. The thought revolted her. So why was it so tempting, particularly when she loved Britt? He glanced down at where her fingertips pressed against his bicep. His gaze darkened with an inner pain. Hope pulled her hand back.

"Tell me what's in your head," she said, clearing her throat. "It can't hurt. Besides, I told you about my ghost."

He seemed to consider that for a moment. "This sounds foolish, but I can't shake the feeling of being two people. I've got images in my head about this vault. They feel like memories, but they can't be."

Hope sucked in a breath and prayed he hadn't heard the anticipation in it. "Don't fight it," she advised softly. "Just run with it, no matter how outrageous it sounds."

McLean gave her a mistrustful look. After a long moment, he traced a finger along a big gouge down the vault's left side. "This happened on the way to Manzanita from San Francisco. A wagon wheel dropped into a rut. The strain of the uneven weight broke an axle. The ropes snapped like cobwebs, and the vault slid to the ground in the middle of the road. For two weeks other wagons had to drive around it until men could build a hoist and gather a mule team to lift it onto another wagon."

Her heart leapt. That part of the vault's history she hadn't known, but it had the ring of truth about it. "Britt didn't mention it in any of our conversations. But according to the journal entries, he wasn't part of the original transport efforts but was very much involved in getting the vault back on a wagon and into town."

"Then I could have read the journal and used my imagination to fill in the rest." He swallowed.

"Not likely," she answered quietly. "And that still doesn't explain what you know about Britt's birthday in the Gold Saloon."

"If Britt . . . tampered with my mind, then I could have all sorts of things rattling around in there that don't belong."

The questions never changed. Had Britt tried to reprogram Richard's brain? Was he too weak to communicate, struggling right now to find a way to let her know he hadn't been completely destroyed? Hope wanted to weep.

McLean returned to studying scratches on the vault, and she gave him a speculative look. Could Britt have moved *in* there? She didn't see how. No matter how tempting being alive again was, and how worthless he'd judged Richard to be, Britt would never take over another man's body. He believed too deeply in not interfering with the living even to consider it. Yet . . .

On the chance that Britt was in the house but unable to communicate, she closed her eyes and projected all her love for him, willing its strength to permeate every corner of Hawkings House. She couldn't tell if it worked or not, but the effort made her feel better.

"What I wouldn't give to turn back the clock," she whispered into the stillness, praying Britt could hear her. "You'd never have followed that ambulance."

"What?" McLean asked over his shoulder.

"Nothing," she said. "Hungry?"

He gave a lopsided grin. "I'm always hungry. I don't remember food ever tasting this good."

Neither spoke as they went into the kitchen. Having to

analyze each action to see whether it had come from Richard or Britt was taxing beyond belief.

As she pulled vegetables from the fridge, he leaned against the counter where he could easily talk to her. That was fine until he crossed one ankle over the other and patted his shirt pocket. How many times had she seen Britt do that!

Oh, please God, let him be in there! She wanted so badly for him to be unharmed that she'd accept any explanation and condition. *Just don't let him be destroyed.*

Maintaining her composure required physical activity. Holding still was emotional suicide, so she sliced and chopped vegetables for stir-fry. The knife hit the wooden cutting board with a gratifying "thwack" as she worked, the project giving her something constructive to focus on. The rice went on to boil next. Then she thin-sliced part of a roast and dumped it and the vegetables into the wok. Hot oil and juices splattered and popped.

A few seconds later, Richard breathed deeply, a euphoric smile on his face. "What are you fixing? It smells wonderful."

Stunned, Hope turned to him. "You hate stir-fry."

He froze. "I do?"

"I made it for you once, and you told me not to bother ever again. You were pretty insulting about it."

His expression tightened, and she regretted throwing the past in his face. Her own memories of their marriage were far from healed, but hitting him now with a past he couldn't remember wasn't fair. Neither was cooking a meal she'd known he would hate.

"Richard would be," he said quietly, "but that's not how McLean behaves."

She understood his militant need to disassociate himself from Richard. Any normal person would do the same. But in his case, she doubted it was healthy. Their gazes collided, then skittered away.

He took a discreet sniff in the direction of the stove. "I think I'll like this."

In moments she had the meal finished, and she retrieved her serving bowls from an upper shelf.

He started to set the table, but stopped, holding the forks

and napkins in one hand and the plates in the other. "I never helped you in the kitchen, did I."

"No," she said, setting down the bowl of rice and the platter of meat and vegetables. "But I guess McLean does."

His blue eyes—so like Britt's—looked tormented. She couldn't deal with this. Neither of them could.

"Let's eat," he whispered, leading the way to the dining room.

"Good idea." As she served up her plate, he gave her a bewildered look. "Now what's wrong?"

"You don't say grace?"

Hope blinked. "You're an agnostic." He opened his mouth to speak, and she held a hand up to stop him. "Don't tell me. McLean isn't."

"I don't think so. Last night I was too hungry to think about anything except the next bite of food."

Hope didn't think she couldn't handle any more surprises. "Then let's pray."

They both bowed their heads, and McLean offered a prayer of simple eloquence like nothing she'd ever heard.

He avoided her gaze afterward and forked a large bite of rice and meat into his mouth—with his right hand!—and moaned in appreciation. A large quantity of his meal disappeared before he raised his head again. "Hope, I've never eaten anything this wonderful in my life. I'm sure of it."

"You don't remember Chinese food at all?"

He shook his head and readied another bite. "No, ma'am, I don't."

Hope nearly fainted. *Ma'am. He called me ma'am.* She stared deep into his eyes. Britt's eyes.

"Britt?" she choked out. "Are you in there?"

Richard's gaze snapped to hers, and he pulled back from the table. His body language projected a horrified denial.

"Are you *both* in there?" she whispered, unable to stop the choking question.

He shoved his chair the rest of the way back and rose to his feet. "Why do you keep asking that! I'm already half out of my mind. Don't finish the job. Please!"

They swapped darting glances.

"You're right," she said. "This has got to stop. I have an idea." She motioned for him to follow her upstairs. "I should have thought of this earlier."

The wariness on his face intensified, but he followed her to the third floor.

"Everything is just as Britt left it," she said, feeling her way into the darkened room. "Wait a minute until I have the light burning." She patted around on the desk for his matches.

"Burning?" he echoed.

A moment later, the warm glow of the old-fashioned hurricane lamp answered for her. "He brought in electric lamps." She pointed to them on either side of the couch. "But I thought this one might jog your memory better."

"I assume there's a logical reason why a ghost needed furniture and lights?"

The edge to the question disheartened her. Would he ever believe? "It kept him a little closer to the humanity he lost."

McLean made a sympathetic noise low in his throat, then studied the desk, chair, couch, coffee table and braided throw rug. He took each item's measure, then let his breath out, half in disappointment half in relief.

"Does any of this strike any chords?"

He shook his head. "Not one."

Walking to the desk, he picked up the substance abuse guide. Even in the softness of lamplight, she saw his face go deathly pale. "Richard has never been up here."

"Not to my knowledge."

He sagged down into the chair, book still in hand. "I was reading this."

A bone-deep trembling shook Hope, and she had to hug herself to keep it from showing.

"Here." He flipped to a bookmark. "I wanted to show you this page when you came home from work, but I didn't get to it that night." His expression tightened with the intensity of whatever churned inside his head. "You came home and we went into the parlor to sit by the fire."

"Only Britt could know that."

He gave her a despairing look. "Help me, Hope. How

can I know this stuff?'' His wild-eyed gaze flashed around
the room. "This is my room. My *home*! Not downstairs.
Here!''

Hope's stomach heaved, but she kept the contents down
where they belonged.

All at once, he seemed oblivious to her presence. "I got
the boards for my bookshelf from the discard pile at the
lumberyard. It took me days of reworking them with my
'smoke and mirrors'—as you liked to call it—to plane them
out into something usable.''

"Plane?''

He frowned. "It's a woodworker's term.'' He drew back,
shaking every bit as hard as she was.

Hope wanted to believe she was somehow looking at
Britt in Richard's body, but given how deeply Britt felt
about *his* "noninterference directive,'' he never would have
done such a thing. The only other conclusion brewing in
her head was too horrific to contemplate—that he'd impressed so much of himself into Richard that nothing remained for himself.

No! She wouldn't believe that. Britt was just weakened
someplace and trying to recover. Hadn't he said that after
he and Nestor had tried to drag him on to the afterlife, that
he'd blacked out for three days? Maybe that's what was
happening now, a blackout—just a longer one than before.

"What *else* do you remember?'' The rasp in her voice
made her sound old and infirm.

"That I didn't want to come here. That I knew what
manner of man Richard was. I didn't like him. Never had.
I was ashamed of him. All I wanted was a place to . . .''

"To what?'' Her throat locked up, and the question came
out barely audible.

"A place to *be*. That's all. Just a place close to . . . my
journal. And you had it in your safe. I had no choice but
to come here. The museum fire . . .''

Dizziness swept through her as the impossible demanded
to be voiced and accepted.

"Hope, what does this mean?''

She couldn't give voice to the words. It would make
them too real. "Do you remember anything about the night
of your overdose?''

He shook his head. "Nothing we haven't already talked about."

She couldn't have torn her gaze away from him if her life had depended on it. "What do you think happened?"

"Would you stop sounding like a damned psychiatrist? If I had any idea, I wouldn't have asked you! You know more than I do about all this."

"Then guess. Please! It's important."

His gaze turned inward, and the war on his face intensified. "Britt isn't in me. I won't let him be! I must be Richard McLean. How else could I have his memories?"

Hope realized she was breathing too fast, too hard. It was as if her body thought it was running a marathon. "Are the memories from Richard's perspective, or are they more like looking from the outside in?"

"I'm Richard," he said with fatalistic surety. "I wish to God I wasn't, but I am." After a long pause, he added, "But part of me has to be Britt, too." His expression hardened. "He didn't have the right to play God with my mind."

"Whatever was happening at the hospital that night was bad. Britt was frightened for my safety. His own, too, I think. That's the part that worries me the most. What could be so horrible that it would make a ghost afraid?"

"I don't want Britt's memories in my head. It's immoral!"

His insistence offended her, even though she understood it. "You're remembering things that only each of you could know. Perhaps you—McLean—are a combination of parts of Richard and Britt. It would explain why you can't connect with either."

Again his face turned ashen. "And whatever caused it created enough trauma that I have partial amnesia from both men?"

"The human body does a lot of strange things to protect itself."

"I can't live with that." He shuddered once, then closed in on himself.

"Do you have any choice right now?"

His eyes glittered with resentment.

"This is ridiculous," Hope asserted. "We don't know

anything. Maybe we're just getting carried away with ourselves.''

He didn't answer for a long time. ''Would you mind terribly if I asked you to leave me alone for a few minutes?''

''Take as long as you need.'' As she headed to the stairs, she said, ''I need some breathing space, too.''

''Hope?'' he called after her.

She looked up.

''Thank you for standing by me. I don't think I could handle this alone.''

She forced a smile. ''Somehow I think the problem will get worse before it gets better.''

He nodded in agreement.

''New subject,'' she said, not meeting his eyes. ''We need to go to Chris's and pick up your car and your clothes.''

''I'm staying?''

''Until I find Britt or I give up.'' Since she didn't plan on either, McLean could be here a long time.

He nodded in tense gratitude.

Marshalling her fragile reserve, she walked down the stairs. Once out of sight, she raced to the master bathroom and threw up. The trembling afterward lasted for hours.

Chapter
Fourteen

McLean waited until he could no longer hear Hope's retreating footsteps before he sagged onto the couch. The implication of the evidence staggered him. What if he really was *possessed*? The entire concept of another being occupying his body made him feel defiled. Unless the ghost made his presence known, how would he even *know*? Would he be forced to do things against his will?

Leaning back, he buried his head in his hands. "Is any of this real? Richard is his own person. Britt may or may not be honorable—if he exists at all. So who in the hell does that make *me*?"

He glanced at the sparse furnishings. He knew so much about them, tiny irrelevant details that only their owner could know. Fear crept through him like a smothering blanket. He desperately needed another explanation, but even the books on the shelves mocked him. Subjects ranged through politics—domestic and international—psychology, science and technology, everything a ghost would need to stay abreast of a changing world he could never again be a part of. McLean even found a couple of renovation guides. He knew which books Britt had read, which ones he hadn't gotten to yet. None of them would appeal to Richard's taste for erotic action-adventure stories. As McLean turned away from the shelf, he realized he didn't know what his own tastes were.

"I am not possessed by the ghost of Britt McLean," he said defiantly. "I refuse to be."

Struggling for answers, he searched Richard's memories, mentally hammering at the wall that kept most of them out of his reach. From what little he could find, the man's thinking appeared completely distorted by an addictive personality. He'd locked himself in a never-ending quest to find the perfect high to escape from a life that didn't suit him. Self-examination hadn't been comfortable, so he'd lived how he wanted, digging an ever deeper hole for himself, narrowing his world until he saw nothing but the inside of the hole. With each new level of descent, he'd found it easier and easier to blame Hope.

McLean wanted to shut away the ugliness, but ignoring truths and potential clues didn't make them any less important. Once he learned how he fit into all of this, he could make a plan to get his life on track—unless he was possessed. A life could be mended or built, but if Britt was influencing his mind, he would never be sure which decisions were his own and which ones were the ghost's. Flashes of Britt's life ebbed and flowed within him, living pieces of the man himself, while Richard's sat there doing nothing. Had the ghost paralyzed the bastard? Was he slowly taking over?

Had Britt—in his rage—taken bits and pieces of himself and Richard and combined them into the persona he thought should live within this body? Each possibility terrified him more than the last.

Out of his depth, he needed help, a friend to walk beside him as he fought for self-identity. But he knew only Hope, and she cared only for Britt. A crushing isolation descended, and with it an eerie familiarity he recognized as belonging to Britt.

"Don't do this to me!" he cried out, digging the heels of his hands into his eyes as if he could rub out the images he so desperately needed to organize. "Britt, did you make me love her because you can't love her yourself? Was creating me your solution for her not having a flesh-and-blood

man to care for her? Damn you! Every time she looks at
me, she must be seeing that animal she was married to!"
But am I that animal, only changed?

McLean stayed in Britt's room, afraid to leave, afraid to
go to sleep. He agonized over every scrap of memory, each
showing a life thrown down the sewer. Futilely, he willed
the pieces together into a cohesive whole he could understand. All he accomplished, though, was to deepen the frustration. Eventually, he glanced up and noticed the pale-gray
dawn lighting the east window. Defeated and more worried
than before, he went downstairs and sought out Hope.

He found her still asleep in her room. Apparently she'd
forgotten to shut and brace her door. Or had that been a
deliberate act of trust? She lay curled on her side, facing
him, one arm curled beneath her head, one strap of her lacy
pajama top slid down a shoulder, hair spread invitingly
across the pillow.

Primitive need slammed into him, driving the air from
his lungs. Richard had shared that bed with her, knew every
line and curve of her body. Night after night she'd sub-
mitted to his demands while he'd ignored her needs entirely. He hadn't cared about her. Not then. God, what a
fool. McLean knew he would give anything to make it up
to her.

As he watched her sleep, a memory filtered to the surface. Richard had announced to her one night that it was
time to start a family. She'd looked at him with equal parts
of anger and grief.

"Your drinking is out of hand," she'd said.

"It is not. But that's not what we're talking about here.
I thought you wanted kids."

"I did." Heartache imprinted its pain all over her face.
"I do."

"So what does this have to do with my drinking? Are
only teetotalers worthy of raising a family?"

"I won't raise a child in an alcoholic home. The beer
goes, or there won't be any children."

"What kind of a bitch would use a kid as an excuse to
get me to quit drinking?" The self-righteous arrogance had
accomplished its task of avoiding any personal accounta-
bility. "So if I don't measure up to your standards of per-

fection then I don't get a family. Nice, Hope. Real loving.''

Tears had welled up in her eyes, but he'd only cared about having his own way. He'd stalked from the room, muttering under his breath, but not until after he'd called her a few more names.

The memory sickened him, but like all the others that belonged to Richard, he clung to it. As long as he had them, he still had the chance to figure out who he was and how to retain his own identity.

He wanted to tiptoe into Hope's room, slide beneath the covers and gather her into his arms. More than sex, he needed the comfort of a woman's touch—her touch. But her heart belonged to Britt. Gritting his teeth, he walked down to the kitchen, wrote her a note and set it by the coffeepot where she'd find it. He tried hard to make the handwriting match what he'd seen on the driver's license and on some old notes he'd found, but he couldn't seem to keep the swirls out of it.

Everything in the house had dual memories except the third floor—and that realm belonged exclusively to Britt. He needed to find something undeniably Richard's—the body's owner—from which to establish a base. Were any of his and Hope's guesses about what had happened right? Was he preparing to fight for survival against a threat that didn't exist? Yet how could it not? Rummaging through the remaining clothes in the garage, he found a tattered old jacket and went for a walk.

Hope stumbled from bed and trudged to the kitchen. The auto brew on the coffeepot had broken. Until she treated herself to a new one, figuring out ways to keep her eyes open until the coffee was done was a rotten way to start each morning. She bumped a piece of paper with her elbow. Sleepily she watched it fall from the counter to the floor. A fuzzy-headed thought suggested that she pick it up, but the idea died an ignominious death.

Rather than hover over the pot as it brewed, she retraced her steps to her bedroom to dress. On the way, the open guest room door caught her attention, and she peeked in to check on McLean. The bed was made, but something told her he hadn't slept in it. The house was too quiet. Something wasn't right. Her morning brain fog lifted abruptly, and she ran upstairs to pull on a sweat suit. Then she tore through the house, calling for him. Even as she searched, she knew she wouldn't find him.

"McLean?" she yelled from the hallway. The quiet intensified. Where could he have gone? After another full search of the house and grounds, she forcibly tied her worry on a short leash. McLean was an adult and not accountable to her.

She had scheduled a paperwork-at-home day and decided that the best use of her time was to get at it. Reluctantly she trudge into the music room to begin. For three hours she worked on assorted contracts and listing updates and the whatnot associated with the less fun aspect of being a real estate agent, but most of her attention stayed attuned to listening for any sound indicating McLean had returned.

When she filled a cup to nuke for hot cocoa, she found the note.

Went for a walk. McLean.

The handwriting was a weird mixture of Britt and Richard. Neither, yet both.

"His coat is still at Chris's," she murmured. "That means he's walking around in shirtsleeves in November—again."

After making a pot of coffee, she filled a thermos, snatched up her car keys, wallet and coat, then jogged out the front door. As she drove through the familiar streets of her neighborhood, she looked for any sign of him. Finding nothing, she headed to the park. Maybe she'd get lucky a second time.

Sure enough, he sat on the same table on the far side of the pond as before, this time wearing a threadbare jacket that couldn't be providing much warmth. Better than nothing, though.

The local duck population had surrounded the table and was eyeing him speculatively. At her approach, they scattered, but not too far in case either human had something edible in their pockets.

"McLean?"

He looked up, eyes hollow, expression drawn. He didn't

answer, just looked at her with a longing that squeezed her heart. Again she was struck by the realization that not even in Britt had she seen a man so utterly alone.

Hope swallowed hard. "Did your walk help?"

"The more I think, the worse the possibilities look."

"You, too, huh?"

He frowned a quick question at her then returned to staring at his feet. The unknowns hung in the air so thickly she could almost see them. Without further comment, she poured coffee into the thermos lid and handed it to him.

He wrapped his long, cold-reddened fingers around it. "Thanks."

"I thought you might be half frozen by now. I was right."

After downing several long gulps, he gave her a crooked smile that didn't last very long. Then she waited him out. If he'd made any discoveries, he'd tell her in his own time.

"I walked around, still trying to find Richard," he said, then drained the cup. "All I came up with were shadows of what *was*. I even went to the bar he frequented. The cleaning crew let me in to look around. I told them I'd lost something."

Hope gave him a refill. "That was quite a risk. The cravings—"

"That was the point," he retorted. "Richard should have stood up and taken notice, fought back. He didn't."

"So you haven't had any breakthroughs?" She nearly added "about Britt," but stopped herself in time. The man had enough on his plate.

"Everything about Richard is passive. It's like looking into someone else's photo album or watching their videotapes."

This time, asking wasn't an option. "What about Britt's memories?"

He flashed her a damning look but controlled it in the next breath and wiped it away. "About the same amounts, but they're active. I feel them, understand them, and that scares the hell out of me." The raw, bloody emotions pouring from him made her ache with sympathy.

Unable to stop herself, Hope perched on the table beside

him, then covered his hand with hers. "I don't care what he did or how bad it looks. Whatever this is all about, he had his reasons. You need to trust him."

"Trust?" McLean echoed faintly.

He turned his hand palm-up and threaded his fingers through hers. The possessive desperation in his grip told her she'd done the right thing. Together, they were fighting a battle no one else would ever believe much less know how to help with. Did that play a part in why she felt an otherwise inexplicable attraction to him?

"You'd forgive him any wrong, wouldn't you," he sighed in flat resignation.

The world centered on their joined hands. She looked deeply into his tormented eyes, unable to see Richard at all. Everything was Britt, from the color of his eyes to the fear of having tampered with something he believed he had no right to. Or maybe it was Britt's contribution to a tender and baffled man who called himself McLean.

"If you were to hazard a guess," she said, "how do you think Britt feels about all this?"

His face fell in deeper resignation. Did he have an answer? Or just not like the answer he'd found? Again, she waited him out.

"He's confused and disgusted," he said finally.

"Sounds like Britt." She leaned toward him. If anyone had suggested that she'd ever want Richard to touch her again, she'd have questioned their sanity. But as she looked into those soft blue eyes, she silently begged him to make the slightest move to indicate that if she wrapped her arms around him, he'd welcome it.

"You want Britt, not me," he said, then hopped to the ground.

That hurt. Then again, the truth often did. "Do both of you feel, or just one?"

The too-thin lines of his face hardened. "Stop talking as if—" He stopped himself, closed his eyes briefly, then eased the tension from his body on a long sigh. "I think only Britt and I feel. I'm not . . . connected enough with Richard to tell what he's doing."

She'd never held Britt, never would, but if a piece of him was within Richard, then this was as close as she'd ever come. Without asking, she slid from the table, put her arms around his waist, pressed her body close and laid her cheek against his chest.

First, he stopped breathing. Then slowly, tentatively, he closed her into a tight embrace and groaned. "Hope, I've wanted this ever since I woke up at the hospital."

She didn't ask which person spoke. Better to imagine him as Britt only. Their embrace deepened, shifted on a level she couldn't quite describe, even though neither of them moved a muscle. Was Britt trying to let her know he was here?

"Hold me," she whispered, needing a surcease from the questions that had no rational answers.

Hesitantly, he tucked her head beneath his chin, gently imprisoning her against him. Then she felt his lips on her hair. The poignancy to the kiss brought an answering cry from her heart. She tilted her head back, seeing only Britt's sadly tender expression, the one she knew so well. Every line, every nuance in him mirrored the need coursing through her veins. She closed her eyes as his lips covered hers and pictured Britt's face. Passion inflamed her.

His lips slanted across hers, searching for a deeper bonding with her soul. The sensual onslaught stole away her breath. She couldn't think, couldn't move. In his arms, she felt suspended between heaven and earth. The world beyond them faded into nothingness. They tasted and devoured each other. She undid the buttons of her heavy winter coat and slid her hands beneath the bottom edge of his jacket. The body heat she found there claimed another piece of her senses. His hands roamed over her body. Then his fingertips brushed across one breast, and fireworks went off in her head and low in her belly. She half turned to give him greater access. He stilled, then dragged in a breath on a low moan and stepped back. His hands slid lingeringly down her ribs then fell away.

Hope whimpered. Every nerve ending stood on edge, demanding a return to the fire that burned between them. "What's wrong?"

"You still want Britt, not me."

"How do you know you're not him?"

He gave her a betrayed look. "With nothing of Richard or McLean? I doubt it."

Sanity gradually replaced the sensual fog. Her breath still came heavily, and her body screamed with want. Trembling, she held motionless as he rebuttoned her coat. This might be Richard's body standing here, but it wasn't Richard's soul—at least, he wasn't in control. She just wished to God she knew what was going on.

"Let's go home before you freeze," she said.

Silent, they walked side by side—untouching—to the parking lot. She drove them to Chris's house where he collected his clothes and car, and they convoyed back to Hawkings House. She tried not to think about Britt never having driven a car. If he was in control, wouldn't he have had problems? McLean certainly hadn't. Or had he drawn from Richard's knowledge?

"Richard always seems so far away," McLean said out of the blue as they walked into the kitchen. "I'm afraid of losing him. He's the only one who has the right to be here."

Hope shuddered. "And I'm afraid of you finding him."

She opened a fresh loaf of bread and fixed lunch. Another one of the seemingly endless silences descended as she worked.

She handed him a sandwich. "What if we're approaching this all wrong?"

"What do you mean?"

"Britt had a reason for whatever he did. That's a given."

"Hope, he isn't—or wasn't—a paragon. He had flaws just like everyone else. Cheating the lottery board comes to mind."

She elected not to pursue that one. Turning to face him, she drove her point home. "What if the way you're struggling to grab *all* the pieces is interfering with whatever Britt had in mind?"

"I don't follow you."

"Have you thought of just letting go of everything and give Britt full control?"

McLean pulled back, his jaw slackening in horror. "Are you out of your mind?"

"Not the last time I checked." Hope leaned close to his

face to drive home her point. "I trust him to do what's right, even if you don't. What if Richard destroyed his mind with that overdose, and the only way Britt could help him was to move in and rebuild him from the inside?"

He blinked at that. "That's the most outrageous theory yet, especially since Britt wanted him dead."

Hope gave him a telling look. "Think about what you feel. It mirrors Britt, not Richard. How else can you explain that Britt is more real to you than Richard?"

His expression tightened with anger. "I have a better one. What if Britt got so tired of being dead that he killed Richard and the empty body became a convenience?"

"Faith," she fired back. "Let Britt take over completely and see what happens."

A deep shudder ripped through his body. "What if I do, and you're wrong? What if Richard is alive and my efforts to hang on to him are all that's keeping him from being buried forever?"

She laid her hand on his chest. He was warm with life. His heartbeat steady and strong beneath her fingers, and his ribs rose slightly with his next breath. It reminded her of the tone in Britt's voice when he'd told her how much he longed to feel the sun on his face, air in his lungs and a heart pumping blood through a living body.

"Britt wasn't perfect in life or in death," she said softly. "But his integrity is worth the gamble. The alternative is to keep on like we've been doing, and I don't know how much longer we can handle the not knowing. Do you?"

He closed his eyes and shuddered. Then he put his coat back on and went outside.

McLean raked the back lawn with far more force than it needed. Oak leaves, pine needles and assorted debris flipped up from the winter grass as if they were alive. He half expected Hope to follow him out to continue the discussion, but she apparently knew how badly he needed to be alone. The forced idleness drove him nearly as crazy as the conflict inside his head. The list of projects Richard had neglected was endless. McLean decided that for however long he lived here or was in control of his thought pro-

cesses, he'd do what he could to get her home in respectable order. He couldn't tell her he loved her. Maybe she'd
see it.

Despite his efforts to block out her proposition, the
words echoed in his ears. How could she expect him to
step aside and let a ghost take over his mind? That was—
of course—if Britt was in there to begin with! The concept
appalled him, but he didn't know what else to try. If it was
true, he had to choose between hanging onto Richard—a
man who'd tried to murder Hope—or embracing a ghost
who'd committed an unspeakable act. What of himself, Mc-
Lean? Didn't he have a right to exist, too?

Remembered sensations of holding Hope in the park
added to the dilemma. His blood burned with them. If she
touched him again, would he muster the integrity to turn
her away, or would he selfishly take her to bed and meet
his own needs?

Days passed. Memories traipsed into his head in drips
and dribbles. They changed nothing, and he was no closer
to bonding with an identity. Richard contributed nothing.
Britt's memories, values and mindset enticed him.

The frontier sheriff had spent his life trying to do right,
making an assortment of good choices and bad along the
way, no better or worse than anyone else. McLean wished
he had Hope's faith in Britt, though. Just how badly had
he wanted to be alive again? Enough to steal another man's
body? Or was that passing judgment without hearing all the
facts?

"What are you thinking?" Hope asked one morning as
they hauled a dozen large bags of yard debris to the street
for garbage pickup.

If he answered honestly, he'd have her in bed before she
could sneeze. Did she know how he ached to run his hands
over her skin, to claim her for his own?

She stood at the curb, waiting for an answer. The stress
of not knowing what had happened to Britt showed in the
dark smudges under her eyes. She watched every move he
made, analyzing, speculating. The tension in the air grew
thick until it was hard to breathe.

"Do you plan to stare at me all day? Or are you going
to say something?" she demanded. The brittle edge to her

voice sharpened, then collapsed. "I'm sorry. You have it far worse than I do. Taking out my worry on you isn't fair."

He stared at her a moment longer, stuffing his hands into his pockets to keep from dragging her close. Taking a deep breath, he conquered the longing as best he could, but the effort left only loneliness to fill in the empty places. He preferred battling the lust. That, at least, he could fight with ethics. But what could he do about having no past and about the terrible sense of being cast adrift it created? Or an uncertain right to a future?

"I watch the way you move," she said tentatively when he didn't speak. "Your body language is more like his ghost's was. You even smile like him. That's hard to watch."

"Do I do anything like Richard?" Why was it he hoped that the answer was no when it needed to be yes? Every muscle in his body locked up as he waited for her answer.

"Not that I've seen."

Not unexpected, but nonetheless disappointing. "Nothing?"

Hope pursed her lips and shook her head. "Would you come inside?" she asked. "I have something I want to try."

"That's the same tone you used just before you took me into Britt's room," he said, making no attempt to hide his suspicion.

"Exactly." A fleeting smiled crossed her face. Then she turned toward the house.

McLean had serious reservations about following her, but when she headed into the old music room, he reminded himself that hiding from a truth didn't alter it.

Without looking behind her, she pulled a spiral notebook from a desk drawer and motioned for him to sit down. As he complied, she handed him a pen and retrieved a section of the newspaper from the trash can by the desk. "I want you to write down everything I say. Don't think about it. Just do it."

Suspicion mushroomed into alarm. "What are you up to?"

She ignored him and began to read aloud an article from the front page. He started scribbling. From one corner of her eye she watched him, dictating just faster than he could write.

When he had half a page written, he put the pen down. "This is enough, Hope. What are you doing?"

She took the notebook from his hand and scanned it, looking for who knew what. A tiny whimper escaped. Her breath came in irregular shallow puffs. "This ought to do it," she said, trying to force calm into her voice.

Then she opened the vault and retrieved an antique handwritten journal. The Britt part of him recognized it. Reverently, she opened it to the middle and laid it in front of him, then placed the page he'd just written beside it.

"Did the same hand write both of these?"

He'd remembered trying to make his handwriting look like Richard's and how miserably he'd failed. When she'd sat him down just now, he hadn't had time to think about how the words looked on the page. He'd just moved the pen across the page, his only thought being to keep up and figure out what she was up to.

"Did they?" she repeated.

Dreading what he'd find, he lowered his gaze to the desk and scrutinized both samples, searching for differences. The journal entries were faint from age, but legible. "I don't know. What I just wrote is more flowing. See how the tail on the—"

"In life, Britt's fingers were shorter than yours—at least that's how his ghost's looked. The only variances I see could be attributable to a difference in hand shape." She dug through a drawer and pulled out her address book. Pieces of oddly shaped papers stuck out at all angles like a pinwheel. She sorted through them and laid one on top of what he'd just written. The note was an involved phone message with two phone numbers and about five sentences. The handwriting was crabbed with harsh angles and rigid lines—like the signature on the driver's license and the other samples he'd seen.

"Richard wrote this?" he asked, knowing the answer.

She pressed a fingertip on the note and another on what

he'd just written. "These are too different for the same man to have written both."

Put that way, he couldn't hide from it. Britt had far more influence on him than he'd previously feared. But she didn't push for his conclusions. Instead, she slid the notebook and message out of the way, leaving only the journal.

She tapped on the beginning of a paragraph. "Read."

"He's a nice enough kid," he read aloud. "Not much on seeing things as they are, though. He wants the world to be as he envisions it. I guess there's a little dreamer in every man, at least the ones who are worth anything. I pray it doesn't get him killed before he learns to handle himself. I'll keep an extra eye out." McLean looked at Hope. "I remember this," he said after a moment. There was no conflict of memories. No sense of duality. Like the third floor of Hawkings House, this was Britt's sole domain. The memory was comfortable, untainted by Richard. God help him, but he liked that—a lot. "This youngster was from England. No more than twenty and completely convinced that the American West he'd read about was the place to be a real man. Poor fool. He got beat up three times before he learned the difference between the way miners brawled and that fancy stuff he learned back home."

"Did he ever get himself straightened out?"

In spite of everything, McLean smiled at the memory. "Yeah, he opened up a store in Dry Diggin's, married a local girl and was starting a family when Carbow—"

Hope gave him a level look. "You called the kid a youngster just now. That's not a term Richard would ever use. And the last part of the 'youngster's' story isn't mentioned in any of Britt's journals. Richard couldn't possibly know any of that." She pressed on. "Did you notice you're not fighting your words anymore?" she added.

"What do you mean?" he rasped out.

"What you said just now. It was relaxed. You weren't coming across as an imitation of Richard."

"Is that how I sound?" When worded that way, he knew full that's what he'd been doing. But how could he face the implications? Could he handle that much defeat?

"Let go. If Britt is there, he'll tell us what's going on."

The will to survive reared up. "Absolutely not!"

"But—"

"I don't trust him like you do. You don't know what it was like being dead for two mortal lifetimes. He doesn't want to go back!"

She should have flinched from the anger, but she leaned over the desk until she stood nose-to-nose with him. Then she laid her hand on his arm. "Britt will do what's right."

"What if *I* just disappear? I want to live, too." He drew her fingers to his lips. He wanted her so badly he hurt, but he had no right—whichever man he was.

Chapter Fifteen

The next few days McLean avoided Hope as much as possible without being rude. Several times she tried to get close to him, but he pretended not to notice, afraid of what would happen otherwise. He needed her to stand by *him* through this ordeal because she cared about *him* and not anyone else. He and Britt wanted her. Neither could have her. The graphic nature of Richard's memories with her added to the torment. This was one instance where he appreciated Richard's lack of voice.

"You're frowning," she said, walking up to him as he swept a fresh batch of leaves from the front sidewalk.

"I'm thinking."

She gave him an attentive look.

He changed the subject before what little honor he had dissolved. "I need to find this body's rightful owner. It's not fair to make a decision without Richard's input. If exposure to things that pertained only to Britt made him more clear to me, then maybe exposure to stimuli exclusively Richard's will do the same. This photo-album effect isn't smoothing out at all."

"Are you finding any trace of Richard at all?" Hope's expressive face showed how badly she wanted him to say no. Unfortunately, it was the truth.

"He contributes nothing. No desires, no opinions, no thoughts of any kind. I can only find pictures and impressions, and those are all from before the overdose."

She tried to hide her relief, but her eyes glowed with it. "What about Britt?" she asked, her voice trembling.

"He seems to be . . . fine."

"So he *is* alive? Within you?" She clutched at his arm. Reluctantly, McLean nodded.

"Whole?" Her voice cracked around the single word.

He debated long and hard before he answered that one. "He appears to be. I seem to be thinking more and more like him all the time."

She sucked in a sharp breath and leaned into him, burying her forehead against his shoulder. He fought the need to sweep her into his arms, gritting his teeth from the strain.

"Thank you, God," she breathed. Tears dampened his sleeve. Her grip spasmodically tightened and released several times before she stepped back. "Oh, Britt, you're okay." She gazed up at him, wiping tears from her cheeks. "I've been so scared. Can you hear me?"

"Stop that, Hope!" He moved further away. "He had his life! This isn't his body! His being here is wrong!"

"But—"

"I know what he felt just before he followed Richard to the hospital." McLean couldn't stand to watch her outpouring of love for the ghost, not when he needed it so badly for himself. "Britt wanted Richard's blood. He planned a killing."

The vehemence set her back, but not for long. "Britt may have wanted Richard dead, but he stopped himself before—"

"In his mind, that bastard was a rabid dog that needed to be shot! What does that tell you?"

Her shoulders squared in a battle stance, and she stepped in front of him. "Britt, if you can hear me, I will always believe in you. You're not a murderer."

"Oh, God, Hope!" he cried out. "Britt wasn't perfect. Why can't you see his flaws! I do!"

"McLean, let go and let Britt do whatever it is he"— she made a helpless gesture toward his body that looked a lot like an aborted embrace—"went in there for."

He just didn't have the emotional reserves to pursue this new angle. "I'm going to talk to Richard's mother today. Eddie and Chris, too, if they're not too wasted."

"What are you going to say?" Her body tensed, reminding him of a female predator protecting her mate. At his first slip, she'd pounce.

"That my memory is a mess and ask what they can tell me that might help. Richard should start filling in the blanks."

Her lips pursed and eyes hardened. He suspected that if he did anything to hamper Britt, he'd have a war on his hands.

"What will you do if that doesn't work?" she asked.

"Keep at it." How had this turned into a sparring match? "I also plan to get a job. I have too much time on my hands. That's not healthy, and I need to contribute around here. I don't like being . . . kept."

One side of her mouth lifted in a cat-in-the-cream look. "Kept. That's exactly how Britt would have worded it."

Damn.

"Any specific employment plans?" she asked, forcing him away from any damage control he might think of.

"I have enough of Richard's memories that I could probably function as an investment counselor."

"That might be a problem. Richard burned all his bridges in that area. Lost every one of his clients. Besides, I don't believe Britt could think of a profession more dull."

She had him there. "Britt's professional skills are a century outdated," he conceded. "So, that leaves me with some form of unskilled labor. Won't be the first time I've bent my back to put food on a table."

The corner of her mouth lifted. "*You* have?"

He nearly swore. "Don't, Hope. I'm fighting for my own right to live—and I don't even know if it's mine to fight for. If you have any compassion at all, stop hounding me."

He'd intended to hurt her and, from the shadows that flashed across her face, he'd succeeded. A moment later, she took a short breath, reached up and drew his head down for a fleeting kiss. Her lips were cool from the November chill, and he wanted to drown in them. Love shone in her eyes, and he pretended—if only for a moment—she meant it for him.

"Don't judge Britt until you've studied him as thoroughly as I have and for as long."

As she walked away, he felt his heart rip from his chest and follow her.

"Richard, dear," Ruth McLean gushed as she opened her front door and saw McLean standing on her porch.

He hated being mistaken for that hellspawn, but he didn't have any choice. "Hello . . . Mom."

"Come in." The petite woman stood back and motioned him inside. Her abrupt gestures reminded him of a nervous hummingbird.

As he entered the house, he sifted through Richard's memories, trying to find one of them that had some life to it. The man had been raised here. Surely something about this place would spark an emotional reaction.

McLean studied the immaculate chrome- and glass-furnished living room. The air smelled faintly of potpourri. As Ruth gave him a beatific smile, he recognized her as the ultimate nurturer—well-meaning but oblivious to the difference between loving support and destructive coddling.

"I have been so worried about you since you moved back in with Hope." The defensive note was unmistakable. "She's not good for you. Come home where you belong."

"Hope has never been my problem, Mom," he said softly.

"How can you say that after all the misery she caused you?"

That infuriated him, and he took a moment to calm down before he answered. "Despite what I told you before, Hope was in no way responsible for my alcoholism or drug addictions."

Ruth gasped as if he'd slapped her.

"I drank and used because I wanted to. I liked the buzz. But that's not socially acceptable, so I had to find a scapegoat. Hope was handy."

"I don't believe that for a minute!" The tiny woman rose up to her full height, her dark eyes flashing.

A fresh wave of loneliness and isolation swept into him, breath-stealing in its strength.

"Richard, you deserve so much better than her. Haven't I told you that all along?"

According to Richard's memories, she'd done a lot worse. From infancy, she invented excuses for misbehavior and covered up for him. Disgusted, McLean shook his head.

"Mom, the psychology of chemical dependency is very complex." That knowledge came from Britt's studies. McLean fought down a shudder. "Maybe one day we'll talk about it. In the meantime, Hope did nothing wrong. I'm the one who chose those paths."

"But—"

He held up a restraining hand. "Mom, please. Placing blame is in the past." Then he thought of something. If he was successful in finding Richard, the man would need proper support from his family, not the kind he'd had all along. Lovingly, he put his hands on Ruth's shoulders. "I'm trying to stay clean and sober. If I fail, the best way to love me is to be tough. Don't support my excuses or excesses."

She worried at her hands, her brows pinched. "You're asking me to be mean?"

"No," he added gently. "Just make me stand accountable for my own actions. Go to Al-Anon and learn how." She'd probably learn a lot of hard truths about herself, too. He expected the self-examination that went with it would be painful but ultimately, she'd be much happier. McLean made a mental note to warn Hope that her meetings might get invaded. "Help me the right way."

"I don't like it. You're not the same. What's wrong with you?" She looked up at him with wounded eyes, and he felt sorry for her.

Impulsively, he kissed her on the forehead.

Ruth's mouth dropped open in shock. Hadn't that jackass even kissed his mother once in a while? Again, he searched through the mental photo album but found nothing. A mother deserved some respect and affection from her children. If that wasn't something Richard bothered with, then whatever affection McLean showed her could be all she got for a long time.

"Yes, Mom, I'm sure." He smiled at her. "I don't want to talk about that, though. I came because I need a favor."

"Oh?" Her eyes became avid. He suspected she wasn't happy unless she was working herself into the ground for someone else. Poor thing.

"My memory is like Swiss cheese. I want to sit down and have you tell me about myself. Childhood or recent. Makes no difference. Just talk, and let me listen."

"You're hoping that things will start to click if I pull on the right thread."

He widened his smile. "Exactly. Pretend I'm a stranger wanting to know everything about your son."

For a week, McLean bounced between Ruth's house and the apartment where Eddie and Chris lived, immersing himself in the life of a man he detested. Other than becoming more revolted than before and finding a few inconsequential pages for the mental photo album, he made no progress. Were these scraps nothing more than what remained physically stored in the brain? Old abandoned files? The implication horrified him. Death?

He elected not to discuss it with Hope.

One morning after Hope left for work, McLean headed out to hunt for a job. The constant self-analysis was driving him crazy, and he needed work to focus on.

The department store had already hired its Christmas help, but he filled out an application anyway. By six, he'd filled out four applications and had one interview. Nothing looked promising. As he drove back to Hawkings House in defeat, his eyes caught a HELP WANTED sign at the pizza parlor.

Thirty minutes later, he was wearing a red-checked apron with a hand-printed name tag that said "McLean." He'd written Richard on his application but explained that he preferred his surname. The owner gave him an odd look, but being an ex-military man, he went along with it.

McLean hoped Richard would be highly insulted at lowering himself from a position of significant income to smearing pizza sauce on raw dough, but, as always, no comment came. After he'd been there a couple of hours, he happened to walk by the drink dispenser as Sally, one of the counter girls, filled a beer pitcher. He inhaled deeply. The pungent odor of the brew called to him. But it wasn't a craving, just a pleasant thought. Over a hundred years had passed since his last glass of beer.

"McLean, are you okay?" she asked, touching his arm. "All the color just drained from your face."

"I'm fine," he choked out. Giving her a too-casual shrug, he turned away.

Throughout the rest of his shift, the beer incident increased in significance. Britt's memory and desire had been a natural extension of himself. By closing at ten-thirty, McLean had come to a place where he couldn't escape the most probable conclusion—Britt was inexorably taking over. Discouraged, he returned to Hawkings House. He found Hope in the music room.

Warily, she looked up from her desk. "I expected you before this."

McLean closed his eyes, castigating himself for his stupidity. "I'm sorry. I was so intent on finding work that I didn't think to call." He explained about being hired at the Pizza Palace. "Once I get paid—and it won't be much— I'll give you everything I don't need for gas in the car."

She gave him a sadly longing smile. "Richard always considered his paycheck his own. Giving it all to me is exactly the type of thing Britt would do."

McLean wanted to be sick. "I think I'll go to my room for the night."

"You don't have to." She rose from behind her desk, sexual need riding low in the sultry heat of her voice. He saw it written in every supple line of her body, smelled it in the air between them.

Arousal slammed into him with full force, damning him even more. "Yes, I do, Hope."

"Why?"

"We've been through this."

"So? We'll go through it again." She slid her arms around his waist and gazed up at him, invitation in her eyes.

"After what Richard did to you, how can you want to make love with me?"

"You're not Richard."

"Doesn't looking at his face bother you at all?"

She leaned back, her expression glowing with the quiet confidence of a woman whose soul knew the man she loved. "Watching you running around in his body isn't easy, but I love the man you are. The shell you're occupying can bring us together if you'll let it."

"What are you saying?"

"I love you, Britt McLean."

"How can you defend what I—he—has done!"

"I told you. Because I love you."

His breathing came hard and fast, and he couldn't look at her. "No."

"You have no right or reason to condemn yourself."

"Doesn't he?" He tried to peel her arms away, but she clung to him as if both their lives depended upon it. Maybe they did.

"McLean, I don't care if Richard is dead or buried so deep he can't ever find his way back," she said. "He *earned* his fate. Leave him to it."

Silence descended between them, stretching into ever more profound depths. McLean floundered helplessly in it.

"You can't mean that," he said eventually.

"With all my heart."

His conscience demanded that he step away from her embrace. But he needed the warmth of her body against his, needed comfort far more than sex. If ever a man had the chance to choose his hell, this was it. After kissing her hard and fast, he grasped her wrists, jerked her hands free from his body and pushed her from him. The loss of contact tore chunks from his soul. "Good night, Hope." With his last ounce of will, he fled to the guest room.

For three days, he spent every extra moment at Ruth's, immersing himself in Richard, coming home only after he was sure Hope was asleep for the night. Still, every effort to revive Richard failed. McLean ebbed and flowed in tune to Britt until the two became inseparable. Self-hatred settled in. His earlier conclusion of Britt taking over was wrong.

He wanted to hide from the ugliness of knowing his worst
fears had proven true, but honor—what little he had left—
demanded that he hold himself accountable. The time for
confessions had come. He'd never been a coward, and he
refused to be one now.

After his shift at the pizza parlor ended, he drove to
Hawkings House. But Hope wasn't home. Why? It was
close to eleven. Where was she? By midnight, the worry
sent him out into the night. Heaven knew she'd gone hunting for *him* enough times.

He found her car in the parking lot, her office darkened
and looking deserted. He tried the door. It wasn't locked.
In the shadows, he saw a hunched-over feminine silhouette
at her desk—Hope. She gasped as he stepped inside. She
probably couldn't see him any better than he could see her.

"It's just me," he said in a low voice. "Watch your
eyes. I'm turning on the light." He gave the wall switch a
quick flip. Harsh glare from overhead flooded the room.

"What are you doing here?" she demanded, squinting
and grabbing for a fresh tissue. Her violet eyes were puffy
and bloodshot, and her nose was red. "You scared me."

"You're crying," he said, heartsick.

"What a brilliant observation. Thank you." She drew in
a shuddering breath and blew her nose.

"What's wrong?" He found himself by her desk without
any conscious recollection of having crossed the room.

"The stress finally got to me, and I needed to let it out."

"I'm always hurting you."

"Not on purpose." She blew her nose again. "I understand why you won't let me close, but I can't take any
more. I need you."

He caught himself moving to put his arms around her,
but checked himself. She gave him a level look, and he
groaned.

"That noise was a Britt classic. Richard's groans always
had a whiny note to them."

How often had he longed to hold her, knowing that being
together was impossible? Now he had a chance. To claim
it, all he had to do was betray the man he'd always been.

She blew her nose again. "Any revelations today?"

Choosing his words carefully," he said, "Does acceptance of an old one count?"

Her fingers clenched around the soggy tissue and she held her breath.

The truth came heavy in his mouth. "Ever since I woke up in the hospital that morning, I've done everything in my power to give Richard the chance to demand his right to exist, but I can't find him."

"Not at all?" she asked in a small voice. A tiny glimmer lifted some of the gloom from her eyes.

He didn't want to see it, nor did he want to see her reaction to the next. "I believe Richard is dead." There. It was said.

"Who's McLean?" Her voice cracked.

"He was—is—the result of trying to sort through a dead man's memories and a ghost's. When I woke up, I had no memory at all, not even of how a body worked or how to talk. Richard stopped the night of his overdose. On a subconscious level, Britt could never accept occupying a body not his, so he—*I*—ended up pulling myself apart without realizing it. *My* memories and thoughts build moment by moment, just like any other man. McLean is an identity that my subconscious invented to keep from having no identity at all."

Silence hung electric in the air.

"So Richard is really dead?" The question came out flat, nothing more than a final confirmation of a truth she had already accepted.

"I see no reason to believe otherwise."

Life seemed to fill her at that moment. She drew in a breath that brought with it a freshness he hadn't seen in a long time. Her eyes drifted closed. Her lips moved as if in prayer. "You're one hundred percent Britt McLean? No bits and pieces of anyone else?"

The truth shamed him, but he stood up to it. "I don't know how or why, but yes, it's me."

In a flash, she threw herself into his arms, showering his face with teary kisses. "I've missed you so much," she cried.

At first he could do nothing but accept the tender assault with stunned resignation, drinking it in, knowing he'd never get his fill. Then he hardened himself to his own needs, carefully took hold of her arms and held her from him. "Think about what you're doing."

Her features pinched with bewilderment. "I'm trying to hug the man I adore. Why do you have a problem with that? You love me, too, don't you?"

"You know I do." He turned his face away, unable to stand the confusion in her eyes.

"Britt, what's wrong? You're alive again. Why aren't you celebrating?"

"You don't know how I got this way!"

"Do you?"

"No," he said in a small voice.

"I don't care." She made a slicing motion with her hand. "You're here. With me. Alive. Whole. Nothing else matters."

She reached for him again, but he took her wrists, pressed them together and stepped back. The feel of her soft skin against his palms was heaven and hell rolled into one. He sucked in a breath and forced himself to let her go.

"Hope, how can you say you don't care when you were sitting in your office crying in the dark!"

"It was self-pity and guilt."

"What?"

"Self-pity because all I want is you, and you fight me every step of the way. Guilt because I want Richard to be gone—even if it means he's dead." Her soft features hardened into a determination that unnerved him. "The circumstances of how you came to be a living man again don't matter to me one iota. I want to build a life with a man who is gentle and kind and honorable—you."

"Honorable? Hope, I may have *murdered* the man. I followed him for no other reason than to end his wretched life!"

"So you *do* remember more of that night," she accused.

"Yes, but not enough. I remember letting you believe I'd calmed down more than I had. I remember thinking how easy it would be to stop his heart. The doctors would blame it on the overdose, and you'd never suspect any different. I planned to enjoy it!"

Her gentle features smoothed in shock. With a shake of her head, she dismissed it. "But you didn't. When it came down to the actual killing, you stopped yourself. I know you. I studied you for years. I know how you think, how you feel." She stepped up to him, fists clenched at her sides, then stared into his face. "If he's dead, then he died on his own."

"Listen to yourself, Hope!" He ached with the need to believe her version of the events, but he remembered too clearly the bloodlust. "You can't ignore the facts by willing them away! That night, I was consumed by hatred, jealousy and envy. Richard had a body. He could hold you in his arms and make love to you! Don't tell me about my honor. I know how badly I wanted him dead, and for no more honorable reason than he had something I wanted—life!"

Before he could collect himself, she again closed the distance between them. Unconditional love and trust radiated from her like the inviting heat from a fire. He held himself rigid as she slid her arms around his ribs and pressed her body against his. How many more times would he be able to find the strength to push her away?

"My faith in you is strong enough for both of us, Britt McLean. If you can't believe in yourself, then let me believe for you."

His willpower fractured, and he swept her into a hard embrace. He buried his face in her hair and held her as the only anchor in a world that made no sense at all. He drew in the sweet scent of her hair, the silken texture of it against his face, and the heat of her body through their clothes.

"Hope, you don't understand," he groaned. "There can be no moral way for me to be where I am. It's an abomination."

She lifted her face and laid a feather-soft kiss on his throat. "Whatever you faced that night, you conducted yourself with integrity. You're a good man, Britt. I'll never believe otherwise."

"How can you say that?" He stared down into her loving eyes, torn between remaining true to himself and swallowing the lovely fantasy she wove around his senses. "I was trapped between the living world and death for a hundred and twenty-seven years. That's nearly two mortal life-

times! You can't know what that was like. Then I found
you. And as irrational as this seems, you were *my* woman.
Mine! That bastard wouldn't leave you alone. He had a
perfectly good life that he was throwing away. I appointed
myself judge, jury and executioner!''

The serenity on her face never wavered. ''But you didn't
go through with it.''

He stared at her in wonder. ''What if I regain the rest of
the memory, and I learn that's exactly what I did?''

''Then I'll forgive you.'' Simple. Unadorned. Faith.
''You know what you wanted to do. But you don't know
what you *did.* Until the facts are all in, give yourself the
benefit of the doubt. All men—including ghosts—are innocent until proven guilty.''

''I'm living in a body that isn't rightfully mine. How
much more proof of guilt do you need?'' He turned his
face away, and she took hold of his chin and pulled it back.

''I don't pretend to know much about ghosts or what
they can do or why. But I don't believe for one minute that
anything—not even Richard—pushed you over the edge.
You may have been tempted, but you didn't fall.'' She gave
him another slow kiss on the throat, the highest spot she
could reach without him bending to her. Within that simple
gesture he found more completion than he'd ever experienced with anyone in his combined 164 years.

A new blast of sexual heat slammed into the body he'd
somehow stolen, and he moaned from the impact. When
they'd kissed before, he hadn't known who he was, and
he'd had McLean to act as a buffer. All that was past. He
was Britt McLean, a dead man who'd finally realized his
fondest dream—to feel a heart beating in a chest again, to
know the touch of another human being. And he'd gotten
far more than that—a woman who loved him without reservation, one who clearly needed him to take her to his
bed. The pressure of refusing grew suffocating.

He stared hard into her eyes, desperate to find something
about himself that he could believe in as strongly as she
did. But all he could remember was following the ambulance, calculating the amount of electrical charge needed to
stop Richard's heart.

Hope's eyes drifted shut, and her lips eased apart in invitation. The flames of need and desperation dragged him under, and his lips claimed hers. He took whatever she gave, then demanded more. In his mind, that made him no better than Richard.

A tiny voice of reason clamored to be heard. He couldn't make love to her. He'd undoubtedly killed a man, then blithely moved into the corpse. If that was true, what else was he capable of? "Hope, I want you more than any woman I've ever known. But this body doesn't belong to me. How can I use it for my own—"

She clamped one hand over his mouth. "I don't care whose body you're in, Britt. Make love to me."

Dragging in a long breath, he again inhaled the sweet scent of her. "No."

She whimpered breathlessly. "Stop questioning everything! We're together. That's all that matters."

Was there no reasoning with her? He tried to stay focused on doing what was right, but the purely male part of him reveled in the knowledge that this incredible woman wanted him so badly that nothing else mattered to her. As erotic as that was, it also humbled him.

"Until I know what I did, I can't move on as if nothing happened. Maybe someone else could, but not me."

"What if you never remember the rest of that night? Richard was so drugged up, his brain may have just dumped the memory altogether. Depending on how your memories are being stored in there, maybe you can't retrieve it, either. If that happens, are you going to deny us a life together indefinitely?"

Her relentless pursuit turned his already overheated blood into molten flame. The force sent tremors through him. Logic and ethics began to elude him. "I can't answer that."

"I'll fight for you, Britt," she declared. "Don't think I won't."

"Hope, you're so different now," he groaned. "When I first came to Hawkings House, you couldn't stand up for yourself at all. Now . . ."

Her lips twitched with a suppressed smile. "The mouse

grew teeth, fangs and a backbone. Consider yourself
warned.''

''So I see.'' For a long moment, they stared at each other,
neither willing to bend. ''Come home, Hope. I can't leave
you here. You're not thinking clearly.''

She trailed a finger lovingly down his arm. Even through
the sleeve of his coat, his skin ignited where she touched,
and he shuddered from the heat.

''Britt, how much longer do you think we can hold off
the inevitable?''

''As long as we have to.'' He turned from her and retrieved her coat from the hook by the door. ''Please come
home. I can't sleep knowing you're here by yourself.''

''Maybe home is the best place to finish this discussion.''

The undercurrent turned up his lust a few notches, turning sexual frustration into raw pain. She said nothing more
as she locked up the office, and they climbed into separate
cars. He followed her home, consumed by need and barely
able to pay attention to traffic.

Once home, he locked the front door and followed her
into the ladies' parlor to draw the drapes. Still trying to
fight the fire in his blood, he kept his back to her. As he
turned to go, he caught a glimpse of her from the corner
of his eye.

Hope stood in the middle of the room, calmly tossing
her blouse on the back of the couch beside the blazer she'd
already discarded. She'd kicked off her shoes, and they lay
on their sides on the carpet. Standing in her stockinged feet,
bra and skirt, she was the most sensuous woman he'd ever
seen.

A fresh onslaught of lust ripped through him. The world
tilted. ''Don't do this.''

She unzipped her skirt, dropped it and stepped free. His
mouth went dry. Then she peeled down her pantyhose and
stood before him in a lacy bra and panties, waiting for him
to make a move. When he didn't, she cocked her head just
enough to make her soft brown hair sweep across one
shoulder. No woman could ever have appealed to him
more. The blatant invitation shut down most of his brain.

''Make love to me, Britt.'' She moved toward him.

The right thing to do would be to walk from the room
and pretend he'd seen nothing. But his feet wouldn't work.
The best he could do was hold his arms rigidly at his sides
as she slid her arms around his neck then snuggled against
him. The softness of her bare belly pressed hard against his
erection. With his last shred of willpower, he pulled her
arms down. But before he could step away, she calmly
reached behind her and unfastened her bra.

Her skin glowed in the dim light. Each curve of her body
called to him. He couldn't breathe, and he didn't dare
move.

"If you can look me straight in the eyes and say you
don't want me, I'll go take a cold shower," she challenged.

"I'm not made of stone, Hope."

"That's why I love you." She brushed his chest lightly
with her palms.

Britt was on fire. Then she pressed her body—nude except for her panties—full length against him. Logic, morals
and personal honor burned to ash in the resulting inferno.
A moment later, he and Hope were upstairs in the master
bedroom, his clothes dropped haphazardly across the foot-
board.

Their lovemaking came fierce, lacking in finesse or
charm. He didn't or couldn't think about anything beyond
the primitive need to claim Hope for his own. She gave in
to his every demand, using her body to coax him into asking for more. Birth control was a nuisance and new to him,
but he accepted it. The last complication they needed was
to bring a child into this mess.

When the flames finally died down, she lay in his arms,
limp and sated. Still she draped one arm around him to
hold him in place, keeping him a willing captive. The
sheets and blankets had been thrown to the side in tangled
disarray, showing him every inch of the woman who'd so
freely entrusted him with her body and her heart.

At first he didn't notice the chill, but as she burrowed in
closer to his body for warmth, he pulled the blankets up
around their shoulders.

"Britt?"

"Hmm?" He didn't want to think about anything.

Thinking meant using his conscience, and he didn't have the energy to fight that war right now.

"Do you really love me?"

"Hope, how can you question that! Of course I love you." He held her so tight he worried he might be in danger of cracking her ribs.

"Then promise me no matter what else you learn about that night at the hospital, you'll find a way to accept it and move forward with our lives."

"Don't ask that of me. There are too many unknowns." He sat up and put some distance between them. "I just made love to you with another man's body, a man I loathe! How can you ask me to make it worse? That's obscene."

"What's obscene is the way you existed for the last twelve decades."

"What if he's not really dead? Just buried too deep for me to find now?"

"Then it's even more important for us to take advantage of the little time we have together. Don't throw that away. When the rest of your memories resurface, we'll decide together what to do."

The adoration and faith in every line of her expression humbled him. "I want to, Hope, but—"

"Do you know what your problem is?" she asked, tenderly.

Wariness coiled around him like a snake. "What?"

"Your greatest strength is also your prison. I always admired your ability to stay true to your beliefs regardless of how tempted you were to abandon them. You once wrote that after everything is said and done, all a man has are his character and his convictions. They're the only two things that cannot be taken from him. They can only be lost or sold."

"If you understand that, why are you trying to—"

"I'm not. I want you to listen to that other part of yourself, too. The part that believes in mercy and forgiveness and compassion. You so freely gave that part of yourself to others. Give some to yourself."

With every fiber of his being, he wanted to latch on to her vision of him, but he couldn't forget how badly he'd wanted blood that night.

"Britt, you're fighting a battle. You retreated to what you perceive as your most secure high ground—not necessarily the *best* ground."

He drank deeply of her words, wanting to believe. But was she right? Reverently, he touched her face. "I'll think about it. That's all I can promise."

They made love half the night, loving then sleeping, waking each other with feather-soft kisses and caresses that proved how in tune they were with each other. Never had he known such contentment or such urgency. Each time the loving began again, he gave her everything he had, knowing it might have to last them forever.

Chapter Sixteen

A hard, winter rain drenched Manzanita, the intensity of the storm reminding Britt of the one when Tyler Carbow murdered him. Over a century of winters had passed through these mountains since he'd last experienced a body that wanted nothing more than to shrink away from physical discomfort. The phrase "guilty pleasure" came to mind as he dressed in Richard's ski jacket and insulated pants, then went outside. Tipping his face up to the biting cold and pounding rain, he savored the sensations.

Hope was finishing up her breakfast, and he prayed she wouldn't follow him. He needed time alone to think and some hard manual labor to bleed off some of the tension.

The roof and one wall of the carriage house had fallen in. If he was still here in spring—mortal or back to being a ghost—he would rebuild it. Hope would like that. For now, he needed to beat away the old mortar from the stone so they could be reused. The perfect project. In the garage he found a ten-pound sledgehammer and got to work.

"What are you doing out here?" Pat demanded from behind him. Not what he needed today. He glanced over his shoulder. She had one hand on her hip, the other holding an umbrella.

Britt dropped the sledge hammer on the growing pile of

cleaned stones and stood to face her. "Good morning."

When he didn't answer with an anger to match hers, she raised one eyebrow in speculation and cocked her head.

"I saw you out here when I was parking the car and decided to see what you were up to."

He glanced at her minivan in the drive. "Oh?" The woman was primed for a fight, and he didn't particularly want to give her any ammunition. Best to stay quiet until he learned what her problem was.

"Your tactic to worm your way back into her life was a stroke of genius. Possessed by the ghost of Britt McLean. If you weren't so reprehensible, I'd take my hat off to you."

Cold water dripped down his hair and face. "From what I've seen," he said, "you're the only one who cares enough about her to take on battles that aren't yours to fight. If Hope has discussed the specifics of the situation with you, that's between you and her."

She was not to be dissuaded. "Poor Richard. Of course, you need Hope to help you find out of it's true, yada, yada, yada. Or do you pretend to be Britt when you're crawling into bed with her?"

If Pat had been a man, Britt would have laid her flat. As it was, though, he could understand how the situation looked.

At the rapid splish-splash of footsteps in the mud, they both turned. Hope ran toward them, lips pursed and head held high.

"Hi, there!" she said with exaggerated cheer. "Fighting as usual, I see."

"I stopped by to punch a few holes in his story and ask if you wanted to go shopping. My husband and the kids are having their once a month Dad-and-kids-only playday."

Hope sidestepped the comment about Britt. "So your brood threw you out of the house, huh?" She grinned.

Pat's gaze locked onto Britt's. In that hard-eyed stare he saw an unwavering promise to expose him for a fraud.

"Let's all go in the house and make nice, okay?" Hope laid a hand on his sleeve. She'd put on a coat but no gloves, and was beginning to shiver. "I want you to tell her the whole story. She studies ghosts and haunted places as a hobby. Maybe she can add some insight.''

The idea appalled him. "No one else should know about this, Hope. It's not right.''

Her hand slid down his arm until her fingers curled around his. The simple skin-to-skin touch of the woman he loved battered at his resolve. He squeezed her hand. Pat's eyes snapped fire.

"Britt, I know why you don't want anyone else to know. But we need a friend. Someone who isn't as emotionally involved in this as we are. A clearer head and all that.'' She shrugged. Tightening her grip, she turned toward the house and pulled him along after her.

Once she had them in the ladies' parlor, coats hung and everyone seated by the fire, Britt blew out his breath. Pat watched him like a cat in the mood to play with its food. He didn't like this, not one bit. But Pat wasn't going away, and if Hope needed the support of a friend, then he couldn't bring himself to say no.

"This goes no further," he told the other woman.

Pat raised an eyebrow again, and Hope's lips curved into a victorious smile.

"Right, Pat?'' Hope said, an edge to her voice.

Pat shrugged. "Sure. But don't be too disappointed when I prove that Richard is the same old dirtbag as always, but with a new trick.''

Britt took charge at that point. "Ma'am, as far as I know, Richard is dead. I'm Britt McLean.''

Her eyes flared with incredulity. Then she burst out laughing. "You don't honestly expect me to believe that, do you? That's worse than your first story.''

Britt studied the determination in Hope's best friend's face. He would have left the room then, but Hope took his hand again and was gently threading her fingers through his.

"You want proof," he said.

"That would be nice, yes," Pat drawled.

He took a moment to organize his thoughts. "The night you took Hope to that . . . *establishment*''—the idea that she had gone someplace to watch men dancing naked still offended him—"you wanted her to laugh, to enjoy herself, to break free of her chains. You meant well, but it was too much for her, and you've felt vaguely guilty over it ever since. You have a good heart, Pat, but often you're not long on common sense. That night pointed it out rather graphically to you."

Her mouth sagged open. "You're guessing."

"Am I guessing about the way you watched her during the performances, hoping she'd unwind a little?"

"How could you know that?"

"That was before Richard's overdose. I was still a ghost then, and I was *there*."

"I don't believe you."

"One day you arrived at work before Hope did, and you told Brian about the 'gay guy' Hope had a thing for. You were worried and didn't know if you needed to protect your friend or stay out of it. He told you Hope was an adult and to leave her alone. The advice was what you expected, but you were disappointed anyway. You turned away from him, accidentally knocking a stack of papers from his desk to the floor. Every time you looked at him for the rest of the morning, you were embarrassed even though you tried not to show it."

The roar of a fresh downpour sounded outside, punctuating the tension in the room.

"How would you know any of that?"

Britt leaned forward. "I was there." He explained about his former ability to read emotions. She paled. "You've been lonely most of your life, and Hope is the one friend you feel cares about you—flaws and all."

Hope's eyes rounded. Pat wouldn't look at her.

"You're overprotective of those people who are important to you," he continued, "because you're afraid of losing them."

Pat drew into herself defensively. "Richard wouldn't know that."

"Richard was a fool," Britt spat. "Ma'am, I don't care whether you accept who I am or not as long as you're there for Hope whenever she needs you." He snatched the still-dripping ski jacket off the coat tree. "Write down a list of

questions for me while you two are shopping. In the meantime, I have a project to do.''

Pat grilled Hope for most of the day as they both whittled
down their Christmas shopping list.

"I'm as close to an expert on Britt McLean as there is.
Do you honestly think someone like Richard could fool
me?''

From the overwhelmed shadows in Pat's eyes, Hope
doubted she'd recovered yet from Britt's pronouncements.
Pat slowly shook her head. "There's no way he could. But
that doesn't mean there isn't another explanation."

"I saw him as a ghost. He proved to me then who he
was, and I believe with all my heart that Richard is dead
and that somehow Britt wound up in his body. And if I'm
not very, very careful, once he can prove to his satisfaction
that he's a murderer, he'll commit suicide to put that body
in the ground where he thinks it belongs."

Pat's breath came out in a low whistle. "Shit."

"Will you help me?"

Pat turned glazed eyes on her and nodded. It still took
Hope another two hours to get her friend's mind focused.

"Okay, he lived with sensory deprivation for a god-
awful length of time," Pat said, thinking out loud. "He
wanted to feel a body again. Right?"

"Right." Hope tensed with expectation.

"Well, then, let's feed the flesh." Pat crossed her arms.
"Do I get to talk to him about what it was like being a
ghost?''

"If we're successful, he'll be around a long time. You
can pick his brain all you want."

"Cool." She grabbed Hope's arm. "First stop, the book-
store for a gourmet cookbook. You're going to assault his
little taste buds until he has love handles the size of Man-
hattan.''

Hope hugged her. "Thank you."

Pat shrugged. "That's what friends are for."

By the time Hope returned to Hawkings House, she'd
bought an arsenal of sensory delights, including a see-
through teddy, a pipe and a boxed set of specialty blend

tobaccos. Cancer risk aside, he needed the comfort of something familiar from his former life. Given his knowledge of modern culture, he probably understood the health ramifications and wouldn't stick with the habit long, but she'd seen him pat his pocket looking for his old pipe. The short-term risk was well worth it.

Britt was at work when she came home, and she spent the evening writing out the last of her Christmas cards and trying to figure out other ways to bypass his damnable code of honor.

Emotionally drained, she fell asleep before he got home, and woke up in the middle of the night alone. Pulling on a heavy robe over the teddy, she made yet another endless search through the house. Upstairs, a soft glow emanated from the closet door that led to the attic. Her heart melted with compassion. Walking in, she found Britt sitting in his original desk chair, a book in his lap, the hurricane lamp hanging from a bent coat hanger he'd jammed through a knothole in the cciling.

"What are you doing up here?" she asked softly.

His shoulders slumped and he drew in a sad breath. "This feels more like where I belong than in one of the bedrooms."

"The past—even if the memories are painful—can give us a place to retreat to, especially when the present is uncertain."

He frowned a question at her.

"You wrote that once."

He grimaced, then glanced at the book in his hands, the printed collection of his journals. "After my death, I had almost total recall. I miss it." He looked up at her, frowning. "I thought this would be a good way to regain some of the old memories."

Hope moved close. Still, she restrained herself from touching him. It wasn't easy. He looked up at her with guilt-ridden eyes, and her resolve broke. She laid her hand on his shoulder. First, he went very still. Then slowly, he reached up and covered her fingers with his own. The soft blue gaze pleaded for understanding. Its silent cry of desperation brought a lump to her throat. He was so lost.

"I'll be right back." She retrieved the small bag from

her bedroom and handed it to him. "It's not wrapped. I wanted to give this to you on Christmas morning, but I think you need it now."

"You bought me another present?" The awe in the whispered question melted her heart.

"Merry Christmas, sweetheart," she choked out.

Reverently, he pulled the pipe's gift box and the package of tobaccos from the bag and stared at them with stunned pleasure. "How did you know how much I've missed my pipe?"

Trying not to tear up, she shrugged. "Just a hunch." She left him then. For hours she lay in bed alone, shivering, more from nerves than cold.

Just before dawn, he crawled into bed beside her. He smelled faintly of fine tobacco—not the scent she recognized, but close enough, and she could get used to it. Then he folded her into his arms. She snuggled in close, just needing to be held.

"It took me about an hour to figure out the scheme behind the gift," he said softly. "And the fancy dinner tonight." He dragged his fingers across the sheer fabric of the teddy. "And this."

There was no point denying it. "Is it working?"

His lips hovered near hers for a timeless moment. "I don't know why you love me so much, but no matter what happens, I'll always be grateful for it."

His kiss came soft with promise and devotion. Fire ignited. Just being held was no longer enough. The magic of his touch passed through her skin to her soul. Slowly, they undressed each other, and she slid her hands along his body, feasting on the cool satin of his skin. She didn't know what Britt's original body looked like, but this one had only a light dusting of hair across the chest. He was still painfully thin, but a good diet was filling in the gaunt places, and she couldn't get enough of just touching him. Any sense of similarity to Richard was lost in the knowledge that inside was the man she loved.

"Forgive me, Hope, but I can't say no to this," he murmured between kisses.

The raging flames in his voice sent her blood's temperature soaring. They slowed down the loving, exploring the lines and contours of each other's bodies.

Eventually, when the time seemed right, Britt unwrapped a condom. "I truly dislike these," he grumbled, trying to hold himself back. "But I could get you with child."

The archaic wording warmed her heart almost as much as did his consideration. "There are other methods," she said, relishing the lighter mood. "We'll find something less intrusive."

Sighing, he rolled her onto her back and gazed down into her eyes. "When I first moved into the attic and learned that a living person cared about me, I felt like I'd been given the most incredible gift in the world. Knowing you love me is even—"

She covered his mouth with her hand, and he kissed her fingers. "If you start talking too much," she said, "you'll start thinking again and ruin the moment. Tell me you love me," she pleaded. "I need to hear it."

He pressed her hand to his cheek, his soft blue eyes liquid in the dark. "No matter what happens, Hope. I will always love you."

They let their bodies speak for them after that. Dawn came and went long before they fell asleep in each other's arms.

The next evening at the Pizza Palace, the heavy crowd kept him too busy to think. Then he heard a male voice that he connected with one of Richard's memories.

"Richard, what are you doing here?"

Britt turned toward a flabbergasted man in his mid-thirties dressed in a dark suit and tie, his hair conservatively cut. He was with two small children and a woman. Britt found more memories. The specifics made him sick. This man, Jerry Wilton, had been a long-standing friend, yet one night Richard had made a pass at his wife. Susan Wilton met Britt's gaze, blushed and looked away. She hadn't refused his advances.

"Is this for real?" Jerry asked.

Britt forced a smile, rifling through more pictures in the photo-album remains of Richard's life. To his knowledge, the man knew nothing of what had happened that night. "I started work here a few days ago."

Jerry's roundish face twisted into a grimace. *"Why?"*

"I was a drunk and worse." Britt despised having to take credit for Richard's problems, but it came with the body. "That's all behind me, but not far enough that I'm likely to find work doing what I'm trained for."

"Even high as a friggin' kite you were a damned good investment counselor. You had an uncanny instinct for the market."

From the corner of his vision he was aware of Susan squirming. "Thank you. But that's all behind me, too."

"In favor of slinging pizza?" Jerry was a good man. Richard had viewed him as gullible, an easy target whose generosity deserved to be exploited.

Shame flooded through Britt that one of his descendants could have been such a self-serving bastard. "Who else would hire a freshly dried-out addict?"

"Me."

Britt blinked, and Susan lost all the color in her face.

"I always liked the idea of the two of us in business together. So how about it? I have more business than I can handle, and I need someone with your qualifications."

Britt searched deeper into Richard's memories. He knew he could do the job. And it paid—by an 1870s perspective—a staggeringly sum money. "You're not worried that I'll start drinking and using again?"

Jerry curled his upper lip distaste. "You won't. I trust you. If you say you're clean and sober, that's it as far as I'm concerned."

The man really was too trusting. And he knew nothing about dealing with addicts. Britt didn't fall into the typical profile, so in this instance, Jerry's trusting nature wouldn't have devastating consequences. One thing he knew for certain. Maintaining a living body was too expensive for a minimum-wage job. "I'd like that, if you're sure."

Jerry extended his hand. "Then blow this taco stand and get yourself down to my office ASAP."

Britt shook on the deal. It took him a moment to figure out the taco stand reference as twentieth-century slang. He still had an uncomfortable amount of holes in his memory, but he'd progressed to the point where he wasn't aware of them unless he reached for something specific and couldn't find it.

Jerry then put in his family's order and herded his wife and children to a table. Britt knew that if he was truly going to take advantage of this opportunity, he had another of Richard's messes to clean up. He waited until Susan brought one of the children from the restroom, then caught up with her before she rounded the corner to the dining area.

"We need to talk."

After flashing him a look of pure hatred, she shooed her young daughter toward the table. "I slept with you once because I didn't realize what a creep you are. The second time was to keep you from telling Jerry. Don't threaten me again. It won't work this time."

Britt felt sick. That part wasn't in the photographs. He wanted to make Richard pay for every wrong he'd ever committed against anyone. Then he shuddered under the realization that perhaps he'd already done just that. "Ma'am, I cannot express to you how deeply I regret past behavior. I was another man then."

The loathing in her eyes deepened. "You want something."

"Only your forgiveness. But not until you believe I've earned it." He bowed his head in a typical nineteenth-century gesture, even though he knew she wouldn't understand. But damn it, if he was going to have to clean up Richard's messes, he would do it in his own way. Having said his piece, he walked away, leaving her to stare after him openmouthed.

He spent the rest of his shift trying to figure out what to do about Hope. If she had her way, he'd never get to the bottom of what had happened that night at the hospital. Staying with her made the temptation to agree too strong. Until he had his conscience satisfied—not that he could imagine a scenario to accomplish the impossible—he needed to put some space between them.

Hope was waiting for him when he came in at eleven-thirty.

"Can we talk?" she asked.

Might as well get it over with. "That would be a good idea."

"I moved the rest of Richard's clothes back into the master closet. I can't see keeping up the pretext of you sleeping in the downstairs guest room."

He closed his eyes. She was pushing for final victory, and he didn't think he could take it.

"I love you, Hope."

Her face opened into the most incredible smile he'd ever seen. The glow in her violet eyes would stay with him forever.

"I will love you until my existence ends, however long from now that may be. But unless I can live with myself, I can't keep sleeping with you."

Her breath rushed out as if he'd kicked her in the stomach. "Denying yourself the fruit of possibly ill-gotten gain, huh?"

He chose not to pursue it. "I'm entering a partnership with Jerry Wilton as soon as I can refresh Richard's memories and make them my own. I'll have enough to support myself until I can figure out what happened that night at the hospital."

He could almost see the frantic thoughts flashing behind her eyes as she scrambled for a counterargument. He recognized it the instant she found something.

"Stop condemning yourself before the facts are in," she said.

"We've gone through this before," he said evenly, determined not to lose control again. "There is no possibility of innocence. Even if he died on his own and I just moved into his unoccupied body, I didn't have the right."

"No matter what you discover about that night, you'll leave his body. You'll return to being dead. I won't be able to touch you or see you in broad daylight ever again." Her voice cracked. "You don't even know if it's possible for you to leave short of a bullet to the brain. You could be permanently welded in there."

"This body isn't mine."

"We'll decide that if the time comes."

.

"No, Hope. I can't think straight when I'm with you. I need to—"

"You're planning to leave me." Her lips sagged apart.

Her intuition unnerved him. "As soon as I get my pay from the restaurant. I'll rent a room at the Wayfarer Inn. Then—"

"That's a roach motel for transients, hookers and winos!"

"It's also all I can afford right now." He brushed past her to hunt down some grocery sacks that he could put some clothes into.

"What if I promise to keep my distance?"

He stopped in the doorway to the dining room but didn't turn around. "Hope, don't."

"You can't possibly want to stay in that filth. The health department closed it down twice last year."

The inflection in her voice changed. Never before had he heard it so calculating. The woman was at war and would never accept defeat.

"Because there is no judge and jury to hear the case you built against yourself, you filled both roles. You also appointed yourself head prosecutor. You found enough evidence to try and convict."

"We've been over this before. I know you don't agree with how I feel, but—"

"I'm not a legal beagle, so I'm making up my own terminology. Sorry if it's not real accurate. I just appointed myself appellate court judge. The defense didn't get its turn, the lower court judge had an extreme conflict of interest, so you get a new trial once the defense—also me—has its case prepared. Got it? In the meantime, the defendant will remain in custody at Hawkings House where he's happy and has someone with more sense than he has."

Even as he turned to face her, he knew it was a mistake, and he braced himself. Her eyes misted, breaking his heart.

"I've studied you since I was a teenager, Britt," she whispered. "I probably know you better than anyone ever has—past or present—yourself included. Convincing Pat that you're real drove that home like nothing else could have."

His willpower crumbled more thoroughly than had the

wall of the carriage house. He couldn't leave her. Murderer or not, he just couldn't walk away. If she believed in him enough to fight for him, then maybe he needed to fight for her, too. "What grounds can you think of for a defense?"

"Not all the evidence is in." She crossed her arms. "But if necessary, I'll plead temporary insanity. You cracked under desperate temptation. The will to live is the strongest instinct in humans and animals alike. You cannot be faulted for that."

"Your parents named you well," he said softly, folding her into his arms. She burrowed in tight as if never to let him go. Selfishly he hoped it was true. "I love you," he whispered.

"I love you, too." She drew back just enough to look up into his face. "The next time you get it into your head to move into that roach motel, remember that your defense attorney and the appellate judge are only a few steps behind you."

"In other words, I can't choose the battle, so I need to choose the location." Risking making love to her at Hawkings House was bad enough. He couldn't imagine how he'd feel if he succumbed to temptation at the "roach motel."

Her lips spread into an approving smile. "That's the idea, Sheriff." She gave him a fleeting kiss. "And since you're not forcing the court to get nasty with you, I won't even try to seduce you tonight." With that, she brushed past him, then stopped. Looking over her shoulder, she asked, "If you try to get all noble and sleep in another room, I'll come after you—nude." With that, she left.

Britt stared after her, amazed. "How could that woman ever have had difficulties asserting herself?"

That night he came to bed, three-quarters convinced that she had more schemes in the works. But she seemed content to sleep in his arms. Still, he lay in bed staring at the ceiling until nearly dawn. Periodically, he cursed himself as twelve kinds of a fool. She was fighting for their love with every weapon she could think of, even if that meant inventing new ones. Could he do no less?

The next day, he worked the lunch shift and clocked out at four-thirty. He took a detour on the way home and drove to the hospital. It was every bit as dark now as it had been on the night of the overdose. The work crew had quit for the night, and he scaled the fence. Using the dubious light of the security lamps, he wandered through what had been the emergency wing. The inner walls were rebuilt and needed only plaster and paint. New light fixtures hung from the ceiling. Neither Richard nor he remembered ever having been here, aside from the isolated memory of him watching Richard's spirit leave its body. What room had that been in? Without the medical equipment to use as a reference point, all the trauma rooms looked alike. For two hours, he wandered the rooms, struggling to regain the lost events before giving up and returning to Hawkings House.

He found Hope in the kitchen, parts of the garbage disposal spread out on newspapers on the counter. A handyman's repair guide lay open beside it.

"What are you doing?"

"It quit working, and I'm trying to fix it."

That offended the vestiges of his nineteenth-century sensibilities. Women had no business making household repairs! Of course, that was probably why she was doing such a conspicuous job of it. "Did you break that thing just to make me feel needed?"

A twinkling laugh filled the air. "No, but I will admit to being very happy when it seized up. I figured if I took it apart, you couldn't resist rescuing your damsel in distress."

"That I can believe," he grumbled, then strode over to the pile of gears, washers and unidentifiable parts. "Here. Let me."

She kissed him between the shoulder blades, then spun away. Not a bad defense attorney. Suppressing a sigh, he studied the pictures and text in the guide. Hope watched him, making no attempt to temper the smile on her glowing face.

"Gloating isn't ladylike," he muttered.

"Innocent until proven guilty, Britt," she said softly.

He refused to answer.

"If you're okay tinkering with the disposal, I'll do dinner."

"Thank you. I'm starving."

"I like putting meat on your bones." Her gaze roamed

over him in lecherous perusal. "The results don't look too bad."

Britt's first reaction was to refuse to dignify her comment with a response, but he needed to find a little faith, even if the best he could do was believe in her faith in him. "Would you like to take a more personal look at your handiwork later?"

Hope's jaw sagged, and her eyes sparkled. "What's this? The defendant actually unwinding a little?"

"It crossed my mind." The byplay sent a ribbon of playful heat arrowing through his veins, and he felt a silly grin cover his face.

With his attention divided, he laid the disposal back on the newspapers, then plugged it in. The simple machine should have started immediately, but it didn't. He reached for it to try something else. The moment his palm connected with the metal casing, an electric current slammed through him like a hammer. He jumped back, his hand and arm aching from the muscle spasm.

"Are you all right?" she asked.

He nodded. Something in the back of his mind came to life and tugged at him. There was an elusive familiarity about that type of pain. He'd experienced it before, in much larger doses. But when?

"You're frowning."

He tried to downplay her concern by shrugging. He didn't know how successful he was. "I zapped myself. Nothing serious."

"I love it when you talk twentieth-century." The sultry backspin told him how much she enjoyed baiting him.

Laughing, he retrieved her rubber jar opener from a drawer and carefully pulled the insulated cord from the wall. "Why don't we make love first, then eat."

Hope turned off the burners on the stove.

The next morning before his shift at the Pizza Palace, Britt drove to Jerry's office and poured over paperwork. The subject matter bored him beyond words. He tried to get Richard to rear his head and offer some enthusiasm. After all, the man had enjoyed his occupation. *Last chance, bastard.* Nothing.

"How are you doing with catching up?" Jerry asked with a smile.

"A lot of this is like reading it for the first time," he hedged.

Jerry patted him on the back. "You'll get it. You always had a sixth sense about this kind of thing."

The instincts belonged to Richard. Britt prayed for a miracle. A client walked in the door and Jerry wandered out to meet him. At noon, Britt took a briefcase full of information home and sat outside on the patio to study.

"Aren't you freezing?" Hope asked, standing in the doorway.

"I needed someplace without walls," he countered.

With a sad smile, she came out and trailed a fingertip along his shoulder. His body's reaction was immediate and annoying.

"Briefcases and cramped offices do not suit you," she said. "You need a job where you can move around." Sadness tinged her voice. "Have you thought about real estate? It's not the same as bringing back criminals, but you won't be cooped up."

Hope made an abortive move as if she'd thought about sitting beside him. It was the type of gesture he was used to from her. He wanted to reach for her hand and draw her down into his lap. A question lit her violet eyes.

"If you're successful at finding an excuse I can live with, I need to make a living."

"In other words, leave you alone so you can study." She bent, kissed him, then darted back inside, leaving a haze of love and contentment behind.

"How can I leave her?" Finding a way to stay looked impossible. Then again, so did finding the willpower to return to that no-man's-land between the living world and the afterlife if he failed.

Chapter
Seventeen

During the next two days, the garbage disposal incident stayed much on Britt's mind. The sense of *déjà vu* grew and wouldn't leave him alone. He'd been dead about five years before he discovered that he generated an electrical charge. In all the time since, he couldn't remember ever having received one. Had he? Was it connected to the night of Richard's overdose? Was he on the verge of a breakthough? Or was this a desperate grabbing at straws? No, the fire at the hospital had been electrical in nature, with multiple points of origin. It had to be connected.

Memories he couldn't reach churned behind the wall of forgetfulness, the pressure building like a winter storm. Images of blue flame flashed in his mind, but he couldn't take hold of the whole memory any more than he could grab the wind. Seeking solitude in the gentlemens' parlor, he closed the door and tried to concentrate. He had to remember!

An hour later, Hope came in, interrupting him. "You haven't spoken two words to me tonight. Are you shutting me out for a reason?" Unshed tears glistened in her violet eyes.

Britt shifted in his chair. They were in this together, and she had a right to know what he was thinking. "For so long, I craved to know the pains and pleasures of a mortal body. I'm liking this, Hope. It's better than I remember. The line between right and wrong isn't so distinct anymore."

The tension ebbed from her shoulders and arms. "Any other conclusion you've come to?" she asked. Her face was hollow from the strain of worrying about him.

"We can't take any more of this not knowing. I have to find answers, not just relegate the moral code I lived by to a closet and pretend it's not there. It would come back later, angry and festering with a resentment that could poison anything we build."

"So what are you saying?"

"This has to stop. Now!" He bolted to his feet and poured his heart into what might well be their last kiss. By the time they came up for air, he was breathing heavily, and Hope hung limp in his arms. "I have an idea."

She blinked in puzzlement at yet another change of direction. He didn't dare explain, because she'd try to stop him. Without explaining, he rummaged through Richard's meager collection of tools until he found a metal, long shaft, flathead screwdriver. Hope trailed behind him to the kitchen.

"What are you doing?" Wariness permeated the question. "I haven't seen this much determination on your face since the night of Richard's overdose."

"Please, Hope, don't interfere. This is something I have to do." It was a stupid thing to say, and he knew it the moment the words tumbled from his mouth. Even without his former ability to read emotions, he felt her apprehension soar.

"What are you up to!" she demanded, stepping in front of him.

"Something that may put an end to this."

"But—"

He brushed past her to the counter. Pulling a large serving bowl from an upper cupboard, he placed it in the sink to fill with water. Then he removed the cover of an electrical outlet. Insulated wires were kinked into a knot, and he carefully drew them out straight enough to give him clean access to the raw ends wrapped around the contacts.

"Talk to me, Britt!" she pleaded. "What possible reason could you have for—"

"This is something I have to try," he whispered.

She pulled herself together enough to look up at him. "What are you doing?"

He shook his head. "You'd only try and stop me."

Appalled fury glittered in her eyes and tightened her features. Before she had the chance to speak, he set her from him. She watched in horror as he removed his shoes, dumped the bowl of water on the floor around his feet, then turned back to the open wires. He gripped the metal shaft of the screwdriver, gritted his teeth, then laid the head on the hot wire.

A burst of spasming pain hit as the electrical jolt flung him across the kitchen. Stunned, he lay on the floor, unable to move. The missing memories began to cascade, picking up speed until he could hardly take them in. Once again, he was hovering above the ambulance as it raced toward the hospital.

Never in his life had he felt such hatred toward anyone as he did the man on the gurney. The ambulance crew unloaded a barely conscious Richard at the hospital's emergency entrance, a monitor lay on the gurney by his feet. Electrodes ran from it to his chest. Britt didn't know what the myriad of lines on the monitor screen meant, but the crew's worry came through quite clearly. They swung down the gurney's legs and all but ran into the emergency room.

"Is this your drug overdose?" a short, wiry, white-coated man asked as he and a team converged on the gurney. The name badge read Dr. William Marin.

"He refused to tell us what he took, and he's going downhill fast."

An alarm blared. As one, the group looked at the monitor.

"Shit! Flat line."

Britt hadn't spent much time reading up on emergency medicine. It was a subject that hadn't interested him other than being intrigued by all the staggering advancements since his day. But as the doctors fought to restart Richard's

heart, he wished he understood more about what he was
seeing. They sent electric shocks through the body, forced
air into his lungs, then shot a syringe full of fluid into his
chest. None of it helped. Richard was a hair's breadth from
death, and Britt couldn't have been any happier about it.
He wouldn't have to do anything after all.

Britt's absolute lack of compassion bothered him, but not
enough to change his mind. Richard saw nothing of life
past his next drink, needle or packet of powder. His world
began and ended with his own wants and needs. A modern
psychiatrist probably had a good name for it.

Britt extended his senses. Richard made no attempt to
struggle for life. Instead, he self-indulgently floated along
for the ride, his spirit still in his body but only partially
attached. Walking the fence between life and death was
nothing but a new game to play.

As much as Britt ached to live again, the attitude infuriated him. *"Don't be a fool, boy!"* he yelled, projecting
his voice fully into the plane only the dead could hear.
"You can fight this! Find your backbone."

"They'll be sorry when I'm gone," came Richard's
drugged reply.

Britt knew that if he could read Richard's thoughts and
not just the emotions, then the man was far closer to death
than he'd realized.

A male nurse frowned up in the general direction of the
ceiling where Britt floated. Apparently she was one of the
sensitive ones. If he needed to say anything else, he'd best
be very careful. Then a double-imaged ripple slithered
across Richard's body. Britt swore. He'd been with enough
people when they'd died to recognize the spirit's final separation from the flesh.

For so long, he'd craved to be encased in a living body
again that seeing anyone—even a man like Richard—throw
one away grieved him beyond measure. *"No!"* he moaned.
"Don't!"

The essence that was Richard McLean rolled free, floating away from its earthly confinement. At first he looked
around, puzzled. Then he studied his translucent hands and
arms, brought them to his equally translucent torso and experienced, for the first time, touching himself without the

sensation of living tissue connecting with living tissue.

"Don't do this!" Britt was frantic. *"You don't know what you're giving up."*

Richard swiveled his gaze toward Britt. *"So this is what you look like,"* he snorted, his mind cleansed from the toxins that had assaulted him.

The nurse didn't react. Richard was far too new to be heard by the living.

"I don't understand," muttered the doctor. "Why isn't this man responding? By all rights, he should be responding."

"Listen, boy. It's not too late." Britt pointed to the medical team frantically trying to revive him. *"They can save you. Why are you* willing *yourself to die?"*

Richard's brows lowered in contempt. *"I was scared of you?* He swore in disgust. *"Satan, my ass. You're nothing!"*

"Get back into your body where you belong. I'll help you any way I can. Just don't do this!"

Richard threw his head up and laughed. Some new ghosts, like newborn babies, didn't have much coordination, and the sudden motion set him into a slow backspin that he squirmed helplessly to stop. Britt loosed a small electrical current and righted him.

"Leave me alone. I don't want your help." His face twisted with disdain. *"You made my life hell."*

"You did that to yourself," Britt snapped back. He floated above Richard to gain a height advantage. *"Those doctors are trying to save your worthless hide. Now get back in that body before it's too late. This isn't a game. Death is forever!"*

Richard's laugh was incredulous. *"Oh, no, you don't. You bossed me around enough. Besides, this has possibilities."* He stood upright, his control improving with each second that passed. Then he floated across the room. His smile slid into a malevolent grin. *"Oh, yeah! I could get used to this."*

Britt knew if he still had blood, it would be running cold right now. His earlier impressions had been correct. Richard wasn't simply flawed, he was as inherently evil as Tyler Carbow.

Richard glanced down at the body he'd occupied for thirty-seven years. It lay there abused and helpless, but not even that elicited any compassion from him. He turned away, unconcerned that he'd thrown out a priceless gift— life—like yesterday's garbage. An explosive envy ignited in Britt.

"I really piss you off, don't I?" Richard observed, taking in Britt's emotions.

Having another ghost read him was a rare experience, but he'd never found it annoying until now. *"You have no regard for anyone. People mean nothing to you other than a means to an end. Cattle to be exploited."*

Richard studied his hands again. Then he looked up and laughed. *"You're dead and hate it. Tough. I think it's great."*

Britt pulled his hat down low, cautiously extending his senses beyond the hospital walls. Where was the tunnel of light? It usually showed up sooner than this. *"You think so, do you?"*

Ignoring him, Richard floated upward experimentally.

"Let's give it up, people," the doctor said on a defeated sigh. Grief and regret billowed from the trauma team in a unified wave.

Dr. Marin looked at the wall clock. "Death is declared at eleven-seventeen P.M."

He sighed again and peeled off his mask and gloves. The other members of the team did the same. One of them covered Richard's body with a sheet.

"Damn it!" Marin tossed the gloves and mask into the biohazard can. "He should have responded."

The team comforted each other in hushed tones as they filed from the room.

Richard couldn't even be bothered to look. When Britt had died, he'd alternately stayed with his family and stood vigil over his body to keep the coyotes away. He'd wept when Nestor and the other searchers found him, and again when they told Lucinda he was gone. His biggest grief was over her fear for the future. But Richard gave no one—not even his parents—so much as a casual thought. It wasn't right!

For the next minute or two, Richard tested his new abilities. The speed at which he was learning to maneuver was uncanny. Then again, the bastard wasn't encumbered by the shock, denial and grief Britt had known upon his own death. An uncluttered mind worked much more efficiently.

"I can't understand why you have a problem with being dead," Richard muttered. *"Look at what we can do."* He spun some figure eights around the trauma room.

What Britt witnessed unnerved him. Also, where was the light? Why wasn't Richard being called away?

"Who are you?" Richard demanded.

"Do you care?"

"Not particularly." Richard shot through a wall, then back. He streaked around the room again, brushing hard against a nurse filling out a form. She jumped at the cold and dropped the clipboard.

"What on earth?" she said, hugging herself and rubbing the chill from her arms.

Richard howled with glee. *"Oh, this is good."* He aimed straight for her.

"Leave her be," Britt ordered. He moved in front of the nurse and deflected Richard with a mild electrical charge. The air crackled, then filled with the acrid stench of ozone.

"You did that to me before. Didn't like it much." His expression turned inward. *"Oh, now I see how this works."* He released a charge at Britt. It was weak, and Britt absorbed it. But the implications frightened him.

"You're scared," Richard howled with glee. *"A nice switch, if you ask me."*

Britt had been with a number of people when they died. The people he'd known in life had been startled but pleased to see him. The light came at various times after death, but only with Evie had it taken this long. Where was it? More seconds passed, and Richard's abilities increased tenfold. When Britt had died, he'd been alone and had no teacher to show him the skills. Richard wasn't so hampered.

Alarm climbed on top of the envy and hate. Then, like a breath of air, he felt the warmth and encompassing presence of the light. He turned toward it in relief. As always, a twinge of hope rippled through him that maybe this time, he'd be called, too. But as always, no gentle beckoning drew him. As always, the light came for one specific person, and it was never him.

The phenomenon resolved itself into the clear form of a tunnel, the clouds within roiling in their unseen currents of energy. When Britt saw what awaited Richard, he protectively backed away from it. Perhaps God had delayed the light, mercifully giving Richard a few more moments before pulling him into the fate he'd woven for himself.

Richard spared the light a marginal glance then shot from the treatment room down the long hallway to the horseshoe-shaped nurses' station by the front doors. Britt followed. The light shifted without appearing to move. Whatever plane of reality it operated on, the rules of mortal physics clearly did not apply.

"You can stop pestering me any time," Richard muttered. *"I've got things to do. Starting with . . . "* He cocked his head. *"Speaking of which, she's here."*

Britt fanned out his senses in every direction. Terror raced through him. Hope had just entered the hospital and stood at the information desk.

"Excuse me. I'm looking for my . . . husband, Richard McLean."

She didn't want to be here, but her worry for Britt had overruled everything else. That puzzled him. What did she think could happen to him?

"She's in love with you?" Richard shrieked. *"That bitch!"* He aimed for the wall as Hope walked into the empty waiting room, looked around and called to Britt.

Britt blocked him, sliding into the corridor just below the ceiling. Fingers of blue lightning blistered the air between them. *"Leave her alone."* The order came low, unbending.

Dr. Marin walked into the waiting room. Britt sensed his dread at having to deliver the worst possible news to a patient's wife.

Richard laughed and came straight at Britt. This time he had his electrical "claws" out, and the charge was far greater than Britt could absorb. He deflected it, watching as it snaked along the inside wall of the waiting room. The sound caught both Hope's and the doctor's attention. Damn.

"Hi, Hope," Richard singsonged, clearly enjoying his newly acquired ability to see through walls.

The malevolent undertones increased Britt's concern.

"It was bad enough having you on my back all the time," Richard continued, *"but now I find out you had a thing going with a ghost all that time. You are one sick bitch."* He blasted past Britt.

Britt shot into position between Richard and Hope, shoving Richard backward with enough force to send him through five walls before he got himself stopped. The impact created an electrical backlash that blew out half the fluorescent lights.

"You will not *touch her,"* Britt snarled.

"Like hell, I won't." Richard laughed. *"She's getting a taste of what you gave me. Serves her right. Were you two working together all along?"*

"She can't hear you."

"Why not? I heard you, didn't I?"

"Communicating with the living is a skill I don't plan to show you. By the time you have it she'll have died from old age. Now back off and go on your way." He glared pointedly toward the light.

Richard glanced over his shoulder at it, his expression turning inward. Death's pull had to be taking its toll. Then he came at Britt again, this time with twice the power as before. For the first time in a very, very long time, Britt questioned his indestructibility. The two connected again, both grappling for control. He loosed the strongest charge he was capable of producing. He didn't think about it first, just did it, like throwing a punch in a saloon brawl. Richard shrieked in rage as the impact threw him out through the back wall of the hospital. Lights, equipment and computer monitors exploded. Wiring overheated in the walls and ignited.

Hope and Dr. Marin ran into the corridor. The staff scrambled in the dark. From one of the trauma rooms, someone screamed for emergency power. Britt swore. He hadn't realized the repercussions. This was a hospital! Patients needed crucial, life-sustaining machines, and he and Richard were destroying them.

"Damn you, Hope!" Richard shot inside and made a straight line for her. *"You can hear me. I know you can!"*

Britt grabbed him, but Richard's momentum was too great to stop. More wiring burst into flames as the two tumbled through the air. Fire lapped at the wooden framing in the walls. Emergency lights glowed dimly in the thickening smoke.

Hope looked right at him. "Britt!"

He didn't think he was visible, but that hadn't stopped her from sensing his presence before. "Hope, Run!" he barked. "Get out of here! Don't look back!" He hated the sound of fear in his own voice, hated more showing Richard how to be heard.

"What?" she asked. "Why?"

"No matter what happens," he called back, "know that I love you. Go!"

An oversized front window had shattered, leaving a gaping hole. The automatic doors had jammed, and a crowd of people fought to open them. Hope bypassed them, then vaulted through the window and out into the parking lot.

Richard cursed him, then tried for a stranglehold on Britt's throat. In the context of their existence, it was a pointless attempt, but the contact created another explosion. More fires started from overloaded wires. Walls burned in a dozen places as he and Richard fought for control.

Richard no longer wanted petty revenge. He wouldn't stop until he'd killed Hope. Britt gathered himself to loose another charge. This one he narrowed to a tight beam. It drove that hellspawn backward like a club to the chest. Behind Richard in a corner of the ceiling, the tunnel glowed with unearthly patience. Richard's sheet-covered body lay below, alone and unattended. How much time had passed? Hours, as it seemed? Or mere minutes? Was it too late?

Richard cast a contemptuous glance at the light as if it had no more relevance to him than anything else in the room.

"Your cruelty and selfishness have destroyed everything good you ever had," Britt yelled. *"You either return to your body now or go where you really belong."*

The light shifted, appearing closer, although it never moved.

Richard gasped as he tried to shake off its pull. *"You*

make it sound like being alive is some great prize."

Good. Richard had kept his words on the spirit level.

Britt looked at Richard's body, a hollow ache of envy piling back into the emotional chaos.

Richard's face opened in incredulity, and he laughed. *"Go for it,"* he sneered. *"You want my corpse? You want life? It's all yours. I'm happy where I'm at."* He attacked Britt again.

Richard had only been dead a short time, but Britt was barely able to hold his own. From the depth of his soul, he knew that unless he did something fast, he was in deep trouble. Moreover, if he lost, Hope was in mortal danger.

As they struggled, they brushed past Richard's body, and the sheet fell to the floor. The light shifted. Britt could almost touch it. With one violent twist, he spun Richard toward it, and felt the light's penetrating grip take final hold.

Richard resisted, screaming under the realization that he'd encountered a force that could not be defeated. Britt backed away, gathering himself for one final push, but a mind-numbing blast of raw power shot up his leg. Stunned by the first pain he'd felt since Evie had tried to drag him with her to the afterlife, it caught him off guard. He glanced down at what seemed to be the source. He'd put his foot through the corpse's leg.

The sensation escalated into white-hot agony, blanking out his ability to think. Helpless under the numbing onslaught, he looked back at Richard.

"Well, Satan. Looks like you have a few problems of your own."

Richard's vindictive glee would stay with Britt forever. As a last act of defiance, Richard released an electric charge. Unprepared, Britt couldn't deflect it. He fell hard into the corpse's abdomen. Nothing, not even being burned alive, could hurt as bad as this! How could the mind endure it! His mouth sagged open from an agony too great to scream.

A fireman yanked open the trauma room door, glanced at Richard's body and ran for it. In one motion, he grabbed the footrail, kicked off the brake and dragged the gurney out behind him. The force of the man's desperate flight to

save someone he didn't know was already dead unbalanced
Britt, and he sprawled full out into the body.

Britt sensed more than saw the moment Richard saw
himself for what he was, saw that no paradise waited for
him, only the realm of the damned. With a single blood-
curdling shriek, Richard slid into the tunnel's core. It
sucked him in, then vanished, leaving behind its strangely
profound quiet that not even the shouts of the living could
penetrate.

The fireman rounded a corner, and the side of the gurney
slammed into a wall as he raced for the parking lot. It
jostled Britt like sand in a bucket. Consciousness slid and
rippled, becoming harder to hold. White pain gave way to
needle-sharp tingles that stabbed through him like exploding embers. He couldn't think.

His spirit expanded and flowed, filling every bone, muscle and cell of the dead man's body. The hell that awaited
Richard couldn't have been this bad. Helplessly, Britt
fought to stay conscious, terrified of what might happen if
he failed.

The fireman bounced the gurney over the sidewalk curb
and down onto the parking lot's asphalt. Britt's mind
screamed in silence. Beneath the agony, he became vaguely
aware of a growing warmth. A heart quivered, then pulsed
drunkenly, driving blood through veins. The chest rose as
the lungs drew in air. Oxygen-starved brain cells soaked up
the needed gift.

The pain began to ebb, and after 127 years, Britt felt the
heat and security of being surrounded by flesh and bone,
and tasted the sweet air that fed it.

An unnamed blackness descended, and he struggled to
swim its depths, but he couldn't tell which direction to go.
The blackness became a quiet rest, and time slid away.

Gradually, the strange sensations lifted, and he became
aware of something strapped to his face, a mask of some
kind. He locked onto the feel of it to give him direction.
Dragging his eyes open, he stared into the hovering face of
a man he'd never seen, a man in a fireman's suit, holding
a tiny light in a narrow, metal tube. What was it called?
Shouldn't he know?

"It's all right," the stranger assured him. "We got you
out, and you're going to be just fine."

What was this man talking about! Nothing made sense.
Where was he? The air in the mask on his face smelled
sweet, like a spring day in a grassy meadow. Why did
everything seem so out of place? Thinking hurt.

"I don't have any paperwork on you. Can you tell me
your name?"

His name. He thought about that for a moment. What
was it? Panic boiled through him. Why didn't he know his
own name? He tried to ask, but only a garbled noise fell
from his throat. His heart pounded, and breathing came
hard and fast.

"It's okay. We'll straighten everything out. Just rest a
bit. I've got other people to check on, but a doctor will be
with you soon."

Hope watched in horror as Britt laid the screwdriver against
the live wire. The electrical jolt shot him across the room.
He sprawled on the floor like a rag doll. She screamed and
ran to him. Dropping to her knees, she cradled his head in
her lap. Drunkenly, his eyes opened, twitched, closed and
reopened.

"What is wrong with you?" she yelled. "What were you
trying to do? Kill yourself?"

"That hurt," he mumbled on a deep groan.

"Of course it hurt, you idiot!" Tears filled her eyes as
she held him close and kissed his cheek. "Britt, what were
you thinking of?"

"When I zapped myself on the garbage disposal, it felt
familiar," he said breathlessly, trying to regain his bearings. "Made the memories close enough to touch." His
eyes gleamed as she helped him shakily get to his feet. "I
thought if I—"

"Electrocuted yourself, you'd solve a lot of problems all
at once. It didn't work, did it!"

He cleared his throat and tried to take a breath that didn't
shake. "Actually, it did." He took another breath. This one
came more smoothly.

"You remember?" Her voice lifted with fearful anticipation.

Still collecting himself, he sat up, drew her into his arms

and held her in silence. The truth was too profound for words, and he tightened his hold, quietly nuzzling her hair. He hurt all over.

Drawing back, Hope scrutinized his face. "Talk to me, Britt."

"I didn't kill him." Each syllable came choked with unshed tears of relief. Haltingly at first, then with more composure, he related the events of that night. "I had no choice about moving into his body. I had no way to stop it."

With each word he spoke, joy welled up higher and higher in Hope. "I knew there was an explanation," she said, half laughing, half crying. "I *knew* it!"

"Yes, you did." He kissed her long and hard. "I don't know if the amnesia was caused by the drugs in Richard's system or the trauma of being drawn into his body. There will probably never be any way to find out for certain. It doesn't matter. I'm not the monster I'd been afraid—"

"You should have listened to me." She hadn't noticed the fresh batch of tears coursing down her cheeks until Britt lovingly wiped them away.

A slow grin covered his face. Never had she seen such joy.

"I'm a living man again," he said, as if experimenting with the feel of those words on his tongue for the first time. "This body is a gift of circumstance. Not something I stole."

With gentle fingers, Hope traced the line of his mouth, reveling in the knowledge that he'd never leave her, that she could touch him anytime she wanted. They had their miracle. "You'd better take very good care of that body, too," she warned, hardly able to contain her happiness, "because I have every intention of growing old with it."

"Yes, ma'am." He laughed again.

Hope knew she'd never get tired of hearing that sound.

"My divorce from that body isn't final until tomorrow. How about I call my attorney and see about canceling it?"

"I'd like that." From the amusement in the laugh lines on his face, he was clearly enjoying her take-charge attitude.

Mouse no more, she thought. "In fact . . ." She cleared her throat. "Britt McLean, will you marry me? I want to be married to all of you, not just the body.''

He looked chagrined. "I was going to ask *you*."

"Well, I beat you to it. Legally it'll be more like a renewal of vows, but we'll know differently. I'm so glad Richard's parents gave him your name as his middle name." She was blithering and knew it, but she couldn't seem to stop. "That will make retraining everyone to call you Britt much easier. We'll rework the logistics as we go. We also need to call Pat. She may have some ideas, and—"

Britt kissed her into silence, and she felt the rumble of his laughter against her lips. When they came up for air, he brushed the hair from her face and drew his hands down her arms. Love shone from him like a beacon. "I want to spend the rest of my very human life with you, Hope. I want to walk in the sun with you, have children with you and build a life together here in this house."

"Will you keep up with your journals?"

"I suppose. Why?"

"When you're out doing whatever you decide to do for a living and I start missing you too much, I want your words to keep me company."

From his awed expression, she must have touched him deeply. She nearly started crying all over again. "What about adopting kids in addition to having our own?"

He stood, then swept her into his arms. "Sounds like I need to find myself a *very* well-paying job. But why don't we discuss it in bed?"

She laughed in joyous abandon. "I like how you think, Sheriff McLean. Lead on."

Presenting all-new romances—featuring ghostly heroes and heroines and the passions they inspire.

❤ Haunting Hearts ❤

☐ *A SPIRITED SEDUCTION*
   by Casey Claybourne   0-515-12066-9/$5.99

☐ *STARDUST OF YESTERDAY*
   by Lynn Kurland   0-515-11839-7/$6.50

☐ *A GHOST OF A CHANCE*
   by Casey Claybourne   0-515-11857-5/$5.99

☐ *ETERNAL VOWS*
   by Alice Alfonsi   0-515-12002-2/$5.99

☐ *ETERNAL LOVE*
   by Alice Alfonsi   0-515-12207-6/$5.99

☐ *ARRANGED IN HEAVEN*
   by Sara Jarrod   0-515-12275-0/$5.99

FRIENDS ROMANCE

Can a man come between friends?

❏ A TASTE OF HONEY
by DeWanna Pace   0-515-12387-0

❏ WHERE THE HEART IS
by Sheridon Smythe   0-515-12412-5

❏ LONG WAY HOME
by Wendy Corsi Staub   0-515-12440-0

All books $5.99

DO YOU BELIEVE IN MAGIC?

MAGICAL LOVE

The enchanting new series from Jove will make you a believer!

With a sprinkling of faerie dust and the wave of a wand, magical things can happen—but nothing is more magical than the power of love.

❑ *SEA SPELL* by Tess Farraday   0-515-12289-0/$5.99

A mysterious man from the sea haunts a woman's dreams—and desires...

❑ *ONCE UPON A KISS* by Claire Cross

0-515-12300-5/$5.99

A businessman learns there's only one way to awaken a slumbering beauty...

❑ *A FAERIE TALE* by Ginny Reyes   0-515-12338-2/$5.99

A faerie and a leprechaun play matchmaker—to a mismatched pair of mortals...

❑ *ONE WISH* by C.J. Card   0-515-12354-4/$5.99

For years a beautiful bottle lay concealed in a forgotten trunk—holding a powerful spirit, waiting for someone to come along and make one wish...

VISIT PENGUIN PUTNAM ONLINE ON THE INTERNET:
http://www.penguinputnam.com

Prices slightly higher in Canada

Payable in U.S. funds only. No cash/COD accepted. Postage & handling: U.S./CAN. $2.75 for one book, $1.00 for each additional, not to exceed $6.75; Int'l $5.00 for one book, $1.00 each addition-al. We accept Visa, Amex, MC ($10.00 min.), checks ($15.00 fee for returned checks) and money orders. Call 800-788-6262 or 201-933-9292, fax 201-896-8569; refer to ad # 789 (7/99)

Penguin Putnam Inc.
P.O. Box 12289, Dept. B
Newark, NJ 07101-5289
Please allow 4-6 weeks for delivery.
Foreign and Canadian delivery 6-8 weeks.

Bill my: ❑ Visa ❑ MasterCard ❑ Amex _____(expires)

Card# _____

Signature _____

Bill to:

Name _____

Address _____ City _____

State/ZIP _____ Daytime Phone # _____

Ship to:

Name _____ Book Total $ _____

Address _____ Applicable Sales Tax $ _____

City _____ Postage & Handling $ _____

State/ZIP _____ Total Amount Due $ _____

This offer subject to change without notice.

TIME PASSAGES